Setup

Elgin shone his light in my eyes, then swept it through the back of the car. "What's in the case?" he asked.

Next to me, Bubba glanced back and sighed. "It's a guitar, Elgin. What do you think?" Then to me, "I need to see a license and the papers on the vehicle, sir."

"You guys want to show me some ID here?"

Bubba stared right through me. "The papers."

"Slow and easy," said Elgin.

I had a pretty good idea what was coming. I reached for the glove compartment, for the insurance papers. I moved very slow, keeping my hand in the flashlight beam.

When my fingers were just about to the glove compartment handle Elgin swore loudly and drew his 9 mm and yelled: "Gun!"

Bubba was quick. On the count of one, he had his semi-auto in my ear and his other hand around my neck. By the count of five I had been dragged bodily over the car door and slammed onto the pavement. . . .

The Widower's Two★Step

Rick Riordan

Bantam Books

New York Toronto London Sydney Auckland

The Widower's Two-Step
A Bantam Book/May 1998

ISBN 978-0-553-57645-0
Published simultaneously in the United States and Canada

Bantam Books are published by Bantam Books, a division of Random
House, Inc. Its trademark, consisting of the words "Bantam Books" and
the portrayal of a rooster, is Registered in U.S. Patent and Trademark
Office and in other countries. Marca Registrada. Random House, Inc.,
New York, New York.

PRINTED IN THE UNITED STATES OF AMERICA
OPM   11   10

To Becky

Acknowledgments

Salud y muchas gracias to the many people who helped me with this book—Dorothy Sherman, president of GrayZone Investigations; Glen Bates and Bill Chavez of the ITS Investigative Agency; Wiley Alexander of the *San Antonio Express-News*; James Morgan of the Bluebonnet Palace; Sgt. Tony Kobryn of the Bexar County Sheriff's Department; Dan Apperson of the Alameda County Coroner's Office; Steve Hanson, chief investigator of the Bexar County Medical Examiner's Office; Detective Jim Caruso of the San Antonio Police Department homicide division; Dr. Jeanne Reesman, English department chair, University of Texas at San Antonio; Alexandra Walsh of the Recording Industry Association of America (RIAA); and Katrine Hughes of the International Federation of Phonographic Industries (IFPI). Continuing thanks to Gina Maccoby and Kate Miciak; Jim Glusing and Patty Jepson for their stories of South Texas; Maria Luna for her patient help with *Español*; the entire Presidio Hill School gang; the Medina Mud Band; Lyn Belisle; and above all to Becky & Haley Riordan.

So hold on, little darlin', 'cause the music is stern,
Twirl 'round the cradle 'til your soul starts to burn,
And don't say the next dance we won't get a turn
'Cause the Widower's Two-Step is a hard one to learn.

—"THE WIDOWER'S TWO-STEP,"
Brent & Miranda Daniels

The Widower's Two★Step

1

"Could you please tell your kid to be quiet?"

The guy standing in front of my park bench looked like he'd stepped off a Fleetwood Mac album cover, circa 1976. He had that Lindsey Buckingham funhouse-mirror kind of body—unnaturally tall, bulbous in the wrong places. He had the 'Fro and the beard and the loose-fitting black martial arts pajamas that just screamed mod.

He was also blocking my camera angle on the blue '68 Cougar across San Pedro Park, eighty yards away.

"Well?" Lindsey wiped his forehead. He'd walked over from his tai chi group and sounded out of breath, like he'd been working the moves too hard.

I checked my watch. If the lady in the Cougar was going to meet somebody, it should've happened by now.

I looked at the tai chi guy.

"What kid?"

A few feet to my left, Jem made another pass on the swing set, strafing Lindsey Buckingham's students as he came down. He made airplane sounds at the top of his lungs, which was a lot of lungs for a four-year-old, then pointed his toes like machine-gun barrels and started firing.

I guess maybe it was hard for Lindsey's folks to concentrate. One of them, a short ovoid woman in pink sweats, was trying to squat for *Snake Creeps Down*. She ended up rolling on her rump like she'd been shot.

Lindsey Buckingham rubbed the back of his neck and glared at me. "The kid on the swings, dumb-ass."

I shrugged. "It's a playground. He's playing."

"It's seventy-thirty in the morning. We're practicing here."

I looked over at Lindsey's students. The pink ovoid woman was just getting up. Next to her a little Latina lady was doing her moves nervously, pushing the air with her palms and keeping her eyes tightly shut as if she was afraid of what she might touch. Two other students, both middle-aged Anglo guys with potbellies and ponytails, lumbered through the routine as best they could, frowning, sweating a lot. It didn't look like anybody was achieving inner tranquility.

"You should tell them to keep their feet at forty-five degrees," I suggested. "That's an unbalanced stance, parallel footing like that."

Lindsey opened his mouth like he was about to say something. He made a little cough in the back of his throat.

"Excuse me. I didn't know I was talking to a master."

"Tres Navarre," I said. "I usually wear a T-shirt, says 'Master.' It's in the wash."

I looked past him, watching the Cougar. The lady in the driver's seat hadn't moved. Nobody else was in the San Antonio College parking lot.

The sun was just starting to come up over the white dome of the campus planetarium, but the night cool had already burned out of the air. It was going to be another ninety-degree day. Smells from the breakfast taqueria down on Ellsworth were starting to drift through the park—chorizo and eggs and coffee.

On the swing set Jem came down for another run.

"Eeeeooooooowwww," he shouted, then he made with the machine guns.

Lindsey Buckingham glared at me. He didn't move out of the way.

"You're blocking my view of the parking lot," I told him.

"Oh, pardon me."

I waited. "Are you going to move?"

"Are you going to shut your kid up?"

Some mornings. It's not bad enough it's October in Texas and you're still waiting for the first cold front to come through. It's not bad enough your boss sends her four-year-old with you on surveillance. You've got to have Lindsey Buckingham in your face, too.

"Look," I told him, "see this backpack? There's a Sanyo TLS900 in there—pinhole lens, clear resolution from two hundred yards, but it can't see through idiots. In a minute, if you move, I might get some nice footage of Miss Kearnes meeting somebody she's not supposed to be meeting. My client will pay me good money. If you don't move I'll get some nice footage of your crotch. That's how it works."

Lindsey scratched some sweat droplets out of his beard. He looked at the backpack. He looked at me.

"Bullshit."

Jem kept swinging higher and shouting louder. His skinny brown legs were pinched into an hourglass shape by the swing. When he got to the top he went weightless, silky black hair sticking up like a sea urchin, his eyes wide, his smile way too big for his face. Then he got a look of evil determination and came swooping down on the tai chi students again, machine guns blazing. The OshKosh B'Gosh Luftwaffe.

"Don't suppose you guys could move your class," I suggested. "Nice place over there by the creek."

Lindsey looked indignant. " 'What is firmly established cannot be uprooted.' "

I would've been okay if he hadn't quoted Lao-tzu. That tends to irritate me. I sighed and got up from the bench.

Lindsey must've been about six feet five. Standing straight I was eye level with his Adam's apple. His breath smelled like an Indian blanket.

"Let's push hands for it, then," I said. "You know how to push hands?"

He snorted. "You're kidding."

"I go down, I move. You go down, you move. Ready?"

He didn't look particularly nervous. I smiled up at him. Then I pushed.

You see the way most guys push each other—hitting the top of each other's chest like bullies do it on television. Stupid. In tai chi the push is called *liu*, "uproot." You sink down, get the opponent under the rib cage, then make like you're prying a big tree out of the ground. Simple.

When Lindsey Buckingham went airborne he made a sound like a hard note on a tenor sax. He flew up about two feet and back about six. He landed hard, sitting down in front of his students.

On the swing, Jem cut the machine guns midstrafe and started giggling. The ponytail guys stopped doing their routine and stared at me.

The lady in the pink sweats said, "Oh, dear."

"Learn to roll," I told them. "It hurts otherwise."

Lindsey got to his feet slowly. He had grass in his hair. His underwear was showing. Standing doubled over he was just about eye level with me.

"God damn it," he said.

Lindsey's face turned the color of a pomegranate. His fists balled up and they kept bobbing up and down, like he was trying to decide whether or not to hit me.

"I think this is where you say, 'You have dishonored our school,' " I suggested. "Then we all bring out the *nunchakus*."

Jem must've liked that idea. He slowed down his swing just enough to jump off, then ran over and hung on my left arm with his whole weight. He smiled up at me, ready for the fight.

Lindsey's students looked uncomfortable, like maybe they'd forgotten the *nunchaku* routine.

Whatever Lindsey was going to say, it was interrupted by two sharp cracks from somewhere behind me, like dry boards breaking. The sound echoed thinly off the walls of the SAC buildings.

Everybody looked around, squinting into the sun.

When I finally focused on the '68 blue Cougar I was supposed to be watching, I could see a thin curl of smoke trailing up from the driver's side window.

Nobody was around the Cougar. The lady in the driver's seat still hadn't moved, her head reclined against the backrest like she was taking a nap. I had a feeling she wasn't going to start moving anytime soon. I had a feeling my client wasn't going to pay me good money.

"Jesus," said Lindsey Buckingham.

None of his students seemed to get what had happened. The potbellied guys looked confused. The ovoid lady in the pink sweats came up to me, a little fearful, and asked me if I taught tai chi.

Jem was still hanging on my arm, smiling obliviously. He looked down at his Crayola-designed Swatch and did some time calculations faster than most adults could.

"Ten hours, Tres," he told me, happy. "Ten hours ten hours ten hours."

Jem kept count of that for me—how many hours I had left as an apprentice for his mother, before I could qualify for my own P.I. license. I had told him we'd have a party when it got to zero.

I looked back at the blue Cougar with the little trail of smoke curling up out of the window from Miss Kearnes' head.

"Better make it thirteen, Bubba. I don't think this morning's going to count."

Jem laughed like it was all the same to him.

2

"What is it with you?" Detective Schaeffer asked me. Then he asked Julie Kearnes, "What is it with this guy?"

Julie Kearnes had no comment. She was reclining in the driver's seat of the Cougar, her right hand on a battered brown fiddle case in the passenger's seat, her left hand clenching the recently fired pearl-handled .22 Ladysmith in her lap.

From this angle Julie looked good. Her graying amber hair was pulled back in a butterfly clasp. Her lacy white sundress showed off the silver earrings, the tan freckled skin that was going only slightly flabby under her chin, around her upper arms. For a woman on the wrong side of fifty she looked great. The entrance wound was nothing—a black dime stuck to her temple.

Her face was turned away from me but it looked like she had the same politely distressed expression she'd given me yesterday morning when we'd first met—a little smile, friendly but hesitant, some tightness in the wrinkles around her eyes.

"*I'm sorry,*" she'd told me, "*I'm afraid—surely there's been some mistake.*"

Ray Lozano, the medical examiner, looked in the shotgun window for a few seconds, then started talking to the evidence tech in Spanish. Ray told him to get all the pictures he wanted before they moved the body because the backrest was the only thing holding that side of her face together.

"You want to use English here?" Schaeffer said, cranky.

Ray Lozano and the tech ignored him.

Nobody bothered turning off the country and western music that was playing on Julie Kearnes' cassette deck. Fiddle, stand-up bass, tight harmonies. Peppy music for a murder.

It was only eight-thirty but we were already getting a pretty good crowd around the parking lot. A KENS-TV mobile unit had set up at the end of the block. A few dozen SAC students in flip-flops and shorts and T-shirts were hanging out on the grass outside the yellow tape. They didn't look too interested in getting to their morning classes. The 7-Eleven across San Pedro was doing a brisk business in Big Gulps to the cops and press and spectators.

"Tailing a goddamn musician." Schaeffer poured himself some Red Zinger from his thermos. Ninety degrees and he was drinking hot tea. "Why is it you can't even do that without somebody getting dead, Navarre?"

I put my palms up.

Schaeffer looked at Julie Kearnes. "You can't hang around this guy, honey. You see what it gets you?"

Schaeffer does that. He says it's either talk to the corpses or take up hard liquor. He says he's already got the lecture picked out he's going to give my corpse when he comes across it. He's fatherly that way.

I looked across the parking lot to check on Jem. He was sitting in my orange VW convertible showing one of the SAPD guys his magic trick, the one with the three metal hoops. The officer looked confused.

"Who's the kid?" Schaeffer asked.

"Jem Manos."

"As in the Erainya Manos Agency?"

" 'Your full-service Greek detective.' "

Schaeffer's face went sour. He nodded like Erainya's name in this case explained everything.

"The Dragon Lady ever hear of day care?"

"Doesn't believe in it," I said. "Kid could catch germs."

Schaeffer shook his head. "So let me get this straight. Your client is a country singer. She prepares a demo tape for a record label, the tape turns up missing, the agent suspects a disgruntled band member who would've been cut out of the record deal, the agent's lawyer gets the brilliant idea of hiring you to track down the tape. Is that about it?"

"The singer is Miranda Daniels," I said. "She's been in *Texas Monthly*. I can get you an autograph if you want."

Schaeffer managed to contain his excitement. "Just explain to me how we got a fiddle player dead in the SAC parking lot seven-thirty Monday morning."

"Daniels' agent figured Kearnes was the most likely suspect to steal the tape. She had access to the studio. She'd had some pretty serious disagreements with Daniels over career plans. The agency thought Kearnes might've stolen the tape at someone else's prompting, somebody who stood to gain from Miranda Daniels remaining a local act. As near as I could tell that wasn't the case. Kearnes didn't have the tape. Didn't mention it to anybody over the last week."

"This is not explaining the dead body."

"What can I tell you? Yesterday I finally talked to Kearnes, told her straight what she was being accused of. She denied knowing anything but seemed pretty shaken up. Then when she bolted out the door this morning I figured maybe I'd been mistaken about her innocence.

Maybe I'd stirred things up and she'd arranged to meet with whoever'd asked her to steal the tape."

Ray Lozano moved Julie's fiddle case off the passenger seat. He sat next to her. He began picking fragments out of her hair with tweezers.

"Stirring things up," Schaeffer repeated. "Nice fucking method."

One of the campus cops came over. He was a heavy guy, a former boxer maybe, but you could tell he hadn't dealt with homicides before. He approached Julie Kearnes the way most people do the first time they see a corpse—like an acrophobic sneaking up to the railing of a balcony. He nodded at Schaeffer, then looked sideways at Julie.

"They want to know about how much longer it'll be." He said it apologetically, like *they* were being unreasonable. "She committed suicide in the bursar's parking space."

"What suicide?" Schaeffer said.

The big guy frowned. He looked down uncertainly at the gun in Julie's hand, then the little hole in her head.

Schaeffer sighed, looked at me.

"She was shot from a distance," I explained. "You shoot yourself point-blank the wound splits like a star. Plus the entrance and exit wounds here are angled down and the caliber of the gun is probably wrong. The shooter was up there somewhere." I pointed to the top of a campus building where there was a series of big metal air-conditioning units making steam. "She was carrying the .22 for protection. Fired it when she was hit because of a cadaveric spasm. The bullet's probably embedded in the dashboard."

Schaeffer listened to my explanation, then waved his free hand in a so-so gesture.

"Make yourself useful," he told the campus cop. "Go tell the bursar to park it on the street."

The big man walked away a lot faster than he'd walked up.

A crime scene unit detective came over and pulled

Schaeffer aside. They talked. The CSU guy showed Schaeffer some ID and business cards from the dead woman's wallet. Schaeffer took one of the cards and scowled at it.

When Schaeffer came back to me he was quiet, drinking Red Zinger. His eyes over the thermos cup were the same color as the tea, reddish brown, just about as watery.

He handed the card to me. "Your boss?"

The words LES SAINT-PIERRE TALENT were printed maroon on gray. Centered underneath in smaller type it said: MILO CHAVEZ, ASSOCIATE. I stared at the name "Milo Chavez." It did not invoke feelings of goodwill.

"My boss."

"I don't suppose you came across any reasons why somebody would want to kill this lady. And don't tell me the fucking demo tape was that good."

"No," I agreed. "It was not."

"You look for large debts, irate boyfriends—the kind of background work real P.I.s do when they're not minding three-year-olds?"

I tried to look offended. "Jem's a mature four-and-a-half."

"Uh-huh. Why meet somebody here? Why drive the seventy-five miles from Austin to San Antonio and park at a junior college?"

"I don't know."

Schaeffer tried to read my face. "You want to give me anything else?"

"Not especially. Not until I talk to my client."

"Maybe I should let you make that call from a holding cell."

"If you want."

Schaeffer dug a red handkerchief the size of Amarillo out of his pants pocket and started blowing his nose. He took his time doing it. Nobody blows his nose as often and as meticulously as Schaeffer. I think it's how he meditates.

"I don't know how Erainya got you this case, Navarre, but you should shoot her for it."

"Actually I know the agent's assistant, Milo Chavez. I was doing Chavez a favor."

Ray Lozano was talking with the paramedics about how to move the corpse. The crowd of college kids outside the police tape was getting bigger. Two more uniforms were leaning on the side of my VW now, watching Jem put his magic rings together. The cowboy fiddle tunes were swinging right along on Miss Kearnes' cassette deck.

Schaeffer finally put his handkerchief away and looked down at Julie Kearnes, still clenching her .22 like she was afraid it might jump out of her lap.

"Hell of a favor," Schaeffer told me.

3

 All the way back to the North Side I had to give Jem a lecture about not taking bets on magic tricks from the nice policemen.

Jem nodded like he was listening. Then he told me he could do six rings at a time and did I want to bet?

"No thanks, Bubba."

Jem just smiled at me and pocketed his three new quarters in his OshKosh overalls.

It would've been faster to take McAllister Freeway back to Erainya's office, but I headed up San Pedro instead. Going north on the highway, twenty feet off the ground the whole way, all you see are the hills and the Olmos Basin, a few million live oaks, an occasional cathedral spire, and the tops of some Olmos Park mansions. Clean and forested, like there's no city at all under there. San Pedro is more honest.

For about two miles north of SAC, San Pedro is the dividing line between Monte Vista and the beginning of the West Side. On the right are the old Spanish mansions, huge acacia and magnolia trees, shaded lawns with Latino gardeners tending the roses, Cadillacs in the wraparound flagstone drives. On the left are the boarded-up apartment blocks, the occasional mom-and-pop ice house selling fresh watermelons and Spanish newspapers, the two-room houses with kids in Goodwill clothes peering out the screen doors.

Go two miles farther up and the bilingual billboards disappear. You drive past white middle-class housing developments and run-down shopping centers from the sixties, streets that were named after characters in *I Love Lucy*. The land gets flatter; the ratio of asphalt to trees gets worse.

Finally you get to the mirrored office buildings and the singles apartment complexes clustered around Loop 410. Loopland could be in Indianapolis or Des Moines or Orange County. Lots of character.

Erainya's office was in an old white strip mall off 410 and Blanco, between a restaurant and a leather furniture outlet. The parking lot was empty except for Erainya's rusty Lincoln Continental and a newish mustard-yellow BMW.

I pulled in next to the Lincoln and Jem helped me put up the ragtop on the VW. Then we got our respective backpacks out of the trunk and went to find his mom.

The black stencil sign on the door said, THE ERAINYA MANOS AGENCY, YOUR FULL-SERVICE GREEK DETECTIVE.

Erainya likes being Greek. She tells me Nick Charles in *The Thin Man* was Greek. I tell her Nick Charles was rich and fictional; he could be anything he wanted. I tell her she starts calling me Nora I'm quitting.

The door was locked. The miniblinds across the glass front of the office were pulled down. Erainya had stuck one of those cardboard black and white pointing hands over the mail slot, pointing right.

We went next door to Demo's and almost collided with a stocky Latino man on his way out.

He wore a three-piece suit, dark blue, with a gold watch chain and a wide maroon tie. He had four gold

rings and a zircon tie stud and smelled strongly of
Aramis. Except for the bulldog expression, he looked like
the kind of guy who might offer you credit toward a purchase of fine diamond jewelry.

"Barrera." I smiled. "What's new, Sam—you come by
to get some pointers from the competition?"

Samuel Barrera, senior regional director for I-Tech
Security and Investigations, didn't smile back. I'm sure
at some point in his life, Barrera must've smiled. I'm
also sure he would've been careful to eliminate any witnesses to the event. The skin around his eyes was two
shades lighter brown than the rest of his face and bore
permanent oval rings from all those years wearing FBI
standard-issue sunglasses, before he'd retired into the private sector. He never wore the glasses these days. He
didn't need to anymore. The glossy, inscrutable quality
had sunk directly into his corneas.

He looked at me with mild distaste, then looked at
Jem the same way. Jem smiled and asked Barrera if he
wanted to see a magic trick. Barrera apparently didn't.
He looked back at me and said, "My conversations are
with Erainya."

"See you later, then."

"Probably so." He said it like he was agreeing that a
sick horse probably needed to be shot. Then he brushed
past me and got into his mustard-yellow BMW and
drove away.

I stood watching the intersection of 410 and Blanco
until Jem tugged on my T-shirt and reminded me where
we were. We went inside the restaurant.

Two hours before the lunch crowd, Manoli was
already behind the kitchen counter carving gyro strips off
a big column of lamb meat. It seemed like every time I
came in the column of lamb got skinnier and Manoli got
thicker.

The place smelled good, like grilled onions and fresh-
baked *spanakopita*. It wasn't easy to get a Mediterranean
feel in a strip mall, but Manoli had done what he could—
whitewashed walls, a couple of tourist posters from

Athens, some Greek instruments on the wall, bottles of Uzo on each table. Nobody came here for the decor anyway.

Erainya was sitting on a bar stool at the counter, talking to Manoli in Greek. She wore high heels and a T-shirt dress, black of course. She looked up when I came in, then lifted one bony hand and slapped the air like it was the side of my face.

"Ah, this *guy*," she said to nobody in particular, disgusted.

Manoli pointed his cleaver at me and grinned.

Jem ran up to his mom and hugged her leg. Erainya managed to tousle his hair and tell him he was a good boy without softening the look of death she had aimed at me.

Erainya's eyes are the only thing big about her. They're huge and black-irised, almost bug-eyed except they're too damn intense to look funny. Everything else about her is small and wiry—her black hair, her bony frame under the T-shirt dress, her hands, even her mouth when she frowns. Like she's made out of coat hangers.

Erainya slid off the bar stool, came up to me, and frowned some more. She stands about five feet tall in the heels, but I've never heard anybody describe her as short. A lot of other things, but never short.

"You got my phone message?" I asked.

"I got it."

"What did Barrera want?"

"Let's get a table," she told me.

We did. Manoli sat Jem on the counter and started talking to him in Greek. Jem doesn't understand Greek, as far as I know, but it didn't seem to bother either of them.

"All right," Erainya said. "Give me details."

I told her about my morning. About halfway through she started shaking her head no and kept shaking it until I'd finished.

"Ah, I don't believe this," she said. "How is it you convinced me to let you do this case?"

"Masculine charm?"

She scowled at me. "You look good, honey. Not that good."

Erainya smiled. She looked out the restaurant window, checking the office. Nobody was beating down the door of the Erainya Manos Agency. No crowds were queuing up for a full-service Greek detective.

"Why was Barrera here?" I asked again.

Erainya slapped the air. "Don't worry about that *vlaka*, honey. He just likes to check up on me, make sure I'm not stealing his business."

It was a point of pride so I nodded like I believed it. Like Barrera needed Erainya's divorce cases and employee checks to stay afloat. Like his security contracts with half the companies in town wasn't enough.

For the millionth time, I looked at Erainya and tried to imagine her back in the days when that competition had been real—back when her husband Fred Barrow was still alive and in charge of the agency and Erainya was Anglicized as Irene, the good little assistant to her husband the sort-of-famous P.I. That was before she'd shot Barrow in the chest. Then he'd been sort-of dead.

The judge had said it was self-defense. Irene had said God rest Fred's soul. Then she'd cashed in her husband's stocks and returned to the Old Country and come back a year later as Erainya (rhymes with *Transylvania*) Manos, tan and very Greek, mother of an adopted Moslem Bosnian orphan whom she'd named after somebody in a novel she'd read. She'd taken over her husband's old agency and become an investigator like it had been her destiny all along. Business had been sliding ever since.

Two years ago, when I'd just moved back to town and was thinking about going legit as a licensed investigator, one of my dad's old SAPD friends who didn't know Barrow was dead had recommended Fred as the second-best P.I. in town to apprentice with, just after Sam Barrera.

After Sam and I had decidedly failed to hit it off I'd gone to Fred Barrow's office address and discovered in the first thirty seconds I was there that Erainya was the trainer for me.

Is Mr. Barrow here?

No. He was my husband. I had to shoot him.

"That's it on the Kearnes case, then," Erainya was saying. "You got what—twenty hours left?"

I hesitated. "Jem says ten."

"Ah, only ten? It's twenty. Anyway, we've got other things to do."

"You said I could do *this*."

Erainya tapped her fingers on the Formica table. They sounded hard, like pure bone.

"I said you could try, honey. Somebody gets murdered, that's the end of it. It's a police matter now."

I stared at the picture of Athens behind her head.

Erainya sighed. "You don't want to have this conversation again, do you?"

"What conversation? The one where you explain why you can't pay me anything this week, then you ask me to baby-sit?"

Her eyes got very dark. "No, honey, the one where we talk about why you want to do this job. You spend a few years in San Francisco doing arm-breaking for some shady law firm, you think that makes you an investigator? You think you're too good for a regular caseload—you'll just keep churning the ones that interest you?"

"You're right," I said. "I don't want to have this conversation again."

Erainya muttered something in Greek. Then she leaned toward me across the table and switched to English midsentence.

"—tell you this. You think you're a big deal, coming back to town with your Berkeley Ph.D. and whatever. Okay. You think you're too good to apprentice because you've been on the streets awhile. Okay too."

"I did teach you the trick with the superglue."

She used both hands this time, going out on either side

of her face like she was slapping people sitting next to her.

"Okay, so you show me one thing. It's even all right you think you want to do this because your dad was a cop. You think you want to do personal favors once in a while, do something out of charity—all right, fine. But that's not what you do to make a living, honey. The job is hard work, which you keep trying not to notice, and mostly it's not personal. You sit in a car for eight hours with intestinal problems taking pictures of some sleaze-ball because another sleazeball paid you to. You look at old deeds and talk to boring credit bureau men that aren't even good-looking. You keep the police happy, which means you stay away from anything where people end up dead. Mostly you don't make much money so, yeah, maybe you do have to take your kid along some-times. I'm talking about the bread-and-butter work. I don't know if you can handle that part of it, honey. I still don't know that about you."

"If you're not going to recommend me to the Board," I said, "now would be a good time to say so."

The coat hangers that made up Erainya's body seemed to loosen a little bit, and she sat back in her chair. She looked out the window again, checking for clients. Still no lines outside the office.

"I don't know," she said. "Maybe not. Not if you can't take a case when it's good and drop a case when it's bad. As long as you're operating under my license I can't risk you getting it revoked."

I examined her face, trying to determine why the warning she'd thrown out so many times before had a harder edge this time.

"Barrera said something to you," I guessed. "He's got pull with the Board. Was he pressuring you about me?"

"Don't be dumb, honey."

"I just watched a woman get murdered, Erainya. I'd like to know why. I could at least—"

"That's right," she said, sitting forward again. "You shake up that Kearnes woman one day and she runs out and gets herself killed the next. What does that tell you about your methods, honey? It tells me you should listen sometimes. You don't blow a surveillance because you're getting impatient. You don't ring the subject's doorbell and ask them to confess to you."

The rims of my ears felt hot. I nodded. "Okay."

Fingers on the Formica. "Okay what?"

"Okay maybe I'll quit. Withdraw. Un-apprentice. Whatever you call it."

She waved her hand dismissively. "Ah, what, after this many months?"

I got up.

She stared at me for a few seconds, then looked back out the window like it didn't matter one way or the other to her. "Whatever you want to do, honey."

I started to leave.

When I was at the door she called me. She said, "Think about it, honey. We could treat it as time off. Tell me next week."

I looked over at Manoli, who was telling Jem something in Greek. It must've been a fairy tale, by the tone and the gestures he was using.

"I told you today, Erainya."

"Next week," she insisted.

I said sure. Before I could leave, Jem looked over and asked me what kind of party we would have when my hours got to zero. He wanted to know what kind of cake.

I told him I'd have to think about it.

4

When I got back to 90 Queen Anne my landlord Gary Hales was out front watering the sidewalk. It looked like he was doing a good job. A few new cracks had sprouted. A couple of slabs that had started to buckle up last week were buckling up a little more. Gary's got a gray thumb.

"Howdy," I told him.

He looked at me like he was trying to figure out who I was.

Gary's a pale guy, kind of quivery, his skin washed-out blue and his face all liquid. Looking at him with a garden hose is kind of disconcerting because you're never really sure where the stream of water stops and Gary starts.

"Ye-uh," he said. "Your lady friend's come by."

I sighed. "You let her in?"

A ripple went across his mouth. Maybe it was a smile. Gary's a sucker for the sweet-talking ladies.

"You old dog," I said. "What'd she promise you this time?"

Another ripple. "Ye-uh. Should make her a key, I reckon."

I walked around to the right side of the house. The yard was crunchy with pecans and mesquite bean pods and red bougainvillea petals, the closest we get to fall colors in South Texas.

Ninety Queen Anne was a decaying two-story craftsman in a state of major denial. It had a dignified facade, intricate woodwork around the windows, a huge bougainvillea-draped front porch where you could sit out of an evening and sip your margarita. But the white paint had started to peel a long time ago, and the green shingled roof sagged in the middle. Sometime in the 1950s the whole house had shifted on its foundations so the right half drooped slightly backward. My mother said it looked paralyzed. I preferred to think of it as extremely relaxed.

When I got to the porch of my in-law apartment Carolaine Smith was standing in the doorway, letting the air-conditioning escape. She was holding the telephone toward me.

Carolaine had on her anchorperson costume—a white silk blouse and conservative blue skirt and blazer, her dark blond hair done up big, brushed away from her face, her makeup heavy for the cameras. Only her prescription glasses were out of costume. They were large black mousy jobs left over from her days as a small-time reporter, back when she still called herself Carolyn. She only wore the glasses now when she wanted to see.

"So who's Annie at First Texan?" she asked. "She sounds cute."

"No comment."

"Asshole."

Carolaine handed me the receiver.

Annie at First Texan had pretty much the same question

about Carolaine, but she finally agreed to give me the information I'd asked her for last Friday about Julie Kearnes.

Carolaine went into the kitchen, where it smelled like something was burning. I stood in the middle of the living room and looked around. My laundry had been put away for me. The futon was put back into couch position. The swords were off the coffee table and back in the wall rack. Robert Johnson had climbed to the top of the closet and was hiding between two shoe boxes.

He peered out at me hopefully.

I shook my head to tell him that Carolaine was still here.

He made a low growl and disappeared back into the shadows.

Annie started telling me about Julie Kearnes' checking account. Biweekly direct deposits from something called Paintbrush Enterprises—$250 each, steady for the last two months, which was as far back as Annie had pulled the files. A few sporadic paychecks from a temp employment firm in Austin. All other deposits in cash, probably gig money, none of them large amounts. Three overdrafts at H.E.B. Central Market. The usual monthly bills. Julie's balance at the moment was $42.33. About forty dollars more than mine.

Annie told me I owed her big-time for risking her job.

"Like Garth Brooks," she suggested. "And dinner at La Margarita."

I said it would be fine with me if she had dinner with Garth at La Margarita. I wouldn't stand in the way. Annie called me some unflattering names and hung up.

Carolaine pulled a cookie sheet out of the oven and said, "Damn."

I think the things on the sheet had been *chiláquiles* in a former life. Strips of corn tortilla and bacon were curled up and smoking. The cheese was brown and the jalapeños were gray. It smelled pretty bad.

"Tinfoil on the top," I suggested. "And turn it down to three hundred degrees next time. That old Wedgewood's like a nuclear reactor in there."

"Damn it," Carolaine said, pushing up her glasses. "I've got to be back at the studio for the noon broadcast."

"Rowww," Robert Johnson complained from the closet.

I looked down at the burned food, then at my clean living room. "You shouldn't have done all this."

"No big deal."

"No," I said. "I mean you shouldn't have done it. You shouldn't keep getting Gary to let you in and setting up house. You don't clean your *own* apartment this much. It makes me nervous."

She leaned back against the sink and raised her eyebrows. "You're welcome."

I stared out the kitchen window at the crepe myrtle.

Carolaine dropped her hands on her thighs. "Jesus, Tres, what am I supposed to do? I've hardly seen you this month. You cancel dinner dates on me three times in a row, you leave me waiting outside the Majestic for an hour with two goddamn concert tickets, then I try to do something nice for you—"

"I'm sorry. It's been a hard morning, Carolaine."

Sarcastic smile. "I bet. Still following some woman around Austin. Peeping through her windows with binoculars at night. Poor guy."

"She was murdered."

The smile flickered around the edges, then disappeared.

She listened while I told her the story. She kept her expression soft and sympathetic, but her eyes weren't totally focused on me. They were moving slightly back and forth like they were reading math equations, maybe calculating what the murder meant for my job prospects.

When I was done Carolaine folded her arms. "What did Erainya say?"

"That I was handling it wrong anyway. End of case."

"What did you say?"

"I quit."

After a moment of stunned silence Carolaine looked at her watch. Then she took her purse off the counter and rummaged for something inside. She was trying not to let it show, but I could see the relief loosening up her shoulder muscles.

"So what now?" she asked.

"I don't know. It depends on what Milo Chavez wants."

"You mean you might keep working for him, unlicensed—like the work you did before?"

She said *before* like it was a euphemism for something one didn't talk about in polite company.

"Maybe," I admitted.

"The last time you did this man a favor it almost got you killed, yes?"

"Yes."

"I don't understand—I don't see why you can't just . . ."

She stopped herself. The corners of her mouth tightened.

"Say it," I told her. "Why can't I just use my degree and get a real job teaching English somewhere."

She shook her head. "It's not my business, is it?"

"Carolaine—"

"I have to leave, Tres." Then she added without much optimism, "You could come back to the studio with me. We could get takeout, spend the afternoon in my dressing room like old times. It might do us some good."

"I have to call Milo."

The frost set in. "All right."

Carolaine closed her purse, then came up and kissed me very lightly without ever really looking at me. She smelled like baby powder. There were a few freckles on her nose that the makeup hadn't quite covered.

"Sorry I bothered you," she said.

The front door slammed behind her.

Robert Johnson came out of the closet as soon as he heard Carolaine's car start. He looked out the window suspiciously, then gave me a look of death he must've learned from Erainya Manos.

"You want to play Anne Frank when people come over," I said, "don't blame me."

He came over and bit me on the ankle, lazily, then headed for the food dish.

Some days everybody wants to be your friend.

5

At sunset the sky turned the color of cooked eggplant. Seven million grackles descended for a con-
vention in the trees and phone wires above the
city. They sat there making a scratchy high-pitched sound
that was probably screwing up the sonar of every sub-
marine in the Gulf of Mexico.

I stood in the kitchen reading the *Express-News* late
edition. I had just started on my third Shiner Bock and
was starting to get mercifully numb in the extremities.

Julie Kearnes had had the good sense to get murdered
on a slow news day. She merited a small story on A-12. I
received honorable mention for making the 911 call. The
staff writer had done some homework. He wrote that
readers might remember Kearnes for her song "Three
More Lonely Nights," recorded by Emmylou Harris in
1978, or for Julie's more recent work as fiddle player and
backup singer to rising local star Miranda Daniels. The
police had no leads in the killing, no murder weapon, no
useful witnesses.

The writer mentioned nothing else about Julie Kearnes—none of the immaterial stuff I had learned from following her around town, talking to her neighbors, going through her garbage. For instance that Julie's favorite food was Thai. That she shopped at the same New Age stores my mother liked. That Julie had played fiddle in country bands since she was six but secretly, at night, preferred to listen to Itzhak Perlman. That she drank cheap white wine and owned a parrot.

None of that made it into the *Express-News*—just the fact that Julie Kearnes now had a hole in her head.

The last part of the article talked about what a pain it was having the SAC parking lot cordoned off all morning for the investigation. It quoted some grumpy students who'd had to park several blocks away from class.

I thought about Julie Kearnes all dressed up nice, fiddle beside her in the '68 Cougar. I thought about the real downside of surveillance—not the boredom, like most P.I.s will tell you, but the times when the subject starts to become a real person to you.

I drank more beer.

I'd had no luck with the telephone. I'd paged and left messages for Milo Chavez but his secretary Gladys insisted that he couldn't be reached. Milo was somewhere in Boerne, working on a major event. Gladys acknowledged that a major event in Boerne was an oxymoron, but she still said there was nothing she could do for me. Yes, she had heard the news about Julie Kearnes. Yes, the police had been by. Yes, she had left messages for Milo about it. No, she still couldn't reach him. No, reaching Les Saint-Pierre himself, God of Talent Agents, was out of the question. Why not try back tomorrow?

I thanked her and hung up the phone.

I was ready to turn in for the day. Unfortunately, time and tide and my weekly dinner at Mother's house would wait for no man.

I went to the bathroom and looked at myself in the mirror.

"You can do this," I said.

Robert Johnson looked up at me sideways from the leaky faucet that doubled as his watering hole. He offered no words of encouragement.

I showered and dressed fancy—jeans with no holes, my Bay to Breakers T-shirt, my deck shoes, the newer ones that didn't yet resemble baked potatoes.

Then I put the top down on the VW and headed north on Broadway toward Vandiver Street, blasting tinny *conjunto* music from my AM radio all the way through downtown Alamo Heights. When I stopped at the light on the corner of Austin Highway a couple of guys in tuxedoes and Stetsons in the Mercedes next to me looked over and stared.

Once you get to Vandiver it's easy to find my mother's house, even in the dark. You just go down the row of white post-WW II houses until you find the pink adobe bungalow with the green porch light. Understated.

Nobody met me at the door so I let myself in.

Mother was burning frankincense tonight. The Christmas lights were blinking in the pencil cactus, and the hot tub out on the deck was bubbling happily to itself, ready for a party. The general theme of the house was Ethnic Eclectic—Mexican curios next to Japanese kimonos next to African burial masks.

Two guys I'd never seen before were playing pool in the dining room. They were about my age. They wore tight jeans and boots and denim shirts with the sleeves rolled up to show their triceps.

They nodded at me and kept playing.

I went down the steps into the kitchen, where Mother and Jess were watching TV. Carolaine was on, doing an advertisement for the ten o'clock news. She said she'd have the latest on the North Side apartment fire.

"Tres, honey." Mother got up, squashed my cheeks together with both hands, and kissed me. "I hope tortilla soup is all right."

Mother was dressed for Zimbabwe. She had on a multicolored caftan and a long black shawl. Her ebony earrings were shaped like the stone heads on Easter

Island and her forearms had so many silver bangles on them they looked like Slinkys. She was around fifty-five and looked thirty-five, tops.

Jess told me howdy and went back to watching the Oilers game. Jess graduated from Heights a couple of years before I did. We played varsity together. I think he was Young Boyfriend number three or four since my mom had gotten her divorce, burned her pot roast recipes, and reinvented herself as a New Age *artiste*.

"I expect a full report," Mother was saying. "How is Carolaine? We never miss the KSAT news anymore. You should tell her to wear that green dress more often, Tres. It's very flattering."

I told her Carolaine was fine and no we were not living together yet and no I didn't know when or if we would be. Mother didn't like the "if" part very much. She looked disappointed that I wasn't living in sin yet. She told me she recommended it highly.

"Huh," Jess said. He kept his eyes on the ball game.

Mother went to stir the soup. She added a bowl of boiled chicken and stewed tomatoes to the broth. I came over to the counter and started chopping cilantro for her.

"And work?" Mother looked sideways at me, intently.

"Maybe not so great. I've got one job to finish. After that . . ."

She nodded, satisfied, then pushed a strand of black hair back over her ear.

Out of habit I tried to spot any sign of gray. There wasn't any. God knows I'd snuck plenty of looks into her medicine cabinet for Miss Clairol and never found anything more incriminating than vitamin E, rosemary essence, and a few healing crystals. Mother looked at me again and smiled, like she knew what I was thinking and enjoyed it. It was a game she'd been winning for a good fifteen years.

"Well," she said, "I happened to talk with Professor Mitchell at UTSA."

I chopped the cilantro a little harder. "Mother—"

"Please, dear, we were just touching base."

"Touching base."

"Of course. It must've been ten years since I did that art show with his wife."

In the other room one of the young rednecks broke a setup and the other one whistled appreciatively. Jess tossed his beer can toward the trash and made it. The Oilers were winning.

"So you just happened to run across Mitchell's phone number in your book."

"That's right."

I slid the cilantro off the knife blade and into the pot. The *cebollas* were already grilled and the sour cream was ready. Strips of fried corn tortilla were in a bowl to the side, ready to be stirred in.

I wiped off my hands.

"And while you were on the phone—" I prompted.

Mother shrugged. "All right. I did ask if there were any openings in the English department."

I looked down longingly at the big knife I'd been using.

"Well, really, Jackson. He was very helpful."

Only my mother calls me by my first name and lives. She likes to put me in my place next to the first two Jackson Navarres—my father and my grandfather. The third in a long line of hopeless males.

The phone rang. My mother tried to look surprised and failed miserably.

"Good Lord, who could that be?"

I bowed to the inevitable and said I'd get it. Mother smiled.

I took the phone out onto the deck next to the hot tub, picked up the receiver, and said, "Professor Mitchell?"

A moment of surprised silence on the other end, then a fatherly voice said, "Now this isn't Tres, is it?"

I told him it was. He laughed and gave me the standard knee-high-to-a-grasshopper reminiscences about how long it had been and how glad he was I'd gotten out of puberty. I said I was too.

"Your mother told me you were job hunting," he said.

"Yeah, about that—"

I wanted to apologize for my mother thinking that college teaching jobs grew on trees and fell when ripe as soon as one's parents made phone calls to old friends.

Before I could, Professor Mitchell said, "I made your appointment for eleven o'clock Saturday. It's the only day we're all available to interview."

I hesitated, then closed the glass door to the kitchen to shut out the pool game and the TV.

"Pardon?"

"Your mother's timing was perfect as usual," Mitchell said. "Big stir-up in the department, the hiring committee just forming. So happens I'm on it. Eleven o'clock. Will that time work for you?"

A polite no would've done just fine. *Sorry, my mother's just meddling in my life again and I have a very bright future in private investigations.* I kept waiting to hear myself say no. I watched through the glass door as Carolaine came on the television again, this time for a newsbreak.

Maybe what made me weaken was Carolaine's face. Maybe it was a week with almost no sleep, doing surveillance, minding a four-year-old. Or the fact that whenever I closed my eyes now I saw Julie Kearnes in her '68 blue Cougar, people with white rubber gloves picking fragments out of her hair with tweezers. When I finally responded to Professor Mitchell I didn't say no. I said, "Eleven o'clock Saturday. What the hell."

My mother's voice came on the upstairs phone line. She sighed and said, "I've died and gone to heaven."

Professor Mitchell started laughing.

6

The good news Tuesday morning was that Gladys the secretary was able to negotiate a lunch meeting for me with Milo Chavez. Actually, Milo was meeting with somebody else, but Gladys figured it might be okay if I dropped in for a few minutes—seeing as there was a homicide to talk about and all.

The bad news was that lunch would require money.

I tried the ATM on Broadway and Elizabeth but it played stubborn with me. It told me my checking balance was insufficient for the minimum twenty-dollar withdrawal. I tried for a cash advance from credit. Somewhere in New Jersey, the people at VISA laughed long and hard.

Plan C. I called my old friends at Manny Forester & Associates. By nine-thirty I had three subpoenas Manny's normal errand boys had been unable to serve. By eleven o'clock I'd found two of the invisible men, dropped the papers at their feet, and gotten away with no more than a few cuss words and a steak knife waved in my face. Not my idea of fun steady work, but at fifty dollars a subpoena it wasn't bad emergency income.

The third delivery was for a repeat customer—William Burnett, a.k.a. Sarge. I served process on him at least once a month thanks to Manny Forester's zealous efforts on behalf of Sarge's wife and creditors. Sarge just kept on smiling and lighting his cigars with the subpoenas, moving from downtown bar to downtown bar. He and I were to the point now where we took turns buying each other beers every time I tracked him down. He'd tell me all about his days in the coast guard down in Corpus Christi.

Thanks to Sarge's stories and the hospitality of the Cantina Azteca I was thirty minutes late for lunch.

When I finally got to Tycoon Flats on North St. Mary's, the tables in the burger joint's courtyard were filling up with college kids from Trinity and lunch-hour businessmen. It was overcast and humid. Heavy kitchen smoke drifted through the mesquite trees into the laundry lines of the unpainted houses behind the restaurant. The whole neighborhood smelled like well-done bacon cheeseburgers.

Milo Chavez wasn't hard to spot. At a green picnic table halfway across the courtyard sat 350 pounds of human boulder, neatly packaged in fifty-two-inch pleated gray trousers and a white dress shirt that had probably been custom-tailored from most of a hot air balloon. He wore gold accents from his stud earring to his Gucci loafer buckles. His hair was newly razor-cut to a thin black stubble, which made his coppery face seem even more huge. The Latino Buddha, with fashion sense.

Sitting across from Milo was an older Anglo man who was trying to impersonate a navy pilot. I might've fallen for the pressed khakis and aviator's glasses, but the leather flight jacket was overkill. His mouth was too soft, his gray-blond eyebrows a little too twitchy and nervous for a navy man.

He was frowning and holding out his fingers in Cat's Cradle position and speaking to Milo in low but insistent tones. I caught "I will *not*" several times.

I tried to read Milo's face, but there was nothing there except Milo's standard sleepy, almost bovine calm.

Of course that didn't mean anything. Milo had looked calm when he'd run into me at Mi Tierra the week before and told me about the demo tape problem that might lose his agency a million-dollar contract. He'd looked calm at our high school senior party when he'd shoved Kyle Mavery's face into the sour cream dip for making snide comments about Chavez's parents having green cards. He'd looked calm in college after we'd just been shot at by a Berkeley house owner whose neglected dog Milo and I had decided to liberate. He'd even looked calm two years after that when he was fired from his first job at Terrence & Goldman Law Offices, after Milo's brilliant idea for tracking down a material witness had landed me in the IC unit at San Francisco General. After many years of on-and-off friendship, I still could never tell when Milo was about to crack a joke or erupt into violence or convince me to do something dangerous and stupid that would sound, coming from Milo, like the sanest course of action in the world. Hanging around him for any length of time did not rate highly on the Tres Navarre fun-o-meter.

I plopped down with my Shiner Bock longneck and my basket of curly fries next to the pilot. I flicked him a salute. "Permission to come aboard?"

The pilot stared at me. "Who the hell—"

Milo gave me a slight shake of the head. "Tres Navarre, meet John Crea. Miranda Daniels' producer."

"*Ex*-producer," Crea amended.

"Pleased as punch." I looked at Milo. "I've been calling you since yesterday morning, Chavez. I'm beginning to feel unloved."

Milo raised his hand, then returned his attention to Crea. "You can't walk away from this, Johnny. You going to give up your ten percent of the final project?"

Crea laughed. His eyebrows twitched. "There isn't going to be any final project, Chavez. You're talking about fifty more hours in the studio by next Friday. Only spec time. That's crazy. Even if I wasn't fed up with the fucking redneck scare tactics—Jesus, did you *see* the bullet hole, Milo?"

"Les is working on things," Milo promised.

Crea stabbed the picnic table with his middle finger. "If Les is working on things I want to know why he's unreachable while I'm getting shot at. Where is the son of a bitch?"

"I told you. Nashville. The developmental deal with Century—"

"The developmental deal is history. I came here to see Les, and some money, and some serious signs that I'm going to get protection." He glanced at me briefly, snorted. "I don't see anything like that. I've got other things to do, Milo. *Adios.*"

John Crea got up, straightened his jaw and his aviator glasses and his flight jacket, and left in a wake of Old Spice. He did it so fast I forgot to come to attention.

Milo stared at his food, then at mine. He reached over, appropriated the largest fry in my basket, and began uncurling it meticulously between his massive fingers.

"He dresses almost as snappy as you," I said.

Milo's features move slowly if they move at all. You pretty much have to rely on his eyes. Now they were dark and concentrated. Angry.

"Johnny used to manage Mel Tillis," he told me. "They did a show once on an aircraft carrier, the whole road crew got those flight jackets. It kind of went to Johnny's head."

"What was he talking about just now?"

Milo ate the smallest bite of fry. "More trouble with Miranda's Century Records deal. Sunday night somebody took some potshots at Crea as he was coming out of the studio, around midnight. He heard a pop, pop, took him a few seconds to realize it was a gun. Police came, found a slug in the doorway, said they'd get right on it."

"A sniper. Like with Julie Kearnes. Thanks for telling me."

"I was meaning to, man."

"Sure. Right after you got through laying flowers on Julie's grave."

Milo gave me a bland look. "Kearnes made my life hell. She stole from us. What do you expect me to do—cry?"

"No. I wouldn't expect that from you. But Julie Kearnes didn't steal your damn demo tape, Milo."

I told him about my last few days of surveillance, up to and including my falling out with Erainya, and my feelings that maybe I'd be looking for some other kind of work in the not-too-distant future.

Milo finished dissecting and eating the curly fry. He produced an individual Wetwipes packet from his pocket, ripped it open, and began wiping the grease off his fingers carefully, cleaning under his nails. I caught the scent of lemon.

"I'm sorry, Navarre. Is that what you want to hear? You want to cut loose from this and leave it to the police, nothing's stopping you. Les and I will figure out something."

"Bullshit."

Milo's black eyes drifted back toward me. "What was that?"

"You and Saint-Pierre aren't figuring out a damn thing, Milo, and your problem is bigger than a missing demo tape. People are getting shot at here; one of them is dead. What the fuck is going on?"

He gave me the look of a bull that was just a little too sleepy to charge. "You know who Les Saint-Pierre *is*, Tres? Every artist that's come out of Texas since 1980, Les has either booked their dates or managed them or both. Miranda Daniels isn't the first artist he's gotten flack for stealing from her local sponsors, for taking her to the big league. He's handled worse."

"Why am I not convinced?"

Milo put his hand flat on the picnic table. He drummed his fingers slowly, one at a time, like he was making sure they all still worked. "I like this job, Navarre. It's not just legal commissions, you know? I'm starting to sell my own dates at fifteen percent. Miranda Daniels gets the Century Records deal, people are going to start knowing my name."

"I'm still not hearing any answers."

"Are you willing to keep working for me?"

"I've worked for a lot of lawyers, Milo. You know what I hate about it? They always have to test you. They give you one small corner of a case and wait to see how you'll handle it. Sometimes that caution works out okay. More often it leaves you operating with a dangerously incomplete picture and somebody winds up hurt. Seeing as we've known each other for fifteen years, seeing as we've been down this road before, I figured we'd be skipping the test stage. I guess I was wrong."

Milo tapped his fingers. "All right."

"All right, what?"

"I made some calls about you over the last week, after you agreed to look at Julie Kearnes."

"Calls," I repeated. "What kind of calls?"

"Roger Schumman, for one. He said you did nice work—said you threw a loan shark through his office window extremely well. Manny Forester had good things to say, too. Seems you know how to get discreet results with skip traces. He said if all his thugs had Ph.D.s maybe they'd be as reliable as you."

"You called for references. On me."

Milo shrugged. "It's been a long time since San Francisco, Navarre. I figured you'd turn out to be good at this kind of work. I was glad to find out I was right."

"No more tests, Milo. What's going on?"

Milo started to say something, then stopped. He tapped his fingers. "Les isn't in Nashville. He's been missing for over two weeks."

I took a plastic knife, reached over, and cut off half of the uneaten cheeseburger in Milo's basket. "And you haven't told the police, even after what happened to Julie Kearnes?"

"It's not that simple. Les—" Milo searched for the right phrase, something legally neutral. Finally he gave up. "Les screws up a lot. He's eccentric. He drinks, he has some other bad habits. Sometimes he'll go off on a binge for a few days and we'll have to cover by saying he's out of town, like we're doing now. I can't be sure—"

"Has he ever been gone this long before?"

Milo shook his head. "But still—" His voice trailed off in disappointment, not buying what he was about to say.

"You think his disappearance might be connected to the missing demo tape," I said. "And the gunshots at John Crea. Now Julie Kearnes' murder. You think it might all be part of a package—somebody pissed off because of this deal you're working on."

"That's what I'm afraid of."

"The wife hasn't reported Les missing?"

The look of distaste on Milo's face told me Mrs. Saint-Pierre was not his favorite subject. "Let me tell you about Les Saint-Pierre and his wife and the police. About six months ago, the last time Les took off, Allison went to Missing Persons. You know what they told her?"

I ate some cheeseburger. I waited.

"They told her Les was *already* missing. For seven years. Seems a former girlfriend had the same problem with him disappearing, reported Les and forgot to let the police know when he'd come home. The Bureau never bothered to follow up, take him off the rolls. Can you believe that?"

"It's been known to happen. MPB is flooded with domestics that are resolved ninety percent of the time before they're even assigned."

"Yeah, well. This time Allison isn't in any hurry. Les joked from time to time about running away to Mexico.

Allison figures maybe he finally did it and she's not crying any tears."

"We're not talking just Missing Persons this time, Milo. Homicide is going to want to talk to Les. You've got to tell them."

Milo pulled on the back of his neck. "It's more complicated than that, Navarre. It's one thing for our clients to think Les is eccentric—that he slips out of pocket for a few days now and then. That his wife reports him gone after a fight or whatever. People can give him some slack there because he's Les Saint-Pierre. But the minute somebody hears a rumor he's honest-to-God missing—that *I'm* looking for him, that it's just Milo holding down the fort—"

He raised his hands off the table. "I need to find Les. Quickly and quietly. And I don't have time to shop around for help."

"You know how to flatter a guy."

He reached into his pocket and pulled out a money roll only Milo could've carried without his pants bulging obscenely—fifty-dollar bills wrapped as thick as a Coke can.

"Your boss doesn't like the case, we can cut out the middle man."

"No," I said. "I don't have my own license. At this point it looks like I might never."

"That's just as well."

"I told you, I'm thinking about getting out of this line of work."

Milo put the cylinder of money sideways on the table and rolled it in my direction. "You're going to look into Kearnes' murder anyway, Navarre. You couldn't put down something that happened on your watch—I know you better than that. Why not let me pay you?"

Maybe I felt like I owed him. Or maybe I was thinking about how long I'd known him, off and on since high school, always reconnecting with each other at the least opportune moments like bad acoustical echoes.

Or maybe I'm kidding myself. Maybe what swayed

me more was that roll of money—the prospect of paying my rent on time for once and not having to borrow grocery money from my mother.

I heard myself saying, "What exactly do you want me to do?"

7

The Les Saint-Pierre Talent Agency was a gray and maroon Victorian on West Ashby, across the street from the Koehler Museum.

Even without a sign in front you could tell the old residence had been converted for business. The power-color combination, the uniform blinds on the windows, the well-kept but totally impersonal landscaping, the Texas flag windsock hanging on the empty front porch—it all screamed "office building."

There were two cars already parked at the bottom of the hill in front. One was a tan Volvo wagon. When I met Milo on the sidewalk he was staring at the other— a glistening black pickup truck that looked like it had been converted at great expense from a semi rig. It had wheels just shy of monster size, tinted windows with security alarm decals on the corners, orange pin-striping, mud flaps with silver silhouettes of Barbie doll women on them. The cab looked like it could sleep four comfortably.

Milo said, "This isn't my day."

Before I could ask what he meant, he turned and lumbered up the steps.

Inside, the Victorian was all hardwood floors and cream-colored walls. A staircase led up from the main foyer. The double doorway on the right opened into a reception area with a couple of wicker chairs, a mahogany desk, a fireplace, and a Turkish rug. A very big Anglo man in his early fifties was sitting on the edge of the desk, talking with Gladys the receptionist.

When I say *very big* and I'm standing next to Milo I have to correct myself. This guy wasn't like Milo, but he was big by any other definition. Tall and barrel-chested. Thick neck. Powerful hands. He had the build of a derrick worker.

Despite the heat he wore a denim jacket over his white shirt, new blue jeans, black Justin boots. He was twirling a Stetson on one finger while he talked.

When he saw Milo, his smile hardened.

"*Hola*, Mario."

Milo walked placidly to the desk and picked up a stack of mail. He didn't look at his visitor. "Fuck you, Sheckly. You know my name."

"Hey now—" Sheckly spoke with the twangy, hard-edged accent of a German-Texan, someone who'd grown up in the hill country around Fredericksburg, where many of the families still spoke a brand of cowboy *Deutsch*. "Play nice with me, son. I just dropped by to see how things were coming along. Have to make sure you're doing right by my girl. You remind Les about that contract yet?"

Milo kept flipping through his mail. "Les is still in Nashville. I'll tell him you dropped by. The contract's right next to the toilet where he left it."

Sheckly's laugh was a rich chuckle. He kept twirling the Stetson. "Come on now, son. You want to dispute our agreement, you've got to put me in touch with the boss man. Otherwise I'm expecting Miranda in the Split Rail studio come November first and I'll tell you what else—you send Century that demo and I'll send them a copy of my contract, see if they want to sink their money into a girl who's gonna bring their legal department a mess of business."

Milo opened another letter. "You know where the door is."

Sheckly got up from the desk slowly, told the receptionist, "You think about it," then started walking out.

In front of me he stopped and offered to shake. "Tilden Sheckly. Most people call me Sheck."

Up close, it looked like all the unnecessary pigments in Mr. Sheckly's face had drained into his tan, which was dark and perfect. His eyes were so bleached blue they were almost white. His lips had no red at all. His hair had probably been thick and chocolaty at one time. It had faded to a dusty brownish-gray, uncombable tufts that looked like clumps of moth wings.

I told him my name.

"I know who you are," he said. "I knew your father."

"Lots of people knew my father."

Sheck grinned, but it wasn't friendly. He looked like I'd missed the joke. "I suppose so. Most of them didn't contribute as much as I did."

Then he put on the Stetson and said good-bye.

When he was gone Milo turned to Gladys. "What did he mean, 'think about it'?"

Gladys said Sheck had offered her a secretarial job with a fifty percent pay raise. She said she'd turned him down. She sounded a little wistful about it.

Milo stared at the space on the desk where Sheck had been sitting. He looked like he was contemplating putting his fist through the mahogany. "You do those calls yet?"

Gladys shook her head. She launched into a long story about how some club owner in San Marcos had called and complained that Eli Watts and His Sunrisers had torn up the hotel room he'd rented for them and now he wanted the agency to pay the damages. Gladys had spent her entire morning trying to smooth things out.

I thought the desk was going to get it, but slowly Milo's meaty fists unclenched. He mumbled something under his breath, then led me down the hall and into his office.

Everything in the converted parlor had been custom-made for Milo's comfort—two massive red leather chairs, a half-ton oak desk with a twenty-one-inch computer monitor and a candy bowl the size of a basketball, bookshelves that started as high as most bookshelves stopped and went all the way to the ceiling. The only thing small was Milo's rosewood Yamaha acoustic in the corner, the same guitar he used to bring on our drunken college road trips into the Sonoma wine country. There was still a crescent-shaped dent near the sound hole where I'd thrown a beer can at Milo and missed.

I sat across the desk from Milo.

On the right wall were framed pictures of Les Saint-Pierre's past and present artists. I recognized several country stars. Nobody recent. Nobody I would've considered huge.

Prominently displayed in the center was a photo of the Miranda Daniels Band—six people at a bar in a honky-tonk, all facing out toward the camera and trying to look casual, like they lined up that way every night. Julie Kearnes and Miranda Daniels were shoulder to shoulder in the middle, sitting up on the bar with their cowboy boots crossed at the ankles and their denim skirts carefully arranged to show some calf.

Miranda looked about twenty-five, her hair dark and shoulder-length, just curly enough to look tangled. Petite body, almost boyish. An unremarkable face. In this shot she was smiling, looking out the corner of her eye at Julie Kearnes, who got caught mid-laugh. With the air-brushing you almost couldn't tell Julie was older than Miranda.

The two good old boys on their right were in their sixties. One had a trimmed white beard and a healthy belly. The other was tall, with no body fat at all and thinning, greasy black hair. The men on the left were younger, both

in their forties, one with longish blond hair and a thick
build and an Op T-shirt, the other with dark curly hair
and a black cattleman's coat and black hat and a scowl
that was probably supposed to be James Deanesque but
didn't quite make it. The cattleman looked quite a bit
like Miranda Daniels, but twenty years older.

On the wall behind the picture was a pale square halo
that told me the band's photo had superseded somebody
else's whose picture had been slightly larger.

Milo followed my eyes to the photo on the wall.

"They're not important," he assured me. "The old
fart with the white beard is Miranda's dad, Willis. The
guy in the Wyatt Earp outfit is her big brother, Brent.
You know—knew—Julie. The thin greasy one is Ben
French. The burly surfer reject is Cam Compton."

"Miranda's brother and her dad are in the band?"

Milo spread his hands. "Welcome to Hillbilly World.
Funny thing is, until about two years ago Miranda was
considered the *un*-talented one in the family. Then Tilden
Sheckly, the lovely human being you just met, took an
interest in her."

"Sheckly is part of your problem."

Milo reached for his candy bowl. "Butterscotch or
peppermint?"

"Definitely butterscotch."

He threw me a roll of midget Life Savers, then took
two for himself. "Sheck owns that big honky-tonk on the
way to Medina Lake, the Indian Paintbrush. You know
the place?"

I nodded. Anybody who'd ever driven toward Medina
Lake knew the Indian Paintbrush. Plopped next to the
highway in the middle of several hundred acres of rock
and dirt, the dance hall looked like the world's largest
portable john—a white corrugated metal box big enough
to accommodate a shopping mall.

"Paintbrush Enterprises," I speculated. "The company
who's been sending Julie Kearnes biweekly deposits."

Milo stared at me. "Do I want to know how you got
access to her bank account?"

"No."

He cracked a smile. "Sheck is known for promoting pet acts. Usually pretty younger women. He lets them open for his headliners on weekends, sometimes gets them into his house band. Sooner or later, he gets them into bed. He manages their careers for fifty percent of the profit, milks them as long as he can. Once upon a time that was Julie Kearnes. Julie acted like a good girl, so even when she stopped bringing in crowds Sheckly kept her on the payroll—doing his spreadsheets, designing promotionals, occasionally opening for somebody. Miranda Daniels was going to be Sheckly's next project. Then Les signed her out from under Sheck's nose."

"And Sheckly still thinks he owns her."

Milo nodded.

"And you and Les disagree."

Milo unwrapped his Life Savers and dumped them in his mouth. He brushed his hands, slid out the side drawer of his desk, and produced a legal-sized document. "You heard Sheckly mention a contract just now?"

I nodded.

Milo slid the paper across to me. "Before we signed Miranda Daniels, Sheck had all kinds of plans for her. He was going to put her first album out on this little regional label he owns—Split Rail Records. He was going to tour her around small clubs in the States and Europe, be her sugar daddy. He probably stood to make about a quarter of a mil off her. Miranda stood to make shit—minimal sales and no national exposure. That was Sheck's plan, only he never put anything in writing. Probably he couldn't imagine Miranda'd be crazy enough to cross him.

"Then Les signed her away from him. Sheck screamed and hollered but there wasn't much he could do. The band was mostly Sheck's old protégés—Julie, Cam Compton, Ben French—but there wasn't much they could do either. They went along with the new arrangement. It wasn't until Les got Century Records interested in hearing Miranda's solo demo tape that Sheckly suddenly waltzed into our office with *that*."

I scanned the document. It was a poor-quality photostat of an agreement dated last July, signed by Tilden Sheckly and Les Saint-Pierre as Miranda's manager. All the legalese seemed to boil down to one main promise: that Tilden Sheckly would have first option on any performances or recordings by Miranda Daniels for the next three years.

I looked at Milo. "This means Sheckly could veto the deal with Century Records?"

"Exactly."

"Is the contract valid?"

"Hell, no. Les screamed bloody murder when he read it. It's a forgery, the oldest bluff tactic in the book. Sheckly's just trying to scare away a potential buyer and Les wasn't about to fall for it."

"So what's the problem?"

"The problem is it's a very effective bluff. Major labels are skittish about new talent. To prove the contract invalid Les would have to go to court, make Sheckly produce the original document. Sheckly could delay for months, drag things out until Century lost interest in Miranda or found another place to sink their money. The window of opportunity for a deal like this shuts pretty damn quick."

"And Les isn't around to challenge it."

Milo held his hand out for the contract. I gave it back. He stared at it distastefully, then folded it and filed it away.

"Les said he had a plan to get Sheckly's balls in a squeeze, something to make Sheck withdraw the contract and do anything else Les told him to do. Les had been spending a lot of time with Julie Kearnes since we took over management of the band. Les said she was going to help him out."

"Blackmail?"

"Knowing Les, I don't doubt it. I warned him to be careful of Julie Kearnes. She'd been working too long with Sheckly; she was still taking his money. Julie was sweet to Les but I saw her other side. She was bitter, short-tempered, jealous as hell. She complained about how Miranda was going to go down the same way she had, that it was just a matter of time. Julie said Miranda should be more grateful, keep Julie around for all her experience once Miranda signed with Century."

He sighed. "Les wouldn't listen to me about Kearnes. They'd gotten pretty close over the last month. I'm not sure how close, to tell you the truth. Then he disappeared. I was hoping if you kept tabs on Julie"—Milo rapped his knuckles lightly on the desk, he scowled—"I don't know what I thought. But it looks like Sheckly got his problems solved very neatly. First Les. Now Julie. Whatever they were planning to do to get Sheck's claws off Miranda Daniels, it isn't going to happen now."

I found myself looking again at the photo on the wall—at the unimpressive face of Miranda Daniels. Milo must've guessed my thoughts.

"You haven't heard her sing, Navarre. Yes, she's worth the trouble."

"There's got to be other country singers around. Why would a guy like Tilden Sheckly get bent out of shape over one that broke out of the stable?"

Milo opened his mouth, then closed it again. He looked like he was reorganizing what he wanted to say. "You don't know Sheck, Navarre. I told you he lets some of his well-behaved artists like Julie Kearnes stick around after they're washed up. One of Sheck's *less* cooperative girls ended up at the bottom of a motor lodge pool. Freak swimming accident. Another male singer who tried to get out from under Sheckly's thumb was busted with a gram of cocaine in his glove compartment, got three years of hard time. The deputies in Sheck's county handled both cases. Half of the Avalon Sheriff's Department works security at the Paintbrush on their off hours. You figure it out."

"Still—"

"Les and Sheck had a history, Tres. I don't know all the bloody details but I know they've been at each other's throats over one deal or another for years. I think this time Les went a little too far trying to twist Sheckly's arm. I think Sheckly finally decided to solve the problem the way Sheck knows best. I need you to tell me for sure."

I unwrapped a butterscotch and put it in my mouth. "Three conditions."

"Name them."

"First, you don't lie to me. You don't withhold anything again. If I ask you for a top ten list you give me eleven items."

"Done."

"Second, get better candy."

Milo smiled. "And third?"

"You bring in the police. Talk to the wife, set it up any way you want, put the best face on it, call it a silly necessity to your clients—but you level with SAPD about Saint-Pierre being gone. You have to get his name into the system. I won't poke around for two or three more weeks, then find out I've been failing to report another homicide. Or a killer."

"You can't seriously think Les—"

"You said Julie and Les were getting close. Julie is now dead. If the police start looking around and can't find Saint-Pierre, what are they going to think? You've got to level with them."

"I told you—I can't just go—"

I got my backpack off the floor and unzipped the side pocket.

It was an old green nylon pack, a holdover from my grad days at Berkeley. It served me well in investigative work. Nobody cares much about grad students with backpacks. Nobody thinks you might be carrying burglar tools or recorders or fat rolls of fifty-dollar bills.

I took out Chavez's money and put it on his desk. Then I stood up to leave.

"Thanks for the chat, Milo."

Milo leaned back and pressed his palm to the center of his forehead, like he was checking for a fever. "All right, Navarre. Sit down."

"You agree?"

"I don't have much choice."

The phone rang. Milo answered it with a "hello" that was mostly growl.

Then his entire disposition changed. The emotion drained out of his voice and his face paled to the color of caffe latte. He leaned forward into the receiver. "Yes. Yes, absolutely. Oh—no problem. Les, ah— No, no, sir. What if—no, that's fine."

The conversation went on like that for about five minutes. Somewhere in the middle of it I sat back down. I tried not to look at Milo. He sounded like an overwhelmed ten-year-old listening to Hank Aaron explain why he couldn't sign the kid's baseball card.

When Milo hung up he stared at the receiver. His fingers wrapped around the wad of money, almost protectively.

"Century Records?" I asked.

He nodded.

"It's getting hard on you."

"I didn't want to run the entire agency, Navarre. We've got seven other artists touring right now. I've got promoters breathing down my neck about deals Les didn't even mention to me. Now Century Records—I don't know how I'm going to hold the deal together when they find out Les is gone."

"So walk away."

Milo seemed to turn the words around in his head. They must have rolled unevenly, like rocks in a tumbler.

"What do you mean?"

"Let the agency collapse if it has to. You've got your law degree. You seem to know what you're doing. What do you need the charades for?"

Milo shook his head. "I need Saint-Pierre's clout. I can't do it on my own."

"Okay."

"You don't believe me."

I shrugged. "Somebody once told me my problem was thinking too small—that I should just take a chance and throw myself into the kind of work I really liked, the hell with what people said. Of course that advice got me a knife in the chest a week later. Maybe you don't want to follow it."

Milo's eyes traced a complete circle around the room, like they were following the course of a miniature train. When they refocused on me, his voice was tightly controlled, angry. "Are you going to help me or not?"

"The Century Records deal is that important to you?"

Milo made a fist. "You don't get it, do you, Navarre? Right now Miranda Daniels is making about fifteen-hundred a gig—that's payment for the *whole* band, if she's lucky. She has minimal name recognition in Texas. Suddenly Century Records, one of the biggest Nashville labels, says they're interested enough to offer a developmental deal. They give her money for a demo, thirty days in the studio, and if they like what comes out of that, she's guaranteed a major contract. That would mean over a million dollars up front. Her price per gig would go up by a factor of ten and my commission would go up with it. Other people in the industry would suddenly take me seriously, not just as Les Saint-Pierre's step-and-fetch-it. You have any idea what it's like having somebody dangle that possibility in front of you, and knowing that a jerk like Tilden Sheckly could screw it up?"

I nodded. "So what's our deadline?"

Milo looked down, unclenched the fist, rubbed his hand flat against the desktop. "Miranda's master demo is due to Century next Friday. I've got that long to get the recording redone and to figure out a way to keep Sheck quiet about this forged contract. Otherwise there's a good chance Century will renege on their offer. Ten days, Navarre. Then, if all goes well, maybe I'll take your advice. I'll ask Miranda to let me represent her and let the rest of the agency go to hell."

There was a knock on the door. Gladys stuck her head in and said that Conwell and the Boys were here for the five minutes Milo had promised them last week. They'd brought a tape.

Milo started to tell Gladys to send them away but

then changed his mind. He told her they should come on down.

When she closed the door again Milo said, "Unsolicited demo tapes. I could build a house out of what we've got in the back room, but you never know. I try not to blow people off."

He pushed the money back to me.

"Just ask Gladys for the files on your way out—she'll know what you mean. It's some background material I put together, stuff you would need to know."

"You assumed I would stay on the case."

"Read the files over. And it's about time you met Miranda Daniels. She's playing at the Cactus Cafe in Austin tomorrow night. You know the place?"

I nodded. "Julie Kearnes' death isn't going to make you cancel the gig?"

My comment might as well have been a sneeze for all it registered. "Just come check Miranda out. See what the fuss is about. Then we can talk."

I didn't protest very hard. I dropped the roll of fifties back in my bag and promised to think things over.

When I was at the door Milo said, "Navarre."

I turned.

Milo was staring through me, into the hallway. "It'll be different this time. It's not like—it's not like I feel good about the way things happened back then, okay?"

It was the closest he'd ever come to an apology.

I nodded. "Okay, Milo."

Then Conwell and the Boys were pouring in around me, all grins and new haircuts and coats and ties. Milo Chavez switched moods and started telling the musicians how glad he was they could drop by, how sorry he was that Les Saint-Pierre was out of town.

I heard the easy laughter of the meeting all my way down the hall.

8

On my way out of the office Gladys gave me a thick gray mailing envelope and told me to have a nice day.

The chances of that happening went down considerably when I got outside and noticed Tilden Sheckly's black truck still in front of the agency. Sheckly himself was across the street, reclining in the passenger seat of my VW bug.

The afternoon was so humid the metal on the cars steamed. With the convertible top up, my VW would be about as comfortable as a pressure cooker. The fact that Sheck had probably been waiting there for a while cheered me up.

I walked around to the driver's side but didn't get in. Sheck was reading a book that I'd left on the floorboard. He'd taken off his Stetson and his denim jacket and set an S & W revolver on the dash.

"I know the cars look alike," I sympathized. "But yours is the one with the pin stripes."

Sheck smiled up at me from his book, my book.

I knew a kid in third grade who liked to set living things on fire with no warning. One minute you'd be sitting there laughing with him about the latest episode of *H. R. Puffinstuff* and the next he'd be holding a match to the shredded newspaper in the class guinea pig cage. His face never changed—small bright eyes like pilot lights, a wide friendly smile that was totally disconnected from his brain. He looked so sweet the teachers tolerated him right up to the day he poured gasoline in a sandbox full of kindergartners and tried to set it ablaze.

Sheck's smile reminded me a lot of that kid.

He hefted my book of medieval drama. "You really understand this muck?"

He turned a page, then tried to read aloud a few lines from the Wakefield *Cain and Abel*.

"Not bad," I commented. "They'd pronounce the 'I' *Eee*. Like *Eee* am wondering what this guy is doing in my car."

Sheck patted the driver's seat. "Come on in."

"I make it a policy not to sit next to people with guns."

He seemed to notice the revolver for the first time. "Oh, hell, son. Give this old man a handle—see why I carry him around."

He picked up the gun by the cylinder and offered me the stock.

"You're supposed to empty the chambers first, aren't you?"

Sheck laughed. "What perfect world do you live in, son? Just take the damn gun."

"Thanks, no."

He shrugged, then put the .41 back on the dashboard. "I'll be sorry when the revolver is history. Everybody nowadays is hot for semiauto, got to have a twelve-round magazine. Truth is this old man never got a chance—finest damn revolver ever made. You know what it is?"

"Smith & Wesson M58," I said. "M & P style."

Sheck nodded approval. "You're a gun lover."

"I know guns," I corrected. "I don't love them much."

That statement apparently made as much sense to Sheck as the Middle English. He tried to interpret it, failed, then decided to keep talking.

".41 caliber round was perfect evolution, you understand—all the punch of a .44 with the velocity of a .357. This is the kind of gun your dad carried on the force back in the seventies. You know why they canned it?"

I said I didn't.

"Police were firing hot loads with it, full Magnum capability. The muzzle blasts were scaring all the lady cops." He laughed. "Then public relations started thinking the citizens would get mad—cops with Magnums blowing away all those helpless victims of society down in the barrio. A damn shame."

"What do you want, Mr. Sheckly?"

Sheck put his finger in the book and closed it, like he'd be coming back to it in a minute. Maybe he wanted to see how things worked out with Cain and God.

"I's just curious what kind of stories your *compadre*'s been telling you. I figured you'd be walking out of there with a big retainer and a bigger load of horseshit."

"Why exactly did you figure that?"

Sheck glanced to his right and smiled, like there was somebody there he wanted to share the joke with. "Come on, son. Old Milo'd love to think I'm the boogeyman causing his every little problem."

"Every little problem. You mean like Miranda Daniels' producer getting shot at, her demo tape stolen, Julie Kearnes murdered—those kinds of little problems?"

Sheckly kept smiling. "Hell, son, I ain't the one who decided Miranda needed a national deal. You understand Century Records only wants *her*, don't you? The rest of the band—those boys don't stand to get nothing from this except a handshake. You want to know who's angry enough with Milo Chavez to cause some problems, you just think about that goddamn Century deal."

"That's funny," I said.

"What is?"

"You keep saying Milo. Les is the one with the agency. Is there some reason you're not worried about him?"

Sheck's smile didn't waver at all. "All right. Let me ask you about that. If Les Saint-Pierre is so all-powerful smart, what makes him hire a three-hundred-pound wetback to sell country music to redneck bars? That make any business sense to you?"

He raised his palm. "I'm serious now, not trying to be mean here. I just don't get what was going through Les' head. I sure as hell wouldn't be out of town as much as he's been, leaving *Gordo* in charge. I'll deal with anybody I need to; don't get me wrong. But there's club owners a lot worse than me, they see Chavez coming—" He shook his head regretfully. "That kind of thing's gonna really hurt Miranda's job prospects."

I looked at the blue S & W on my dashboard.

"Mr. Sheckly, it's hot out. The only air-conditioning I've got in this convertible is called 'fourth gear.' I'd like to get moving."

"I'm just telling you, Tres—I worry about my friends the Danielses. Willis and me go way back. I care about his daughter doing all right. This agency's charging ten percent for booking, old Les is gettin' forty more for management. For fifty percent of my career, if I was Miranda, I'd expect a damn sight better service."

"And you're the better service."

"That's right."

"I hear you did wonders for that other girl you sponsored—the one in the swimming pool."

Sheck let out air between his teeth. "You could do yourself a favor right now and forget whatever horseshit Chavez's been feeding you. I'll do right by Miranda. You think some spic lawyer's gonna play straight with you about that? You think your daddy would be arguing against me here?"

I counted to five. "Sheck—you like Sheck, right?"

He nodded.

"Honest, Sheck—I appreciate the concern. The thing

is, the only load of manure I've come across today has been dumped in my passenger seat. I'd like it out of here."

Sheck's face darkened but his eyes stayed as bright and colorless as high-octane fuel. "That was a mistake, son. I can overlook one mistake. When I was younger I thought I was hot shit, too."

"Are you going to get out of my car?"

Sheck put my book back on the floorboard. He took his revolver off the dash and got out of the car.

"I thought to level with you, Tres, because I knew your father. I never had any beef with him; I don't see any reason to have one with you. You want to talk, come on out to my place some night. I'll buy you a beer. But you get yourself tangled on the wrong side of the barbed wire when it comes to Miranda Daniels, I'll eat you for lunch."

There was no anger in his voice, no violent edge.

He turned and walked with easy confidence across West Ashby, back to his truck. He didn't even bother to holster the S & W.

9

 I got home around sunset, changed into exercise clothes, and ran through the basic stances, five minutes each, then twenty minutes of silk reeling exercises.

Afterward I lay on the floor until the sweat started to dry and the air-conditioning felt cold again. Robert Johnson climbed up onto my chest and sat there, staring down at my face.

"What?" I said.

He yawned, showing me the black spots on the top of his mouth. His breath was not pleasant.

I made our standard dinner—Friskies tacos for him, *chalupas* for me. I showered and changed, then drank a Shiner at the kitchen counter.

My green neon KMAC wall clock read seven-oh-five. Erainya Manos would still be at the office, typing up the daily client reports. The professors at UTSA would probably be in their offices too, preparing for night classes or yawning as they waded through bad under-

graduate essays. I tried to imagine myself in either place.
I couldn't quite do it. All I got in my head was a cartoon
vision of me as Wile E. Coyote, my toes clinging to two
different icebergs, doing the splits as they drifted farther
and farther apart. In my hand a little wooden sign that
read *yikes*!

I looked at the thick gray envelope that was propped
up by the sink. The maroon words LES SAINT-PIERRE TALENT
were printed in the upper right-hand corner. No return
address, just like there'd been no number on the business
card. You either knew what you needed to know to get in
touch with Les Saint-Pierre or you didn't merit the information. Cocky.

I opened the envelope and started to read.

On top of the stack, on a piece of yellow legal paper,
Milo had brainstormed all the personal facts he knew
about the missing talent agent. The list was surprisingly
short. Date of birth April 8, 1952. Place of birth unknown,
somewhere near Texarkana, Milo thought. High school
in Denton, a year of formal music training at North
Texas State before Saint-Pierre had dropped out and
joined the air force toward the end of Vietnam. In '76,
he'd started his music industry career as a song-plugger
for a large Nashville publishing group. He'd been partially responsible for the surge in Texas music that had
happened over the following few years—the birth of the
Austin City Limits TV show with its video-taped studio
concerts, the rise of Willie Nelson and the other Outlaws,
the sudden interest in places like Luckenbach and Gilley's
and Kerrville. Les had been a confirmed bachelor until
three years ago, when he'd met Allison Cassidy in
Nashville. He and Allison now lived in Monte Vista, not
far from the agency's office.

On the back of the page was a list of Les' favorite bars
and hangouts in San Antonio and Austin. That list was
more extensive.

Underneath the legal paper was a portrait studio
photo of the God of Talent Agents. Les Saint-Pierre looked
like a cross between Barry Manilow and an amateur

prizefighter. His mouth was a colorless Cupid's bow and his eyes were dark and soft. Maybe the unsuspecting could even mistake them as sensitive. His nose had started out as a fine thin triangle but had obviously been broken at least once. His neck, his cheekbones, and his brow were all a little too thick, a little too Neanderthal for Manilow. His hair was short and greasy and thinning and his shirt was open to reveal a chest that was robust enough but pale and hairless and somehow hollow-looking. There was a slightly haggard look to his face, and a dangerous quality, too—the kind of omnivorous hunger you see in drug addicts and car salesmen and low-rated talk show hosts.

I skimmed through the rest of the package. A copy of Les' management contract with Miranda Daniels, a copy of the allegedly backdated agreement between Tilden Sheckly and Les, a list of present clients and how much the agency had grossed in commissions in the last six months—just over a million dollars all together. There was a rundown on the last dates Les had personally sold and the last people he had spoken with. Tilden Sheckly and Julie Kearnes were among them.

The last person who'd seen Les Saint-Pierre was the lady who watered his plants. Les had walked out of his house on the morning of October twelfth, told the horti-culturist to lock up on her way out, then vanished into thin air. Neither of his two cars ever left the garage.

Milo had formulated a list of twenty or thirty people Les had antagonized over the years. Tilden Sheckly's name was on top. Several other names were famous country singers. There was no list of Les' friends.

I checked my watch. Still happy hour. I put the gray envelope and a wad of Milo's money into my backpack and headed out to make some friends in the service industry.

Seven bars and a dozen tip-me-and-maybe-I'll-remember-something encounters later, I wasn't much wiser than when I'd started. I told everybody I was an old friend of Les' trying to track him down. The bartender at the

Broadway 50-50 complained that Les had an unpaid tab of $230. The manager at Diamond Rodeo said Les was a bloodsucker but for God's sake I shouldn't tell Les he said so. A singer named Tony Dell at La Puerta told me a great story about how Les had once left him stranded in Korea doing an eight-hour-a-day sweatshop gig that had almost driven Dell to suicide. Dell said no hard feelings and if I could get a tape to Les he had some great new material. Everybody agreed that Les hadn't been around in the last couple of weeks. Nobody seemed too concerned about it and nobody warmed up to me much when I told them I was Les' friend.

It was full dark by the time I pulled in front of the Saint-Pierres' Monte Vista mansion—a three-story white stucco wedge with a half-acre front yard, two-car garage, and just enough lit view around the side of the house to confirm that there was a swimming pool and a tennis court. I rang the doorbell for five minutes.

No Les. No Mrs. Saint-Pierre.

I went back to the VW and sat, pondering a next move. The night clouds darkened and turned the texture of cedar bark. The grackles gave way to the quieter drone of the crickets.

In the yellow dash light I ran my finger around the pages of Milo's handwriting, looking for nightclubs I hadn't yet visited. My finger kept coming back to one in particular.

What the hell.

I drove north to see if Tilden Sheckly still wanted to buy me a beer.

10

I came over the rise of San Geronimo Hill and saw the Indian Paintbrush below. The whole expanse of metal building was lit up stark white like some kind of giant UFO hangar. Its twenty-foot-high trademark neon wildflower blinked one petal at a time, then flashed all at once.

The road sign out front said TAMMY VAUGHN TONIGHT! Underneath, in smaller letters that obviously hadn't been changed in a long time, it said MIR NDA D NIELS EVERY SAT.

Apparently Tammy Vaughn had some draw. The gravel lot was almost full and a line of trucks and cars was still snaking in from the access road. Inside the lot, parking attendants jogged around trying to give directions. Waist-deep clouds of shiny dust were rolling through the crisscrossed headlights.

After parking the VW, I made my way to the ticket window and through an entrance corridor that smelled like a cattle chute. A bouncer in a Confederate flag T-shirt

stamped a little green star on the back of my hand and
sent me on into the main hall.

The place was not small.

A light-gauge bullet shot from the entrance probably
would've fallen short of the neon beer signs mounted
on either side wall. The ceiling would've been a long
shot too.

Along the back wall was an empty stage about fifty
feet wide and five feet high. Speakers the size of coffins
hung from the ceiling, cranking out canned music that
sounded vaguely like Alabama.

The bar stretched out for a good forty yards, manned
by an army of bartenders in matching red Western shirts.
Some of the bartenders were busy filling orders. Most
were not. I walked downstream until I found a particularly bored-looking woman whose name tag read *Leena*.
I ordered a Shiner draft and a shot of Cuervo.

"Sheck around tonight?" I asked.

Leena started to make a distasteful face, then froze,
suddenly wary. "You a friend?"

"Sheck's got friends?"

Leena smiled. "Amen to that."

I told her I was a talent buyer putting together a pro-
motional and I was hoping to run some demos past
Sheck. I had no idea what I was saying and neither did
Leena, but she was more than willing to point out Tilden
Sheckly. He was forty yards away at the edge of the
dance floor, arguing heatedly with a redheaded woman in
a sky-blue jumpsuit.

"I wouldn't count on him being available anytime
soon," Leena told me. "Simulcast rights."

"How's that?"

She nodded again toward the lady in the jumpsuit.
"Tammy Vaughn's manager. She's going to demand some
rights to the radio broadcast. She'll blame the booking
agency for overlooking that when they signed the contract. Sheckly's going to tell her tough shit. Tammy will
end up playing the gig anyway because she needs the
exposure. Here comes the contract."

Sure enough, just at that moment Sheckly produced a piece of paper and held it in the woman's face, like he was inviting her to find any line that supported her demand. The manager brushed the paper away and kept arguing.

"Every damn week," Leena told me. "He'll spend half the night arguing with her, the rest of the night trying to get in her pants."

"Suppose I just left a note in his office," I said.

"Upstairs annex, past the bull ring, next to the studio." She pointed toward the double doors, far off to the right, where the neon bullrider was flickering back and forth on his neon bull. Leena leaned across the bar, gave me a friendly smile. "Now you're gonna have to buy another drink, honey, or I need to quit talking."

I told her thanks, put a dollar in her pitcher, and got up to leave.

Leena sighed. "The night goes downhill from here."

The bull riding arena was dark. Seventeen or eighteen empty rows of seats sloped down toward the circular pit. Nothing there but some red plastic barrels, rodeo clown props, two metal chute gates on the north wall hanging open apathetically. The dirt was scarred and streaked from the last round of boot heels and hooves that had pounded through it. Nobody had raked since then. Sloppy.

A man and a woman were sitting in the top row, arguing about somebody named Samantha. When they saw me they stopped, annoyed, and got up. They moved their conversation back into the dance hall.

The noise of the music and the crowd sounded tinny and far away, like it was echoing from the bottom of an oil tanker. I walked around the perimeter of the arena to a metal door with a sidebar and a white sign that read EMPLOYEES ONLY. I looked for an alarm wire. None. No surveillance camera. I pushed the door open.

Inside was an empty office with cheesy walnut paneling and pink carpeting. There were three metal desks. On the wall were framed posters of Tilden Sheckly's washed-up B-grade artists, Julie Kearnes among them. There was plenty of blank space on the wall for Miranda Daniels a few years down the line. Probably several others, too.

Two doors led out of the room, left and right. The left one said STUDIO and the right said SHECK. I looked for surveillance equipment on the SHECK door and found none.

Okay.

The handle turned.

One look at the layout of the office and I was tempted to close the door and try coming back in again, just to make sure I was seeing correctly.

It looked like a cross between a safari hunter's tent and a Hard Rock Cafe. A huge zebra-skin rug took up most of the floor. A mounted tiger's head glared at me from the wall behind the desk. The ceiling was decorated with deer antlers like stalactites. On the east wall a padlocked gun display glowed from inside, showing off all sorts of rifles and shotguns. On the west wall an identical case was filled with musical instruments—a fiddle, two acoustic guitars, a black electric. I looked closer at the instruments. The fiddle had Bob Wills' name on it, set in mother-of-pearl.

I went to the desk.

After five minutes rummaging I hadn't learned much. The few personal records Sheckly kept were all done by hand, scrawled in a third-grade cursive with all the *b*'s and *d*'s slanting backward and none of the *i*'s dotted. He was a doodler; little stars and curlicues adorned the margins of his notes.

Sheck had been making some calls recently about a trucking company he owned that had apparently been losing stock value. He also had notes on phone calls he'd made with Les, among other agents, discussing the terms of various deals with performers scheduled to play the Paintbrush. As Leena the bartender had indicated, there were several notes about managers and agents protesting Tilden's unstated rights to his radio broadcasts of the headliner shows. Apparently the artists got no percentage of the syndication money and had no say over the mix or content of the show that was recorded.

There were also airline receipts for trips to Europe dating back several years—mostly to Germany and the Czech Republic. Some were made out to Tilden Sheckly. Others to someone named Alexander Blanceagle. On two of the itineraries from early last year Alexander Blanceagle was listed as traveling with Julie Kearnes. I took those.

Last was a folder with a schedule of artists' names next to dates they had performed over the last two years. Some of these names had checks, some stars. There were no notes about Miranda Daniels. No pictures of Les Saint-Pierre with dart holes in his forehead.

I walked back into the main office and tried the second door, the one labeled STUDIO.

It opened easily.

The room on the other side was about twenty by twenty, brightly lit, and completely quiet. The walls and ceiling were white acoustic tile, the floor tan industrial carpet. Clumps of boom microphone stands stuck up here and there like oversized toothpick sculptures. The left wall was covered with milk crates, towers of expensive stereo equipment, and speakers all stacked together haphazardly, many topped with collections of old McDonald's soda cups.

Against the right wall was a ten-foot-long mixing board. A man sat sideways next to it in a battered easy chair, turning control knobs and listening through Walkman-style earphones.

He was oddly built, muscular but gangly, his face angular and goofy-looking with freckles in a raccoon pattern across his nose and ears that, if not pinned back by headphones, would have made perfect little radar dishes on the sides of his head. A standard-issue Hayseed. The only thing not comical about him was the bulge under his beige windbreaker, right about where a shoulder holster would go.

He was most definitely drunk. A near-empty bottle of

Captain Morgan's sat next to him on the console. His eyes were heavy-lidded and his fingers were having trouble with the sound board controls.

I stepped into the room.

When Hayseed finally noticed me, he took a few seconds of blinking and frowning to decide I wasn't just another stack of musical equipment. He brought the easy chair into upright position and spent some time trying to connect both his feet to the floor. He got his hands working, groped up the side of his head until he found the earphones and removed them.

"Evening," I said.

He looked at me more closely and his ears turned red. "Goddamn Jean—"

He said *Jean* the French way, the Claude Van Damme way.

I was about to correct him when he stood up and began staggering toward me, reaching for the now-exposed black butt of his gun with one unsteady hand.

That pretty much decided me against the diplomatic approach.

11

I met Hayseed halfway across the room and heel-kicked him in the shin to take his mind off the gun. He grunted, stumbled forward one more step, his hands moving down instinctively toward the pain.

I grabbed his shoulders and forced him backward. When he tipped over the side of the easy chair, his knees went up and his butt sank and the back of his head hit the mixing board. The equalizer lights did a crazy little surge. His bottle of Captain Morgan's toppled over, speckling the controls with rum.

Hayseed stayed put, his arms splayed and his knees up around his ears in hog-tie position. He made a little groaning sound in his throat, like he was showing displeasure at a very bad pun.

I extracted a .38 revolver from his shoulder holster, emptied its chambers, threw gun and bullets into a nearby milk crate. I found his wallet in the pocket of his windbreaker and emptied that, too. He had twelve dollars, a driver's license that read ALEXANDER BLANCEAGLE,

1600 MECCA, HOLLYWOOD PARK, TX, and a Paintbrush Enterprises business card identifying him as Business Manager.

I looked at the mixing board. Rows of equalizer lights still bounced up and down happily. A bank of CD burners and digital disc drives were daisy-chained together, all with beady little green eyes, ready to go. There were six or seven chunky one-gigabyte cartridges scattered across the board. I picked up the earphones Alex had been wearing and listened—country music, recorded live, male singer, nothing I recognized.

Behind the chair was an unzipped black duffel bag filled with more recording cartridges and some microphone cords and a bunch of paper folders and files I didn't have time to look through.

Blanceagle's groaning changed pitch, got a little more insistent.

I helped him untangle his legs from his ears, then got him seated the right way again. His clothes fit him like a short-sheeted bed and his once nicely combed hair was doing a little swirly unicorn thing on top of his head.

He massaged his shin. "I need a damn drink."

"No, you damn don't."

He tried to sit up, then decided that didn't feel too good and settled back in. He tried to make some thick, fuzzy calculations in his head.

"You ain't Jean."

"No," I agreed. "I'm not."

"But Sheck . . ." He knit his eyebrows together, trying to think. "You look a little—"

"Like Jean," I supplied. "So it would seem."

Alexander Blanceagle rubbed his jaw, pulled his lower lip. There was a little U of blood on the gumline under one of his teeth. "What'd you want?"

"Not to get mistaken for Jean and killed, preferably."

He frowned. He didn't understand. Our little dance across the room might've happened a hundred years ago, to somebody else.

"I'm here about a friend of yours," I said. "Julie Kearnes."

The name registered slowly, sinking in through layers of rum-haze until it went off like a depth charge somewhere far under the surface. Blanceagle's freckles darkened into a solid red-brown band across his nose.

"Julie," he repeated.

"She was murdered."

His eyebrows went up. His mouth softened. His eyes cast farther afield for something to latch on to. Nostalgia mode. I had maybe five minutes when he might be open to questions.

Not that drunks have predictable emotional cycles, but they do follow a brand of chaos theory that makes sense once you've been around enough of them, or been made an alumni yourself.

I overturned a milk crate, shook the electrical cords out of it, and sat down next to Blanceagle. I unfolded one of the airline receipts I'd taken from Sheckly's desk and handed it across. "You and Julie went to Europe together a couple of times on Sheckly's tab. Were you close?"

Blanceagle stared at the receipt. His focus dissipated again. His eyes watered up. "Oh, man."

He curled forward and put the hand with the airline receipt against his forehead, the Great Karnak reading a card. He scrunched his eyes together and swallowed and started shuddering.

I'll admit to a certain manly discomfort when another guy starts to cry in front of me, even if he is drunk and funny-looking and recently guilty of trying to draw a gun on me. I sat very still until Blanceagle got his body under control. One Muddy Waters, two Muddy Waters. Twenty-seven Muddy Waters later he sat up, wiped his nose with his knuckles. He set the airline receipt on the arm of the chair and patted it.

"I got to go. I got to—"

He looked at the sound board, struggling to remember what he'd been doing. He started gathering up the one-gigabyte cartridges, sticking them in his windbreaker pockets that were a little too small to hold them. I handed him one that kept slipping away.

"You're copying a lot of music here."

He stuffed the last of the discs in his pocket, then made a feeble attempt to clean the drops of Captain Morgan's Spiced Rum off the sound board's controls, wiping between the lines of knobs with his fingers. "Sheck is crazy. I can't just—I'm in six years deep now, he can't expect—"

Alex padded his shoulder holster, realized it was empty.

"Over there." I pointed. "Sheckly can't expect what?"

Blanceagle glanced over at his unloaded gun in the milk crate, then at me, suspicious how I'd pulled that off.

"What was your name?" he asked.

I told him. He repeated "Navarre" three times, trying to place it. "You know Julie?"

"I was tailing her the day she got murdered. Maybe I helped it happen by applying pressure on her at the wrong time. I don't feel particularly good about that."

Alex Blanceagle pulled together enough anger to sound almost sober. "You're another goddamn investigator."

"Another?"

He tried to maintain the glare but he didn't have the attention span or the energy or the sobriety for it. His eyes zigzagged down and came to rest on my navel.

He muttered unconvincingly, "Get out of here."

"Alex, you've had some kind of disagreement with Sheck. You're clearing out your stuff. It's got to be in connection with the other things that have been happening. Maybe you should talk to me."

"Things will work out. You don't worry about Sheck, you understand? Les Saint-Pierre couldn't do it, I'll take care of it myself."

"Take care of what, exactly?"

Blanceagle looked down at his half-packed duffel bag and wavered between anger and wistfulness. Maybe if I'd had more time and more Captain Morgan's I could've eventually plied him into a temporary friendship, but just then the door of the studio opened and my stunt double came in.

Jean did look enough like me that I couldn't label Alex a complete idiot for making the mistake. Jean was much thicker in every part of his body, though, slightly taller, his black hair curlier. He was also less comfortably and more expensively dressed—black boots, tight gray slacks, a black turtleneck, a gray linen jacket. It must've been a thousand degrees in those clothes. His left hand casually held a gray and black Beretta that matched his outfit perfectly. His eyes were the same color as mine, hazel, but they were smaller and amorally fierce as a crab's. Put me on the GNC high-cal high-fiber diet and force me to dress that way and I probably would've looked the same.

Jean looked around calmly. He zeroed in on the shoulder holster under Alex Blanceagle's windbreaker, dismissed it, then noticed Blanceagle's full pockets and the duffel bag. Finally he looked at me. That took a little longer.

Eyes still on me, Jean asked Alex a calm, three-word question in German. Blanceagle responded in the same language—a negative answer.

Jean held out his hand.

Alex struggled to his feet. He limped over to us, trying to keep the weight off his recently kicked shin. He started fumbling with his pockets, pulling out the recording cartridges one by one, and handing them to Jean.

Two of the discs clattered to the floor. When Alex bent over to get them, Jean kicked him in the ribs just hard enough to send Blanceagle sprawling. Jean did it without anger or change of expression, the way a kid might push over a roly-poly bug.

Alex stayed on the carpet, blinking, reorienting himself, then began the process of getting his limbs to work.

Jean's next question, still in German, was aimed at me.

I shrugged helplessly. Jean looked at Alex, who was now up on one elbow and seemed quite content to stay that way.

Blanceagle squinted up at me for a long time. He said,

slowly and deliberately, "He's a steel player, for God's sake. I forgot to reschedule the fucking base track session tonight, is all."

Jean scrutinized me one more time, trying to burn a hole in my face with those little crab eyes. I tried to look like an ignorant steel guitar player. I managed the ignorant part pretty well.

Finally Jean nodded at the door. "Get out, then."

His English was perfect, the accent British. A German-speaker with a French name and a British accent. It made about as much sense as anything else I'd come across so far. I looked down at Alex Blanceagle.

"Don't worry about those base tracks," Alex told me. "I'll take care of it."

There was absolutely no confidence in his voice.

As I left, Jean and Alex were having a very quiet, very reasonable conversation in German. Jean did most of the talking, slapping the gray and black Beretta against his thigh with a casual carelessness that reminded me very much of his boss, Tilden Sheckly.

When I got back to the main room I could've stuck around longer. Tammy Vaughn was just starting her first number, "Daddy Taught Me Dancin'." I wasn't a country fan but I had heard it once or twice on the radio and Tammy sounded fine. The two hundred or so folks on the dance floor looked like a paltry crowd in the vastness of the hall, but they were hooting and hollering their best. Tilden Sheckly was standing by the sound board, still having a lively argument with the woman in the sky-blue jumpsuit. I could've asked a lot of questions, done some two-stepping with big-haired women, maybe met a few more nice men with guns.

Instead I said good-bye to Leena the bartender. She was busy now, a bottle of tequila in either hand, but she told me to stick around for a while longer. Her break was coming up soon.

I told her thanks anyway. I'd had enough of the Indian Paintbrush for one night.

12

When I woke up Tuesday I stared at the ceiling for a long time. I felt queasy, disoriented, like I'd been looking through someone else's prescription lenses too long. I groped along the windowsill until I found the business card from Julie Kearnes' wallet. The words on it hadn't changed.

LES SAINT-PIERRE TALENT
MILO CHAVEZ, ASSOCIATE

Milo's wad of fifties was still there, too, not much lighter for my night on the town.

Finally I got up, did the Chen long form in the back-yard, then showered and made *migas* for myself and Robert Johnson.

I checked the latest *Austin Chronicle*. Miranda Daniels was scheduled to start at the Cactus Cafe at eight P.M. After doing the dishes, I called my brother Garrett and left a message telling him surprise, we had plans tonight. I love my brother. I love having a free place to sleep in Austin even more.

I tried Detective Schaeffer at SAPD homicide. Schaeffer wasn't in. Milo Chavez wasn't in either.

I peeled off a stack of Milo's fifties, enough for my October rent, and left it in an envelope on the counter. Gary Hales would find it. Maybe, if things went well between now and next Friday, I would be able to spring for November too. But not yet.

I left extra water and Friskies on the kitchen counter and a piece of newspaper where Robert Johnson would, inevitably, throw up when he realized I was gone overnight. Then I headed out for the VW.

I hit Austin just after noon and spent a few more fruitless hours visiting Les Saint-Pierre's hangouts, talking to people who hadn't seen him recently. This time I claimed to be a songwriter trying to get my tape to Les. I told everybody I had a great new surefire hit called "Lovers from Lubbock." I found it difficult to generate much excitement.

After a late lunch I swung by Waterloo Records on North Lamar and found a Julie Kearnes cassette from 1979 in the bargain bin. I bought it. There were no recordings by Miranda Daniels yet. There were quite a few CDs in the Texas Artist section on Sheckly's Split Rail label—such household names as Clay Bamburg and the Sagebrush Boys, Jeff Whitney, the Perdenales Polka Men. I didn't buy them.

I drove north on Lamar, right on Thirty-eighth, into Hyde Park, following the route I'd taken last week on surveillance. I turned left on Speedway and parked across the street from Julie Kearnes' house.

The Hyde Park neighborhood is not quite as snooty as the name implies. It's equal parts college kid, aging hippie, and aging yuppie. It's got its share of bad elements—sleazy laundromats, dilapidated student housing, Baptist churches. The streets are quiet, shaded by live oaks, and lined with quaintly run-down 1940s starter homes.

Julie Kearnes' place was just run-down, not quaint. Back in the sixties it had probably been what my brother Garrett called a "hobbit house." Above the door a round stained-glass peace sign window was now grimy and broken, and the comets and suns that had once been painted along the trim of the roof and windows had been thinly whitewashed over. The yellow front lawn was shaded by a pecan tree so infested with web worms it looked like a cotton candy stick. About the only thing that looked well tended was Julie's planter box underneath the living-room window, full of purple and yellow pansies. Even those were starting to wilt.

Afternoon traffic on Speedway was heavy. An orange UT shuttle went by. Ford trucks with lawn mowers and rakes and whole Latino families in the back cruised for unkempt front yards. A good number of seventies Hondas and VW bugs puttered down the street with peeling bumper stickers like UNREAGANABLE and HONOR THE GODDESS. Austin, the only city in Texas where my car is inconspicuous.

Nobody paid me any attention. Nobody stopped at the Kearnes residence. If the police had been here they hadn't left any obvious sign.

I was about to cross the street and let myself in when a guy stuck his head in my passenger's side window and said, "I thought that was you."

Julie's across-the-street neighbor had horselike features. He smiled and you expected him to bray or nuzzle you for a sugar cube. His salt-and-pepper hair was clipped close around the ears, gelled, spiky on top. He wore a blue button-down shirt tucked into khaki walking shorts, tied with a multicolored Guatemalan belt, and when he leaned into the car I didn't so much smell him as experience one of those surrealistic fifteen-second designer cologne ads.

He grinned. "I knew you'd be back. I was sitting on my love seat having an espresso and I thought: *I bet that police detective will be back today.* Then I looked out the window and here you are."

"Here I am," I agreed. "Listen—was it Jose—?"

"Jarras. Jose Jarras." He started to spell it.

"That's great, Mr. Jarras, but—"

Jose held up one finger like he'd just remembered something vitally important and leaned farther into my car.

"Didn't I tell you?" he said, lowering his voice. "I told you something funny was going on."

"Yeah," I admitted. "You called it."

I wondered what the hell he was talking about. Maybe Julie's murder had made the *Austin American-Statesman*. Or maybe Jose was just percolating some of the great theories he'd offered me Saturday morning—how Miss Kearnes needed his help because the Mafia was after her, or the Feds, or the Daughters of the Republic of Texas.

Jose narrowed his eyes conspiratorily. "I started thinking about it after I talked to you. I said to myself, why would the police be so interested in her? Why are they staking out her house? She's got one of those drug-dealer boyfriends, doesn't she? She'll have to go into the witness protection program."

I told Jose he had a hell of a deductive mind.

"Poor dear's been super agitated," he confided. "She's stopped making those sugar cookies for me. Stopped saying hello. She's been looking like—well."

He waved his hand like I could easily imagine the crimes against fashion the poor dear had been perpetrating. I nodded sympathetically.

"She had that visitor Saturday night . . ."

"I know," I assured him. "We were watching the house."

The visitor had been one of Julie's girlfriends, an amateur aromatherapist named Vina whose innocuous life story I'd already delved into. Vina had come over to Julie's with her essential oil kit around eight and left around nine. I didn't want to tell Jose that the chances of Vina being a mafia hit man were pretty slim.

Jose leaned farther into my car. Another inch and he'd be in my lap.

"Are you going to break in?" he asked. "Check for traps?"

I assured him that it was standard procedure. Nothing to get alarmed about.

"Oh—" He nodded vigorously. "I'll let you get to work. Aren't you supposed to give me your card, in case I remember something later?"

"Give me your hand," I told him.

He looked uncertain, then thrust it at me. I took my permanent black marker off the dashboard and inscribed Jose's palm with Erainya's alternate voice-mail number, the one that says: "You have reached the Criminal Investigations Division."

He frowned at it for a minute.

"Budget cutbacks," I explained.

When I got to Julie's front door it took me about two minutes to find the right dupe for the dead bolt. I leaned leisurely against the door frame, trying different keys and whistling while I worked. I smiled at an elderly couple walking by. Nobody yelled at me. Nobody set off any alarms.

A licensed P.I. will tell you that committing crimes in the line of work is a myth. P.I.s gather evidence that might be used in court, and any evidence gathered illegally automatically ruins the case. So P.I.s are good boys and girls. They do surveillance from public property. They keep their noses clean.

It's ninety percent true. The other ten percent of the time you need to find out something or retrieve something that's never going to see its way into court, and the client—usually a lawyer—doesn't care how illegally you do it as long as you don't get caught and traced back to them. They'd just assume use somebody unprincipled and unlicensed who can play a discreet game of hardball. That's how I'd worked for five years in San Francisco— unprincipled and unlicensed. Then I'd moved back to Texas, where my dad's old friends on the force had put increasing pressure on me to get licensed and work right.

None of them wanted the embarrassment of busting Jack Navarre's kid.

I jimmied the side bolt. Then I took the two days' worth of mail from Julie's box and went inside.

The kitchen smelled like lemon and ammonia. The hardwood floors had been swept. Copies of *Fiddle Player* and *Nashville Today* were neatly stacked on the glass-topped fruit crate that served as a coffee table. There were fresh cut flowers on the dining table. She'd left an orderly home for someone who was never coming back to it.

I sat on the sofa and went through the mail. Bills. A letter from Tom and Sally Kearnes in Oregon and a pix of their new baby girl. The note said *Can't wait for you to see Andrea! Love, T & S.* I stared at the pink wrinkly face. Then I placed the photo and letter upside down on the coffee table.

I did a quick sweep of the back rooms. No messages on the answering machine. Nothing to look at in the garbage can except molding coffee grounds. The only thing interesting was on the top shelf of Julie's bedroom closet. Buried under a down comforter was a two-tone brown suitcase like you'd see in a vaudeville act.

Inside on top were photos of Les Saint-Pierre. There was Les drinking beer with Merle Haggard, Les accepting an award from Tanya Tucker, young Les in a wide-collared pink shirt, big curly hairdo, lots of polyester, standing next to a similarly dressed disco cowboy who was probably famous once but whom I didn't recognize.

Underneath the photos were lots of men's clothes, packed more like someone had been emptying drawers than picking things for a trip. It was all socks and jockey shorts. Or maybe that's what Les Saint-Pierre wore when he traveled. Maybe I'd been going to the wrong vacation spots.

I put the suitcase back.

In the den a green, hungry-looking parrot was sitting on its polished madrone branch. He told me I was a

noisy bastard and then went back to scratching raven-
ously at his cuttlebone.

I found some pistachios for him in the kitchen. Then I
sat down at Julie's IBM PS/2 and stared at a dark screen.

"Dickhead," the parrot croaked. He cracked a pistachio.

"Pleased to meet you," I said.

The corkboard behind the computer was cluttered
with paper. There was a dog-eared picture of Julie
Kearnes as a young fiddle player, her auburn hair longer,
her body slimmer. She was standing next to George
Jones. There was a more recent picture of the Miranda
Daniels Band with Julie in the forefront. The photo was
surrounded by concert reviews clipped from local papers,
a few sentences about Julie Kearnes' fiddle playing high-
lighted in pink. One front-page feature from the
Statesman entertainment section showed just Miranda
Daniels, standing between a stand-up bass and a wagon
wheel with a fake sunset backdrop behind her. The title
boldly announced: "The Rebirth of Western Swing: Why
a new breed of Texas talent will take Nashville by
storm."

A smaller corkboard to the left was more down-to-
earth. It displayed $250 check stubs from Paintbrush
Enterprises, also Julie's schedule and hourly pay scale for
several jobs she'd taken through Cellis Temps in the last
few months to make ends meet—basic word processing
and data entry for an assortment of big corporations in
town. Whether or not Miranda Daniels was going to
take Nashville by storm, it didn't look like Julie Kearnes
had been in any immediate danger of becoming affluent.

I looked through Julie's floppy disks. I opened the
horizontal cabinet and took out a thin stack of mildewed
blue folders. I was just starting to look through one
labeled "personal" when the front door opened and a
man's voice said, "Anybody home?"

Jose tiptoed into the study, smiling apologetically, like
he needed to pee real bad.

He looked around at the decor and said, "I *had* to
see."

"You're lucky I didn't shoot you."

"Oh—" He started to laugh. Then he saw my face. "You don't really have a gun, do you?"

I shrugged and turned back to the files. I never carry, but I didn't have to tell him that.

Jose unfroze and began looking around the room, picking up knickknacks and checking titles on the bookshelf. The parrot cracked pistachios and watched him.

"Dickhead," the parrot said.

I gave the bird some more nuts. I believe in positive reinforcement.

On a quick look, Julie's "personal" file seemed to deal mostly with her debts. There were plenty of them. There was also some paperwork from Statewide Credit Counseling that suggested Julie had entered into debt negotiation about two months ago. The house, the parrot, and the '68 Cougar she was murdered in seemed to be her only assets. It looked like she had two mortgages on the house and was about one of Sheckly's paychecks away from becoming homeless.

I started Julie's IBM, figuring I'd do a quick check, take the hard disk with me and look at it more leisurely later on if anything seemed of worth.

There was nothing of worth. In fact, there was nothing at all. I sat there and stared at an empty green screen, a DOS prompt asking me where its brain had gone.

I thought for a second, then turned off the machine and pried off the casing. The hard drive was still in its slot. Erased, but not removed. That was good. I wrestled it out, wrapped it in newspaper, and stuck it in my backpack. A project for Brother Garrett.

"What is it?" Jose asked.

He'd come up behind me now and was peering over my shoulder, fascinated by the open computer. The cologne was intense. The parrot sneezed.

"Nothing," I said. "A lot of it. Somebody has tried to make sure there's nothing to be found on Julie Kearnes' computer."

Jose said, "It must've been that man who came over."

I stared at him. "What man?"

Jose looked exasperated. "That's what I was talking about outside—the man who came over Saturday night. You said you knew about him."

"Wait a minute."

I did a mental checklist. Saturday night, the night before I'd confronted Julie myself. There hadn't been any man. I'd pulled standard surveillance, methods even Erainya couldn't have found fault with. I'd watched the house until eleven-oh-five, which had been lights out plus thirty minutes. At that point you can figure the subject is down for the count. I'd chalked Julie's tires, on the off chance she'd go somewhere during the night. Then I'd driven home for a few hours sleep before heading back to Austin at four-thirty the next morning.

"When did this guy come over?" I demanded.

Jose looked proud. "He banged on Julie's door at eleven-fifteen. I remembered to check my clock."

The parrot ruffled his feathers and squawked, "Shit, shit, shit."

"Yeah," I agreed.

13

When it came to snooping Jose was a pro.

He remembered that the visitor had woken up Julie Kearnes at exactly eleven-fifteen on Saturday night. He remembered the man going inside and arguing with Julie in her living room for eight minutes twenty seconds. Jose had seen them through the window. He could describe the guy well—Latino, stocky, well dressed, in his late fifties. Around five feet eight, maybe 230 pounds. His car had been a BMW, goldish color. Jose gave me the license, though after hearing the description of the visitor I was pretty sure I didn't need it.

Jose apologized that he'd only heard a few lines of their argument when the visitor came storming out of Julie's house. Something about money.

Jose said Julie Kearnes had been holding her .22 Lady-smith when she came onto the porch the second time, like she was chasing the guy out.

"She didn't fire it." He sounded disappointed.

I told Jose he'd done a great service for his country

and hustled him out the door. He vowed to call the number on his hand if he remembered anything else.

I went back inside Julie's house and stared at the disassembled computer. I looked at Dickhead the parrot, who'd just finished his last pistachio and was now eyeing my nose. Hungry, thirsty, alone.

"Robert Johnson wouldn't like you," I told him.

The parrot turned his head upside down and tried to look pathetic.

"Great," I said, and held out my arm.

Dickhead flew over and landed on my shoulder.

"Noisy bastard," he said in my ear.

"Sucker," I corrected.

When I got to Guadalupe Avenue, otherwise known as *the Drag*, the sidewalks and crosswalks were clogged with students just getting out of their afternoon classes. The five-block stretch of shops and cafes bordering the west side of campus boasted an impressive selection of human flotsam—graying hippies, homeless people and street merchants, musicians and soapbox preachers, sorority girls. Across the street from the chaos, the big peaceful live oaks and white limestone buildings and red-tiled roofs of UT stretched out forever, like Rome or Oklahoma City, someplace that had absolutely no concept of limited space.

The Drag probably wasn't the best place in Austin to get some serious thinking done. On the other hand, nobody was going to bother me sitting on the sidewalk outside the Student Co-op with a parrot on my shoulder.

Maybe Dickhead would volunteer a few choice expressions for the passersby. Maybe if I put out a hat somebody would drop coins in it. Meanwhile I could watch time pass on the UT tower clock and think about my favorite dead woman.

Julie Kearnes' finances didn't look good. Reading through them a little closer I could see how much pressure she'd been under. She'd been getting harassing reminders from the bank that held her mortgages, from all the major credit card companies, from a local Musicians' Credit Union.

The debt negotiation she'd started might have helped, eventually, but not if she lost her biweekly paychecks from Sheck because she'd been getting too close to Saint-Pierre. Not if she lost her only paying gig with Miranda because of the Century Records deal. The temp jobs she'd been doing to fill in the cracks wouldn't have been enough to sustain her and pay the debts.

So maybe she'd decided to do some dirty work. Maybe she'd found herself getting crushed to death between Les Saint-Pierre and Tilden Sheckly and had to play both ends against the middle. Steal a demo tape for Sheckly or go bankrupt. Find some dirt on Sheckly for Les Saint-Pierre or lose your gigs.

She'd known Sheckly for years, worked in his office for most of that time, took trips to Europe with his business manager. She'd been in a position to find dirt.

Maybe what she'd dug up had been a little too good. Les had disappeared before he could play his hand. Julie had gotten nervous. She'd been pressured by some unwanted visitors over the weekend, including me. Then finally she decided to set up some kind of emergency meeting Monday morning with someone she needed help from but didn't trust. She'd taken her .22, driven to San Antonio, and walked into her own murder.

People get desperate, play in a league over their head, they often get killed. Certainly not the fault of the dashing investigator who'd only come in at the end of Act V.

Maybe. The scenario didn't comfort me any. It also didn't explain the suitcase full of Les Saint-Pierre's intimate apparel sitting in Julie's closet two weeks after he'd disappeared. Or the man in the gold BMW who knew enough about surveillance to spot me and out-wait me at Julie Kearnes' on Saturday night.

On the street, three guys in studded leather coats and green porcupine hairdos walked by smoking clove cigarettes. A group of girls in matching wrinkled flannel, with long tangled hair and bleached white skin, stopped for a minute to ask me if I knew a guy named Eagle.

Flannel in Texas requires a real commitment. Until the cold fronts start coming in, anything except shorts and flip-flops requires real commitment. I told them I was impressed. Dickhead even whistled. The girls just rolled their eyes and kept walking.

By seven o'clock the sky was turning purple. The grackles started coming in from the south again and a curve of black clouds slid in from the north, smelling like rain. The last wave of college kids flooded across Guadalupe, dispersing to seek coffee shops or frat parties.

I checked my brain for new revelations on Les Saint-Pierre and Julie Kearnes, found I had none, then got up and dusted the street grime off my jeans. I went back to my VW and locked Dickhead inside with some pistachios and a cup of water.

I walked across Guadalupe Avenue to the pay phone.

When I called my own machine, the Chico Marx voice said, "Oh, broda, you gotta plenny messages."

Carolaine Smith had called, canceling our weekend plans because she had an out-of-town special assignment. She didn't sound particularly shaken up about it. Professor Mitchell had called from UTSA, asking me to bring a curriculum vitae and a dossier when I came to my interview on Saturday.

Erainya had called, reminding me she needed to hear by next week whether I was coming back to work and by the way could I take Jem for a few hours tomorrow night. It would mean a lot to him. I could hear Jem in the background singing the Barney the Dinosaur song at the top of his lungs.

My next call was collect, person-to-person to Gene Schaeffer at the SAPD homicide office. Person-to-person was the most expensive calling rate I could think of. As usual Schaeffer accepted the charges graciously.

"What a privilege," he said. "I get to pay money to talk to you."

"We should form a calling circle. You, me, Ralph Arguello."

"Screw yourself, Navarre."

Ralph Arguello is one of my less reputable friends. I made the mistake of introducing Arguello to Schaeffer once, thinking they could help each other on a West Side murder case. The problems started when Ralph offered Schaeffer a finder's fee for any unclaimed goods the detective could send to Ralph's pawnshops from the SAPD evidence locker. Schaeffer and Ralph did not come away from the encounter with a warm fuzzy feeling.

"I assume you have an excellent reason for calling," Schaeffer said.

"Julie Kearnes."

The walk light on Guadalupe changed. Students drifted across, their faces now featureless in the dusk.

"Schaeffer?"

"I remember. The fiddler. I assumed you had enough sense to get off that case."

"Just curious what you'd found."

He hesitated, probably wondering if hanging up would be enough to dissuade me. Apparently he decided not. "We found nothing. The job was clean and professional; only a few custodians in the SAC building that time of morning and nobody saw anything. Weapon was a high-powered rifle. Hasn't been found yet and I doubt it will be. Your client's going to have to look elsewhere for her missing demo tape."

"It's a little more than that, now."

I told Schaeffer about Les Saint-Pierre's disappearance. I told him about Miranda Daniels' problems getting out from under Tilden Sheckly's thumb and Milo's theory that Les might have used information from Kearnes in some kind of botched blackmail attempt. I told him about the man who had been arguing with Julie Kearnes Saturday night.

Quiet on the other end of the line. Too much of it.

"I figured you'd want to know about Saint-Pierre," I said. "I figured you'd want to find him, clear up some of those pesky questions, like is he still alive? Did he get Kearnes killed?"

"Sure, kid. Thanks."

"The guy in the BMW. Who does that sound like to you?"

"What do you mean?"

"Don't let's obfuscate, Schaeffer. You know damn well it's Samuel Barrera. He was at Erainya's not two hours after Kearnes got gunned down. Alex Blanceagle at the Paintbrush hinted that another investigator besides me had been poking around. Barrera's in this somehow—not one of his twenty operatives but Barrera himself. When was the last time Sam had a contract so juicy he handled it personally?"

"I think you're jumping to some large conclusions."

"But you'll talk to Sam."

Schaeffer hesitated. "As I remember, Barrera turned you down for a job. A couple of years ago when you were shopping around."

"What's that got to do with it?"

"What was it he told you—you weren't stable enough?"

"Disciplined. The word was *disciplined*."

"Really stuck in your craw, didn't it?"

"I got a trainer. I stayed with the program."

"Yeah. To prove what to who? All I'm saying, kid, you would be ill-advised to go forward on this Sheckly case, to see it as some personal competition between you and Barrera. I'm advising you, as a friend, to drop it. I know for a fact Erainya isn't going to cover your butt."

I stared up at the phone lines above me. I counted rows of grackles. I said, "You called it the *Sheckly* case. Why?"

"Call it whatever you want."

"He's already talked to you, hasn't he? Barrera did, or some of his friends in the Bureau. What the hell is going on, Schaeffer?"

"Now you're sounding paranoid. You think I can get pressured off a case that easy?"

I thought about his choice of words. "Not easy at all. That's what scares me."

"Let it go, Tres."

I watched the lines of grackles. Every few seconds another little rag of darkness would flit in from the evening sky and join the congregation. You couldn't identify the screeching as coming from individual birds, or even from the group of birds. The sonar static was disembodied, floating noise. It echoed up and down the malls between the limestone campus buildings behind me.

"I'll think about what you said," I promised.

"If you insist on continuing, if there is anything else you need to tell me, anything that needs reporting—"

"You'll be the first to know."

Schaeffer paused. Then he laughed dryly, wearily, like a man who had lost so many coins in the same slot machine that the whole idea of bad luck was starting to be amusing. "I'm brimming with confidence about that, Navarre. I truly am."

14

Wednesday night during midterms, to hear a
country band, I hadn't figured the Cactus Cafe
would exactly be standing room only. I was
wrong. A small whiteboard sign out front said: MI-
RANDA DANIELS, COVER $5. There was a line of about
fifty people waiting to pay it.

Most of them were couples in their twenties—
clean-looking young urban kickers with nice haircuts and
pressed denim and Tony Lama boots. A few college kids.
A few older couples who looked like they'd just driven in
from the ranch in Williamson County and were still
trying to adjust to being around people instead of cows.

At the back of the line, two guys were having an argument. One of them was my brother Garrett.

Garrett's hard to miss with the wheelchair. It's a custom-
made job—white and black Holstein hide-covered seat,
dingo balls along the edges, bright red wheel grips set
close to the axle like Garrett likes them, nothing motor-

ized, a Persian seat cushion designed for a guy whose weight distribution is different because he has no legs.

He's plastered the back of the chair with bumper stickers: SAVE BARTON SPRINGS, I'D RATHER BE GROWING HEMP, several advertising Nike and Converse. Garrett enjoys endorsing athletic shoes.

The chair's got a beer cooler under the seat and a pouch for Garrett's one-hitter and a bicycle flag-on-a-pole that Garrett long ago changed to a Jolly Roger. Garrett kids about putting retractable spikes on his wheels like they had in *Ben Hur*. At least I think he's kidding.

The guy he was arguing with had patched jeans and a black T-shirt and longish straw-colored hair. If I'd still been in California I'd've pegged him for a surfer—he had the build and the windburned face and the jerky random head movements of somebody who'd been watching the crests of waves too long. He was blowing cigarette smoke at the floor and shaking his head. "Naw, naw, naw."

"Come on, man," Garrett protested. "She's not Jimmy Buffet, okay? I just like the tunes. Hey, little bro, I want you to meet Cam Compton, the guitar player."

The guitar player looked up, annoyed that he had to be introduced at all. One of his brown irises had a bloody ring around it, as if somebody had tried to smash it in. He studied me for about five seconds before deciding I wasn't worth the trouble.

"You and yo' brother get your brains in the same place, son?" His accent was pure Southern, too rounded in the vowels for Texas. "What you think? She's gonna get eaten alive, isn't she?"

"Sure," I said. "Who are we talking about?"

"Son, son, son." Compton jerked his head toward the cafe door. He flicked ashes at the carpet. "Miranda-*fucking*-Daniels, you idiot."

"Hey, Cam," Garrett said. "Calm it down. Like I told you—"

"Calm it down," Compton repeated. He took a long drag on his cigarette, gave me a smile that was not at all friendly. "Ain't I calm? Just need to teach a bitch a lesson, is all."

Several young urban kickers in line glanced back nervously.

Compton tugged on his T-shirt, stretching the blue-gray markings above the breast pocket that had probably been words about six hundred Laundromats ago. He pointed two fingers at Garrett and started to say something, then changed his mind. Garrett was down a little low to be effectively argued with. You felt like you were scolding one of the Munchkins. Instead Cam turned to me and stabbed his fingers lightly into my chest. "You got any idea what Nashville's like?"

"Do you need those fingers to play guitar?"

Cam blinked, momentarily derailed. The fingers slipped off my chest. He jerked his head randomly a few times, trying to regain his bearings on the waves, then looked back at me and gave another close-lipped smile. Everything under control again. "She's gonna get one album if she's lucky, son, a week of parties, then *adios*."

"*Adios*," I repeated.

Cam nodded, waved his cigarette to underscore the point. "Old Sheck knew what he was doing, putting her with me. She ditches Cam Compton she ain't going to last a week."

"*Oh*," I said. Sudden revelation. "*That* Cam Compton. The washed-up artist from Sheckly's stable. Yeah, Milo's told me about you."

I smiled politely and held out my hand to shake.

Cam's forehead slowly turned scarlet. He glanced at Garrett, then held up the lit end of his cigarette and examined it. "What'd this son of a bitch just say?"

Garrett looked back and forth between us. He pulled his scraggly salt-and-pepper beard, the way he does when he's worried.

"Can I talk to you?" he asked me. " 'Scuse us."

Garrett wheeled himself out of line toward the men's room. I smiled again at Cam, then followed.

"Okay," said Garrett when I joined him, "is this going to be another Texas Chili Parlor scene?"

He gave me his evil look. With the crooked teeth and the long hair and the beard and the crazy stoned eyes, my brother can look disturbingly like a chubby Charles Manson.

I tried to sound offended. "Give me some credit."

"Shit." Garrett scratched his belly underneath the tie-dyed *I'm With Stupid* T-shirt. He produced a joint, lit it, then started talking with it still in his mouth.

"Last time I took you out we ended up with a three-hundred-dollar bar tab for broken furniture. They won't let me in the Chili Parlor for dollar magnum night anymore, okay?"

"That was different. I'd burned that guy for worker's comp fraud and he recognized me. Not my fault."

Garrett blew smoke. "Cam Compton isn't some out-of-work schmuck, little bro. He's been on *Austin City Limits*, for Chrissakes."

"You know him well?"

"He knows half the people in town, man."

"Seems like an asshole to me."

"Yeah, well, you pass around good shit and give out backstage passes to major shows, you get a little leeway in the personality department, okay? You invited me here and you're buying the beer. Just don't embarrass me."

He wheeled himself around without waiting for an answer. Cam had disappeared inside the club. Probably gone to wax his guitar or tune his surfboard or something.

Garrett flashed his blue handicapped placard and made some noise and got us back to the front of the line, then inside.

The Cactus Cafe was an unlikely music venue, just a long narrow room off the corner of the Union lobby, a stage not much bigger than a king-sized bed, a little bar in back that served beer and wine and organically correct snacks. Not much in the way of atmosphere, but for fifteen years this had been one of the best places in Austin to hear small bands and solo acts. In Austin that was saying a lot.

I followed Garrett through the crowd. He drove over as many feet as he could getting past the bar and to the far wall. I had to stand next to him, pressing against the thick burgundy drapes and hoping the window didn't open and spill us all out into the rain on Guadalupe Avenue. I had enough room only if I used one foot and kept my Shiner Bock close to my chest.

"Good crowd," I said.

"I caught her last month at the Broken Spoke," Garrett said. "You wait."

I didn't have to. Just as Garrett was about to say something else applause and hoots started up behind us. The band emerged from the back room and began pressing through the crowd.

First onstage was the pudgy, white-bearded man from the photo on Milo's wall. Willis, Miranda's dad. He looked like a Texas version of Santa Claus—hair and whiskers the color of wet cement, a jolly red face, a well-fed body stuffed into Jordache jeans and a beige collarless shirt. He limped onto the stage with a cane, then substituted a stand-up bass for it.

Next came Cam Comptom, looking not overjoyed. He stared out at the audience grudgingly, like he was afraid they were all going to pester him for autographs. When he plugged in his Stratocaster he put a blue pick in his mouth along with several frizzy strands of his hair.

After him came a mousy librarian-looking woman who was apparently Julie Kearnes' replacement on the fiddle. Then an elderly rail-thin drummer—that would be Ben French. Then a fortyish acoustic guitar player with a dark-checkered shirt and black jeans and a black Stetson that was slightly too small for his head—Brent, Miranda's older brother.

Miranda herself was not in the lineup.

Daddy Santa Claus leaned on his bass and straightened his straw hat and waved at one of the older couples in the audience. Willis might've been standing on his front porch picking for a few friends, or doing an impromptu hoedown at the local Elks Club. The rest of the band looked stiff, nervous, like their families were being held at gunpoint in the back room.

After a few minutes of general cord fumbling and string plucking, the musicians all looked expectantly at Miranda's brother Brent.

He came up to the mike uncertainly, mumbled "Howdy," then lowered his head so you couldn't see anything except the brim of his black Stetson. Without warning he started strumming his guitar like he was afraid it might get away from him. His dad the bass player, undaunted, looked over at the others, smiled, and mouthed: "Ah one, two, three—"

The rest of the band came in and started grinding through an instrumental version of "San Antonio Rose." The fiddle player sawed out the melody in a watery but fairly competent fashion.

The crowd clapped, but not very enthusiastically. Many of them kept glancing toward the back of the room.

Nobody onstage looked like they were having an exceptionally good time except for Willis Daniels, who tapped his good foot and plucked his bass and smiled at the audience like he was totally deaf and this was the best damn thing he'd ever heard.

The band lurched through a few more numbers—an anemic polka, a version of "Faded Love" during which Cam Compton had a flashback and went into a Led Zeppelin solo, then Brent Daniels' vocal of "Waltz Across Texas." Brent's voice wasn't bad, I decided after the second verse. None of the band members were bad, really. The drums were steady. The bass solid. Cam would've made a better rock 'n' roller but he obviously knew his scales. Even the substitute fiddler didn't miss a note. The players just didn't go together very well. They weren't much of a group. They definitely weren't worth a five-dollar cover.

The audience started to fidget. I wondered if there'd

been a mistake. Maybe they'd all thought Jerry Jeff or
Jimmie Dale was playing tonight. That might explain it.

Then somebody at the bar gave a good "yee-haw" as
Miranda Daniels came out from the back room wearing
all black denim and carrying a tiny Martin guitar. The
applause and whistling increased as Miranda squeezed
her way through the audience.

She looked like she did in the press release photos—
petite, pale, curly black hair. She wasn't knockout beautiful by any means, but in person she had a kind of
awkward, sleepy cuteness that the photos didn't convey.

The band put an abrupt stop to their waltz across
Texas when Miranda got onstage. She smiled tentatively
into the lights—just a hint of her dad's crinkles around
her eyes—then straightened her black shirt and plugged
in her Martin.

She was definitely cute. The men in the audience
would be looking at her and thinking it might not be a
terrible thing to be cuddled up with Miranda Daniels
under a warm quilt. That was my impartial guess,
anyway.

Daddy Santa started an up-tempo bass line going, tapping his foot like crazy, and the audience started clap-
ping. Brent's rhythm guitar came in, more sure than
before, then the drums. Miranda was still smiling,
looking down at the floor but swaying a little to the
music. She tapped her foot like her father did. Then
she brushed her hair behind her ear with one hand,
took the microphone, and sang: *"You'd better look out,
honey—"*

The voice was amazing. It was clear and sexy and
overpowering, not a hint of reservation. But it wasn't just
the voice that nailed me to the wall for the next thirty
minutes. Miranda Daniels became a different person—
nothing tentative, nothing awkward. She forgot she was
in front of an audience and sang every emotion in the
world into the microphone. She broke her heart and fell
in love and snared a man and then told him he was a fool
in one song after another, hardly ever opening her eyes, and

the lyrics were typical country and western cornball but coming from her it didn't matter.

Toward the end of the set the band dropped away and Miranda did some acoustical solos, just her and her Martin. The first was a ballad called "Billy's Señorita," about the Kid from his Mexican lover's perspective. She told us what it was like to love a violent man and she made us believe she'd been there. The next song was even sadder—"The Widower's Two-Step," about a man's last dance with his wife, with references to a little boy. It was unclear in the lyrics how the woman died, or whether the boy died too, but the impact was the same no matter how you interpreted it.

Nobody in the cafe moved. The other band members could've packed up and left for the night and nobody would've noticed at that point. Most of the band looked like they knew it, too.

I glanced over at Cam Compton, who had come to sit next to Garrett in a chair some woman had gladly given up for him. As Cam listened to Miranda his expression slipped from amused disdain into something worse—something between resentment and physical need. He looked at Miranda the way a hungry vegetarian might look at a T-bone. If it was possible to like him less, I liked him less.

At the break the musicians dissipated into the audience. Miranda escaped into the back room. I was trying to figure out the best way to get in to talk to her when Cam Compton made up my mind for me. He downed what must have been the fourth beer someone had bought for him, got up unsteadily, and told Garrett, "Time I had a talk with that girl."

"Wait a minute," I said.

Cam pushed me into the curtains. I didn't have room or time to do anything about it.

When I got to my feet again Garrett said, "Uh-uh, little bro. Cool it, now." Then he saw my eyes and said, "Shit."

Cam was moving toward the back room like a man

with a purpose. A woman got in Cam's way to tell him how great he was and he pushed her into somebody at the bar.

I followed Cam like I was a man with a purpose too. I was going to beat the living crap out of him.

15

The back room of the Cactus Cafe was not exactly the place to go to escape claustrophobia. Crates of organically correct snacks and kegs of beer were stacked to the ceiling along either side, and the back was an explosion of paperwork that had completely overrun the manager's desk and was now crawling up the wall by way of thumb tacks and overflowing onto the floor. Whatever free space might've been left in the corners was now piled with the band's instrument cases.

In the center of the room Miranda Daniels and a blond woman who'd been in the audience were just sitting down at a card table when Cam Compton barged in, followed by me, followed by the club manager. If anybody else wanted to follow *him* they were out of luck. There wasn't even room to close the door.

A lot happened in a very short time. Miranda looked up at us, startled. The woman who was with Miranda rolled her eyes and said, "I don't *believe* this," then started to get up, fumbling with a canister of Mace on her key chain.

The manager tapped my shoulder hard and said, "Excuse me—"

Cam walked over to Miranda, grabbed her wrist, and started pulling her up out of her chair. He was smiling, talking almost under his breath falsely calm and sweet the way you might coax a naughty dog out from under the house so you could whack it hard. "Come on, darlin'," he said. "Come talk to me outside."

The blonde cursed and tried to untangle her Mace and muttered "you son of a bitch" several times. Miranda was saying Cam's name and trying to stay calm and get down low so she wouldn't be pulled toward him.

"Excuse me!" the manager said again.

There were more people outside the doorway now, trying to see into the room—Miranda's brother, her father, a few other guys from the audience who smelled a possible fight. They were all asking what the hell was going on and pushing on the manager who was in turn pushing on me.

Miranda glanced nervously at me, not having a clue who I was or why I was in line to abuse her next, then went back to reasoning with Cam while she pried at his fingers on her wrist, telling him to please calm down.

Cam said, "Just come on outside for a little bit, sweetheart. Just come on out."

The blonde was still having no luck with her Mace. It was either wait for her to get it free or do something myself. I decided on the latter.

I grabbed Cam Compton by his frizzy blond hair, yanked him back from Miranda, and slammed his head into a beer keg.

I'm not sure whether the lovely metallic sound came from the keg or Cam's skull, but it stopped him from pestering Miranda pretty effectively. His legs folded into praying position and his face hit the keg again on his way down to the floor. He curled into fetal position on the linoleum, squinting and trying to figure out how to close his mouth.

Miranda's blond friend stared at me. She had just gotten her Mace out. She pointed at me, then looked at Cam on the floor, realized I wasn't a target, and said, "Shit!"

"You're welcome," I said.

Miranda half sat, half fell back into her chair. She cupped her wrist, rocking back and forth and pursing her lips. Her friend tried to put her hand on her shoulder but Miranda immediately recoiled. "I'm all right, I'm all right."

The manager was not all right. He'd been momentarily stunned by my beer keg routine but now grabbed my upper arm and growled, "That's fucking *it*!"

He picked up the wall phone. Behind him Miranda's dad and brother insisted they get in this very minute.

"Just hold on now!" Miranda's voice was surprisingly loud.

The manager stopped dialing. Miranda's kinfolk stopped pushing their way in.

Miranda held up both hands like she was preparing to catch a basketball she really didn't want. She looked at me, her mouth trying to form a question.

"Tres Navarre," I volunteered. "Milo Chavez asked me to come by. I saw Cam getting a little out of control so—"

I put up my palms. I couldn't think of a euphemism for slamming someone's head into a keg.

"Am I throwing this guy out or what?" demanded the manager.

"Goddamn yes!" roared Miranda's father.

"Gam nam," mumbled Cam.

Miranda and the blonde looked at each other. Miranda sighed, exasperated, but she told the manager to let it go, told her dad and brother everything was fine and I was probably not a lunatic and please get on out.

Miranda's dad took a little more convincing than that. Miranda had to assure him repeatedly she was fine. She told him I was from Milo Chavez. That did not seem to comfort the old man greatly. Finally he shuffled back out into the club, mumbling prophesies of doom about young men who dressed poorly and carried backpacks.

When the crowd had dispersed, the blonde looked down at Cam Compton, who was still pulling himself into a ball. She looked at me and slowly cracked a smile. "So you're from Milo?"

"First-class service at economy prices."

"I'll be damned. Chavez finally did something right. Buy you a beer?"

Miranda looked at her like she was crazy.

Cam mumbled, "Kill you."

I told the ladies, "I'll be right back."

I picked up Cam by his wrists and dragged him outside.

"Very cool," the blonde said as I left the room.

A few people looked down as I dragged the guitarist past the bar and out the door. Some laughed. One said, "Olé Cam."

Garrett wheeled up behind me and followed me out. "Lovely. I suppose I can write this place off my list, too. You should visit more often, little bro. Jesus Christ."

Once we got out into the Union lobby I deposited Cam sideways on a folding table. He was mumbling some feeble threats and trying to spit the hair out of his mouth.

"Just great," Garrett growled as we went back in. "Jimmy Buffett's at Manor Downs in two weeks. Cam knows the keyboardist. I guess I can pretty much forget that backstage pass now."

I told the manager to get my brother a Shiner Bock.

"Fuck that," said Garrett. "You got any LSD?"

When I returned to the back room, Miranda and the blonde were drinking newly opened Lone Stars and talking.

Their conversation cut off abruptly when they saw me.

"Hey, sweetie," said the blonde. She offered me a longneck and a chair. "Your name was—"

I told her again.

"I'm Allison Saint-Pierre. I guess you figured out this is Miranda."

Allison Saint-Pierre. Les' wife. I tried to keep the surprise off my face.

I shook Miranda's good hand. It was soft and warm with no grip at all. "I'm a fan as of tonight."

Miranda gave me a practiced smile. "The first set was off."

"Like hell," Allison said.

They made good foils for each other—Miranda, dark-haired, reserved, petite; Allison, tan and tall with straight blond hair and a smile that had no reservation at all. Allison's white tube top and jeans showed off a good figure, almost too curvy, the kind that would've gotten all the catcalls in middle school gym class. I kept trying to think of her as Mrs. Saint-Pierre. I couldn't quite get my mind around it.

"You've got a name from Chaucer," I told her.

Allison drank her beer, looking at me over the top. Her eyes were green.

"That's a first," she said. "Most guys open with Elvis Costello."

Miranda smiled weakly like she remembered that conversation from every bar they'd ever been in. She also looked like she was used to Allison getting the offstage attention. She sat back in her chair, stared at her drink, and looked relieved.

" 'The Miller's Tale,' " I said. "Alisoun was famous for making a guy kiss her ass."

Allison's eyes looked brighter when she laughed. "Damn straight. I like her already."

"You an English professor, Mr. Navarre?" Miranda asked without looking up. "Milo called you a—what was it?"

" 'A pretty smart arm-breaker,' " Allison supplied. She winked at me.

"I'm gratified," I said. "Where is Milo?"

Allison made a face. She was about to offer some unflattering hypothesis when Miranda cut her off.

"He said he'd try to come late if he could. Some kind of crisis at the office."

Allison gave me a cautious look, probably appraising how much she should say. "I guess you heard about the fun we've been having—the potshots, stolen demo tapes, the occasional murdered fiddle player."

"Not to mention your missing husband."

I wanted to see their reactions. I wanted to judge whether Allison knew that I knew, whether Miranda had been told. Apparently Milo's communication lines had opened up. Miranda looked pained but not surprised. Allison just smiled.

"He'll be back," she insisted, more to Miranda than me. "I know the asshole well enough to know that. Soon as he's through popping pills and screwing debutantes."

She tried for casual disdain and didn't quite make it.

There was an uncomfortable silence. I drank my beer. Miranda pushed on the blue coolant gel in the bag on her wrist, one finger at a time. Allison got restless.

Suddenly she laughed. She leaned across the table toward me and her hair spilled over her right shoulder in a silky line, like somebody pulling a curtain. The front edge swept across the table until it got caught in a ring of water where her beer had been.

"Screw Les, anyway. Miranda was *my* discovery. Did you know that, Tres?"

Miranda started to protest.

"I'm sorry, sweetie. It's not often I get the credit for something like that. I've got to brag."

She took Miranda's forearm. It was meant to be a friendly gesture but with Miranda's despondent face the tableau looked more like Miranda was a little girl Allison was about to drag out of the supermarket.

"Tilden Sheckley did one good thing in his life," Allison told me. "He got Miranda a spot at the South by Southwest Conference last spring. I happened to see her there. We talked for a long time, got to know each other, then I told Les about her. That's how it all started."

"That wasn't Milo's story," I said.

Allison rolled her eyes. "Why am I not surprised? If you're going to watch out for Miranda, the first place to start is with all those people who want to carve her up. She just won't kick butt for herself."

"Please—" Miranda had already made herself very small in her metal folding chair. Now she was picking up the edges of her beer napkin as if looking for a place to hide under it.

"I mean it," said Allison. "Miranda needs to tell people that treat her wrong to go screw themselves. Tilden Sheckley, Milo Chavez, Cam Compton—"

"Even your husband?" I asked.

"Especially him. You're the bodyguard now, you can help me talk some sense into her."

"I'm not a bodyguard." I looked at Miranda.

"That's not a big deal—" she started.

"Don't be so sure," Allison said.

I asked what she meant.

Allison gave me a don't-let's-bullshit look. She was about to elaborate when she seemed to notice for the first time how small the singer was making herself.

Allison tapped a fingernail on the edge of her beer bottle. "We can talk about that later. Miranda still has a set to get through tonight. There's no sense in bringing up—"

She stopped, apparently envisioning things that were graphically unpleasant, then shook her head. "Just forget it. The point is, I hope we'll see you around a lot, Tres. We could use a few more heads bashed in a few more beer kegs."

The door opened. Miranda's brother stepped halfway into the room and said, "Everything okay?"

Brent Daniels looked like he'd been treated to more than one drink since my altercation with Cam. His curly black hair was messed up. His checkered shirt was coming untucked. His eyes were focusing poorly and his face had reddened so much that his scruffy two-day whiskers stood out like a real beard.

He scowled at me, like a protective but not very bright guard dog. I smiled back.

"Everything's fine, Brent." Miranda's voice was suddenly hard. Cold.

Brent looked at Allison for a second opinion, then nodded reluctantly, like he still didn't believe it. "About five minutes, then. I'll be taking Cam's leads."

He closed the door.

"My big brother," Miranda explained. She frowned at her beer napkin, then looked up at me. She tried to rework the smile. "I need to start the next set."

"I'd like to talk to you sometime. Maybe now isn't—"

"There's a party at the Daniels house Friday night," Allison offered. "Miranda wouldn't mind—"

Allison looked at her friend to finish the invitation. Miranda nodded unenthusiastically, then met my eyes and made a quiet counterproposal: "We're taping tomorrow morning. Silo Studios on Red River. You could stop by if you're still in Austin."

She sounded like she wanted it to happen. Allison didn't look too pleased. Maybe that's why I said yes.

"What time?"

"Six," Miranda said, apologetically.

"In the morning?"

Miranda nodded, sighed. "We're working spec time. We have to take what they give us."

"What *Milo* gives you," Allison amended. "Like three hours sleep and gigs in different towns every damn night. I'd love to talk to you, too, Tres. I hope you can make the party."

I said I'd try, then got up to leave.

On my way out I turned. "I like that song, by the way. 'Billy's Señorita.' Did you write it?"

Miranda looked at me hesitantly. She nodded.

"I like the line about roses the color of bruises. I wouldn't have thought of that."

Her face colored. "Good night, Mr. Navarre. I'll tell Milo you came by."

For once, Allison didn't say anything.

When the second set started I was wheeling Garrett out the door, trying to convince him everything was just fine and Cam hadn't suffered any permanent damage since it was only his head I'd smashed. Onstage it was just the drummer using brushes on his trap set and Miranda singing a slow one, her voice low and sensual and powerful, the lyrics about lost love. The one time she opened her large brown eyes I was sure she was looking straight at me.

Then I caught Allison Saint-Pierre watching me from the bar, smiling dryly like she knew exactly what I was thinking. Like she knew that every guy there was thinking the exact same thing.

16

Driving to Garrett's apartment was like driving through a different world. The rainstorm had swept through and the temperature had dropped suddenly into the low seventies. The streets were shiny and wet and the air was clean. It was enough to put anybody in a good mood, except maybe the parrot.

Dickhead was calling me every name in the book, flapping around and telling me just how he felt about being imprisoned in the VW most of the evening.

"Five more minutes," I told him. "Then we get you a new home."

"Noisy bastard," he squawked.

I followed Garrett's safari van down Twenty-sixth toward Lamar. It was about eleven o'clock, and there were still plenty of people hanging out at Les Amis drinking wine by the Franklin stove, talking outside the Stop 'N' Go, smoking in the parking lot of Tula, everybody enjoying the cooler air. Once in a while somebody would recognize the Carmen Miranda and wave. Garrett

would honk back to the tune of "Coconut Telegraph."
The mound of plastic fruit hot-glued to the roof shuddered every time he changed gears. My brother, the local
celebrity.

Garrett's apartment building on Twenty-fourth has
all the charm of a Motel 6. The redwood box stands
five units wide and three high, all the front doors facing south and painted lichen green. You get to Garrett's
door by climbing up three flights of metal stairs and
across a concrete walkway. No elevator. Garrett, of course,
had chosen to live on the top floor so he could sue for
access. Last I heard the case was going well. The landlord
loved him.

Garrett pulled the Carmen Miranda in between
a Harley and a broken washing machine. I parked by the
frat house across the street.

"This is what I get," Garrett complained as he eased
himself out of the van and into his wheelchair. "Home
before midnight. Thanks for the wonderful evening."

Then he saw the parrot and his face brightened
considerably.

"Holy shit," said Garrett.

"Dickhead," said the bird, and flew off my shoulder
onto Garrett's armrest.

It was love at first sight.

"Where the hell did you get him?" Garrett was
stroking the bird's beak. The bird was eyeing Garrett's
beard like it might make a fine nest. I told Garrett that
Dickhead was orphaned. I didn't tell him the last owner
had died violently. Since Jimmy Buffett fans styled themselves "parrotheads" I figured the match was made in
heaven. Or Key West, anyway.

"You approve?" I asked.

The bird was cawing some sweet obscenities in
Garrett's ear. Garrett grinned and invited me up for a beer.

Tres Navarre, etiquette master. You bust a few heads,
you'd better come prepared with a thoughtful "I'm
sorry" gift.

We got upstairs, Garrett taking them on his hands,

pulling the chair after him. When he opened his front door the smell of patchouli nearly knocked me over. Even the parrot shook his head.

"Get yourself a Shiner," Garrett said. "I've got to play a couple of tunes."

Garrett's apartment is a long hallway—living room in front separated from the kitchen by a bar, one tiny bedroom in back. The only thing that keeps the place from feeling claustrophobic is the ceiling, which vaults up from the kitchen toward the front of the building at a forty-five-degree angle. Skylights at the top.

I headed toward the refrigerator and Garrett wheeled himself over to the wall of electronic equipment that doubled as his computer and entertainment system. He turned on the main power switch and the lights of North Austin dimmed. He picked a CD to play.

While I could still hear myself talk I said, "Who's winning?"

You could hear the stereo from the downstairs neighbors just fine. They were playing Metallica. Playing isn't really the right verb for Metallica, I guess. Grinding, maybe. Extruding.

Garrett sighed. "The bastards got new woofers last week. That was pretty bad. Then I got this friend of mine in here—used to do the Sensurround systems for Dolby. You know—the shaking effects they had with those seventies earthquake movies? He cut me a good deal."

"Great," I said. "Earthquakes. After ten years in California, I get to come to Austin for earthquakes."

I looked around the kitchen for something to strap myself to.

When Garrett turned up the volume the bookshelves on the wall started to shake, spilling copies of *The Electric Kool-Aid Acid Test* and *The Anarchist's Cookbook*. The Armadillo World Headquarters posters on the wall vibrated. The parrot started performing acrobatics.

In the moments when there were pauses and my brain fluids started flowing correctly again, I recognized the song as "Bodhisattva" by Steely Dan. We weren't so much listening to it as experiencing it by Braille.

I somehow managed to open a beer and drink it while the building shook. When the song was over it was quiet except for the parrot, who was still trying to punch his way out through the Plexiglas skylight. The downstairs neighbors' stereo had stopped.

Garrett grinned like a madman. "Gotcha."

"Does anybody—" I stopped to readjust the volume of my voice. "Does anybody ever call the cops?"

"Who—Fred?"

Fred the cop. First-name basis. "I guess that answers my question."

Garrett waved his hand dismissively. "You call Fred, that's cheating. Sometimes somebody new moves into a side apartment, they try that for a while. It never lasts long. Now where's that hard drive you want squeezed?"

I gave him the card I'd pulled from Julie Kearnes' computer.

Garrett wheeled himself over to his computer. He pecked at the keyboard. The screen glowed orange, then came alive with a short mandolin riff. Garrett whistled Steely Dan and started mixing and matching SCSI cables from his spare parts drawer.

I sat down next to him in a battered black recliner that had been our father's. After twelve years, the leather still smelled faintly of his Cuban cigars and spilt bourbon. The left armrest was gouged out where I'd used a penknife to dig a foxhole for my plastic army soldiers when I was seven. It was a comfortable place to sit.

"Damn," said Garrett.

"What?"

Garrett started to say something, then looked at me, probably realizing the effort it would take to filter what he was thinking from computerese to plain English. "Nothing."

I drank my beer and listened to Garrett tinkering with hardware. Finally he got the hard drive connected with a loose collection of multicolored spaghetti and clacked a few commands on his keyboard.

"Okay, yeah," he said. "Give it a few minutes."

He toggled to one of his other processors—Garrett has eight, just in case he wants to have a dinner party someday. The screen dimmed, then came up with gray World Wide Web page. The lights of his ISDN router flickered on. He clacked a few more commands.

"What are you working on these days?" I asked.

"Bastards running RNI," Garrett complained.

Every time Garrett talks about the company, he starts with that comment, even though he's been there so long and accumulated so many stock options he *is* one of the bastards running RNI.

"They've got me doing the GUI on an account management program. I make this piece of shit program look really slick, except it still crashes when it merges field data."

"So that's what they're paying you for," I said. "What are you *really* working on?"

Garrett smiled, not taking his eyes off the screen. "Bring the tequila from the kitchen and I'll show you. It requires tequila."

I'm not one to refuse a direct order. I got the bottle from the kitchen and poured some for both of us. My brother and I share an understanding about tequila—it should be Herradura Añejo and it should be drunk straight, no lime or salt, preferably in large quantities.

The parrot was perched on the edge of a bar stool, looking at the shot glasses enviously, his head cocked to one side.

"Sorry, no," I told him.

When I got back to the recliner Garrett had a new program up and ready to demonstrate.

"Okay," he said. "Say you've got some material that's too sensitive to store on your computer. What do you do?"

I shrugged. "Hide it on a disk somewhere. Use a read/write protect program on it."

"Yeah, but disks can be found, and if somebody's good they can break into them with a logic diagram of the disk drive. Or a password tumbler. Disks can also get destroyed."

"So—"

"So you boomerang it."

He selected a file called *Garrett.jpg*.

"Here's my sensitive data—my picture I want to keep but I don't want anybody to see. So I don't keep it myself—I let the net keep it for me. I upload that sucker, encrypt it so it's invisible and innocuous, then program it to bounce around randomly, transferring itself from server to server so it's never in the same place for more than five minutes. It bounces around the net, impossible to find, until I send the retrieval code out for it. Then it comes home."

He clicked on the file and we watched it disappear into the net, erasing itself from the hard drive as it uploaded. Then Garrett punched in a series of numbers. Two minutes later the file downloaded itself back into existence.

"See that?" he said. "The sucker was in Norway. By the time anybody noticed it was there, it'd be on its way to somewhere else."

The picture opened. It showed Garrett sitting in a bar somewhere with a woman on his lap. She had jeans and a motorcycle helmet and a Harley-Davidson T-shirt that she had pulled up to reveal some very ample breasts. Garrett was toasting the camera with a bottle of Budweiser.

"Family photos," I said.

"Biker women," he said fondly. "They understand there are some things only a man with no legs can do."

I tried not to use my imagination. Another shot of tequila helped.

A red light flickered in the corner of the computer and Garrett said, "It's soup."

He toggled back to the processor that had been giving Julie Kearnes' hard drive the Spanish Inquisition. On the screen now was a text document, mostly intact. Only a few nonsense characters attested to its trip through the cyber trash can.

"Names and social security numbers," Garrett announced. He scrolled down to the bottom. "Seven pages. Dates of hiring. Dates of—DOD, what's that, date of death? Looks like several different companies, big Austin firms. This make any sense to you?"

"Company personnel archives—lists of people who died while employed or retired and then died and had their pensions closed out. Looks like about a decade worth of names for almost all the businesses where Julie Kearnes did temp work. She stole this information."

Garrett waved his fingers, unimpressed. "Amateur. Anybody could download these—no company is going to guard discontinued personnel records very seriously. But why bother? And then why trash them?"

I thought about that. An uncomfortable idea started to form somewhere underneath the pleasant buzz of the Herradura. "Can I get a hard copy?"

Garrett grinned.

Two minutes later I was back in the easy chair with a refill of tequila and seven pages of deceased employee names from all over Austin.

Garrett closed down the computer, patted the keyboard like you would a puppy, then pushed himself away from the desk. He started digging around in his wheelchair's side bag until he found a Ziploc full of marijuana. He got out a five-dollar bill and a paper and started rolling himself a joint.

"So tell me about it," he said. "What's with the flies? Why the sudden interest in country music?"

I told him about my last two days.

There are no confidentiality issues when I talk to Garrett. It's not so much that he's incredibly honorable about keeping secrets. It's more that Garrett doesn't ever remember what I say long enough to tell anybody. If it's not about programming or Jimmy Buffett or drugs, Garrett never bothers to save it into the old hard drive.

When I finished talking, Garrett shook his head slowly.

He blew smoke up toward the parrot. The parrot leaned into it.

"You scare me sometimes, little bro."

"How do you mean?"

Garrett scratched his jawline under the beard, using all ten fingertips. "I see you sitting in that chair, drinking and talking about your cases. All you need is a cigar and about a hundred extra pounds."

"Don't start, Garrett. I'm not turning into Dad."

He shrugged. "If you say so, man. You keep playing detective, hanging out in the Sheriff's old territory, working with his friends on the force—the Man's dead, little bro. Murder solved. You can take off the Superman cape, now."

I tried to muster some irritation but the tequila and the easy chair were working against me. I stared at the tips of my deck shoes.

"You think I like being known as Jackson Navarre's kid every time I work a case? You think that makes it easier on me?"

Garrett took a toke. "Maybe that's exactly what you like. Saves you the trouble of growing up and being something else."

"My brother, the expert on growing up."

He grinned. "Yeah, well—"

I leaned back farther in the recliner.

Garrett noticed how short his joint was getting and reached behind him to get a roach clip out of the ashtray. His left leg stump peeked out briefly from his denim shorts. It was smooth and thin and pink, like part of a baby. There were no signs of scars from the train tracks that had long ago severed Garrett's lower third.

"You remember Big Bill?" he asked.

Garrett's favorite strategy. When in doubt, bring up something embarrassing from Tres' childhood.

"Gee, no I don't. Why don't you remind me?"

Garrett laughed.

Big Bill had been a roan stud Dad used to keep out at

the ranch in Sabinal. Randiest, meanest son-of-a-bitch stallion ever born. The horse, I mean, not my dad.

The Sheriff had insisted that I learn to ride Big Bill when I was a kid on the theory that I could then handle any horse in the world. Each time I tried, Big Bill would intentionally head for low-lying tree branches to try and knock me off. On our third ride together he succeeded, and I'd gripped the reins so tightly as I fell that I couldn't let go when I hit the ground. My hands stayed wrapped around the leather straps as Big Bill galloped on for a good quarter mile, dragging me through as many cactus patches as he could find. When I returned home with half the back forty stuck to my clothes and my hair, my father had judged the ride "a little too wild."

"I found his saddle at the ranch last month," Garrett said. "Had it polished up. I've got it back in my bedroom if you want to see it."

"For the biker women, no doubt."

Garrett tried to look modest. "Actually it made me think of my little brother. I still got this image of you, man—nine-year-old kid being dragged behind a runaway horse."

"Okay. I get the point."

"How old are you now, twenty-eight?"

"Twenty-nine," I said. "There's a difference."

Garrett laughed. " 'Scuse me if I don't feel sorry for you. Just seems to me you got time to try some different things, little bro. Maybe you could get yourself a life that doesn't get you shot at so often and your girlfriends pissed off and your old brother kicked out of bars when you come to visit."

"I'm good at my work, Garrett."

"That what your boss says—you're good at your work?"

I hesitated.

"Yeah," Garrett said. "Like I said, you never could let go when you needed to."

"You saying I should've been like you—hop a freight car every time things at home started to get bad?"

It was a mean thing to say, but Garrett didn't react. He just kept smoking and looking at a point somewhere above my head.

After a while the heavy metal music from the downstairs neighbor started up again, rattling the half-empty tequila bottle on Dad's army footlocker that Garrett used as a coffee table.

Garrett looked down at the floor with tired resignation, then he reached over to pick a new CD.

"Hope you can sleep to music," he said.

17

"Mr. Navarro, isn't it?"

Miranda's dad shook my hand with both of his and most of the rest of his body. This was a good trick, considering that to do it he had to put his walking stick in the crook of his arm and lean on his good leg and still keep from falling over.

"Navarre," I said. "But call me Tres."

Willis Daniels kept shaking my hand. His face was bright red, beaming like he'd just run the Iron Man triathlon and loved every minute of it.

"Course. Navarre. I'm sorry."

"No problem," I said. "San Antonio. Navarro. Historical connection. I get that all the time."

We were standing in the doorway of Silo Studio on Red River near Seventh. The studio was a single-story refurbished warehouse with metal-framed windows and brown stucco outer walls the texture of shredded wheat. The main door was at the rear of the building, where the parking lot was.

We were standing *right* in the doorway, me on my way in and Mr. Daniels on his way out and the guy with a dollyful of electrical equipment waiting two feet behind Daniels shit out of luck. Daniels didn't seem to notice him.

The old man squinted and leaned his face into mine, like a preacher about to offer me important words of comfort as I filed out of church. He smelled like wet leather and Pert.

"I apologize for last night," he said. "Hard situation, Cam getting out of control like that. I surely didn't mean to misjudge you."

"Don't mention it."

"Cam was fired, of course."

I nodded amiably.

The guy with the dolly cleared his throat loudly. Daniels kept beaming at me.

With the solid red flannel shirt and black jeans and the curly gray hair now minus straw hat, Daniels looked even more like Santa Claus than he had the night before. He was mighty perky for somebody over sixty who'd played music until two that morning.

"You know you do look Hispanic," he decided. "I suppose that's why I thought Navarro. It's the dark hair. Bit of a swarthy complexion. You don't mind me saying so?"

I shook my head. Swarthy. Maybe I should have kept the parrot. Gotten myself a cutlass.

"I hear you might be coming to our party tomorrow night," he continued. "I surely hope you can make it."

"Do my best."

"Fine."

We nodded at each other, both smiling.

I pointed to the parking lot, the way he'd been heading. "You're not helping with the recording today?"

He looked surprised, then chuckled and let out a whole string of little *no*'s. "Just dropping off Miranda. Old man like me couldn't keep up."

He said his good-byes with more handshaking and

smiling and then finally noticed the guy with the dolly. Daniels made a big deal about getting out of his way and telling him to have a good day.

I watched Daniels drive off in a little red Ford sedan. The guy with the dolly disappeared around the corner of the building.

I crouched down and looked at the cement steps at my feet. Nothing. I looked up at the sides of the walls. The bullet hole was a putty-colored gouge in the brown stucco, about four feet up, just inside the doorway. My index finger fit up to the first joint. The rim of the hole was scarred where the police had removed the slug but I could still get the basic trajectory. I looked south and up. Parking garage next door. Probably the third floor. Probably a .22—a stupid shot from so far away, more effective at scaring than killing, unless you got lucky. The police might've been up there looking for casings.

Still . . .

I took a five-minute excursion next door. I had a nice talk with a parking attendant about garbage collection days, then went up to the third floor and found what I wanted on the first try, right by the elevator. I put my prize in my backpack and walked back to Silo.

The studio's lobby was a remodeled loading dock. There was one door on the far wall marked PRIVATE and a sickly ficus tree in the corner that apparently doubled as an ashtray.

Next to the ficus tree, an Anglo guy in a sleeveless Hole T-shirt and Op shorts was leaning against the wall, reading *Nashville Today*. His head bobbed up and down like he was listening to a Walkman.

"Help you?" he asked.

"Gold records."

He looked up with just his eyes, his face still bent over the magazine. "What?"

"There's supposed to be gold records on the walls."

He scratched his nose, then made a small sideways nod to the door marked PRIVATE, the only other exit from the room. "Studio's that way."

"Thanks. I might've gotten lost."

His obligations to building security fulfilled, he went back to his magazine and his invisible Walkman.

I walked down a long hallway with several cheaply paneled doors on either side. Each had an identical PRIVATE sign. Someone must've gotten them on sale.

The hallway ended in a black curtain so thick it could've been sewn together from flack jackets. I squeezed around the edge into a large circular room where I could hear Miranda singing but at first couldn't see her.

The place smelled like burnt Styrofoam. Duct-taped cords ran along the floor, overhead among the fluorescent lights, up the walls that were apparently constructed from egg carton material.

Spaced here and there around the recording area were gray portable partitions, poofy and overstuffed so they looked more like vertical pillows than walls.

In the center of a V made by two of these was Miranda Daniels. She wore huge black headphones that doubled the size of her head. One large boxy mike was pointed toward her face and another angled down toward her guitar, and with all the wires and cords and the people looking at her from the glassed-in control room I couldn't shake the impression that I was watching some kind of execution.

I skirted the room and walked up five steps into the control area, where Milo Chavez and three other guys were standing at a recording console that looked suspiciously like a *Star Trek* energizer.

Miranda was mid-song—one of the faster numbers I'd heard the night before. The sound was crisp and clear from the two shoe-box-size wall speakers, but it seemed thin with just Miranda's voice and the guitar. The studio acoustics seemed to suck all the excess sound out of her voice so the words just evaporated as soon as they left her mouth.

Milo glanced at me briefly, mumbled a greeting, then continued glaring through the Plexiglas.

One of the engineers was hunched so low over the console I thought at first he was asleep. His head was cocked sideways, his ear only an inch from the knobs like he wanted to hear the sound they made when he turned them. The other engineer was keeping a close eye on the computer monitor. More accurately, he was keeping a close finger on it, tapping the little colored bars as they flickered, like that would somehow affect them. You could see from the greasy smudges on the monitor that he did that a lot. The third man was standing slightly back from the console. From his demeanor and the orders he gave the engineers I guessed he was the new producer, John Crea's replacement, but he looked more like a vice principal—blue polyester shirt, double-knit slacks, white socks with dress shoes. His hair was gray but worn too long, seventies conservative. He had his meaty, furry arms crossed and a frown on his face that made me want to apologize for coming in tardy. A little gold-tinted American flag was pinned on his shirt pocket.

Milo mumbled, "Sorry I missed you last night. I heard you made friends with Cam Compton."

"Somewhere in San Antonio," I said, "there's a big and tall store with a bronze plaque inscribed to you."

Milo frowned and looked down at his outfit—rayon camp shirt, black slacks, oxblood deck shoes that made mine look like poor country cousins. His braided gold neck chain would've hunchbacked a lesser human being.

"You have to get all your clothes custom-made," he said, "you might as well get them made nice. Some of us can't just throw on yesterday's jeans and T-shirt, Navarre."

I checked my Triple Rock T-shirt for stains. "I have two of these. What was the crisis that came up last night?"

Miranda kept singing. She opened her eyes every once in a while to glance up nervously at the control booth, like she knew how she was sounding. She *looked* like she was singing her heart out—taking huge breaths from her diaphragm, scrunching up her face with effort when she belted out the words, but none of the energy of the night before was coming through the speakers. The first engineer tilted his head a little more and said, "I told you she was miked wrong. You and your damn V87s."

The vice principal grunted. The second engineer tapped at the computer monitor a little more.

Milo pointed left with his thumb. We moved a few steps toward the door, just out of earshot from the studio guys.

"Tell me you've decided to help us out," he insisted.

"What happened with you last night?"

He scratched the corner of his mouth, found some invisible particle that displeased him, rolled it in his fingers and flicked it away. "I had a great day. I called around, gently explaining to people that maybe I wasn't exactly sure where Les is. Several major clients bailed. The cops were thrilled. They were about as excited as I thought they'd be. As soon as they get through yawning I'm sure they'll launch a massive manhunt." Milo glared at me accusingly.

"Honesty is next to godliness," I consoled.

"Then I got a call from our accountant. Not good."

"How not good?"

The two engineers were arguing now about the isolation qualities of wide compression mikes.

"Does she *have* to sing with the guitar?" the monitor-tapper pleaded.

The vice principal shrugged, keeping his eyes sternly on the imaginary detention hall below him. "Lady said she felt more comfortable that way."

The other engineer grumbled. "Does she *sound* like she's comfortable?"

Milo kept staring forward. "Apparently Les hasn't been telling me everything. Some of the commission checks haven't been going into the main account. A few days ago one of our checks for some equipment rentals bounced. There are also some creditors I didn't know about."

"Bad?"

"Bad enough. The agency costs fifteen thousand a month to run. That's bare-bones—phone bills, transportation, property, promo expenses."

"How much longer can you keep afloat?"

Milo laughed with no humor. "I can keep the creditors at bay for a while. I don't know how long. Fortunately our clients pay us; we don't pay them. So they don't have to find out right away. But by all rights the agency should've folded at the start of the month. Les had made arrangements to pay our bills then and there's no way he could have."

"About the time he disappeared."

Milo shook his head. "You had to put it that way, didn't you?"

Miranda strained her way through another verse.

"Look," one of the engineers was saying, "it's a Roland VS880, okay? Pickup isn't the problem here. You don't need the goddamn digital delay if she's singing it right, man. The lady's a cold fish."

"Just try it," the vice principal insisted. "Put a little through her headphone mix, see if that warms her up."

Finally I told Milo about my last two days.

Milo stared at me while I talked. When I finished he seemed to do a mental countdown, then looked out the Plexiglas again and sighed.

"I don't like any of that."

"You said Les joked about running off to Mexico. If this plan he had to get Sheckly was dangerous, if it went bad—"

"Don't even start."

"Stowing away funds from the agency, pulling deceased identities from personnel files—what does that sound like to you, Berkeley Law?"

Milo brought his palms up to his temples. "No way. That's not—Les couldn't do that. It's not his style to run."

Milo's tone warned me not to push it. I didn't.

I looked back down at Miranda, who was just finishing the last chorus. "How bad will all this affect her?"

Milo kept his eyes closed. "Maybe it can still work. Silo's been paid through next week. Century Records will need some heavy reassurances, but they'll wait for the tape. If we get a good one to them on time, if we get Sheckly off our backs . . ."

Miranda finished her song. The sound died the instant she stopped belting it out. Nobody said anything.

Finally the engineer asked halfheartedly, "Do another take? We could try to feed her just the basic tracks. Move the baffles around."

Miranda was looking up at us. The vice principal shook his head. "Take a break."

Then he leaned over the console and pushed a button. "Miranda, honey, take a break for a few minutes."

Miranda's shoulders fell slightly. She nodded, then started slowly toward the exit with her guitar.

Milo watched her go out the black curtain.

"You wanted to talk to her," he mentioned.

"Yeah."

"Go ahead, first door on the left. I'd have to be positive with her. Right now that's not possible."

He turned and concentrated on the recording console like he was wondering how hard it would be to lift and throw through the Plexiglas.

18

Miranda was lying on a cot with her forearms over her face and her knees up. She peeped out briefly when I wrapped my knuckles on the open door, then covered her eyes again.

I came in and set my backpack on the little round table next to her. I took out my bag of Texas French Bread pastries and a .22 Montgomery Ward pistol. Miranda opened her eyes when the gun clunked on the table.

"I thought you could use some breakfast," I said.

She frowned. When she spoke she exaggerated her drawl just a little. "The croissants put up a fight, Mr. Navarre?"

I smiled. "That's good. I wasn't sure you'd have a sense of humor."

She made a square with her arms and put them over her head. She was wearing a cutoff white T-shirt that said COUNTY LINE BBQ on it, and there was a small oval of sweat sticking the fabric to her tummy where the guitar had been. The skin under her arms was so white that her faint armpit stubble looked like ballpoint pen marks.

"After the last few mornings I've had in the studio," she said, "you've got to have a sense of humor."

"Hard to get the sound right. The engineers were saying something about the microphones."

Miranda stretched out her legs. She looked at her feet, then kicked her Jellies off with her big toes. "It's not the microphone's fault. But that ain't what you're in here to talk about, is it? I'm supposed to ask you about the gun."

I offered her a chocolate croissant. She seemed to think about it for a minute, then swung her legs onto the floor and sat up. She shook her head so her tangly black hair readjusted itself around her shoulders. She moistened her lips. Then she bypassed the chocolate croissant I was holding and went straight for the only ham and cheese. Damn. A woman with taste.

She nudged the .22 with her finger. Country girl. Not somebody who was nervous around guns. "Well, sir?"

"It's the gun somebody used to shoot at John Crea. I found it in the third-floor garbage bin at the parking lot next door."

Miranda tore a corner off her croissant. "Somebody just left it there? And the police didn't—"

"Hard to underestimate the stupidity of perps," I said. "Cops know perps are stupid and they try to investigate accordingly, but sometimes they still underestimate. They overlook possibilities nobody with any sense would try, like using a .22 Montgomery Ward pistol for a hundred-yard shot and dropping the gun in the garbage on their way to the elevator. Police are thinking the shooter must've used a rifle and carried it away with him and ditched it somewhere else. That's what a smart person would do. Most people who get away with crimes, they don't do it smart. They do it stupid enough to baffle the police."

"So—you taking the gun to the police?"

"Probably. Eventually."

"Eventually? After what happened to poor Julie Kearnes, shot the exact same way—"

I shook my head. "Poor Julie was killed by a professional. Whoever left this was an amateur. Similar incidents, both people connected to you, but they weren't done by the same person. That's what I don't get."

"If I could help—"

"I think you can. You know Sheckly a lot better than I do."

Her expression hardened. "I don't know him that well. And no, he wouldn't have anything to do with this."

"Somebody's trying to make things difficult for you since you started courting Century Records. You have any theory?"

Miranda took a bite of my ham and cheese croissant. She nodded her head while she chewed. After she swallowed she said, "You want me to admit Tilden Sheckly is a hard customer. Yes, sir. He is. He's got a bad temper."

"But—"

She shook her head. "But Sheck wouldn't do those things. He's known Willis, shoot—he's known all the families in Avalon County for a million years. I know what people think, but Sheck's always been a gentleman with me."

She looked up at me a little tentatively, like she was afraid I might contradict her, might ask her to prove it.

"If he's such a great guy," I said, "why did you sign with Les Saint-Pierre?"

Miranda pressed her lips together, like she'd just put on lipstick.

"You heard of that lady who played out at the Paintbrush a few nights ago, Tammy Vaughn?"

"I saw her."

Miranda raised her eyebrows. Apparently she hadn't figured me for a country music fan. I liked her for that.

"A year ago," Miranda continued, "Tammy Vaughn was where I am. She played mostly local gigs—South Texas, Austin. Mostly dance halls. Then she got a good agent and signed with Century Records. They're the only major label with a Texas office, did you know that? They've started paying attention to the talent down here, picking out the best, and sending them on to Nashville. Now Tammy's playing for fifteen thousand a night. She opened for LeAnne Rimes in Houston. She's got a house in Nashville and one in Dallas."

"And Sheckly can't do that for you."

"My dad's barely paid the mortgage on his ranch for as long as I can remember. He does contracting all day and music all night and he won't ever be able to retire. We won't even talk about Brent. The idea of being able to help them out . . ."

"You're telling me it was just the promise of money?"

She thought about that, apparently decided to be honest. "No. You're right. I signed with Les because of the way he talked, that first time we met. Something about Les Saint-Pierre—you can't just tell a fella like that no. Besides, Sheck or not—sometimes you have to make choices for your career. You don't always get to make everybody happy."

"Allison," I said.

Miranda frowned at me. "Pardon?"

"That's an Allison Saint-Pierre line, isn't it?"

Miranda looked uncomfortable. She put the croissant down half-eaten and brushed her fingers. She stared at the .22.

"What about Cam Compton?" I asked.

Miranda took her eyes from the gun. Slowly she worked up a smile. "Does he have it in for me? No, sir. Cam—I know you ain't going to believe this after last night, but Cam is basically harmless. You know how they say, dogs always look like their masters?"

"Uh-huh."

"I'm serious now. Cam's nothing but the poodle version of Tilden Sheckly. He tries awful hard to look wicked and dangerous and like he's got all this violent side ready to let loose, but comes right down to it, he wouldn't do nothing if Sheck didn't say 'sic 'em.' Even then he wouldn't have the brains to do it right."

"You think so. Even after last night."

"I know. Cam's got himself a little music store down in S.A., bought it after he got this one hit record over in Europe somewhere, about ten years ago. Cam'll go back to that, go back to working the house band at the Paintbrush. Two weeks from now he'll forget all about Miranda Daniels. He's got nothing riding on my chances one way or the other."

Sounding pleased, like she'd just reconvinced herself, Miranda stretched back out on her cot and examined the ceiling. "You know Jimmie Rodgers recorded his last session two days before he died? The tuberculosis was eating up his lungs so bad he had to lay down in a cot in the studio between songs, just like this here. I keep thinking about that."

"Should I put the gun away?"

She smiled nicely. "No, sir. It's just that Jimmie Rodgers' last sessions sound so good. It's depressing."

"You're not doing too badly."

She didn't look encouraged.

"Your family supportive about your career?" I asked. "Your mom?"

She studied seven or eight ceiling tiles. "She's dead. A long time ago. Milo didn't tell you that?"

I shook my head. "Sorry."

"I guess there's no reason he should have. I don't think about it much."

She moved her lips a little more, like she still couldn't get them aligned quite right. "But that wasn't your question again. Yes, Dad is real supportive. He's amazing, how he keeps going. You can say what you please about Tilden Sheckly, Mr. Navarre, but Sheck encouraged Dad to stay with me when we put the band together, to play at any gig he could, and that's been my biggest comfort. We got a stand-in bassist for him when we do bigger gigs, but still—he's an old workhorse. If it hadn't been for his music when I was growing up, all the Ernest Tubb records and the Bob Wills—that and my mother singing in the kitchen—"

She drifted off. I concentrated on my croissant and let her mind work around to wherever it wanted to go for a few moments.

"What about Brent?"

Miranda's eyes became clearer and cooler. "He's supportive."

"You didn't seem happy with him last night."

"You have siblings?"

"Brother and a sister. Both older."

"You get along with them all the time, Mr. Navarre?"

"Point taken."

She smiled dryly. "You seem like a nice fella. You were asking last night about 'Billy's Señorita.' That's about the only song I wrote myself, Mr. Navarre. The others are Brent's, did you know that?"

I said I didn't. I tried not to look too surprised.

"It's funny about how they sound in the studio," she said at last. "Ace was telling me—"

"Ace?"

She did a mental rewind, then smiled. "John Crea. My old—my ex-producer. He liked to be called 'Ace,' what with that flight jacket and all."

"I bet he did."

"Anyway, Ace was telling me how some singers have to reproduce what makes them so good onstage in order to sound right in the session. Drugs, audiences screaming at them, what you please. Some got to turn their backs to the control booth or sing in the dark. Ace told me about this one rock and roll fella had to hang upside down to get the blood going right before he sang. I ain't kidding you. Ace said whatever I needed to make the songs sound right, he'd make it happen."

"Do you know what you need?"

I could see her framing the right answer, her face hardening up with a level of seriousness that didn't seem natural for her. Then she looked at me and decided to discard it. She softened again and smiled. "No. I just keep imagining myself hanging upside down in the dark with a bottle of whiskey, singing—*Billy rode out last night . . .*"

She got that far singing the line, then cracked up. "Don't help me to sound any better, but it sure keeps things lighter in my mind."

A buzzer sounded down the hall from the recording area. Miranda puffed up her cheeks and exhaled.

"That'd be the master, calling me back. You like to stay—watch me sweat out a few more bad takes?"

I shook my head. "I should pay some other visits in town before I head back to San Antonio. You didn't answer my question."

She looked me in the eyes. She tried to keep the smile playful, but it was a strain for her. "What question was that, Mr. Navarre?"

"Who do you think is causing you so much grief, if not Sheckly or Cam? Anybody you know who would like to see you miss your big chance?"

She looked down, her hands on the edge of the cot and her shoulders bending into a U. She was short enough that she could hang her legs over the side and sweep the flats of her feet back and forth.

"I didn't mean to undercut Allison's invitation to our party," she said. "You're welcome to come tomorrow."

"Thanks."

"Allison has been my best friend the last few months. She's been so good to me."

"You're still not answering my question."

When Miranda stood, we were close enough to slow dance. I saw green flecks in her brown irises I would never have noticed otherwise. She spoke so softly I barely heard her.

"The funny thing is, Allison Saint-Pierre's about the only person who truly scares me to death. You asked and I told you. Isn't that a terrible thing to say about a friend?"

Milo Chavez wrapped his knuckles on the door. "There's the champ."

He moved past me and wrapped a huge arm around Miranda's shoulders. Miranda unlocked her eyes from mine and smiled up at Chavez. Her head rested on his chest. She let some of her tiredness show.

"It's going pretty rotten, Milo."

"No," Milo insisted. He'd found his positivity. He beamed the best smile I'd ever seen him beam. I was almost convinced myself, almost ready to believe our recent conversation about his missing boss and the missing funds had been a daydream. "You wait, Miranda. Give it another week, you'll see. You'll be amazed. You're going to listen to yourself on the finished tape and think: 'Who's that star I'm hearing?' "

Miranda tried for a smile.

As they were walking down the hall together, Milo was rubbing Miranda's shoulders like a boxing coach and telling her how great she was doing. Miranda took one backward look at me, then returned her attention forward. The buzzer blared again, calling them inside.

19

 I called my information broker from the pay phone at the Whole Foods Market complex on North Lamar. One of Kelly Arguello's housemates, I think it was Georgia, answered the phone, a little breathless like she'd been doing her morning aerobics. When I asked for Kelly she said, "I'm not sure if she's in. Who is this?"

I told her.

"Oh." Her voice went up half an octave. "Kelly's in. Hang on."

The phone smashed against something.

I heard Kelly laughing a long time before she got the receiver. She was telling Georgia to shut up.

Clunk. "Tres?"

"Kelly. How's school?"

She made a German *ch* sound in the back of her throat. "Midterms. Contractual law. Any more questions?"

"I've got a missing person to track, need some paperwork collected on him. If you're too busy—"

"Did I say that? Are you in town?"

I hesitated. "Yes."

"Come over. I think I've still got a Shiner Bock in the fridge."

I stared at the roof of the parking garage at the other end of the lot. It was lined with giant papier-mâché groceries—strawberry, eggplant, milk. I said, "I could just E-mail the information if you need to study or something."

"You know better than that."

After Kelly hung up I stood there, glaring up at the huge papier-mâché chicken. Any resemblance to persons real or fictional was purely coincidental.

When I was first starting my apprenticeship Erainya had two words to tell me about finding an information broker: *law students*. They're happy to see even small amounts of cash and they don't ask questions except occasionally "Where's the beer?" They're used to working like dogs, they're bright, and they know how to get the best results out of bureaucracies. All that is a lot more than you can say for most of the people who run information services.

Unfortunately my law student helper had turned out to be a little more than I bargained for. Considering the person who referred her to me was her Uncle Ralph, I don't know why I was surprised.

When I got to Kelly Arguello's house in the neighborhood of Clarksville she was in front clipping back a huge mass of honeysuckle that was taking over her exterior bedroom wall and threatening to grow into her window.

Kelly's not hard to spot. She's a girl who'd catch your eye anyway, but since she's moved to Austin and put purple highlights in her hair it's doubly easy.

"I love this stuff," she said when I came up behind her. "Unfortunately, so do the bees."

"You're allergic?"

Without looking away from her work she widened her eyes and nodded several times. "The little guys buzzed in my window all summer long. This is the first morning it's been cool enough to do some pruning. If we keep this place for the spring semester I'm going to have to trade rooms with Dee."

She got her weight balanced on the ladder, then reached a little farther across the window. She was wearing a surgeon's green scrub shirt and men's white swim trunks that should've done a good job hiding her figure but somehow didn't. She still showed off the lean, smoothly sculpted body of a teenaged swimmer. She was twenty-one, barely, but no bartender in his right mind would've failed to card her. Her purple and black hair was pulled into a ponytail that swung back and forth every time she clipped.

"You're going to fall," I said.

"Well, hold the ladder, stupid."

I held the ladder, looking sideways so my face wasn't in Kelly's swim trunks. I concentrated on the house next door.

"Your neighbors are gardeners, too."

Kelly made a "sshhh" sound, though nobody could've heard me. The next-door neighbor's front yard consisted of dirt, ragweed, an old chevy chassis set on cinder blocks, and a brown Frigidaire leaning against an oak tree.

"I've got this idea." Kelly stuck out the tip of her tongue as she tried to clip a vine. "Me and Georgia and Dee are thinking about quitting law school and going into the yard appliance business. You know—selling old washing machines and refrigerators that people can set in their front yards. You drive around this side of Austin you'll see there's obviously a big demand for them. What do you think?"

"I think your uncle would be proud of you."

She smiled. There aren't many times I see the likeness between Kelly Arguello and her uncle. I see it when she smiles. Though, on Kelly, thank God, the smile doesn't have the same maniacal edge.

She leaned out for one last curl of honeysuckle that hung over the window. "Okay. Enough for now. There's a cooler on the porch. Get that Shiner Bock."

"It's ten-thirty."

"You want a light beer instead?"

I took the Shiner. Kelly drank a Pecan Street Ale. We sat on her wooden porch swing while she booted up a little blue portable computer, then started copying the information I had so far on Les Saint-Pierre.

The laptop beeped unpleasantly. She cursed, held it aloft by the screen, resettled herself so her bare feet were pulled up under her, then put the computer back in her lap and hit the delete key several times.

"New toy?" I asked.

She wrinkled her nose, rabbit style, and kept it that way for a few seconds.

"Ralph?"

She nodded. "I told him I was saving up for one. Next thing I know he's bought it for me. He's always doing that."

"He's just upset you got all those scholarships. Had his heart set on paying your way through college."

"Probably he'd beat up my professors if they didn't give me straight A's."

"That's not true," I insisted. "He'd *pay* to have them beat up."

She didn't look amused. She kept typing, squinting as she tried to read Milo Chavez's handwriting.

"*Lo hace porque le importas,* Kelly."

She acted like she hadn't heard me.

"You want all the paperwork on this guy?" she asked. "Like last time?"

"Get his marriage certificate. DMV. Credit. He's also got an air force record. We can at least get his date and nature of discharge on that. Check the tax rolls, especially deeds, building permits—"

"Basically everything," she summed up. She flipped through some more papers, gaining confidence in the task until she hit the personnel files from Julie Kearnes' computer, all seven pages worth. "Whoa."

She scanned a few lines, looked up at me wide-eyed. "What the hell?"

"Part of our problem. This guy might be a vanisher."

She nodded slowly, trying to decide whether she should pretend she was following me or not. "Yeah?"

"Let's say you were into something dangerous."

"Like what?"

"I don't know. But you know you're going to be making some enemies and you want to leave yourself an escape hatch. Or maybe you're just unhappy with your life anyway and you've been planning to skip for a long time, then something bad comes up and you figure the time is ripe. Either way, you want to disappear off the face of the earth for a while, maybe forever. What would you do?"

Kelly thought about it. It can take law students a while to turn their training around—to look at the illegalities that are possible rather than the legalities. When they finally start thinking in reverse, though, it's scary.

"I'd start constructing a new identity," she decided. "New ID, new credit, completely clean paper trail. Maybe I'd butter up somebody who had access to employee files for some big corporations, like these."

She scanned the printouts more closely. "I'd look for somebody deceased who was about my age, somebody who died far away from their town of birth so their birth and death paperwork would've never met up. I could order their birth certificate from their home county, get a new social security number with that, then a driver's license, even a passport. That about right?"

I nodded. "A plus."

"People really do this?"

"A couple of hundred times a year. Hard to get figures because nobody ever advertises success."

"Which means—" She started to recalculate the job I was asking her to do. "Holy shit."

"It means we have to narrow the field. We have to find the most likely candidates from those files who might make viable new Les Saint-Pierres—males in their late forties who were born out of state and died fairly recently. There shouldn't be too many. Then we have to find out if any of those dead folks have requested new ID paperwork in the last, say, three months."

"That could still mean five or six names to track. And even then we might miss him. *If* he really did disappear."

"That's true."

"How long do we have?"

"Until next Friday."

She stared at me. "That's impossible. I'll have to get down to Vital Statistics today."

"Can you do it?"

She raised her eyebrows. "Sure. I can do anything. But it's going to cost you."

"How much?"

"How about dinner?"

I plinked the rim of my beer bottle. "Kelly, your uncle owns a very large collection of guns."

"What—I can't ask you to dinner?"

"Sure. I just can't accept."

She rolled her eyes. "That's such bullshit, Tres."

I stayed quiet and drank my beer. Kelly stuffed the personnel files back into the folder and returned to typing. Every once in a while the fragrance of clipped honeysuckle would drift across the porch, a strange smell for mid-October.

I pulled five of Milo's bills from my backpack and handed them to Kelly. "You run into any unusual expenses, let me know."

"Sure."

She dug back into the folder and pulled out Les Saint-Pierre's photograph. "Yuck."

She tried to shape her expression like Les'. She couldn't quite get the eyebrows right.

Across the street a businessman stumbled out his front door and spilled coffee on his tie. He lifted both arms in a Dracula pose and swore, then walked more carefully toward his BMW. His duplex looked like it had been built in the last twelve hours—all white aluminum siding and the lawn still made up of little green squares that hadn't grown together. The house next to his was an old red shack with a store on the side that sold ceramics and crystals. Austin.

"What was it like growing up without your mother?" I asked.

Kelly lifted one eyebrow, then looked at me without turning her head. "What makes you ask that?"

"No reason. Just curious."

She stuck out her lower lip so she could blow away the strand of grape-colored hair that was hanging in her face. "I don't think about it much, Tres. It's not like I spent my childhood thinking I was different or anything. Dad was always around; five or six uncles in the house. Things were just the way they were."

I swirled the last ounce of beer in my bottle. "You remember her at all?"

Kelly's fingers flattened on the keyboard. She stared at her doorway and, momentarily, looked older than she was. "You know the problem with that, Tres? Your relatives are always telling you things. They remind you of things you did, the way your mom was. You mix that with the old photos and pretty soon you've convinced yourself you have these memories. Then if you want to stay sane you bury them."

"Why?"

"Because it's not enough. You grow up with men, you have to learn to deal with men. The fact you don't have a mom—" She hesitated, her eyes still searching for something in the doorway. "With a mom, I guess you get some intuition, some understanding and talking. With a bunch of guys in the house, little girl has to take a different tack. Learn sneaky ways to get them to do what you want. Good training for working in law firms, actually. Or working for you."

"Thanks a lot."

Kelly smiled. She looked through the other documents in my packet, found little that would help her, then resealed the manila envelope. She closed the laptop.

"I'll call you as soon as I get something," she told me. "You're heading back to S.A.?"

I nodded. "You want me to tell your uncle anything?"

Kelly stood up so quickly the porch swing started moving cockeyed. She opened the screen door. "Sure. Tell him I'm expecting a dinner out of you."

"You want to get me killed."

She smiled like I'd guessed the exact thing she had in mind, then shut the door behind her and left me alone on the porch, the swing still zigzagging around.

20

There are two state-run rest stops between Austin and San Antonio, leftovers from simpler times before developers plopped convenience stores and outlet malls at hundred-yard intervals all the way down the highway.

I resisted the urge to pull into the first, even though Kelly Arguello's Shiner Bock was working its way through my system, but by the time I'd passed through New Braunfels my bladder was twisting itself into funny little balloon animals. I decided to exit at the second rest stop.

I made such haste parking the VW and shuffling up the steps toward the john that I didn't take much notice of the pickup and horse trailer I'd parked behind.

Nor did I take much notice of the guy next to me at the urinal. He smelled faintly of cigarette smoke and the checkered shirt and the profile of his face looked familiar, but there is no space quite so inviolable as the space between two men at the pee trough. I didn't look at him until we'd both suited up and were washing our hands.

"Brent, right?"

He clamped his hands on the paper towel a few times, frowning at me. He hadn't changed clothes since yesterday, nor shaved. The bags under his eyes were puffy, like the extra tequila from last night's gig had drained into them.

"Tres Navarre," I said. "We met last night at the Cactus, sort of."

Brent threw away his towel. "Cam Compton's forehead."

"Right."

"I remember."

Brent looked past me, out the entrance of the john. I was standing between him and the exit, which made it difficult for Brent to get around me. He obviously wanted to. Two men having a conversation in the bathroom was only slightly less awkward than acknowledging each other at the urinal. Maybe I should compensate by offering him some Red Man. Mention the playoffs. Bubba etiquette.

"You with Miranda?" I asked.

He looked around, uncomfortably. "No. Just the equipment."

"Ah."

He shuffled a little more. I took mercy and stepped aside so we could both walk out at the same time.

The rest stop was doing a pretty good business for a weekday. Down on one end of the grassy oval island the picnic benches were overflowing with a huge Latino family. Fat men in tank tops drank beer while the women and children streamed back and forth between the tables and their battered station wagons, bringing ice chests and boxes of potato chips and marshmallows. A little dog was doing circles around the kids' legs. The far curb of the turnout lane was lined with semis, the cabs dark and the drivers inside sleeping or shaving or eating,

staring at the horizon and thinking whatever it is
truckers think.

A local Baptist church had set up an outereach table
at the bottom of the bathroom steps. Several perky
blond-haired women offered DUI fliers and free pocket
Bibles and donuts and coffee. A green posterboard sign
announcing CHRIST LOVES TRAVELERS, TOO flapped in the
humid wind.

Brent Daniels wasn't thrilled when he realized we had
parked next to each other—my VW right behind his
pickup and trailer.

Brent's rig was a white Ford with brown stripes. The
windows were tinted almost pure silver, making it impossible to see inside the cab. The trailer was a one-horse
job, brown metal, with the words ROCKING U RANCH
thinly painted over in a beige-brown that didn't match
the rest of the metal.

"Equipment in a horse trailer," I said. "Inventive."

Brent nodded. "Cheaper than a van. Willis got a good
deal on it."

We stood there. I wasn't quite sure why Brent was
staying to talk. Then I realized that for some reason he
wanted me to leave first.

When you've got an advantage, I say press it.

"I was talking to Miranda about your music this
morning. She said you wrote most of the songs. Said you
were real supportive about her recording them."

Brent hooked his fingers on the door handle of the
Ford and hung them there. His expression was hard to
read, mostly gruff apathy with maybe a little dry amusement around the edges. With the facial stubble a day
thicker I could see that some of the whiskers were
coming up white, like his dad's.

"Supportive," he repeated. "That a fact?"

"She seems to think so. You ever try to record on your
own? Make it in Nashville? You've got some nice songs."

That brought the amusement a little closer to the surface. A tic started going in Brent's left eye, like he was
trying to smile but was having a short-circuit problem.

"Ask Les about that," he said. "I'm forty-two, didn't even start writing—" He caught himself, decided to change tack. "I didn't start writing until about two years ago. Most artists making it—fifteen to eighteen, some even younger. Miranda's barely okay at twenty-five. Les says you're over thirty as an artist, you're pretty much dog-meat."

"Les said that, huh? What is Les—forty-five?"

Brent ticked his eye a little more. "Guess the rule don't apply to agents."

We both looked out at the highway as another semi roared by at plane-engine volume. Some raindrops were splattering the asphalt noncommittally, once every few seconds. The wind was slow, heavy, and hot, and the clouds couldn't seem to decide what to do—break up or move in. They made the low hills an even darker green, almost purple.

"How about the rest of the band?" I asked. "Mr. Sheckly seems to think you folks'll be left out in the cold if Miranda's record deal goes through. Anybody besides Cam upset about that?"

Brent lost whatever smile he might've been starting to accumulate. He scuffed his boot on the curb, a small sign of impatience. "Suppose you'd have to ask them, wouldn't you? Julie's dead. Cam's fired. Pretty much leaves Ben French and the family, don't it?"

Behind us a trucker was flirting with one of the Baptist women, calling her Sweet Thing. She was trying to keep her polyethylene smile in place, talking about how Jesus wanted the trucker to have some coffee and stay awake out there on the road. Her tone wasn't very convincing.

"You got a day job?" I asked Brent.

"Nope. How about you?"

Ah. A hint.

Brent kept his fingers hooked on the door, making no move to open it. I looked at the silvered window of the cab and saw nothing but me, bubbly and smeared in the glass.

"I didn't know better," I told Brent, "I'd think you didn't want to open that door."

Brent looked at his boot, then sideways at the Latino mutt dog, which was now doing tight orbits around the metal poles of the breezeway.

Brent smiled at the little dog.

"You working for Milo?" Brent asked me.

"That's right."

Brent nodded. "You best get at it, then."

He opened the door of the cab and got in, trying not to be too quick about it. I tried not to be too obvious about looking, but there wasn't much to see—just a woman's tan feet crossed at the ankles, propped up on the window in the miniature backseat like she was sleeping back there. She had painted toenails and a little gold ankle chain.

Brent closed the door and was lost behind the window tinting.

The truck pulled out and a big plop of warm rain landed squarely on my nose.

The Baptist lady breathed a sigh of relief because the flirtatious trucker had just left. She called over to me and offered me a donut. I told her thanks but Jesus would have to find somebody else. All she had left were the jelly-filled variety.

21

"It's registered," Ralph Arguello told me.

He slid into the backseat of his maroon Lincoln with me, then returned the Montgomery Ward .22. Chico pulled the car out of the pawnshop parking lot and headed south on Bandera.

"You were in there all of five minutes," I said.

"Yeah. Sorry so long. My friend at the data entry office, she does all the firearm slips for the pawnshop detail. Sometimes I don't want to wait, she'll do a pre-screening for me, you know? Today she was a little busy."

"You get the owner's name and address?"

"What do you think?"

"I think you probably got his grandmother's maiden name and his favorite flavor ice cream."

Ralph grinned. *"Que padre, vato."*

When Ralph grins he gives the Cheshire cat a bad name. He makes psychopaths nervous. Maybe it's because you

can't really see his eyes, the way they float behind the
inch-thick round lenses. Or maybe it's the red color his
face turns, same as one of those chubby diablo masks
they sell in Piedras Negras. When Ralph grins it could
mean he's made an easy thousand dollars or he's had a
good meal or he's just shot somebody who was annoying
him. It's hard to tell.

He handed me a piece of paper from the front pocket
of his white linen guayabera. In Ralph's meticulous, tiny
block print it said: C. COMPTON 1260 PERRIN-BEITEL SA TX
78217.

"I got a story about this guy," Ralph offered.

That was no surprise. It was a rare and boring San
Antonian Ralph Arguello didn't have a story about.

I read the name C. Compton again.

"Tell me your story."

Ralph produced a joint and started carefully pinching
the ends. "Your man Compton works for that kicker
palace, the Indian Paintbrush. You know the place?"

"I know it."

"You remember Robbie Guerra—halfback from
Heights?"

I had no idea, as usual, where Ralph was going, or
where his information had come from, but I nodded.
"How is Robbie?"

"He's dead, man, but that's another story. Six months
ago we had this nice deal going with a restaurant supply
company and some of the places they delivered to. The
Indian Paintbrush was one. Every tenth crate set aside,
Robbie and me'd pick it up, everybody involved gets a
little cut. Compton was some musician or something, but
he worked day shifts with the business manager, too,
some guy—"

"Alex Blanceagle. Freckles. Big ears."

"—that's right. Anyway, Compton and Blanceagle
knew about our deal with the crates, they got their share,
everything was *suave*. Then one night Robbie and me
accidentally skimmed from the wrong shipment, okay? It
happens sometimes. We came by on the guard's Coke

break, like normal, everything looked cool, we started taking these big brown cardboard cylinders off the loading dock. We thought maybe they were full of copper piping or something because they were heavier than shit but we figured hell, goods are goods. Five seconds later we had all these *gabachos* with guns in our faces—Blanceagle and Compton and two German guys screaming in Kraut. Robbie and me got a talking-to, half of it in Kraut, with guns at our heads the whole time. Blanceagle was all yelling like he never saw us before and telling us we were lucky to walk away alive. So we said *chupa me*. That was the end of one restaurant supply deal."

Ralph lit the *mota* and took a long drag. He might've just been telling me about his last birthday party for all the agitation he showed.

"Describe these Germans."

Ralph gave a pretty accurate description of Jean, the man with the Beretta from Sheckly's studio. He described another guy who didn't sound familiar.

"What was in the cylinders?"

Ralph blew smoke. "*No se, vato.* All those rednecks and Nazis pointing guns at my ass I wasn't going to ask for no peeks. Probably KKK training kits, right?"

We drove in silence down Bandera for a few miles, under the Loop, into a residential area where the houses looked like army bunkers, flat and sunken behind old brick privacy walls and overgrown pampas bushes. There was some fresh gang graffiti on the walls. A phone booth on the corner of Callahan had been pried out of the ground and laid flat across a bus bench. On top of it was a line of empty MD 20/20 bottles that a little shirtless boy was hitting with a stick.

The sky wasn't helping the general impression that this whole neighborhood had recently been stepped on. A layer of gray clouds was pressing down low, like insulation material. The air had heated up again, and now it was just hanging there, stagnant and heavy.

After a few blocks Chico leaned his head back and asked Ralph in Spanish if he wanted to stop by Number Fourteen, since we were passing by. Ralph checked his gold Rolex and said sure. Then he got Mr. Subtle out from under the driver's seat and loaded it. Mr. Subtle is his .357 Magnum.

"The homeboys been making noise," he said. "*Pinche* kids."

"Number Fourteen," I said. "Catchy name."

"Hey, man, you get over twenty pawnshops, you try naming them all."

He stuck Mr. Subtle in his jeans, underneath the guayabera. Most people couldn't wear a Magnum like that and look inconspicuous. Most people don't have Ralph's girth and his XXL linen shirts.

Chico found a Def Lepard song on the radio and turned it up. Probably still on the Top Ten in San Antonio.

"So," Ralph said, "you see my niece when you were up in Austin?"

"She's doing fine. Good worker, just like you said."

Ralph ticked. "She's going through this *con crema* phase, man. I don't get her sometimes."

"*Con crema?*"

"You know what I mean. She won't speak Spanish. Only dates white guys."

"No kidding."

Ralph nodded, shifting a little in his seat. I shifted in my seat. We stared out the windows. He decided to change the subject.

"Speaking of *con crema*, man, you hanging out again with that *cabron*, Chavez?"

I hadn't told Ralph anything about the case. Not that that mattered. Ralph had probably found out about my meeting with Chavez the day it happened. Anything that went on within the city limits, Ralph usually knew about it in time to start placing bets.

"Milo's tangled into something, Ralphas. I told him I'd try to help out."

"Yeah." Ralph grinned. "*Pinche* bastard ever figure out what he wants to be when he grows up?"

I had never been quite sure when or how Milo and Ralph had met. They'd simply always known and disliked each other. All three of us had gone to Alamo Heights, of course, but as far as I knew the two men had never exchanged a word, never acknowledged each other. I'd never been in a room with both of them at the same time. Aside from being North Side Latinos, the two could not have been further apart. Ralph had come from poverty, from a factory shantytown where his father had died of cement dust in his lungs and second-generation natives still kept fake green cards because it was easier than making *La Migra* believe their nationality. Ralph had made it through high school on the strength of his football playing and cunning and a straight-edged razor and the certain unwavering knowledge that someday he would be worth a million dollars. Milo had come from a placid, well-off family. He was one of the few Latinos who had been accepted in the white circles, been invited to Cotillion dances, even had a white girlfriend. The news that he'd toyed with music after high school, then business, then finally persevered through a law degree caused no surprise among his old friends, no excitement. No feeling that he'd tackled insurmountable odds. The fact that he'd changed jobs again, gone into the country music industry, would generate, at best, a few amused smiles.

"Milo's doing all right."

Ralph laughed. "Isn't he the one almost got you killed out in San Francisco?"

"That's one interpretation."

"Yeah. You remember that shit we used to drop in water in chemistry class? What was that—"

"Potassium."

"That's it. Boom, right? That shit is you and Chavez, man. I can't believe you're talking to that *pinche* bastard again. You thought about that offer I made you earlier?"

"I wouldn't be into it, Ralphas. I got enough worries."

Ralph blew a line of marijuana smoke against the window. He shook his head.

"I don't get you. I been trying since high school and I still don't. You push a guy off a smokestack ten stories up—"

"Special circumstances. He was going to kill me."

"You break some *pendejo*'s leg just because an old lady asked you to, for no money."

"He was ripping off her social security checks, Ralphas."

"Now you work for Chavez when you know he's going to fuck you up, man. Then I offer you five hundred a week easy, doing the same kind of shit, and you tell me you're not into it. *Loco.*"

Chico had been quiet so far. Now he turned his head slightly and said, "Fuck him."

I looked at Ralph.

Ralph took another toke. "Chico's new."

"I got that."

Chico kept his eyes on the road, left hand on the wheel, and huge right arm draped along the top of the bench seat. He had LA RAZA tattooed in very small letters on his deltoid. His hair was covered with a yellow bandanna, tied in back, pirate-style.

"Fuck him," he said again. "What you need his pansy ass for, man?"

Ralph smiled at me. "Eh, Chico, this guy's okay. I saved his ass from some shitkickers in high school."

"*You* saved *me*?"

"Yeah, man. You remember." Then to Chico: "Changed his life, man. Became this martial arts badass. He's good."

Chico grunted, unimpressed. "Guy I knew in the pen did tae kwon do. Kicked the shit out of him."

We kept driving.

Pawnshop Number Fourteen was in a five-unit strip mall just off Hillcrest, sandwiched between the Mayan Taco King and Joleen's Beauty Shop. Number Fourteen's bright yellow marquee said WE BUY GOLD!!!! The windows were painted with pumpkins and witches and smiling cartoon dollar signs that didn't quite go with the burglar bars and the shotgun displays aside.

A gallery ran in front of the mall, covered by a metal awning held up by square white posts. Leaning against the posts outside Number Fourteen were two young Latino guys, maybe seventeen, both in black jeans and Raiders jackets. They would've made good fullbacks if they'd been in school. Sitting on the sidewalk between them, leaning back on his elbows, was a much skinnier kid who'd evidently done his clothes shopping with the fullbacks. On all of them the clothes were huge and baggy, but especially on the skinny guy. The three of them looked like a family of elephants who'd gotten a group rate on liposuction.

Ralph and Chico walked up to them. I followed.

None of the kids moved, but the skinny one in the middle smiled. He had the pointiest chin I'd ever seen, with a little spiky tuft of adolescent beard at the tip. It made the lower half of his face look like it had been fashioned out of a stirrup.

"Boss man," he said. "*¿Que pasa?*"

Ralph smiled back. "Vega. You want to take your *chiquitas* here and play somewhere else? You're cramping my business, man."

I got the feeling Ralph and Vega had gone through this a couple of times before. They looked at each other, both smiling, waiting for something to break.

What broke was our new man Chico's patience. He detached himself from Ralph's side and said, "Fuck this."

He walked up to the skinny kid and lifted him by his jacket with one hand. Maybe that would've been impressive if the kid hadn't weighed ninety pounds, or if Chico hadn't planted his legs apart and given Vega a beautiful opportunity to knee him in the balls.

Vega's knee was mostly bone, and what he lacked in weight he made up for in ferocity. As he kneed Chico,

Vega's face tightened and his teeth clenched so hard his tuft of beard almost touched his lower lip.

Chico grunted, dropped the kid, then doubled over and started turning around in slow motion. Chico's face was the same color as his bandanna. One of the fullbacks kicked him from behind and Chico went sideways onto the asphalt groaning: *"Mierda, mierda."*

I looked at Ralph. "He's new."

"Yeah."

Vega adjusted his baggy clothes and sat back down, smiling again. He rubbed his little beard and told his buddies what a big tough *pachuco* Chico was. They laughed.

"Oh, man," said Vega, "you had some customers come by today, Boss, but they didn't look like a good type of people, right? We told them no way. We're looking out for you good."

About then a scrawny gray-haired man shuffled out of the pawnship, looked at Ralph a little fearfully, and started apologizing in Spanish.

"Mr. Arguello, I swear I didn't know they were out here. I chased them off twice already."

Then the old man started waving a rolled-up newspaper at the three kids, halfheartedly telling them to go away. Nobody paid him any attention. The kids were looking at the .357 Magnum Ralph was now holding.

"You know, *vato*," Ralph said to me casually, "used to be you had just *La Familia* coming to you. Least they were adults, right? Now you've got these *pinche* kids, think just because they can beat up their math teacher they got a right to protection money. Sad, man. It's really sad."

Vega looked at the gun in Ralph's hand like it was a big joke. "You gonna shoot me, Boss Man?"

Vega wasn't afraid. Maybe you don't get afraid when you're seventeen and you've got your set behind you and you know guns the way other kids know skateboards.

On the other hand, I didn't like the way Ralph was smiling. I'd seen Ralph use a .22 like a staple gun on a guy who'd touched his girlfriend in a bar. Ralph had been smiling the same way as he stapled the guy's palm flat against the wooden counter.

"We got guns," Vega said. "Like in the middle of the night. Outside your house, right?"

Chico was on his hands and knees now, taking noisy breaths and mumbling that he was going to kill them.

Vega looked down and said, "Good dog."

That got another laugh from his fullbacks.

Ralph was perfectly still, frozen. I figured I had a few seconds before he made up his mind what part of this kid's body he was going to blow a hole in.

"You three need to leave," I said.

Vega looked at me for the first time. "Who's this, Boss Man? This your girlfriend?"

Before Ralph could shoot, I grabbed Vega's ankles and pulled. The kid went back off his elbows and hit his head on the cement edge of the stairs. I dropped him just as his fullback buddies realized they needed to act.

I don't often use *Ride the Tiger*. Usually you don't get opponents attacking the way a tiger does, from above. As the first kid jumped me I slid into bow stance and swept my arms up in a circle, my right hand rolling against his chest and my left hand against his leg. He flew over me like he'd been bounced over the top of a spinning wheel. I didn't look behind to see how he landed on the asphalt of the parking lot.

The second kid tackled me from the side. I hooked his baggy jacket, turned my waist hard, and flipped him over my knee. He landed on his butt with a muffled crack.

By the time I saw Vega move out of the corner of my eye and saw the flash of metal and I turned, it would've been too late.

There was a *click*.

The kid was propped up on one elbow, a long knife in his hand, the tip frozen six inches away from my thigh. Ralph was kneeling next to him, smiling calmly, the muzzle of his .357 pressed hard into Vega's eye. Vega's head tilted up at the same angle as the barrel, as if he was looking into the eyepiece of a telescope. His free eye was twitching violently.

"The man put you on the ground, *ese,*" Ralph told him amiably. "You got any sense, that's where you stay."

The three of us stayed frozen for a couple of centuries. Then, finally, Vega's knife clattered against the pavement. "You're dead, Boss Man. You know that?"

Ralph grinned. "Twenty or thirty times, *ese.*"

Ralph took Vega's knife, then stood up and put away Mr. Subtle. I looked around. The guy I'd knocked on his butt was still on his butt. He was staring at me. His eyes were watering and he was tilting sideways, trying to get away from the pain. The guy I'd thrown into the parking lot was trying to stand up, but it looked like his left shoulder was glued to the pavement. I think maybe his collarbone was broken.

I got the kids to their feet and started herding them out of the lot.

They shuffled down Bandera, Vega shouting back at me that they knew where I lived and my family was dead. I called after Vega that his buddy would need a doctor for the collarbone. Vega shot me the finger. His eye was still twitching from the cold, oily nudge of the .357 muzzle.

When I came back to the front door of Number Fourteen, Chico was sitting on the sidewalk, trying not to throw up. He looked up at me resentfully.

"Lucky shot," I said. "I thought you had him."

The old man with the rolled-up newspaper was trying to explain to Ralph that everything was fine and he would have it under control from now on. He looked nervous.

Ralph grinned at me and brought out a clip of money and peeled off a few bills.

"Least I can do, man."

The going price for beating up teenagers was two hundred dollars. A lot more expensive than a few .357 rounds. I gave the money back to Ralph.

"No thanks."

Ralph shook his head in amazement. "So you wouldn't be into it, eh, *vato?*"

He laughed. Then he turned and went into Number Fourteen to check on business.

22

There are definite disadvantages to teaching a four-year-old to tell time. As soon as I walked in Erainya's front door at six that evening Jem looked up at me from the dining-room table, pointed at his Crayola Swatch, and told me I was late. We now had only thirty minutes before our movie started at the Galaxy. He didn't want to miss the previews.

He scooted out from the table and rushed toward me. Instead of our usual full-tackle hug he screamed "Watch!" as he ran, then proved how well he'd been practicing his moves by landing a flying kick in my crotch.

There are also disadvantages to teaching a four-year-old martial arts.

I wiped away a few tears and limped with him into the kitchen, assuring him he was learning the basics just fine.

The kitchen smelled like burnt fila and garlic. It always smelled like Erainya had just been cooking, though I'd never actually caught her doing it. I suspected she'd snuck an entire sweatshop full of Greek cooks back from the old country and kept them locked in the basement when she had company over. Of course this was the same woman who'd shot her husband, so I'd never gotten the courage to actually check her basement. No telling what or who else I'd find down there.

Erainya handed me a three-section paper plate loaded with Mediterranean food. It was so thickly covered with Saran Wrap I couldn't tell exactly what was underneath the wrap. I only knew it was food because Erainya handed me a plate like that every time I came over. Apparently my uncertain employment status hadn't changed the ritual.

"Just in time," I said. "I was beginning to think I might have to go shopping this month."

"Ah." She slapped the air next to her ear, but she did it listlessly, like her heart really wasn't in it today. She was wearing a pullover black shirt and dark slacks, which meant something was up for tonight. Erainya only forgoes the standard T-shirt dress when she knows she's got some crawling or running or breaking in to do. "Just leftovers. Some *kibbeh*. *Dolmades*. *Spanakopita*. There's a little *melitzanosalata*—what's . . . eggplant salad, I guess you'd say."

Erainya's first language was English, but every once in a while she likes to forget how to translate something from Greek. She says thinking in Greek clears her soul.

Jem raced to the bedroom to get his sneakers. When he disappeared down the hallway Erainya said, "You thought things over, honey? About the job?"

"I'm thinking. I have an interview lined up. For a college position."

Erainya gave me the black eyes. "I thought you couldn't stand the idea of a dusty office and a tweed suit."

"Maybe that was sour grapes. Nobody ever offered me a dusty office and a tweed suit."

Erainya slapped air. "Not that I care—not like I want you back if you won't work right. I'm not losing my license over you being an idiot, honey."

"Sam Barrera speak to you again?"

"I don't know nothing about Sam Barrera's cases and I don't know nothing about what you're doing on your time off, you understand that?"

"Sure."

Erainya glared at the dishrags. "I'm not going to let that *ouskemo* tell me what to do, neither. Maybe he's got some friends in a lot of places. He doesn't own me."

I nodded. We were quiet, listening to Jem throw toys and other large heavy objects around his bedroom, apparently looking for just the right fashion statement footwear.

"Be good to know some background on a guy named Tilden Sheckly," I said. "About some shipments he's been processing through his dance hall, especially any connections he might have in Europe. Like for instance if your friend in Customs knew anything—what's her name?"

"Corrie. I didn't hear any of that."

I agreed that she hadn't.

Jem came back wearing purple Reeboks. He showed me how the heel-lights flickered when he bounced up and down. He'd also put a Casper the Ghost mask on his head with shafts of his thick black hair sticking out of the eyeholes. I told him he looked great.

Erainya started loading up her purse while Jem told me about what his Halloween costume was going to be. The costume apparently had nothing to do with the Casper mask. He told me how many hours and minutes were left until six o'clock Sunday, when he was going trick-or-treating. Then he told me about the movie he was taking me to—something with marsupials that transformed into cosmic warriors.

Erainya packed her cassette recorder, her Mace canister, her obligatory box of green Chiclets, and five Kleenex folded into triangles. She deliberated over her key chain, rubbing her thumb on the little gold key that opens her gun cabinet.

Then she looked up and realized I was watching her.

Her eyes turned hard as obsidian. She stowed the keys in her purse and zipped it.

"Is two hours going to be enough time?" I asked.

I tried to keep my voice casual, disinterested. Erainya responded the same way.

"Sure, honey. Fine."

Jem gave up explaining the virtues of outer space marsupials to me. He climbed back onto a stool at the kitchen counter and started coloring a picture of Godzilla.

"The Longoria case?" I asked.

Erainya hesitated long enough to confirm it. "It's nothing, honey. Don't worry about it. I'll just be able to run some checks faster while Jem's out with you."

Jem colored a red halo around Godzilla's head, focusing his energy into the tip of his marker with a level of concentration no adult could match.

"Erainya—"

She cut me off with a look. When she spoke she addressed the top of Jem's head.

"Don't you waste time worrying about the wrong person, honey. I can tell you all about it next week when you're back at work."

I didn't answer.

Erainya muttered something in Greek that sounded like a proverb. She sighed and put her purse on her forearm.

"I'll meet you back here by nine. And no damn candy at the theater, huh?"

Jem complained a little about that, telling her we always got Dots and Red Vines, but he knew better than to push it. He just shut his mouth and let his mother rewrite the rules as ridiculously unfair as she wanted. That's a lesson everybody learns eventually with Erainya.

23

 After the movies I dropped Jem off at Erainya's house and flipped a coin, Compton or Blanceagle. I was half hoping the coin would land on its edge and I could go home.

Instead it came up Blanceagle. I headed out for the address I'd seen on Alex's driver's license, 1600 Mecca.

Mecca Street, like its namesake, is a place most people only get to once in their lifetime, only with the help of Allah, and only after many tribulations. Once you do find the road, it twists illogically through the Hollywood Park subdivision, disappearing and then reappearing, following what was once a creek bed through the rolling hills just inside Loop 1604.

I took 281 North and gave myself up to the hajj as soon as I exited, praying that someday I'd find Alex Blanceagle's house.

Hollywood Park was showing its age since I'd been there last, almost ten years before. The pseudo-ranch houses that lined the streets were now more weathered, the lawns that had been grafted with fruit trees and turf grass now regressed in spots to the original scrub brush, mesquites, and cactus.

On most blocks the pristine look of affluent Gringo-land had given way to more down-to-earth realities—plastic daisy pinwheels in the yards, porches overflowing with tricycles, windsocks, political signboards, pumpkins, and paper skeletons.

Blanceagle's house was in one of the nicer areas, with half-acre lots and expensive cast-iron mailboxes and the occasional white split-rail fence. The house itself was a two-story affair, half limestone, half cedar siding, set far back from the road. I parked a block down on Mecca, then walked up the gravel driveway toward the front porch, my backpack in hand.

No exterior lights. Dim illumination from behind an upstairs curtain, more from around the side of the house—kitchen window, maybe. I was almost to the porch before I realized that the front door wasn't really painted black. It was just completely open.

I stood to one side on the porch and let my eyes adjust. Then I moved inside and stood against the wall.

A man's living room, lit only by the glow from the hallway on the right and from the staircase on the left. There were two large easy chairs and a mismatching love seat, all ugly and functional. A big-screen TV and cabinet of stereo equipment. A bookshelf that was mostly filled with CDs stacked sideways. A bar in the corner. A sliding-glass door that led out to a back porch. There was also a strange combination of smells that I didn't like at all—very old cigarette smoke, mildew, dead rat.

I listened. Faint clinking sounds came from down the hallway, from the kitchen.

I should've left right then.

Instead I walked down the hallway, into the kitchen and into the line of fire of Sam Barrera, senior regional director of I-Tech Security and Investigations. He was sitting behind the butcher-block table eating a gallon-sized bowl of Corn Pops and his little .22 was pointed at exactly the spot my forehead appeared as I came into the room. There was no surprise on his face when he saw me. With his free hand he put down the spoon and wiped a dribble of milk off his chin. He said, "Drop the backpack. Come in and turn around."

"Hey, Sam. Nice to see you too."

I did what he told me, very slowly. With a guy who'd been a special agent for the FBI for sixteen years, you're better off not taking liberties. Sam came around the table and patted me down. He smelled as usual like Aramis.

He took my wallet. I could hear him rummaging through the backpack, setting things out on the counter, then sitting back down behind the table. His Corn Pops hadn't even stopped crackling.

"Look at me," he ordered.

I turned.

Sam was wearing a charcoal three-piece and a maroon tie. The gold rings made his right hand almost too chunky to hold the .22. He gave me his standard frown and hard, glassy eyes.

He held up my roll of money from Milo Chavez and showed it to me. Then my studio photograph of Les Saint-Pierre. Then my business card from the Erainya Manos Agency.

He waited for an explanation.

"I'm a tidge bit curious myself," I told him. "Finding a high-profile corporate dick in somebody else's kitchen, eating their Corn Pops with a spoon and a .22—I don't come across this scenario often."

"I was hungry. Mr. Blanceagle isn't going to need them."

I looked at the ceiling. The smell of dead rat was fainter in the kitchen, but still present. When the realization finally hit me, it hit hard.

I don't know why some things knock a hole in my gut and others don't. I've seen a dozen dead bodies. I've seen two people killed right in front of me. Usually it doesn't get me until much later, in the middle of the night, in the shower. This time, even without Blanceagle in front of me, even considering I'd only met the guy once, something gave way like a trapdoor under my rib cage. The idea of that poor schmuck being upstairs dead, the guy who'd looked so drunk and pathetic and outclassed at Sheckly's studio who had done me the small favor of calling me a musician to get me out the door—the idea of him being reduced to a rodent smell got to me.

Embarrassing, with Sam Barrera there. I had to swallow a couple of times, press my hands against the bumpy texture of the kitchen wall behind me.

"Upstairs?"

Barrera nodded.

"Two days ago," I guessed. "Shot with a Beretta."

Barrera started, a bit uneasy at my guesswork.

"See?" I said. "You passed up a hell of a trainee."

"I'll live with it. Go look. I'll wait."

It was almost easier than staying there in the kitchen. At least upstairs, if I threw up, I wouldn't have Barrera looking at me.

My feet were heavy on the staircase.

I breathed as shallowly as I could but it didn't help. After only two days dead in a cool house, the smell shouldn't have been this cloying. Somehow, though, every time I smelled that smell it seemed worse than the time before.

Alex was facedown on a queen-sized bed in the same clothes he'd worn at the Indian Paintbrush. His left limbs were extended and his right limbs curled into his body, so it looked like he was rock climbing. The sheets were in a state of disarray that conformed to his posture, a clump of fabric gathered in his right hand. Fluids had crusted his face to the bedspread. There were flies.

I stood at the doorway for a long time before I could make my feet cooperate. I forced myself to go closer, look for entrance wounds. There were two—a clean round hole in the back of the beige windbreaker, maybe shot from ten feet away, the other in Blanceagle's temple with the edges of the flesh starred and splitting, very close range. Hard to be sure without stripping him, checking for lividity, but I was pretty sure the body hadn't been moved. He'd walked into his bedroom, somebody behind him. They'd shot him in the back. He fell forward onto the bed. They came up and finished it off. Simple.

The rest of the room looked fuzzy, like all the light was bending toward the corpse. I tried to focus on the bedstand, the dresser, to look without touching.

There was a shoe box on the bureau top, full of correspondence that looked carefully picked through. Drawers were open. A pair of rubber gloves was draped over the top one and the chair was pushed out as if someone had just gotten up from it. Sam Barrera's work, half-finished. Maybe it was possible that even Barrera got the creeps, alone in a dark house, going through paperwork with a dead man right next to you on the bed. Maybe even Barrera had to take a Corn Pops break from that kind of work.

I didn't throw up. I somehow made it all the way back down the stairs, back into the kitchen where Barrera was still eating, one hand holding the .22 flat against the tabletop.

"Can I sit down?" I asked.

Barrera examined my face, maybe saw that I wasn't doing so hot. He waved at the stool opposite his.

I sat, took a few breaths. "I take it you haven't called the police."

Sam lifted his right ear just slightly, like God was telling him something. "Blanceagle's been dead two days. He can wait another few hours. Now I'm going to ask you what I asked Erainya: What's your business with Blanceagle? With Les Saint-Pierre?"

I stared at Barrera's cereal bowl, the little gold ball bearings in the white grease. My stomach did a somersault.

Barrera said, "Try some. It'll help. Corn products are good."

"No thanks. Erainya doesn't have any business with Blanceagle. I'm on my own."

"On your own," he repeated.

"That's right."

"Unlicensed."

I nodded. Sam shook his head and looked sour, like his worst assumptions about human nature had just been confirmed.

"Tell me everything," he ordered.

"And then?"

"And then we'll see."

I told him the basics. Sam asked a few questions—what did Jean look like, what exactly had Les Saint-Pierre told Milo Chavez about his plan to force Tilden Sheckly's cooperation. Twice Barrera dug out handfuls of dry Corn Pops from the box and ate them, one pop at a time.

When I was done talking he said, "I've already spoken with Detective Schaeffer at SAPD. I'll talk to the Hollywood Park police. You were never here tonight. You are not working on this anymore."

"Just like that."

"Tell Mr. Chavez he'll have to do the best he can for his artists. Tell him Les Saint-Pierre will probably show up on his own sooner or later and there's no problem with Tilden Sheckly as far as you can determine."

"And that Santa Claus is getting him a nice tricycle for Christmas."

Barrera frowned at me. He flexed his fingers and the gold rings rubbed together with a sound like seashells.

"This thing with the singer, Miranda Daniels," he said. "This is a sideline. Forget it. You think it has anything to do with Saint-Pierre disappearing, you think a guy like Tilden Sheckly would waste his time with murders over a recording contract—" Barrera paused. "You don't know what you've stepped into, Navarre. I'm telling you to step back out."

"There're some shipments going through the Indian Paintbrush," I said. "Something from Germany—big heavy cylinders. Blanceagle said the arrangement has been going on for about six years. Les Saint-Pierre found out about it from Julie Kearnes, who probably got it from

Alex Blanceagle. Les threatened to expose the business to
keep Sheckly from pressing his claims on Miranda
Daniels. Les miscalculated—either how bad the information was or how violently Sheck would react. Now Les
has disappeared and the two people who helped him get
his information are dead. How am I doing?"

"Not well," Barrera said. "Shut up."

"You spoke to Alex Blanceagle at least once before—
he told me another investigator had been poking around.
You were in Austin Saturday night arguing with Julie
Kearnes after I knocked off surveillance. At the time she
wouldn't cooperate; she shooed you out of the house
with a gun. By Sunday night, after I'd rattled her too,
maybe after she'd gotten some calls from Sheck's people,
she was scared enough to set up a meeting with you in
San Antonio. Somehow Sheck found out about it. Julie
still didn't trust you so she came armed, without any
information written down. She got to your rendezvous a
little early or you got there a little late and she got shot in
the head. You got there, found a murder scene, and
decided it was safest to drive on by and ask questions
later. Who are you working for, Sam? What is Sheckly
hiding that's worth killing people?"

Barrera stood up slowly, checked his gold watch.
"Gather your stuff. Go home and stay there. I'm going to
call it in."

"You've got five full-time operatives just at the San
Antonio office, fifteen more regionally. You've got a
dozen national clients subcontracting investigations
through you. If you're here in Blanceagle's living room
yourself, taking trips up to Austin to argue with Julie
Kearnes in person, this has to be big. Something your
friends on the Bureau lined up for you, maybe."

"Your other option is that I turn you over to some of
the agencies involved."

"*Some* of the agencies?"

"People far out of your league, Navarre. They could
make very sure you stay quiet. They would also have
some hard questions for Erainya Manos about the way

that you're operating. We could be looking at a revoked license for her, a guarantee your application never comes up for review. That's all before we bring in the D.A."

"You'd be such a bastard?"

Sam looked at me dispassionately. There was no implied threat. It was a simple multiple-choice test.

"All right." I started to gather up my money, my burglar's tools, my photos and paperwork. I stuffed it all into my backpack. My fingers didn't work very well. My stomach still felt fluttery, warm.

Sam Barrera watched me zip my bag. I wouldn't say he relaxed, but his eyes got a little less intense. He put his gun in his belt, behind his coat. He tilted his head sideways, stretching his neck muscles, and the little shiny black square of hair on top of his head glistened.

"You said six years," he told me. "That's about right. Maybe someday I'll show you my file cabinets, show you how a real case is put together. Maybe I can explain to you what it's like, all that buildup and documentation only to find an informant you've been courting disappeared, then another one shot in the head the day you wanted to interview him. Then to have somebody like you waltz in and act like you own the situation. You're not doing Erainya any favors following this line of work, kid. You're not doing yourself any favors. Go home."

I picked up my bag, got unsteadily to my feet.

"And Navarre—" Sam said, "you didn't find anything. Nothing to indicate Les Saint-Pierre's whereabouts. No documentation you can't explain."

It took me a second to realize he was actually asking me a question rather than giving me another order. I stared at him until he felt obliged to add, "Saint-Pierre was supposed to give me some information. It wasn't up there in Blanceagle's bedroom and it wasn't in Julie Kearnes' house."

I shook my head. The only piece I hadn't told Barrera about was the personnel files, and those weren't blackmail material. At the moment they seemed a petty thing

to hide, a grudgingly small way to get some revenge on
Barrera.

"Nothing," I told him. "I found nothing. Just the way
you thought, Sam."

He scrutinized my face, then nodded. When I left, he
was just starting to talk to the Hollywood Park police on
the phone, explaining to them exactly how they were
going to handle his problem.

24

Milo's green Jeep Cherokee honked in my driveway at ten o'clock Friday morning.

I opened the passenger's side door and said, "I don't believe it. She's alive."

Sassy the basset hound sat up on the seat and yawned. Her tongue rolled into a long bologna canoe. She did a little shuffle on her front paws and snorted. Maybe it was a friendly greeting. Maybe she was having a doggie coronary.

"How old are you?" I demanded. "You make a deal with Satan?"

Sassy panted. She turned her head to the left, trying to see me through her one eye that was milky with cataracts. Where the other eye should've been was a sagging canyon of gray crusty fur.

"Sassy's plugging along okay," Milo admitted. "Got an abscess I have to drain every week."

He showed me one of Sassy's silky brown ears that normally would've made a perfect size ten and a half shoe liner. Today it looked like someone had sewn a squeeze bulb into it. Sassy kept grinning and panting as Milo examined the abscess. She turned her head side to side like somebody was calling her but she couldn't figure out from where.

I'd thought of Sassy as old when we'd dognapped her from her abusive former owners in Berkeley eight years ago. By now Sassy must've been pushing twenty. In canine years, she'd been around since the Civil War.

It wasn't easy moving her into the backseat. Imagine a sack of bowling balls with stubby feet and bad breath. When we finally got under way Milo broke out the extra-soft geriatric dog biscuits for her and beer for us. He poured the beer into coffee cups.

We exited Loop 410 on Broadway and headed south listening to Sassy chew. Most of the biscuit fell out the side of her mouth, but she went at it with gusto anyway.

I handed Milo a single typewritten sheet of paper.

He glanced at it as much as he could without losing his beer or running off the road. "This is—"

"My first report."

He frowned. "Your *report*? Am I paying extra for this?"

"Erainya Manos is trying to instill me with some nasty habits—following procedures, writing daily reports to clients, stuff like that."

He handed it back to me. "Give me an audio version."

I told him about Alex Blanceagle's murder. Then I told him what Samuel Barrera had said, about the party line I was supposed to give Milo to blow the case off. Sassy was apparently interested. She kept sticking her nose between the seats, trying to slobber her biscuit residue into my beer.

When I finished Milo said, "And you still think Les disappeared on his own?"

"I think it's a strong possibility. I think he was using Julie Kearnes in more than one way. He got her to steal some personnel files from her temp jobs, probably sold her on the idea that they'd be running off together, even brought over a suitcase as a show of good faith. Then he ditched her."

"And she didn't say anything to anyone. Why?"

"She couldn't go bragging about what she'd been doing, helping Les blackmail Sheckly. Maybe she was hoping Les would still come back for her. Maybe she just didn't want to admit she'd been had."

"But you're not certain of any of that."

"That's why I want to look around Les' house."

"You've seen what Sheckly is like, Navarre. Now Alex Blanceagle is dead. It doesn't take a genius to figure out what happened to Les."

We drove a few blocks in silence.

Milo could've been right. It would've been a lot easier on Milo to think his boss hadn't voluntarily left him waist-deep in trouble. It would be a lot easier on me to believe Les Saint-Pierre was just another corpse waiting to be found. Corpses are stationary targets.

Otherwise, if Les Saint-Pierre had adopted a new identity with Julie Kearnes' help, then even with Kelly Arguello and me working overtime to find him, the chances of tracking him down were slim. The chances of tracking him down by next Friday, when Miranda's demo was due to Century Records, were virtually nonexistent. If Sheckly insisted on his bogus first option contract, there would be no effective way of challenging him. Miranda would go back to Sheckly's stable. She'd become another has-been artist waiting to happen.

"You're not following this Barrera guy's advice," Milo noticed, "about getting off the case."

"No, I'm not."

"Even though it could get you in trouble. And your boss. Why?"

I didn't have an immediate answer. I threw another biscuit into the backseat, hoping Sassy's nose would follow it. No such luck.

I turned my coffee mug in little half circles against my thigh and watched the businesses on Broadway go by—the abandoned Whopper Burger, the Witte Museum, the Costume Shop.

"Maybe I don't appreciate how Barrera called Miranda's problem a sideline. Maybe I don't appreciate how certain people are getting run over and Barrera treats them like they're small fish in a big pond. Some corporate client is paying him five or six figures to get them some justice, that much I'm sure of. I keep thinking about Julie Kearnes and Alex Blanceagle and how many more people are going to get killed before Barrera considers it worth his client's financial while to do something."

Milo nodded. "I can't do five or six figures."

"Beer in a coffee mug counts for a lot."

Milo took a right onto Hildebrand. He used huge arm movements to turn the wheel, like he was steering a boat. He had to hunch over to see out the windows that were made for normal-sized drivers. "He's wrong, you know."

"Who?"

"Barrera. He's wrong about you not being cut out for this kind of work."

I stared at him. "Finding occasional corpses? Spending most of my time tracking paperwork in county courthouses and getting doors slammed in my face? You think this work you got me into is fun, Milo? Past seven years, it's been like what people say about war—hours of boredom punctuated by seconds of terror. Take it as a daily routine, it starts to grate on you."

Milo smiled ruefully. He shook his head. "You're kidding yourself, man. What's that martial arts style you do—tai chi, right?"

"So?"

"The slowest style there is, the one that would drive most people crazy with impatience. What'd you study at U.C.—the Middle Ages?"

"So?"

"So it figures. You're *medieval* all fuckin' over, Tres. Kind of guy who'd work seventeen years on one illuminated manuscript, or spend twelve hours getting into a suit of armor for a three-second joust—that's you, Navarre. Process wasn't hard, you wouldn't enjoy it."

"I think I've just been called stupid."

The corner of Milo's mouth crept up.

He drove us over McAllister Highway, past Trinity University, and into Monte Vista. We turned left on Main.

"Your father still live over here?" I asked.

Milo nodded. "Got nominated for Rey Feo at Fiesta last year. He was all excited."

I tried to remember what kind of businesses Milo's father owned. Auto supply stores, maybe.

I tapped the small icon of the Virgen de Guadalupe that Milo had glued on his dashboard. "Your folks finally got you back into the Church?"

"Huh. Not exactly. The Virgen's for business."

"Pardon?"

Milo shook his head sadly. "I didn't tell you why Les hired me?"

"Because you did his legal work?"

"No. That was a nice fringe benefit, but no. Les wanted to get into the Tejano market. I finally got Les to drop the idea and give me Miranda Daniels, but for a while there I was driving all around town trying to sign wannabe Selenas."

I frowned. "What did you know about Tejano music?"

Milo pinched the skin of his forearm. End of explanation.

"Your prospective clients liked the Virgen?"

Milo shrugged, looking at the Lady of Guadalupe like she was a purchase he still wasn't completely satisfied with. "Some of them. Put them at ease, frame of reference. It was bad enough I'd speak to them in English."

I nodded. I'd spoken with Milo in Spanish only enough to know that he wasn't as comfortable with it as I was. There were plenty of Latinos who would consider Milo's lack of fluency a personal insult. A cultural lobotomy. I could almost see Ralph Arguello grinning.

"Can't be the only reason Les hired you," I said.

Milo made a sour face. "No. Not the only reason. Les also needed someone because. he'd just forced his previous assistant to quit. They weren't seeing eye to eye on business decisions."

"Who was his previous assistant?"

"Allison Saint-Pierre."

For no reason I could see, Sassy barked once, growled a little, then went back to her biscuits. Maybe Milo had her trained.

"Speaking of the happy couple," Milo said.

We pulled in front of the Saint-Pierres' white stucco mansion.

There were no cars in the driveway, but Brent Daniels' brown and white pickup with the horse trailer was parked on the curb.

Milo scowled at the truck. "Why the hell did he do that?"

"What?"

"Brent dropped the equipment here. That was stupid."

"Maybe—"

Milo was already shaking his head. "Shouldn't be anyone here this time of day except maybe the cleaning staff. Come on."

"But—"

Milo was already out of the car. Sassy needed help getting to the ground, but after that she waddled behind him at a pretty good clip.

Milo had a key to the front door. Assuming nobody was home, he unlocked the dead bolt and let us in. That was a mistake.

The front door led directly into a living room the size of a small church sanctuary. The walls were whitewashed stucco, striped with alternating columns of window and Oaxacan wall hangings that each must've represented the year's work of an entire village. There was a brick fireplace against one wall and a full bar against the other. The three white sofas around the fireplace would've taken up most of any other living room, but here they seemed ridiculously small, huddled together in the corner of a Sautillo-tiled wasteland. Plopped with apparent randomness around the rest of the room were pedestals displaying artwork—some folk art, some bronze sculpture, some ceramic vases. All valuable but totally unrelated to each other.

There were two people together on the edge of the nearest white sofa but before I could really process what I was seeing Brent Daniels had jumped sideways and was straightening his checkered shirt and his jeans.

That left only Allison Saint-Pierre on the edge of the sofa, leisurely tightening the belt on her white terrycloth robe.

Her blond hair was disheveled, her face a beautiful shade of red like she'd just taken an invigorating swim in ice water.

"Sweetie," she said to me. "Don't you knock?"

25

 Allison took a cigarette from a teak box on the coffee table. She lit it with a ceramic roadrunner that had the business end of a lighter sticking out of its mouth, then held the cigarette with all five fingers, like a cigar.

We were sitting around the fireplace on the big white sofas. Milo crossed his arms and glared at Allison. I looked at the flecks in the iced tea the maid had just poured me. Sassy dozed contentedly with her head hanging off the sofa and her rump in Milo's lap, her tail thwacking against his belly. Brent Daniels was frowning at his own zipper, which he'd probably just realized was still half-down.

"This is fun," Allison decided.

If she was at all uncomfortable being half-disrobed in front of three men and a basset hound, she did a good job hiding it. She hooked her left foot behind her right knee, then made a feeble attempt to nudge the terry-cloth back over her thigh with the bottom of her iced tea glass. It was quite a nice thigh.

Next to her on the couch was a folded-over section of newspaper. I could see half a headline—DANIELS SET— and half a photo of Miranda. Allison caught me looking at it.

"You read this yet?" she asked.

When I shook my head she glanced at Milo, silently asking him the same question. It was the first time she'd acknowledged Chavez's presence.

"I've seen it," Milo muttered.

I looked at Milo for elaboration. He didn't look back.

Allison grinned at me. "Pressure's on, sweetie. This morning's *Recording Industry Times*. They did a nice write-up on Miranda, found out her demo is going to Century Records next week. Apparently one of their in-house reviewers caught a show of hers last week—said if the tape was half as good as the concert, Miranda Daniels was going to be Century Records' next chart-buster. That's the kind of article creates a nice buzz going into a contract negotiation. Chalk up another one for Les Saint-Pierre."

Her eyes glittered with amusement. Milo's did not. Brent shifted uncomfortably, eyes still fixed on his zipper.

Allison continued, unfazed. "We were smart, we'd use this to sweeten the deal. Get Brent better than fifty percent on the song royalties, go for a multi-record contract. Screw Les, anyway. We could do better."

"*We?*" Milo scratched the base of Sassy's tail. "You going to start managing again, Allison?"

She kept smiling. She lifted her pinkie as the cigarette burned down, but there was nothing dainty about the way she did it. "That depends."

Milo sipped his tea. "Geez, I don't know. You think the agency could afford it? You willing to start collecting commission payments outside the bedroom?"

Allison's expression hardened instantly. She shook her head, like she'd just asked herself a silent question and had decided the answer was no. "You're a complete ass-hole, Chavez."

Milo nodded his thanks.

"Brent?" Allison stretched out his name, making her voice sweet again like she was about to ask for a really huge favor.

Brother Daniels looked at her. She waved her cigarette toward the front door. She smiled nicely.

Brent frowned. He reluctantly undraped his arms from the top of the couch, stood, then zipped his pants. He looked at me like he wanted to say something.

"Bye bye, sweetie," Allison said, dismissing him. "Thanks again."

Brent closed his mouth, lost a very brief stare-down with Allison, and left. Allison looked me in the eye, daring me to speak. I didn't.

"I've been staying in Austin with friends," she explained. "Miranda's party being tonight and all, I thought I'd come back to town. Brent was nice enough to drive me down."

"Uh-huh," Milo said.

Allison set down her glass very slowly. "You want to say something about that, Chavez?"

"Don't act so sensitive, honey. Not like Les would be surprised. Not like it's the first time you've tried to sleep your way in good with a major client."

Allison stood and dropped her cigarette. She took two normal steps toward Milo and then two very quick ones, making fists right before she came down on top of him. Sassy extruded out the middle like a sausage coming out of the grinder. Milo's tea glass toppled off the sofa and shattered on the tiles.

By the time I realized just how ferociously Allison was hitting, it was too late for me to do anything. With difficulty Milo managed to grab both of Allison's wrists and launch her sideways, off her feet and onto the floor, but in that short amount of time she'd done her share of damage.

Milo had a red, fist-shaped welt burning under his

right eye and another on his temple. Allison's fingernails had ripped two dotted lines of blood and skin across his neck. Milo's baby-blue button-down was wrinkled and splattered with tea.

A little stiffly, Allison sat up on the floor. She'd just missed landing on any broken glass. Her robe had come open and the space between her breasts was tan and lightly freckled. She pushed her hair out of her eyes. She was a little out of breath but her tone was surprisingly calm.

"Soon as I get the agency, it's going to be such a pleasure firing you."

Milo dabbed a finger on his neck. "Sure. In the meantime, we got problems. Tres wants to look around upstairs."

Allison took two deep breaths. She stood up. When she readjusted her robe her fingernails left little bloodstains on the terry-cloth.

The maid materialized with a hand broom and dustpan. She walked over and began casually cleaning the broken glass, like this was an event that happened every day about this time.

Allison brushed off her palms and looked at me. Her green eyes still had all the friendliness of a crocodile's. "Sure, sweetie. Excuse me. I'm going to get a gun so I can kill Milo if he's still in my house when I get back."

There was nothing in her tone that even remotely hinted at a joke.

After she left the room Milo sat forward and rested his chin in one hand. Sassy came up to him and started licking a gash Allison had made on his forearm.

"What is it with you two?" I demanded.

Milo looked at me sadly, then decided not to try an explanation.

"Go on, bud," he said, waving toward a staircase. "Take your time."

"And if she comes back with a gun?"

Milo stared at the doorway Allison had gone through.

"Her aim is off. She tends to pull to the left. Don't worry unless you hear more than one shot."

As I headed toward the staircase, the maid was sweeping up the ice cubes and glass shards, offering Milo some Spanish words of consolation that I was pretty sure he couldn't understand.

26

 Allison could've been standing in the doorway of Les' room for a long time. I'm not sure. I was sitting at Les' desk with my back to the door, sorting through shoe boxes full of old letters and photographs and getting dizzy from trying to understand Mr. Saint-Pierre.

The task should've been simple. I had the man's whole life in front of me, neatly packaged and labeled in little boxes. Still, I felt like a drunk taking a DUI test. I kept trying to put the old finger on the nose in the center of my face and I'll be damned if the nose didn't move every time.

Allison watched me at least long enough to identify which shoe box I was pulling letters from.

"That's his 'Gotcha' box," she said.

I'd like to think I didn't visibly jump, but Allison was grinning when I turned around.

She'd changed into a peach polo shirt and black Mylar

bike pants and white Adidas. She wore fingerless net gloves. If you didn't know to look, you wouldn't have noticed the stiffness in her left side where Milo had thrown her to the floor.

I pulled another letter from the box that Les had labeled "Correspondence."

"He's shown you these?" I asked.

Allison widened her eyes. "Oh, no, he didn't *show* me."

She came in and sat on the very edge of the bed. From ten feet away, I caught the scent of Halston. Her legs made a V in front of her, only the heels of her Adidas touching the carpet. She looked around with mild interest like this was the first time she'd been in Les' bedroom.

"I'm sorry about downstairs." She sounded like she was apologizing for a random nudge in an elevator. "Milo gets to me."

I stared at her.

She tried to mimic my expression—eyes wide, mouth slightly open. "Problem?"

"No. I suppose not."

"Look, sweetie, you grow up with four brothers in a little hick town, you learn how to fight. If I sat around acting pretty and taking shit from guys like Chavez I wouldn't have lived past sixth grade."

I decided it was safest to return my attention to the letter I'd been reading.

It was poorly typed on onion-skin paper. All the *o*'s were solid black circles and the *a*'s were cocked to the right. It read:

Dear Jason:
I really appreciate what you said you would do
for me and I hope you like the songs and your
publishing company will decide to take them for
your catalogue. I am really willing to work hard as
a staff writer and really had a wonderful time with
you this weekend too. Please call soon.
Patti Glynn

The letter was dated five years ago. Patti had stapled her picture to the back of it just in case Jason forgot who she was. She was cute—roundish face, feathery brown hair, widely spaced eyes lit up with hope.

There were at least twenty letters like that dated as far back as 1982, many with photos attached, all from different women addressed to a different man's name. Sometimes they were to Larry the label head and sometimes to Paul the producer. Sometimes, along with veiled references to nights of passion, they mentioned checks they were sending. One woman wrote that she'd enclosed five hundred dollars because she believed Jason-Paul-Larry was going to buy just the right birthday present that would put her name in solid with the Artists & Repetoire director at EMI-Capitol.

I looked up at Allison. "These letters—"

"Sure," she said. "They're all to Les."

"Les had a reputation. He had real connections. If he wanted to use women he didn't have to lie about who he was. Why—?"

Allison paddled the toes of her shoes back and forth a few times. "I never confronted him about it, but I think I know what he'd say. He'd tell you it was harmless fun. He'd say he was weeding the crop of would-bes and if they were really this stupid, they would fall for the first con man they met in Nashville anyway so he might as well save them the trip."

I couldn't quite grab on to Allison's tone. It wasn't resentment. More like wistfulness.

"You think it was harmless fun?"

Allison smiled, picking at the netting on her palm. "No, sweetie. I think Les had an addiction. He was hooked on making himself the answer to everybody's problem—at least until you left the room or signed his contract or whatever. The less you mattered to him, the crazier he could afford to get offering you what you wanted to hear, and the more he liked it. Do you see?"

"I'm not sure."

She shrugged. "I guess you'd have to meet him. It

doesn't matter. The point is he couldn't have stopped selling confidence if he wanted to. He was a hell of an agent."

"So why would he want to vanish?"

Allison crossed her legs at the ankles and hunched forward, tapping her finger on her chin like she was pretending to think. "Gosh, Tres. Aside from the fact that he could never get out of his job any other way, that he was a natural-born son of a bitch, that his client list was eroding so bad he had to pin his hopes on unknowns like Miranda, that he was drinking or snorting or popping most of his profits, that he and I fought every time we saw each other—I just can't imagine."

I stared at my lap, where I'd been collecting the most useful things from Les' desk drawers.

I held up a black leather shaving kit full of pill bottles and bags. I pulled out one Ziploc with a dozen white tablets in it.

"Amphetamines?" I asked.

Allison shrugged. "I can't keep track. He drinks Ryman whiskey straight. The pills change. I think that's Ritalin."

"The stuff they give hyperactive kids?"

She smiled. "That's my husband."

I dug through the other things—a '69 Denton High School yearbook, then some more photographs of Les with various music industry types.

"There's no will," I said.

"He won't make one. He was clear on that. He enjoys the idea of people fighting over his stuff when he's gone."

I shuffled through some other papers without really looking at them. I kept coming back to the photo of Patti Glynn.

"You said Miranda needed protecting from your husband. Is this what you meant?"

The idea seemed to amuse her. "I said she needed to kick butt for herself, sweetie—that's different than being protected. And God, no. Les wouldn't have messed with Miranda. Not like that, anyway."

"Because she has real talent?"

"Partly. Partly because of the way Miranda is."

"Country girl, naive, a little too sweet for her own good. Seems like just the kind Les liked to prey on, not too different from the girls in this box."

Allison smiled, disappointed. "I could say a lot of things, sweetie, but Miranda's my friend. You make your own conclusions."

I tried to read into that, but all I saw in her face was stubbornness. And maybe just the faintest tinge of resentment.

I looked down at the correspondence box. "These other women. Didn't they eventually figure out who Les was? Didn't they get angry? Cause problems?"

Allison frowned, like she was trying to remember some trivial detail from her prom night. "They got taken by Les for a few nights, maybe a few hundred dollars. They felt good that their careers might be going somewhere, then most of them faded back into the woodwork in Plano or Dimebox or wherever the hell they came from."

"You were one of them."

She flashed me exactly the same look she'd given Milo before she'd attacked him. It took her about thirty seconds to mentally stand down.

"No," she said. "You know the difference, sweetie? I got my revenge. I married the bastard."

"Not much of a last laugh."

Allison spread her fingers apart so she could examine the netting between them. "Good enough."

"If you're right, if Les vanished on his own, I bet he left you nothing in the bank and all the payments on the house and the credit cards and no guarantee of any income from the agency, at least not without a court fight. You can't even collect life insurance until you get him declared legally dead, and that could take years."

Allison's anger melted into a little smile, like I'd just made a pass she had no intention of accepting but she appreciated the offer. She stood to leave.

"That's why I'm so glad you're here, Tres. You're going to bring old Les home to me."

She left me alone, staring at the picture of Patti Glynn but wondering this time if there was something besides innocence there, some latent potential for maliciousness that needed to be stomped on. For a disturbing moment, I thought I might be understanding Les Saint-Pierre.

I put the lid on the shoe box and decided it was time to leave.

27

 Cam Compton's Monster Music was a two-story white cube on Perrin-Beitel Road, right next to the Department of Public Safety. The bottom floor was the store, with burglar-barred windows and a five-car parking lot and silver doors plastered with brand-name guitar stickers. The top floor was Cam's residence. His front door was on the side of the building, accessed by a metal staircase and a narrow concrete walkway. There was one large picture window so Cam could look out every day and enjoy the scenery—an endless stream of gawky adolescents and bulldog-faced patrolmen engaged in the American ritual of parallel parking between the orange cones.

I tried upstairs first and got no answer. Then I tried the music store, which for a Friday afternoon was not exactly crawling with customers.

The guy behind the sales counter said, "Cam can't talk."

I looked over the guy's shoulder, through the glass

wall into the room where Cam was giving a guitar lesson
to an adolescent kid whose acne was the same shade of
red as his Stratocaster.

Cam was hunched over, examining the kid's fingers as
the kid moved them on the fret board. Cam's forehead
had a pancake-sized yellow and purple hickey on it from
our last meeting at the Cactus Cafe. He had a heavy
drinker's swollen morning-after face and rumpled clothes
that suggested he'd crawled out of bed and down the
steps just in time for this lesson. Probably a normal week
in the life of a superstar guitarist.

I looked back at the salesman. He was a large man.
Flabby large, with arms that had mass but no muscle
lines. His face hadn't seen a razor blade or a toothbrush
or even a nose hair clipper in a mighty long time. He had
a Harley-Davidson T-shirt with cigarette burn holes on
the belly.

"Cam's looked better," I said.

Harley grinned. "Some guy's been leaning on him.
Some big ass motherfucker—private detective or something. He slammed Cam's head into a wall. Then last
night he came back and did Cam's ribs."

"You saw this?"

Harley leaned closer to me. "Naw, but you know
what I told Cam—I said take me along next time. I'll put
that dick motherfucker in a vise grip."

I smiled appreciatively.

The slow, distorted power chords of Bad Religion
seeped through the glass window of the practice room.
Cam nodded his head and the adolescent smiled. Talent
under development.

"He'll want to talk to me," I told Harley. "Tell him it's
the dick motherfucker."

Harley started to laugh, then he saw I was serious. He
scratched his beard. He pointed at me with his thumb
and tried to frame a question.

"I don't know about the ribs," I amended. "I just did
the forehead. And it was a beer keg. You get prettier
bruises with a beer keg."

Harley searched his beard with his fingers a little more. Then slowly he cracked a grin. He turned and started what he'd been doing before I came in—hanging guitar straps on a rotating display.

"Cam ain't much of a boss," Harley told me. "Be my guest."

I walked into the practice room. Cam was nodding his head and saying encouraging things about the adolescent's F-chord. Then they both saw me.

I winked at the kid and told him to keep up the good work with the F-chord. Then I looked at Cam, whose purplish forehead was turning almost flesh color. "How you feeling?"

"Got a student," he managed to say.

"He can practice." I turned to the kid. "I bet you know 'Glycerine' already, don't you, Slick?"

The kid got that elated light in his eyes that beginning guitarists get when they actually know a request. He looked down and dutifully began plinking out the Bush song.

"Let's talk," I told Cam.

"Why you think I'd want to—"

"I went to see Alex Blanceagle last night. He looks a lot worse than you do. Jean paid him a visit."

Cam's beady, bloodshot eyes move an inch farther apart. He looked around uncomfortably, at his student, at Harley who was grinning sideways at us through the glass, waiting for some kind of show to start.

Cam put his guitar pick between his lips and spoke around it. "Upstairs. And you ain't gonna fuck with me again, y'hear?"

I held up my hands. Truce.

Harley looked disappointed when he saw we were taking our conversation elsewhere. Cam led me out into the afternoon heat, then up the stairs and into his place. He headed straight for the refrigerator.

His apartment was about the same size as mine—one main room, closet, bathroom, side kitchen. An unmade twin bed set flush against the south wall was occupied by

piles of laundry that still retained the upside-down shape
and crisscrossed texture of laundry baskets, like Jell-O
out of the molds. I counted three guitars in the room—
two electrics in open cases on the floor, one black Ova-
tion twelve-string on a corner tripod stand. The coffee
table was a Sears appliance box covered with spare
guitar tuning pegs and string packets and old Olympia
cans and an extra large Funky Bird, the kind with the red
hair and the hat and the big butt that bobs up and down.
Instead of chairs Cam had guitar amps. The posters on
the walls were all from the store downstairs—peeling
advertisements of bikini girls showing off the latest thing
in mixing boards or speakers or trap sets. The only thing
in the room that reflected care and meticulous upkeep
was the CD collection. That took up three levels of cinder
block and board shelving.

I walked over and looked through the titles while Cam
was rummaging for beer. The CDs were all kinds, rock
and jazz and country guitarists, heavy on the Eric
Clapton and the Chet Atkins and too light on the Blind
Willie McTell for my taste. The titles were perfectly
arranged in alphabetical order except that the top shelf
started with Cam's own releases. I was surprised how
many—at least fifteen different CDs. I pulled one. The
cover art was a bad photocopy of Cam's face, with his
name and the title "American Cowboy" and the rest of
the liner notes in what looked like Cyrillic script. Russian? Czech? I checked the other titles. Most were similar
foreign releases. Only one was labeled Split Rail Records,
dated five years ago and entitled *The Best of Cam
Compton*. Probably went platinum, that one.

Cam opened himself an Olympia and walked over to
the bed like he was in pain. He knocked the laundry off
and sat down slowly, elbows out, the way you'd lower
yourself into an extra-hot bathtub.

"Your ribs are taped," I said. "Somebody gave you a
talking-to last night."

"What the fuck business is that to you?"

I took the stack of Compton's own CDs and went over

to an amp and sat down, facing him. I started flipping through the jewel cases. "Interesting discography. Bulgaria. Romania. Germany. You must have had some success over there."

Cam studied me warily. His one eye with the bloody ring around the iris was almost closed. His urge to play silent was duking it out with his urge to talk about himself. The latter finally won.

"Good market in Europe," he admitted. " 'Specially since the Eastern parts opened. Had me a number ten song for a week in Yugoslavia 'fore the country broke up."

"That so?"

He nodded morosely, like the whole political mess had been a plot to get him off the charts. "Course Germany's always loved Texas stuff—horses, cowboy hats, country music. They cain't get enough of that shit. Sheckly had me touring some honky-tonk clubs over there four or five times. Good money."

"Yeah?" I held up the CD I'd been looking at earlier. "What's this—Russian?"

Cam grunted. He was drinking more beer, warming up to the subject. "Fan sent that to me with a real nice letter. Said it wasn't playing right anymore and she loved it, could I please send her a copy of the American original. Good-looking girl, too."

"You sent it?"

"Couldn't. There is no original. It's a bootleg of one of my shows in Munich. Half the titles in there are boots. Hell, half the titles in Europe. Now you gonna tell me about Alex B.?"

I put the CDs aside. "I came here to help you, Cam."

He stopped with his beer can halfway to his mouth, put the can down. "That a fact? You get me fired one day, now you're gonna help me."

"Alex Blanceagle was shot dead."

He blinked, kept his eyes closed a second too long. "And what's it got to do with me?"

"He was talking to a man named Samuel Barrera about Sheckly's business. In particular those shipments you've been helping process through the Indian Paintbrush."

Cam put together a smile. He rubbed the bruise on his forehead. "I ain't been close to Sheck for a long time, son. Last help I gave him was signing up with Miranda's band. Look where that got me. Sheck has some other kind of problem, it ain't mine."

"I know different, Cam. Samuel Barrera's ex-FBI and he's very good. He'll come talking to you eventually. With something like this he'll have Customs involved, the State Attorney, the D.A. You want my guess, Sheck and his friends know something is coming. They know Les Saint-Pierre caused a leak and they're plugging up any places where it might've come from—Julie Kearnes, Alex Blanceagle, you. If I were you, I'd be worried."

Cam looked at his beer, thought for about five seconds, then decided to laugh. "Tha's bullshit."

"Ask Alex Blanceagle if it's bullshit."

I opened my backpack and pulled out Cam's .22 Montgomery Ward. I set the gun next to me on the amp.

"You could've killed John Crea, Cam. Not likely, but possible."

Cam looked at the gun and his eye ticked. "What you going on about now? What's that for?"

"I suppose the demo tape's around here somewhere, too. You wouldn't be smart enough to trash it. You think I should give this to the police, Cam, tell them where I found it? I could tell them what idiot it's registered to and how he probably forgot to wipe the inside of the chamber for prints. They put this together with the Julie Kearnes murder, the way that was done, guess who's going to get the blame?"

Under his bruises, Cam got red-faced. He stood up real slow, holding his beer can as if he were about to throw it. "Wait a goddamn minute—"

"When it comes to Sheckly's helpers you're at the bottom of the food chain, Cam. I bet he didn't even pay you—I bet he just knows how to get you riled up, how to put ideas in your head of things he wants done. He's got absolutely nothing to lose, using you, and when people come knocking on his door with warrants for larger problems, you're the first sacrifice he's going to toss out. Sheckly's got you set up pretty good."

Cam's eyes narrowed. The anger got diffused and tangled up inside him. He lowered the beer can. "And what you think I should do, son—sit there and enjoy the knife in my back? How you think that feels? There's a time not too long ago I's in Miranda Daniels' corner pretty fierce—even after she got with Mr. Saint-Pierre. I used to drive her to the Paintbrush every night—nice and friendly. We'd talk about the business. She and me had an understanding. I's gonna look after her; she's gonna be my ticket somewhere else besides here." He waved a hand around at the apartment. "Look to you like I'm getting anywhere?"

"You figure she owes you," I said.

"Damn right."

"You figure the whole world owes you. You got an ego so big you collect your own bootlegs, Cam. Probably autograph them for yourself too. I think your perception of what Miranda promised might be a wee bit twisted."

He took a step forward. "You asking for something, son, you're going to get it."

"Knock it off, Cam. I want to get Miranda extricated from Sheckly, so her deal with Century Records can go through. You could give me the leverage I need to do that."

Cam laughed harshly. "Heard that before."

"You mean from Les?"

Cam shook his head in disgust, walked stiffly into the kitchen, pulled another beer from the refrigerator. "Ask little Miss Daniels. Ask if I didn't tell her, first time she came crying to me about Sheck's contract on her. I figured a Century Records deal, hell, she was going to take me along for sure. We'd be set. I told her somebody wanted to get a little pull with Sheck, all they had to do was look into those shows he's been taping for radio. Maybe get close to Julie Kearnes, ask Julie to pull some

files here and there from the Paintbrush computers, ask
her about those trips to Europe with Alex B."

I stood very still. The only sound was the hum of Cam
Compton's refrigerator and the traffic on Perrin-Beitel.
"You told Miranda all this."

"That's what I'm saying."

"And if somebody was to dig where you said to dig—?"

Cam gave me his close-lipped smile. "Not like every
sound man who's ever worked the Paintbrush doesn't
know. Not like the headliner artists don't know, son. It's
rankled them for years. Just nobody can prove it. I tell
you, what do I get?"

"I'll introduce you to Sam Barrera, make sure he cuts
you a fair deal."

"Price would be higher than that, son."

"Somebody's already kicked in your ribs, Cam. You
think you can afford to wait around for a better offer?"

Cam's smile dissolved. "Get the fuck out, then."

"You should talk to me, Cam."

He went across the room, retrieved his .22 from the
guitar amp. He held it lazily in my direction, never
mind the chambers were empty.

There wasn't much more I could say.

I opened the door. The heat immediately sucked into
the room around me, along with the traffic sounds and
the smell of exhaust.

As I left, Cam Compton was standing in front of his
music collection, his .22 wedged in his armpit. Cam was
examining one by one the stray CDs I'd taken out, using
his grubby T-shirt to wipe the front of each jewel case
before he put it back in its proper place.

28

That night it took more than a little self-convincing to get myself out of the house, away from the possibilities of a simple *chalupa* dinner and my medieval drama book and maybe even some sleep, to drive out instead to the address Miranda Daniels had given me—her family ranch house near Bulverde.

It had been less than a year since an inheritance case had taken me out that direction, but I was amazed by the urbanization, how much farther I had to go to start smelling the cedars and the fertilizer.

San Antonio grows in concentric layers like a tree. It's one of the few ways the town is orderly.

My grandfather rarely went farther from downtown than Brackenridge Park, unless he was looking for deer to shoot. My mother used to think Scrivener's fabric store on Loop 410 was the edge of town. In my high school years the outermost boundary of the known world was Loop 1604, and even inside the loop it was still mostly tracts of live oak and cactus and broken limestone.

Now I could drive past 1604 and halfway to the village of Bulverde before I was ever out of earshot of a convenience store.

The sky behind me was city gray-orange and ahead of me rural black. Just above the hills, the full moon made a hazy white circle behind the clouds.

I exited on Ranch Road 22, a narrow two-laner with no lighting, no posted speed limits, plenty of curves, and nothing on the shoulders but gravel and barbed wire. A killway, my dad would've called it.

In my gore-loving adolescent days I used to pester the Sheriff to tell me about all the traffic accidents he'd handled on little ranch roads like RR22. He usually said no, but one night he'd gotten drunk enough and fed up enough to tell me in graphic detail about a particularly nasty head-on collision. He told me murder scenes were nothing compared to car accidents, and then he went on to prove it. I never asked to hear any more of his work stories.

I swerved once to avoid a dead deer. Fence posts and mile markers floated into my headlights and out again. Occasionally I passed a billboard advertising a new housing development that was about to be built—CALLE VERDE, FINE LIVING FROM THE 120's. I bet the folks who'd moved out here for a retirement in the country were pleased about that. The 7-Elevens and H.E.B.s would be coming in next.

The turn for Serra Road was unmarked, despite what Miranda had told me, and it wasn't much wider than a private driveway. Fortunately I could see the Daniels' party all the way from RR22. A quarter mile or so across a dark pasture, lights were blazing in the trees and a fire was burning. There was the distant hum of music.

I bumped along Serra Road with rocks pinging into the wheel wells of the VW. The air was the temperature of bathwater and had a strange mix of smells— manure, wood smoke, gasoline, and marigolds. One more right turn took me over the cattle guard of the Daniels' property.

Their front yard was a full acre of gravel and grass. A dozen pickup trucks were parked around a granddaddy live oak several stories tall and hung from root to top with white Christmas lights. One of the pickup trucks was a huge black affair with orange pin-striping and silver Barbie doll women on the mud flaps. I wondered if there could be two such trucks in the world. Not with my luck.

The house itself was low and long and white, with a front porch that stretched all the way across and was now spilling over with people. Willis Daniels and his stand-up bass were the center of attention. He and a small bunch of grizzled cowboy musicians, none of them from Miranda's group, were burning their way through an old swing number—Milton Brown, if my memories of my father's 78 collection served me right. All the players were drunk as hell and they sounded just fine.

Smaller clumps of people were gathered around the property, drinking and talking and laughing. Half a dozen were throwing horseshoes by the side of the house, their light provided by a line of bare bulbs strung between a mesquite tree and a toolshed. Some women in dresses and boots and lots of silver jewelry were gathered around a campfire, helping bleary-eyed kids roast marshmallows. All of the pickup truck cabs were dark and closed but not all of them were vacant.

Next to the oak tree two men were talking—Brent Daniels and my buddy Jean.

Brent was wearing the same dingy checkered shirt and black jeans he'd been wearing the last three times I'd seen him. They weren't getting any prettier and neither was he. His black hair looked like day-old roadkill. He was shifting uncomfortably from foot to foot.

Jean wore a dark blue linen jacket, slacks that were a little too tight around his middle, a white collarless silk shirt, black boots, and a silver bracelet. His hand was clutching Brent's shoulder a little too firmly and he was leaning close to Brent's ear, telling him something.

When Jean realized somebody was watching their conversation he cast around until he found me. He locked his fierce, indifferent little eyes on me for a second, finished his statement to Brent, then pulled away and laughed, patting Brent's shoulder like they'd just shared a fine humorous story. Brent didn't laugh. He turned angrily and walked toward the house.

Jean leaned back against the oak. He put his heel on the trunk, produced a hand-rolled cigarette, and began fishing around his pockets for a lighter. He watched me as I walked toward him.

"The steel guitar player."

"It's honest work."

Jean lit his cigarette, nodded. "No doubt. Honest work."

"Why are you standing out here in the dark?" I asked. "Your boss too embarrassed to bring you into the party?"

Jean narrowed his eyes. He mouthed the words *your boss* like he was trying to interpret them, like he was suspicious he'd just been insulted.

"Sheckly," he decided.

"Yeah—the big ugly redneck. You know."

In the glow from the white Christmas lights, Jean's smile looked unnaturally luminous. The fierceness in his eyes didn't diminish at all. "I see."

"You did a hell of a job clearing out Alex Blanceagle the other night."

No response. Jean took a drag on the cigarette, turned his head, and blew smoke leisurely toward the porch. The old drunk musicians had launched into something new—an instrumental that sounded vaguely like Lester Scruggs. A couple of women were do-si-doing with each other on the sidewalk.

I looked toward the front door. Brent Daniels now stood next to an ice-filled garbage can, drinking a beer as fast as he could. Several people were talking to him but Brent wasn't paying them any attention.

"What was that about?" I asked Jean.

He followed my gaze, caught my meaning. "I told Brent Daniels I admired his sister. Her music. I said I hoped she would tour Europe soon."

"Like Cam Compton used to. Make a nice courier system, wouldn't it? Good cover, touring with a band, with lots of equipment, if you had goods you wanted to deliver to a lot of places in Europe."

Jean blew more smoke. He gave me the crab eyes. "Do you intend to provoke, Mr. Navarre, or are you simply an idiot?"

"I'm not usually like this," I confessed. "Usually I don't find so many corpses in one week. You usually leave so many?"

Jean smiled coldly. "An idiot," he decided.

He disengaged his back from the tree and was leaning forward to say something when some commotion erupted around the side of the house.

Somebody by the shed yelled "Ohhh!" like he'd just seen a great triple play. A woman shrieked. A crowd of people started to converge around the horseshoe pit. Some were swearing, a few laughing. Willis Daniels' hoedown faltered to a stop as the musicians got up to see what was going on.

A drunk cowboy staggered away from the scene, laughing, telling people what had just happened in a loud enough voice that Jean and I could hear him fine. Apparently Allison Saint-Pierre had just knocked Tilden Sheckly out cold with a horseshoe.

I looked at Jean.

He tossed his cigarette down in a leisurely way. It bounced off a root and disappeared in the crack between two other roots, then dimmed to a little orange eye. Jean looked up at me and smiled, almost pleasantly this time.

"*My boss,*" he said with satisfaction.

Then he turned and casually walked in the opposite direction, into the dark.

29

Sheckly wasn't out cold, exactly. Just slightly cooled down.

I nudged my way through the spectators and found him sitting in the dust, his fingertips on his temples and a look of complete dismay on his face. He was dressed in black from boots to shirt. His Stetson lay near-by, knocked from his head. Below Sheck's left eye, the cheek looked like a cross-section of a rare filet mignon. An inch higher and the horseshoe would've blinded him.

An older woman squatted next to him, patting his shoulders and trying to console him. Her words came out slurred. The margarita in her other hand sloshed at a forty-five degree angle.

A couple of cowboy types stood on the other side. They seemed anxious to lend the rich man a bandanna, or an arm to lean on, or a gun to shoot Allison Saint-Pierre. Anything he needed.

Sheckly shook his head a couple of times. He dabbed at his ruined cheek with the back of his fist, looked at the blood on his knuckles, and regained some color in his face. Then he tried to get up and failed. He rallied again, staggering to his feet with the help of the cowboys.

"I'm gonna kill that crazy bitch."

The men murmured agreement.

Sheckly blinked. He stumbled, huge and awkward as a drugged horse.

He scanned the crowd, targeted me briefly, and seemed to make a foggy connection. Then his eyes kept moving.

Allison Saint-Pierre was nowhere to be seen, though a few people were looking in the direction of the ranch house and shaking their heads as they speculated about her. I went toward the house.

When I bumped into Willis Daniels on the porch he turned around and grabbed my upper arm and for a second I thought the old man was going to clobber me with his cane. I hardly recognized him. The Santa Claus smile had vanished. His eyes blazed. His cement-colored hair was flattened into sweaty bangs against his forehead.

He looked disappointed when he saw I wasn't someone he wanted to clobber. At least not at the moment.

"Damn it," he muttered, lowering his cane.

"Allison went this way?"

Willis raised his cane again and shook it at nobody in particular. Then he glared in the direction of the horse-shoe pit and began grumbling things about Mrs. Saint-Pierre that weren't fit for Santa's elves to hear. I went inside.

Stringed instruments decorated the walls. A couple of kids slept on a Naugahyde couch in the living room while their parents told Aggie jokes and mixed drinks in the kitchen. The door to the first bedroom down the hall was open. A woman I didn't know had passed out on the bed in the middle of a pile of cowboy hats. The door to the second bedroom was ajar and Allison's voice came through in a tone so shaky it made me wince—like

an E-string tuned to the point you just knew it was going
to snap in the guitarist's face.

"He pushed me down!" she yelled. "I'm not going to
just stand there like you and—"

"Allison—" Miranda's voice was only slightly more in
control. "You should look at yourself, girl."

I opened the door.

They were both standing by the bed. Miranda looked
like a young square dancer in her full-length denim skirt
and white blouse and bandanna around her neck. She
wore no makeup, but the color in her face looked
healthier than usual because she was angry. Her eyes
were bright brown.

She picked a twig out of Allison's hair. She had plenty
to choose from. Allison had smudges of dirt on her face
and dust all down her side. Her red blouse had come
untucked from her jeans. She had the same murderous
look I'd seen in her eyes that afternoon, but now her eyelids were swollen and red, a few tears smeared in with
the dirt.

Miranda saw me before Allison did. The singer's
shoulders relaxed just slightly. She said nothing but her
posture invited me in. If I'd been alone in a room with
Allison right then, I would've welcomed company too.

"What happened?" I asked.

Allison started. She had a little trouble bringing me
into focus. She took a shaky breath before she could
answer me with something besides a scream.

"Sheck."

"He pushed you. So you figured you'd just brain him
with a horseshoe?"

Allison splayed her fingers and brought them up to
her ears. "He moved too fast. I swear to God the next
time—"

Her voice broke. However violent a show she was
used to staging, however much she normally got away
with, this time she'd surprised herself. The muscles in her
face had started loosening up.

"There can't be any next time," Miranda said.

"You could've succeeded in killing him, Allison," I said. "Easily."

Allison managed to refocus on me. "You're the one who slammed Cam's head into a beer keg, Tres. What—it's okay for *you* to act that way?"

Miranda gave me a look I couldn't quite read. She seemed to be willing me to say something.

I'm not sure why, but just then the room we were standing in came into clearer focus. I realized it must be Miranda's. The burgundy and blue quilt on the bed, the miniature wooden horse on the desk, the dried arrangements of sage and lavender along the windowsill all seemed right for her. A tiny blond Martin guitar was propped in the corner. A few Daniels family photographs were framed in silver on the nightstand. It was a strange room—sparse and orderly but also cozy, definitely feminine. Normally I would've guessed it belonged to a little girl with a tidy mother, or perhaps to somebody's grandmother.

Miranda kept giving me a silent request.

I looked at Allison. "Why don't I drive you home? You need to get out of here."

Wrong answer. Miranda tightened her lips, but she said, "That's a good idea."

Allison collected herself. She was just about to agree, I think, when Tilden Sheckly barged into the room.

He moved like he was still groggy, but he managed a pretty hideous facsimile of his regular grin. The left side of his face was still mostly blood and dirt. His unruly gray-brown hair was flattened on top by sweat in the shape of his missing hat.

"Allison Saint-Pierre," he croaked. "I think we need to talk."

Sheck walked toward her. I made the mistake of trying to stop him, figuring that he was still dazed.

The next thing I knew I was sitting on the rug with my jaw feeling like it had just been branded. There was either blood in my mouth or dark beer—Guinness, maybe. I don't remember Sheckly's upper cut at all. I certainly didn't have time to block it.

"I'll talk to you in a minute, son," Sheckly said unevenly. He was focusing a little to the left of my eyes. "We'll have some words about trespassing in people's offices. Right now, stay out of my way."

He grabbed Allison by the wrist.

Allison managed to break Sheckly's grip and rake the bad side of his face with her fingernails, but Sheck looked like he'd expected that. He winced and swayed backward and then smiled, like he'd just been given permission to try again with a little more force.

"*Sheckly,*" Miranda said, soft but insistent.

"Miranda, darlin'." He kept trying to get his mouth to work right, to have that normal smooth tone to it. "This ain't your fault, honey. I know that. But you understand what your friend here did? At your Daddy's party? You think I'm gonna let her walk away from that—would that be right?"

Allison tried for another slap and got her wrist intercepted. The back of Sheck's other hand struck her across the mouth with a sound like a leather belt snapping.

Miranda stood frozen, staring at Sheckly's fingers around Allison's wrist. I had no luck trying to get off the floor.

Sheck was raising his hand to strike again when Brent Daniels stepped into the doorway and cocked the hammer of his shotgun.

Brent didn't need to say anything. Sheck knew the sound of a double-aught-six just fine. Sheck's hand froze next to his shoulder, like he was saying the Pledge of Allegiance. He turned around.

When he saw it was only Brent he tried to reconstruct his smile. A little bead of blood dripped off his chin.

"Aw, Christ, son, put that damn thing down. You know I ain't—"

"You step away," Brent insisted.

Brent's voice was even and deadly serious. His eyes were still bloodshot but there was no alcoholic glaze to them. No hesitation and no uneasiness. Brent's eyes were alert and dangerous and I couldn't quite remember why I'd ever thought of him as dim-witted.

"Brent—" Miranda started to say, firmer than before.

"Shut up, Miranda."

Sheckly stepped sideways, toward the foot of the bed. He wiped at his chin. "All right, Brent. It's your house. Just appears to me—"

"Get out, Mr. Sheckly."

Sheck raided his hands slowly, giving up. "All right, son. All right."

He looked at Allison to let her know nothing was finished. He searched his pocket for a handkerchief and realized he didn't have one. He walked toward Brent until his chest was only a few inches from the shotgun's muzzle.

"Can I pass?"

Brent stepped aside silently. Sheckly got a glint of dazed amusement in his eyes.

"Marla would be proud of you, son. Taking up a gun again." He winked, I think. With his ruined face it was hard to tell what was intentional and what was just the flesh going into shock. "You cut a fine figure of a man."

Then, mumbling pleasantly to himself about all the people he was going to kill, Tilden Sheckly left the room.

When he was gone the barrel of Brent's shotgun lowered to the floor. I got to my feet.

Allison collapsed onto the bed. Her hands clenched but they trembled anyway. She gave Brent a crooked smile, winced, dabbed her tongue into the corner of her mouth, and tasted the blood there. "My hero."

Brent was blushing violently, but I don't think it was from Allison's comment. Miranda looked at him with an expression somewhere between outrage and sympathy.

"Oh, Brent—Good Lord, I'm sorry."

"Shut up, Miranda," Brent said again. He was staring at the floor, digging a hole in the rug with the shotgun muzzle. "For once, just shut up."

30

I leaned against a cedar post on the Daniels' back porch, staring across the dark field toward the barn where Brent Daniels had retreated. I could only see what was illuminated by the kerosene lantern Brent had hung at the edge of the roof, and from a hundred yards away that wasn't much. The building was apparently half tractor shed, half apartment. On the side closest to me was a curtained window with no light coming through.

The field between here and there was scarred with black lines of trenches, pocked with mounds of dirt. About thirty yards out was the dark silhouette of a backhoe. Some kind of plumbing work in progress.

My jaw where Tilden Sheckly had hit me throbbed every time my heart beat. My lower gums were puffy, but I hadn't chipped any teeth and my tongue had stopped bleeding from the hole I'd bitten into it. Compared to Sheckly—compared to a lot of people I'd met this week—I counted myself lucky.

Behind me the party sounds were dying down. The taillights of pickup trucks made little red eyes down Serra Road and onto RR22. Above my head, the bug zapper sizzled every time it said howdy to a mosquito. Once in a while somewhere out in the fields a cow or a horse farted. You think I'm kidding. Stay on a ranch sometime—you'll get to know those nighttime sounds intimately.

I'd finished my last beer and was now busy shredding the plastic cup into a flower. Allison Saint-Pierre had ended up getting a ride from someone else. As it turned out there were plenty of guys ready to fight me for the chance. I didn't fight.

I started wondering why I didn't just go around the yard, get in my car and disappear when the screen door creaked open. Miranda Daniels came out and sat next to me on the railing. She'd taken off her bandanna and untucked her white shirt so it fell loose and wrinkled over her skirt. In the black light of the bug zapper her clothes glowed various shades of violet. Her lips were dark purple. The only thing that didn't change color was her hair. It was so black I couldn't tell where it ended in the dark.

"Thanks for waiting," she said.

"Did you get your dad calmed down?"

"I think so. He's ready for me to quit the recording project. He says it's ruining his parties."

"Not to mention his relationship with Sheckly."

When she took a deep breath her collarbone sketched a line underneath her shirt. "Daddy'd like to see me stay a local performer awhile longer, that's a fact. He doesn't trust how fast Les has been taking things. Sheckly and him—they see eye to eye on that."

"And you? What do you want?"

She scraped her thumbnail along her palm like she was stroking out a splinter. "It must look like I'm just going along for the ride, don't it? Letting everybody else take turns steering. Allison's always telling me—" She stopped, shook her head, displeased with herself for taking that detour. "I'm really not sure. I wake up different mornings, I feel different things."

"Allison showed me an article in the *Recording Industry Times* today. They seem to think you'll be rich enough soon to pay off your dad's ranch and buy the rest of Bulverde, too."

Miranda laughed uneasily. "They're assuming Les Saint-Pierre will be around to represent me."

"I spoke with Cam Compton too. He said he'd told you some ways to make the Century deal happen, some ways that Les could get bargaining power against Sheck."

Miranda frowned. She seemed to be casting around in her memories, trying to make a connection. Finally she found it. "You mean about Julie. Something about the headliner shows."

"So he did tell you."

"Cam said a lot of crazy things."

"But you passed the information along to Les."

Miranda shrugged. "I don't— Maybe I did. But not seriously. I told Les it was just crazy stuff. I told him not to do anything stupid on my account."

"But he did. Les started getting close to Julie Kearnes. He started digging for dirt on Sheck."

She shivered. "I don't want to talk about this."

We listened to another caravan of pickup trucks rumble and ping down the gravel road. Willis Daniels' voice was coming from the kitchen window now. He was thanking somebody for coming.

"You asked me to wait," I reminded her.

Miranda nodded, but she didn't say anything.

"If you want to convince me how frightening Allison Saint-Pierre can be, don't worry about it. I've seen the demo."

I think Miranda blushed. It was hard to tell in the bug zapper light.

"No," she said. "I feel bad now, talkin' about her the way I did. The minute you left the studio I felt bad."

"But you're still uneasy about her."

"I don't know. No. Let's forget it."

The expression on her face told me she couldn't forget it, at least not for more than a few hours. She looked out toward the shed, where moths were starting to gather around the kerosene lamp.

"You don't approve of her seeing your brother," I supplied.

Miranda's expression hardened. "Did you understand about Brent? About what Sheckly said?"

"Only that the words hurt."

She sat up straighter, pushing her back and shoulders and head against the cedar post like she was going to get her height measured. "Marla was Brent's wife. She died two years ago."

The words of the song Miranda had sung the other night came back to me, one of the numbers I couldn't believe Brent could've written. "The Widower's Two-Step."

"I'm sorry to hear it."

She accepted the condolence with a shrug. "Marla had diabetes. Juvenile insulin-dependent diabetes."

The way Miranda threw that phrase out, as casually as a doctor might've, told me the disease's name had long ago become part of her family's vocabulary.

"It wasn't treatable?"

"No. I mean yes, it was treatable. That ain't what killed her, not by itself. She tried having a baby."

Miranda looked at me, hoping I could guess the rest of the story without her having to say it. I guessed.

"That must've devastated Brent."

As soon as I said it I realized what a stupid observation it was. The man was forty-two and still living in a barn behind his father's house. He didn't comb his hair or shave and he apparently wore his clothes until they rotted off of him.

"For a while there," Miranda said, "Dad had to lock up the guns because Brent was threatening to kill himself. That's what Sheckly was talking about. Even now, I think about Brent with Allison—the way she might let him down—"

Miranda stared at the lantern across the field. "You know that expression—somebody's life is like a country song? That's us. Mother dying, then Brent and Marla—"

"And you?" I asked.

"It's coming." She said it with absolute certainty. "Mine is coming."

A bug zapper is not normally the kind of illumination that helps me decide a woman is beautiful. But when Miranda looked at me I decided exactly that. I'm not talking about cute—the vulnerable little kitten quality I'd imagined in her when she'd been onstage at the Cactus Cafe. There was a kind of quiet stubbornness in her face now that suited her well, a much older, steadier light than I'd seen before.

"Do you—" I stopped. I wanted to ask if Miranda lived here, in the tidy burgundy and blue room I'd seen. I hoped she'd say no, that the room was just a museum to her childhood. I couldn't figure out how to phrase the question and not sound judgmental. As it turned out I didn't have to. Miranda heard what I was thinking.

"Yes," she said. "I'm afraid I do. Brent—he didn't have much choice about staying here. Me, I guess it's just a matter of laziness."

There were other possibilities, but it would've been meanness to challenge her. Instead I said, "Why wasn't it a choice for Brent?"

"No medical insurance. Marla's medical bills were sky-high. If Brent tried to get work, she would've stopped qualifying for government health benefits. They were forced to stay unemployed. That little shack over there is about all they had, and that only because Daddy insisted. Marla accepted for them. Brent would've been on the street first. He's too proud."

I tried to associate the word *pride* with Brent. It took some effort.

From inside the kitchen Willis Daniels' voice laughed long and hard. He was saying good night to what must've been his last departing guest.

"What did you ask me out here for?" I said again.

Miranda stared at her hands. "Inside—in my room—you didn't understand."

"I guess not. I thought you were asking me to get Allison out of here."

The lights of the last truck headed down Serra Road. As soon as they turned onto RR22, the kitchen erupted with shattering crashing sounds—like somebody sweeping a cane across a counter full of glasses. Willis Daniels yelled four or five obscenities. Then it got quiet again.

"No," Miranda said, not in response to the noise but like she was merely carrying on our conversation. "I wanted you to take *me* out of here. I don't give a damn where to."

31

 I pushed the VW a little too fast, rounding the curves on RR22 at fifty miles an hour.

The wind blew around the convertible, coming at us from behind. It undid Miranda's hair from the scarf she'd tied over her head and swept strands of black forward so it looked like they were in a desperate race to beat the rest of her face out of Bulverde. She made no attempt to push her hair back.

A hundred yards behind us, a car with cockeyed headlights was following leisurely.

"You know how to get to Les' office?" Miranda asked the question so softly that I almost didn't hear her in the wind.

"Sure."

We'd decided I was taking her to the agency's Victorian house in Monte Vista to spend the night. Miranda knew where the emergency key was. She said Les kept a guest room upstairs for touring artists and she didn't think he would mind her staying there.

I was pretty sure she was right about Les not minding.

After a while she reached over and squeezed my forearm. Her hand felt incredibly hot in the cool of the wind. "Thank you. You okay?"

"Sure. My jaw hurts a little."

Miranda let go of my arm. "I'm glad you took that punch."

"Because?"

"For a while there I thought you were Superman, what with smashing people into kegs and bringing croissants and guns to women in need."

I shook my head. "I got red underwear, though. Want to see?"

She smiled. "Maybe later."

We rounded another curve. The headlights cut a swath across the woods. Light brown ghosts moved behind the cedar trees—deer, foxes, possums. The headlights behind us disappeared, then reappeared, still about a hundred yards back.

When we turned south onto I-10 the cockeyed headlights turned with us. Ahead, the clouds glowed above San Antonio.

We were still a few miles inside the Avalon County line when the lights behind us started edging closer.

"About time," I said.

"What?" Miranda asked.

I slowed down to forty and the headlights started to gain, then dropped back for a while. I slowed down some more.

Finally they gave it up. A red light blinked into existence on the top of the car and the hand-siren started. It was a black Ford Festiva.

"What—" Miranda started to say.

"Probably nothing," I lied.

"How many beers did you have?" she asked nervously.

We pulled over.

I looked in my rearview mirror. The guy coming up on the passenger's side looked like a badly shaved orangutan. He had pale skin, brutish features, and a little tuft of orange on the top of his head. One hand held up a flashlight next to his ear and the other hand was under his wrinkled brown blazer.

The guy coming up on my side was a stocky blond in a turquoise polo shirt and slacks. He wore a side arm. Both men were staying close to the car, cautious.

"Phew," I said. "I don't think they're carrying a Breathalyzer."

They swept the convertible with their flashlights from about five feet back. The blond guy came up to my window.

Under different circumstances I would've said he had a friendly and open face—big features, red nose, bristly mustache, wide unwrinkled brow with the hatband impression still engraved on it. Your basic Bubba. Nice guy to drink a beer with.

Different circumstances would've been without the suspicious frown on his face and the light shining in my eyes and his left hand resting on his semiautomatic.

"Howdy," I said.

Bubba frowned some more.

The guy with the orange hair came up next to Miranda and stared at her, almost resentfully. "Miss Daniels?"

Miranda looked startled, then seemed to come up with a name she wanted. "Hey, Elgin. How you doin'? How's Karen?"

I looked at Bubba. "Elgin—that's his code name, right?"

"Shut up, sir."

Sir. Nice. The courteous shakedown.

Elgin scratched his little tuft of orange hair, then stepped back from Miranda's window, then forward again. He looked uneasy. Poor guy had been planning a nice easy evening of police brutality. Two on one. No ladies present. Nobody that knew his name. This wasn't in the script.

"You step out of the car, please, ma'am?"

Miranda looked at me for some kind of advice. I

smiled. She tried to put that same smile on her face when she turned to Elgin.

"Sure, Elgin. I hope there's nothing wrong."

Elgin got her out of the car. He shone his light in my eyes, then swept it through the back of the car.

"What's in the case?" he asked.

Next to me, Bubba glanced back and sighed. "It's a fucking guitar, Elgin. What do you think?" Then to me, "I need to see a license and the papers on the vehicle, sir."

"You guys want to show me some ID here?"

Bubba stared right through me. "The papers."

"Slow and easy," said Elgin.

I had a pretty good idea what was coming. I reached for the glove compartment, for the insurance papers. I moved very slowly, keeping my hand in the flashlight beam.

When my fingers were just about to the glove compartment handle Elgin swore loudly and drew his 9mm and yelled "Gun!"

Bubba was quick. On the count of one, he had his semiauto in my ear and his other hand around my neck. By the count of five I had been dragged bodily over the car door and slammed into the pavement. One eye couldn't see anything. The other could just make out some fuzzy lights. Something large and hard and sharp was boring a shaft between my shoulder blades. I think it was Bubba's knee. It took him another few seconds to pin down my right arm with his free hand in a fairly decent joint lock. He should've been pressing a little closer to the nerve above my elbow. It's more incapacitating that way. I decided not to volunteer the information.

We stayed like that for a minute, maybe less. I couldn't see or hear Miranda, though every once in a while Elgin would say, "Just stay back, ma'am."

Elgin made a show of searching my glove compartment.

It didn't take long for the warmth and wet of the asphalt to soak through my T-shirt. I think there were some pebbles in my left nostril and my jaw was throbbing again. My neck felt like it had been pried half off with a very large bottle opener.

"Yo, Frank."

"You got it?" Bubba-Frank demanded.

"Yeah," Elgin said.

"Get up," Frank told me. No *sir*, this time.

He lifted me to my feet and shoved my chest against the car. He stayed right behind me. Frank and I both looked at Elgin, who was now grinning evilly, holding up a generic .38 with a duck-taped grip.

"I suppose you got a license for that?" Frank asked me.

"Never seen it before."

"He had it," Miranda muttered. Then with a little more certainty: "He had it." She hugged her arms, doing all her pointing with her chin. When she spoke again her tone was almost apologetic. "Elgin, you put it in the car. I just saw you."

Elgin laughed a little too nervously. He waved the .38 in no particular direction. "Come on now, Miss Daniels. You know better—"

"It's called a throw down," I told Miranda. "You're not telling these guys anything they don't know."

"But I *saw* him." Her tone was soft but obstinate, like a child describing an invisible friend.

We were all silent. There were a lot of possible scenarios we could take from here. Most of them I didn't like worth a damn.

Elgin looked at Frank for some backup. I couldn't see Frank's face but from Elgin's reaction I'd say the backup was not forthcoming.

"I swear to God—" Elgin started.

"Jesus," said Frank. Disgust in his voice.

He put me back on the pavement, not so hard this time, and told Elgin to watch me, if he was up to it.

Elgin came over and glared down at me silently. He pointed the .38 casually at my spine. Then he put his boot on the back of my neck and kept it there.

I decided to keep my mouth shut. Sometimes I'm capable of it.

Frank took Miranda back to the black Festiva.

I had a great view of the VW's left rear tire. The treading was getting worn. A car drove by on the highway, slowed down to look, then kept going.

Frank's field radio was telling him something.

After a while Frank came over and told Elgin, "Talk to me for a minute."

They walked away from me. I didn't hear the first part of their conversation until Elgin protested something.

"Bullshit," Frank said, a little louder.

The conversation got too low for me to hear again, but it was clear that Frank was less than thrilled with Elgin. He didn't even call him "sir."

Finally Frank came up to me and undid the cuffs. He got me on my feet.

"Get back in your car."

I did. Miranda joined me, trying very hard not to look at anything. Her scarf had loosened and slipped around her neck and her hair was a tangled black mesh from the wind.

Elgin stared at me angrily for a minute, then caught Frank looking at him and retreated toward the Festiva.

"I apologize for this," Frank told me. "Simple mistake."

"Great," I said. "Tell me about it while I dig the asphalt out of my nose."

Frank shook his head.

"And if I want to make a complaint with the Avalon County Sheriff's Department?"

Frank looked at me blandly. "You don't."

When we drove away Elgin and Frank were just starting to have a collegial conversation, sitting on the hood of their car and yelling at each other. My side began to feel a little bit better.

Then Miranda started crying.

32

The Les Saint-Pierre Agency had gotten in the spirit of the season. Somebody—I was betting Gladys the receptionist—had put a clump of pumpkins on the front porch and a *ristra* over the door. I wondered if Milo Chavez would dress in costume and hand out candy to the would-be recording stars who visited. Somehow I doubted it.

Miranda made it all the way up the steps of the old Victorian before sinking down, without explanation, onto the porch. I set her guitar and her overnight bag by the door, then sat next to her.

It was one in the morning, finally cool enough to be pleasant. I didn't feel pleasant. Most of my body weight had drained into my hands and feet. The only thing keeping me awake was the persistent pain in my jaw and my side.

Miranda must've been operating on even less sleep than I was. She sat with her upper body listing back and forth, like she was correcting her balance on a ship. She'd stopped crying a long time ago but her eyes were teary.

"I'm sorry," she said. "I just couldn't believe about Elgin. He and his wife—she's a cousin to Ben French, my drummer. They came to some of my father's parties. Elgin seemed like a gentleman."

"A gentleman," I said. "Like Tilden Sheckly."

It came out harsher than I intended.

Miranda leaned back until her shoulders touched the wall. She stared across the street at the dark turrets of the Koehler Mansion. "And if I hadn't been there?"

"It's lucky for me you were. Frank and Elgin wanted to give me something to worry about besides Tilden Sheckly's business."

She circled her arms around her knees. She'd taken off her boots in the VW and now her toes stuck out from beneath the folds of her denim skirt. She dug them in, over and over, like she was trying to gather up more of the hardwood porch.

"Sheck was talking to me tonight," she said. "Before all that mess with Allison. He asked me about moving out to the mansion."

"What?"

She put her head back and closed her eyes. "He lives in this old hunting lodge out behind the Paintbrush—got about six million rooms in it. Sheck offered me a whole wing to myself and free time at the studio. Ain't nothing like Silo in Austin, but still. Sheck said I'd be closer to the action that way."

"Uh-huh."

She opened her eyes and kicked me lightly on the shin. "It's not what you think. It would be like an artist colony."

She looked at me uncertainly, like she was hoping against hope that I'd agree. An artist colony, conveniently down the hall from Tilden's bedroom, I bet.

Miranda hadn't moved her bare foot. It still rested against my leg. Maybe she was just too tired to notice.

"Your father would disapprove," I speculated.

But my mind wasn't really on what I was saying anymore. I was looking at Miranda, trying to remember the photograph of her I'd seen in Milo's office five days ago. I was trying to superimpose that image, to see if I could remember why I'd found it so hard to believe that Tilden Sheckly would want to own her.

"Les would discourage me, too," she added. "If Les was around."

I saw what she wanted me to say. I tried to sound as convincing as I could. "Les believed in your career, Miranda. He'd've been foolish not to. If he got himself in trouble with Sheck, it was his doing. Not yours."

Miranda examined my face. She relaxed her shoulders a little. "I just get worried. I'll be glad when this business is decided one way or the other."

"I can understand that. Don't do it."

"Don't do what?"

"Move into Sheckly's place. You should move out of your father's and get something of your own, Miranda. But not Sheckly's house."

She looked at me differently then, not tired, not really asking me any question you could put into words. Her foot was still resting on my leg.

I cleared my throat. "Been a long day. You play tomorrow night?"

"At the Paintbrush. Every Saturday we open for the headliner."

"Well—"

I stood to go. Miranda offered me her hand.

I pulled her up but she didn't let go of my hand. We walked to the door, where Miranda retrieved a spare key from behind the mailbox on the wall.

When she opened the door of the agency the smells of freon and fresh flowers seeped out, leftovers from a hot day.

She turned toward me and smiled. "Good night?"

"Yeah." My voice came out ragged.

I wanted to let go of Miranda's hand so she wouldn't realize mine was shaking a little. She didn't let me.

She moistened her lips. "Maybe—it's sort of uncomfortable, being alone here tonight."

Several different voices were hissing in my ears, Erainya Manos and Milo Chavez and Sam Barrera and a bunch of others—all talking about professional detachment and client loyalty and warning me not to start things I'd regret. Miranda kept smiling and the voices kept getting farther away. With the little reservation I could muster I tried to think of something to say, something polite and witty by way of declining. Instead I mumbled, "Maybe I could just—"

"Maybe so," she agreed.

Miranda's hand tightened on mine. She led me under the *ristra* doorway and inside.

33

It was only the fear of meeting Milo Chavez if he came to work in the morning that got me home to 90 Queen Anne Street before dawn. I caught about three hours of sleep before Kelly Arguello's phone call woke me up again.

"Good God," she said. "What's that noise?"

I rubbed the crud out of my eyes and tried to identify any unusual sounds other than the grinding inside my skull.

Oh.

"Just Robert Johnson," I told her.

"Are you torturing him?"

Robert Johnson kept making his overworked wench-motor noise. I tried to wriggle my foot loose from his front claws. He rolled on his back so he could attack with all four. I rubbed his belly with my toes while he gave my ankle the meat hook treatment.

"Sort of," I said. "I'm late with breakfast."

"You must make a hell of a breakfast."

I tried to get up from the futon. Mistake. I steadied myself on the ironing board, sat down again, and waited for the fuzzy black balloons to go away.

I tried my best to make my brain work while Kelly started giving me the rundown on what she'd found so far about Les Saint-Pierre.

Once again she surprised me. In the world of government paperwork you can't expect much out of forty-eight hours, but somehow Kelly manages. She'd already gotten all of Les' driver's information from DMV—body reports on the Mercedes convertible and the Seville that he'd left behind, his driver's record, previous applications, Allison Saint-Pierre's record. Kelly had written for the incident report on a DUI Les had received last year in Houston. That would take another week at least.

She had submitted a few tons of requests to the Social Security Administration and various state agencies, looking for any recent papers issued for any of the names from Julie Kearnes' personnel files. We'd been a little too liberal in the weeding process, narrowing down the scope to the six most likely candidates for a new Les Saint-Pierre, but even with that many names, tracking paperwork was going to be a nightmare. Kelly planned on following up Monday morning.

"How'd you squeeze DMV so quickly?" I asked.

"No big deal. I told the guy at the desk I was working a grand jury subpoena for the State Attorney's Office. Like that time in San Francisco you told me about. You're right—it works like a charm."

"I wasn't suggesting that as model behavior, Kelly."

"Hey, what? You want me to put the information back?"

I hesitated. Tres Navarre, the moral example. "They bought the State Attorney line from you, huh?"

"Sure."

"Purple hair and all?"

She sighed. "Jesus, Tres, it's not like I wore a nose stud or anything. I can dress business. I look good in a blazer."

I didn't argue the point.

Kelly went on to tell me about Les Saint-Pierre's parents' death certificates in Denton County, which had led her to a probate court settlement on their estate, which had in turn given her a list of real estate inherited by Les. He'd received the small family house in Denton and a vacation house on Medina Lake. Kelly had sent requests to Denton County and Avalon County for copies of the assessor's records on both properties.

"Medina Lake," I repeated. "Avalon County."

"That's what it says here. I'm skeptical about the place in Denton but I'm pretty sure he's still got the lake property."

"Why?"

"I went by Parks and Wildlife. Les has a freshwater sailboat registered."

I whistled. "You're pushing for a bonus, now."

A lot of paper-chasers overlook Parks and Wildlife. I normally wouldn't have tried it myself so early in the process. Usually you start with the obvious and work your way toward the obscure. Fortunately in this case, Kelly worked differently. Her procedure was dictated more by where all the government offices in Austin fell on her bus line.

"It isn't a big boat," she told me. "A twenty-five-footer. He didn't need to get it registered but it looks like he did anyway."

I thought about Les' bedroom, about the labeled shoe boxes that filled his closet, even his illegal drugs and his scams on women all neatly categorized and filed away. Maybe the bastard had been a little too organized.

"Go on."

"He bought the boat at Plum Cove, Medina Lake. I made some calls, got an address for the dry-dock space he's been renting."

I found a pen wedged in the crack behind the ironing board/phone alcove and wrote down the information. "Good stuff."

"Yeah. At least nobody else has asked about the boat."

My pen froze above the paper. "What do you mean?"

"When I was at DMV, the clerk recognized the name Les Saint-Pierre from a few weeks ago. It's an unusual name. He commented that Les must be in a lot of trouble."

"Why's that?"

"Seems I was the second person from the State Attorney that month looking through his records."

34

My mother was squatting in her neighbors' back-yard, painting faux wisteria vines on a pine fence. To get to her I had to step carefully in my dress shoes through a minefield of pie tins filled with various colors.

She was wearing purple overalls and a fuchsia Night in Old San Antonio T-shirt, both speckled with acrylic. The air was warm and stagnate with fumes and Mother was sweating almost as much as the open Pecan Street Ale bottle on the stepping-stone next to her.

She greeted me without looking up. She swirled her brush to form a cluster of pale purple petals. There was a fingerprint the exact same color on the side of her nose.

"You know they sell plants now," I said. "You can just buy them in stores."

Mother suppressed a giggle. I think that was my first indication maybe she'd been sitting in the heat and the paint fumes too long.

"It's trompe l'oeil, Jackson." Then she lowered her voice. "The Endemens are *paying* me."

I looked back at the Endemens' house. Mr. Endemen, a scruffy retired newspaperman, was sitting at his typewriter at the dining-room table. He was trying hard to look busy, but he kept sneaking sideways glances at us through the picture window. He was frowning, like the view hadn't improved since I'd arrived.

"I won't tell," I promised.

Mother finished her petals and looked up at me. She did a double take.

"Well . . ." She raised her eyebrows. "I'm sorry, I thought you were my son."

"Mother—"

"No, you look wonderful dear. What happened to your chin?"

"It's a bruise."

She hesitated. She had noticed something else too—that pheromonal afterglow that only mothers and girlfriends can detect, that aura which told her I had been Up To Something the night before.

Whatever conclusions she came to she kept to herself. She looked down at my ensemble while she stirred her brush through a pie tin. "I don't know if I'd've chosen the brown tie, but it's nice. I suppose conservative is best for an interview."

"A woman in purple overalls is giving me fashion tips."

She smiled. "I'm very proud of you. Would you like to take a medicine pouch for luck?"

"Actually I was hoping to borrow the Audi."

Mother tightened her lips.

She reached past me for her beer bottle. I stepped back so she wouldn't get paint on my black slacks. After she took a sip of Pecan Street Ale she looked up and down the fence at her work so far.

"Mr. Endemen wants grape vines along the top," she mused. "I think that's too much with the wisteria, don't you?"

I thought about it. "You get paid per plant?"

She sighed. "Artistic question. I shouldn't have asked you. I hope you want the Audi just to drive to UTSA?"

I gave her my best innocent look. "No . . . I have some work to do afterward. It would be better if I didn't use my own car for it."

"Some work," she repeated. "Dear, the last time you borrowed my car for some work . . ."

"I know. I'll pay you back for any repairs."

"That's not really the point, Jackson."

"Can I trade cars with you or not, Mother?"

She put down her paintbrush, then wiped her hands on a rag. She pulled her key chain out of her bib pocket with two fingers. "My hands are sticky."

I took the key off the chain. "Thanks."

Mother leaned in close to the fence and traced out a new curl in her vine. Mr. Endemen kept typing in the dining room, looking out the window from time to time to see if I'd gone away yet.

"So," Mother said, "are you nervous?"

I refocused on her. "About the interview?"

She nodded.

"No sweat," I said. "Sitting around with a bunch of professors won't be the worst thing that's happened to me this week."

Mother smiled knowingly. "Don't worry. You'll do fine."

She looked at my face again. For a minute I thought she might bring out a Kleenex, dab it on her tongue, and wipe my cheeks like she used to do when I was five. "I hope we'll see you tomorrow."

"You having your traditional costume party?"

I thought, after all these years, that I could keep the resentment out of my voice. I'm not sure I managed.

She nodded. "It doesn't mean we can't make it a double celebration, Jackson."

"I'll do my best."

"You'll come," she insisted.

When I left she was still deliberating whether or not to go with the grape vines.

The neighborhood private security guy cruised past the front yard as I was opening my mother's white Audi sedan. He saw my dress clothes and for the first time in two years he didn't slow down or look at me suspiciously.

There was an Indian medicine pouch waiting for me on Mother's dashboard.

35

 "I think that went just fine," David Mitchell told me. "Come in, come in."

His office was on the third floor of the Humanities & Social Sciences Building, just down the hall from the interview room. On the office door was a *Peanuts* cartoon of Lucy in the psychiatrist's booth with the little DOCTOR IS IN sign. Professor Mitchell, a man on the cutting edge of humor.

His work space was messy but cozy, filled with crammed bookshelves and dented filing cabinets and dying potted plants. There was a Macintosh computer setup as big as a Hyundai against the back wall. A poster for the Houston Renaissance Festival above that. More Lucy and Linus cartoons were Scotch-taped around the room like hastily applied Band-Aids.

Mitchell offered me a seat and a Diet Pepsi from his private stash. I accepted the seat.

"Well," he said. "Now that we've grilled you, perhaps you have some questions of your own."

He nodded his head encouragingly. He'd done that all the way through the formal interview while his three colleagues—two elderly Anglo men and one Latino—stared at me and frowned and asked me over and over again what exactly I'd been doing since my postgraduate work. When they'd shaken my hand at the end of the hour they'd all looked worried, like they should've worn surgical gloves. Maybe Mother was right. Maybe the brown tie had been a bad choice.

I asked Mitchell some questions. Mitchell nodded his head a lot. He had silver hair and silver sideburns that were trimmed into the shape of fins from a 1950s automobile. His features were pinched and angular and his eyes were beady like a weasel's. A nice weasel. A good ole weasel.

Mitchell gave me some background on the teaching position that had opened up in the department.

Apparently old Dr. Haimer, who as far as anyone could remember had been teaching medieval literature since it was titled "Contemporary Authors," was finally retiring, midterm. Last week, in fact. His two teaching assistants had resigned in protest, leaving Haimer's classes in the hands of other T.A.s and a few American Lit professors who probably thought Marie de France was some kind of bicycle race.

"Medieval just isn't a very popular field," Mitchell told me. "Usually we'd have plenty of lecturers waiting to fill the position in an emergency, but—"

"Why did Haimer leave?"

Mitchell shook his head. "He opposed the establishment of more separate ethnic studies programs. Said it was fragmenting, that the curriculum should have one inclusive canon."

"Oops."

Mitchell looked grave. "He had good intentions. The fact is he said what was on a lot of our minds. But his vote was the only open dissent in the faculty senate. Word got out to the students. Boycotts started, protests on the Patillo, signs that read RACIST. Not the sort of public relations the provost wanted."

"So why me? You don't need another white guy."

Mitchell stared at me like I'd just made an inside joke. "Of course. The committee would prefer someone— 'of diverse gender and ethnicity,' I think is the going term."

"But?"

He shook his head, letting a little more distaste show. "I'll have to speak with Dr. Gutierrez about that in the committee meeting, I'm sure, but let's talk about qualifications, son. We need someone who knows the field, someone with a good background who can relate to the students. Someone young, a teacher more than a publisher. Technically it would only be for the rest of the year—a visiting assistant professor's position—until a more extensive hiring search can be conducted. But still, once you're in, once you make connections on the faculty—"

He nodded more encouragement, letting me get the picture. I got it.

We talked a little more about the interview process, about when I might come back to teach a demo class if the committee decided to go the next step. I wasn't holding my breath for that, but I said I could stay available. Mitchell nodded, content.

He opened the folder I'd given him and ran down my credentials and training from Berkeley. He started shaking his head and smiling.

"You're bilingual."

"Spanish and English. Middle English. Some classical Spanish and Latin, enough Anglo-Norman to get the dirty jokes in the fabliaux."

He whistled silently and closed the folder. "You completed a five-year program in three years. These letters of recommendation are extremely strong. How is it after all that you got into . . ."

He looked for a polite word.

"Thug work?" I offered.

He chuckled. "Let's go with 'investigations.' "

"Just luck. And the fact that the only job I could get with my Ph.D. at the time was tending a bar on Telegraph Avenue. And the fact that a friend of mine introduced me to someone, a criminal lawyer who sort of—took me in."

Maia Lee probably would've laughed at that. "Took me in" was a nice euphemism for teaching somebody to break a window the right way, disarm a security system, do a skip trace, blackmail somebody with photos to keep a civil case from going to trial. Maia's associates at Terrence & Goldman had frowned on her methods until Maia made junior partner.

Mitchell was looking at me, still smiling but with a little more wistfulness in his expression.

"And the fact your father was a lawman," he suggested. "I suspect your mother is right—that had a lot to do with your career getting sidetracked."

I didn't answer. *Sidetracked?*

"So why would you go back to Academia now?" he asked.

I think I told him something about wanting an intellectual challenge and applying real world experience to the classroom, blah, blah, blah. My mind was pretty well disconnected with my spiel by the time someone knocked on the door.

Mitchell excused himself. He went into the hall and mumbled briefly with one of the other members of the hiring committee.

He came back in and sat down. He kept his face impassive.

"That didn't take long," he said.

I got ready to leave, to tell him thanks anyway.

Mitchell broke into a grin. "They'd like to see a demo next week. Dr. Gutierrez said you're the most refreshing candidate he's interviewed in a long time."

When I left Mitchell's office I had a little slip of

paper confirming my demo lesson to the medieval undergrad seminar on Monday. I also had a dazed, sticky feeling, like somebody had already started wall-papering me with *Peanuts* cartoons and Scotch tape.

36

A red Mazda Miata was parked in front of 90
Queen Anne Street with its right tires over the
curb. When I walked around to my side of the
house Allison Saint-Pierre came out my front door and
said, "Hi."

She was wearing white Reeboks, a pleated white skirt,
and a white tank top that wasn't lining up with her bra
straps very well. A terry-cloth sweatband pushed her hair
into bangs. Her smile was alcohol-fortified. Tennis lesson
day at the country club.

She was holding two Shiner Bocks. One bottle was
almost empty. The other she gave to me.

"Damnedest thing," she said.

She leaned sideways in the doorway so I could pass if I
wanted to do the mambo with her.

I stayed on the porch.

"Let me guess. My landlord let you in."

She smiled wider. "Sweet old fart. He picked up that

envelope on the counter and asked me if I knew anything
about this month's rent."

"Yeah, Gary has a thing for blondes. Rent money and
blondes. Maybe if I brought over more blondes he'd ask
less often about the rent."

Allison raised her eyebrows. "Worth a try."

Then she turned inside like her back was hinged to
the doorjamb. I almost thought she was going to fall into
the living room, but at the last minute she put her foot
out and walked in. She said, "Wooo."

I drank some of my Shiner Bock before following her
inside.

Allison had taken Julie Kearnes out of the cassette
deck and put in my Johnny Johnson. She'd pulled an old
Texas Monthly off the windowsill and left it open on the
coffee table. The ironing board was down and the phone
had been pulled out from behind it.

Allison sat on the kitchen counter stool and spread her
arms along the Formica. "Somebody named Carol called.
I told her you weren't here."

"Carolaine," I corrected. "That's just great. Thanks."

She shrugged. Happy to help.

I looked for Robert Johnson but he'd buried himself
deep. Maybe under the laundry. Maybe in the pantry.
Unlike my landlord, Robert Johnson didn't go much for
blondes.

"You send Sheckly a get-well card yet?" I asked.

Allison had a happy drunk going that was about as
thick as battleship skin. My question pinged against her,
a small annoyance but not nearly enough to make her
change course.

"One of his lawyers left me a message this morning—
something about the medical bills." She was turning the
tip of her right sneaker in time to the music. Back, forth,
back, forth.

I waited.

"You're in my apartment for a good reason, I'm sure.
Mind telling what it is?"

Allison appraised me while she bobbed her head,

starting at my feet and working her way up. When she got to my eyes she locked on and smiled, approvingly.

"You look good. You should dress like that more often."

I shook my head. "This outfit reminds me of too many funerals."

"That's where you were this morning?"

"Close enough. Why are you here?"

Allison lifted her fingers off the counter. "You were listed in the book. I felt bad about you getting hit last night."

"You felt bad."

She grinned. "I'm not that terrible, sweetie. You don't know me well enough."

"The guys who know you well enough seem to get flesh wounds."

"Like I said, Tres, I grew up with four brothers."

"How many of them made it to adulthood?"

Her eyes sparkled. No making her mad today. "Maybe I was just curious. Miranda's dad called me this morning. He wanted to know if Miranda was with me last night."

"Yeah?"

She gave me a smirk. "Yeah. Seems she disappeared last night after the party. So did you, for that matter."

She waited for information.

Fortunately for me the phone rang. Allison offered to get it. I told her thanks anyway. I moved the phone to the bathroom doorway, which was as far as it would stretch, then picked up the receiver.

Erainya Manos said, "RIAA."

"Is that Greek?"

The next thing she said *was* Greek, and unflattering. "No, honey, I'm telling you something you never got from me. Recording Industry Association of America. When it comes to enforcing copyright laws in the music industry, they're it. They've got a branch office in Houston. For all of South Texas, they contract through Samuel Barrera."

I looked across the room at Allison. She smiled at me pleasantly, still moving her feet to the Johnny Johnson.

"That's great," I told Erainya. "I'm glad it was nothing serious."

Erainya hesitated. "You got visitors?"

"Uh-huh."

"Just listen, then. Sheckly's been in court half a dozen times the last few years, sued by big-name artists who've appeared at his place. They all claim he's taped their shows for syndication and given them no rights to anything, no percentage."

"I've heard about that."

"They also claim bootleg CDs of their shows have been turning up all over Europe. Excellent quality recordings, made at first-rate facilities. My friends tell me it's pretty common knowledge Sheckly is the one making the tapes, getting a little extra money out of them. He speaks German, goes over to Germany frequently, probably uses the trips to strike some deals, distribute his masters, but nobody can prove it. Since the shows are taped for syndication they could've been copied and distributed at any radio station in the country, by anybody with the right equipment."

I smiled at Allison. I mouthed the words *sick friend*. "Doesn't sound like anything that would kill you. Just a minor annoyance."

Erainya was silent. "It doesn't sound like anything to get killed over, honey. You're right. Then again, how much money are we talking about? What kind of guy is Mr. Sheckly? You got a sense for that?"

"I'm afraid I might. Why haven't they caught this before?"

"I hear Sheckly keeps things pretty modest. Doesn't import the music back into the U.S., which would make it more profitable but ten times easier to bust. He sticks to the European market, only live tapes. Makes him a low-priority target."

"Got it."

"And, honey, you heard nothing from me."

"Room twelve. All right."

"If you can use this to squeeze Barrerra's balls a little bit—"

"I'll do that. Same to you."

I hung up. Allison looked at me and said, "Good prognosis?"

"You mind if I change clothes?"

She pursed her lips and nodded. "Go ahead."

I pulled a T-shirt and jeans out of the closet and went into the bathroom. Robert Johnson peeped out the side of the shower curtain.

"Not yet," I told him.

His head disappeared back into the bathtub.

I'd just taken off the dress shirt and was pulling the sleeves right-side out when Allison came in and poked her finger in my back, touching the scar above my kidney.

It took great effort to control my backward elbow strike reflex.

"What's this?" she asked.

"You mind not doing that?"

She acted like she hadn't heard. She poked the scar again, like the puffiness of the skin fascinated her. Her breath dragged across my shoulder like the edge of a washcloth.

"Bullet hole?"

I turned to face her, but there wasn't much place to back up unless I sat in the sink. "Sword tip. My *sifu* got a little excited one time."

"*Sifu?*"

"Teacher. The guy who trained me in tai chi."

She laughed. "Your own teacher stabbed you? He must not be very good."

"He's very good. The problem was he thought I was good too."

"You've got another scar. That one's longer."

She was looking at my chest now, where a hash dealer had stabbed me with a Balinese knife in San Francisco's Tenderloin District. I put on my T-shirt.

Allison pouted. "Show's over?"

I waved her out and closed the bathroom door in her face. She was still smiling when I did it.

Robert Johnson stared at me as I put on the jeans. He looked about as amused as I was.

"Maybe if we rush her," I suggested. "A two-flank approach."

His head disappeared again. So much for backup.

When I came into the living room Allison had opened another beer and relocated to the futon.

"This reminds me of my old place in Nashville," she said, studying the water-stained plaster on the ceiling. "God, that was bad."

"Thanks."

She looked at me, puzzled. "I just meant it's small. I was living on nothing for a while. Kind of makes me nostalgic, you know?"

"The good old days," I said. "Before you married money."

She drank some beer. "Don't knock it, Tres. You know what the joke was in Falfurrias?"

"Falfurrias. That's where you're from?"

She nodded sourly. "We joked that you only go to college for an MRS." She tapped her wedding ring with her thumb. "I bypassed the degree plan."

She closed all ten fingers around the beer bottle and kicked her feet up on the futon. I stared at the beer, wondering how many it would take for me to catch up with her.

"When I was eighteen I was working during the summer as a secretary at Al Garland's auto dealership." She looked at me meaningfully, like I should know Al Garland, obviously a bigwig in Falfurrias. I shook my head. She looked disappointed.

"I was trying to sing at a few clubs in Corpus Christi on the weekends. Next thing I know Al was telling me he was going to leave his wife for me, telling me he would finance my music career. We started taking weekend trips to Nashville so he could show me how rich and important he was. He must've sunk ten thousand into the wallet doctors."

"Wallet doctors?"

She grinned. "The guys in Nashville that smell small-town money a mile off. They promised Al all kinds of stuff for me—recordings, promotion, connections. Nothing ever happened except I showed Al how grateful I was a lot. I thought it was love for a while. Eventually he decided I'd become too expensive. Or maybe his wife found out. I never knew which. I got left in Nashville with about fifty dollars in cash and some really nice negligees. Stupid, huh?"

I didn't say anything. Allison drank more beer.

"You know the bad part? I finally got up the courage to tell somebody in Nashville that story and it was Les Saint-Pierre. He just laughed. It happens a hundred times every month, he told me, the exact same way. The big trauma of my life was just another statistic. Then Les told me he could make it right and I got suckered again. I was a slow learner."

"You don't have to tell me any of this."

She shrugged. "I don't care."

She sounded like she'd said it so many times she could almost believe it.

"What happened with the agency?" I asked. "Why did Les decide to push you out of the business?"

Allison shrugged. "Les didn't want somebody bringing him back to earth when he went really far out with an idea. He didn't know when to stop. Most of the time, it turned out well for him that way. Not always."

"Such as?"

She shook her head, noncommittal. "It doesn't really matter. Not now."

"And if he doesn't come back?"

"I'll get the agency."

"You sound sure. You think you can keep it afloat without him?"

"I know. Les' reputation. Sure, it'll be tough, but that's assuming I keep the agency. The name is worth money—

I can sell it to all kinds of competitors in Nashville. There are also contracts in place for publishing rights on some hits that are still bringing in money. Les wasn't stupid."

"Sounds like you've been looking into it."

Allison shrugged. Slight smile. "Wouldn't you?"

"You must've run down his assets, then."

"I've got a pretty good idea."

"You know anything about a cabin on Medina Lake?"

Allison's face got almost sober. She stared at me blankly. I told her about the probate settlement from Les' parents' property.

"First I've heard about it."

But there was something else going on in her head. Like something that had been bothering her slightly for a long time was now coming to the forefront. I looked at her, silently asking her to tell me about it. She wavered, then looked away. "You have a plan, sweetie?"

"I thought I'd head out there. Check things out."

I regretted my answer as soon as I said it.

Allison tottered to her feet, held up her beer to check how much was left, then smiled at me. "You'd better drive. I'll navigate."

Then she began that job by trying to locate the front door.

37

Allison was quiet for the first half of the trip. She'd complained bitterly before we left about me making her a thermos of coffee rather than tequila, then making her change clothes into something more utilitarian. I'd found a pair of Carolaine's drawstring Banana Republics and a crewneck pullover in the back of the closet. They fit Allison well. Once we got going, she curled into the passenger's seat of my mother's Audi with her knees on the dash and her face behind the coffee mug and a pair of my mother's purple sunglasses she'd pulled out of the glove compartment. For a while she made occasional "uhh" sounds and I thought she was going to be ill, but once we got out of the city she began to perk up.

She even decided to come with me into the tax assessor's office when we got to Wilming. Wilming was a small county seat consisting of an American Legion Hall and a Dairy Queen and not much else. The assessor's office was open Saturday because it was also the post office and the grocery store. After successfully scoring the deed and the last five years of tax records on Les' property I had to grudgingly admit that having the subject's wife with me, the subject's pretty blond wife, had helped expedite matters somewhat.

When we got back in the car Allison poured herself more coffee and said, "Gaah."

"It's just strong," I said. "You're not used to Peet's."

She shuddered. "Is this like Starbucks or something?"

"Peet's is to Starbucks what Plato is to Socrates. You'll appreciate it in time."

Allison stared at me for about half a mile, then decided to turn her attention back to the tax assessor's documents and the coffee.

She flipped through the paperwork on Les' cabin. "Bastard. Two years ago he changed the billing for the tax statements so they wouldn't come to the house. Exactly when we got married."

"He wanted a place you didn't know about. He might've already been thinking about getting away someday, leaving himself an exit route."

She made a small, incredulous laugh. "What's this billing address in Austin? A girlfriend?"

"Probably a mail drop. A girlfriend would be too risky."

"Bastard. You think you can find this place?"

I shook my head. "Don't know."

We had the exact address for the cabin but that didn't mean much at the lake. Most people had their address registered as a mailbox along the main highway, and there would be hundreds of those, all plain silver, many of them with incomplete or weathered-down numbers. Even if we found the right box it wouldn't necessarily be near the cabin. Most likely that would be a mile or two down some unnamed gravel road, the turnoff marked only by wooden boards displaying the last names of some of the families that lived that way. Often there was no sign at all, no way to find someone out here unless you had word-of-mouth instructions. If you could avoid the notice of the locals, Medina Lake wasn't a bad place for a missing person to hide out.

We passed Woman Hollow Creek, wended our way through some more hills, down Highway 16. The ratio of RVs to cars began to climb.

Allison examined my mother's medicine pouch on the rearview mirror, letting the beads and feathers slip through her fingers. "So how do you know Milo anyway? You two don't seem—I don't know, you're like the Odd Couple or something."

"You know that scar on my chest?"

Allison hesitated. "You're kidding."

"Milo didn't do it. He had this idea. He thought I'd make a good private detective."

The road was too twisty for me to look at Allison's face, but she stayed quiet for another mile or so, the purple sunglasses turned toward me. I missed the noise and the wind and rattling of the VW. In my mother's Audi, the quiet spaces were way too quiet.

Finally Allison laced her fingers together and stretched her arms. "Okay. So what happened?"

"Milo was assistant counsel for defense on this homicide case. His first big job with Terrence & Goldman in San Francisco. He wanted someone who could track down a witness—a drug dealer who'd seen the murder. Milo thought I could do it. He thought he'd really impress his boss that way."

"And you found the guy."

"Oh, yeah, I found him. I spent a few days in San Francisco General afterward."

"Milo's boss was impressed?"

"With Milo, no. With me, yes. Once I got out of intensive care."

Allison laughed. "He gave you a job?"

"She. She offered to train me, yes. She fired Milo."

"That's even better. And a woman, too."

"Most definitely a woman."

Allison opened her mouth, then began to nod. "Ah-ha. Milo wanted to impress—"

"It wasn't just professional."

"But you and her—"

"Yeah."

Allison grinned. She nudged my arm. "I do believe the P.I. is blushing."

"Nonsense."

She laughed, then uncapped the thermos and poured herself another cup of Peet's. "This stuff is beginning to taste better."

We skirted the lake for over a mile before we actually saw it. The hills and the cedars obscured the view most of the way around. The waterline was so far down that the clay and limestone shore looked like a beige bathtub ring between the water and the trees.

Medina wasn't a lake you could get your bearings on very easily. The water snaked around, following the course of the original river that was dammed to make the lake, etching out coves and dead ends, each outlet and inlet looking pretty much like all the others. We might've been searching for Les' cabin the rest of the week if an old friend hadn't helped us out.

About a mile past the Highway 37 cutoff, a black Ford Festiva was pulled off on the right side of the road, opposite the lake. The driver's side window was open and a redheaded orangutan-looking guy was behind the wheel, reading a newspaper.

I drove a quarter mile up the road and then U-ed around. I waited for a semi to rumble by and then pulled in behind it, following close.

"What are we doing?" Allison asked.

"Keep looking straight ahead."

On my second pass the redhead in the Festiva still didn't pay me any attention, but it was definitely Elgin. He had his head firmly buried in the sports page. Advanced surveillance methods. He'd probably figure out to poke eyeholes in the paper pretty soon.

I quickly scanned the area he was staking out. There were no side roads in view. There were no mailboxes. It was just a curve of highway around a hill. On the lake side the road fell away in a steep, heavily wooded slope, so you couldn't really see what was down toward the water, but there were some power lines angling in. That meant at least one cabin and only one way to get down there—past Elgin.

"Elgin without Frank," I said. "Not smart."

Allison looked behind us. "What are you talking about?"

I told her about my encounter the night before with Elgin and Frank on the side of the highway, how they'd introduced my face to the asphalt and offered me a very nice throw-down gun. I told her they were probably sheriff deputies, buddies of Tilden Sheckly.

"What shits," she said. "And they're watching Les' place?"

"One of them at least."

"So we're going to go back and whack him on the head or something, right? Tie him up?"

I chanced a look sideways to see if she was kidding. I couldn't tell. "Whack him on the head?"

"Hey, I've got Mace, too. Let's go."

After her performance with Sheckly the previous evening I thought it prudent not to deride her abilities as a head-whacker. I said, "Let's keep that as a backup plan. Get a fifty out of my backpack."

We kept driving, going back as far as Turk's Ice House.

After five minutes of chitchat with Eustice, the blue-haired store clerk in the flashy satin shirt, we came to an agreement that the cove we wanted was Maple End and no, Eustice didn't recognize Les from his picture and no, Allison hadn't gone to high school with Eustice's daughter. Despite the last disappointment, Eustice agreed to introduce us to Bip, who agreed to loan us his out-board fishing boat for fifty dollars. Bip and his boat were both large grayish wedges, dented up and grungy, and both smelled like live bait. Bip kept grinning at Allison and saying "whuh!" every time he looked away from her. I tried to give him warning looks, to let him know he was putting himself in mortal peril, but Bip paid no attention.

We started the outboard with some effort and pulled away from the dock at Turk's.

The cove widened into the main spine of the lake. A half mile away, on the far shore, the hills were dotted with cabins and radio towers. Occasionally a motorboat would zip by a few hundred yards away; a minute or so afterward we'd find ourselves bobbing up and down as we cut through the wake. By the time we'd turned the boat toward the mouth of Maple End Cove we had lake water up to our ankles and I'd had to move my backpack off the floor and into my lap. Bip had assured us those little holes in the boat would be no problem.

Allison took off her shoes and was about to dangle her footsies over the side when I said, "I wouldn't do that."

She frowned. In the afternoon sun, the purple glasses cast long red reflections down her cheeks. "What? They're already wet."

"It's not the water. It's the moccasins."

I pointed ahead to a spot where the water was rippling a little bit more aggressively than the normal dips and swells.

Allison brought her feet back in.

We passed the floating nest. A dozen or so green and silver whips were twisting into sailor's knots just below the surface.

Allison whistled softly. "Only snakes we had in Falfurrias got made into belts. Hope these guys understand if the boat sinks next to them."

"Me too. Last year a water-skier took a spill into one of those nests. She died instantly."

Allison put her feet up on my bench, one on either side of my legs. Her toenails were painted red. Her pants legs were rolled halfway up her tan calves and fit tight that way, not loose as they would've on Carolaine.

She rested her elbow on her knee and cupped her hand on her chin and blinked her eyes at me. "I believe you made that up, Mr. Navarre."

I shrugged, tried not to smile. We puttered along past the snakes.

The southern tip of Maple End Cove, sure enough, had a huge maple tree jutting from the top of the ridge. Maples are pretty rare in Texas, but this one apparently hadn't heard the news that it wasn't supposed to thrive. It was at least thirty feet tall and blazing with fall colors. The rocky ground around it was littered with burnt orange and apple yellow. At the waterline below, several women were sunbathing on an old floating pontoon dock. There were stairs cut into the rock, leading down to the dock, but they stopped a good twenty feet above, where the waterline used to be.

The cove narrowed quickly as our boat puttered into it. After one curve the banks on either side were no more than twenty yards apart. The water this far back was murky green and smelled of stagnation—scum and leaking septic material and dead fish. The shoreline on the right was fairly steep and thick with cedars and live oaks, all the branches overgrown with spiky Spanish moss. I could glimpse the tops of semis or RVs speeding along the highway above where Elgin was parked.

There were two cabins, both on that side of the cove. The one farther down was a well-kept white-shingled house set almost at the top of the ridge. At the water level was a floating dock, and above that a small patch of lawn grass. A hand-painted wooden sign meant to be read from the water proudly announced: THE HEIDEL-MANS, with daisies and frogs all around the letters. There was a small army of plastic waterfowl with wind-propellers for wings surrounding the sign and a flagstone path up to the house. The windows were all shuttered and no lights were on.

A half acre closer to us was a military-style Quonset hut that jutted out of the slope about halfway between the water and the highway. It had a wooden deck facing the water. The front wall was painted chocolate brown, with a screen door and two windows covered in yellow curtains. The hut's shell was an arc of corrugated

aluminum as dull as the inside of a food can. There was a
metal pipe chimney in the back.

"My husband," Allison sighed. "Wonder if I can
figure out which one of these is his."

I cut the boat's engine and drifted into the tall weeds
by the shore below the Quonset hut. The boat ground
against the rocks as it came to a stop.

There was a dock, sort of. The cement pylons were
still there, and a few boards not yet rotted to splinters. I
wasn't sure I wanted to trust them with my weight.

Ten feet to the left of the dock there was a sunken
boat sticking its prow out of the water. The remnants of
Bip's last customer, maybe.

I sloshed and slipped my way onto dry land. Allison
stayed right behind me. I looked up at the dark windows
and the closed door of the Quonset hut.

If Elgin was smart, if he was keeping watch because he
thought Les might show up here, he'd have his partner
Frank somewhere down here. Maybe at the Heidelmans,
or even inside Les' cabin. Of course if Elgin was smart,
he wouldn't have been so damn easy to spot on the
highway. I figured we had a fighting chance.

We climbed what passed for steps—old boards ham-
mered perpendicularly into the clay of the hill. The stairs
to the deck were on the side of the cabin. Nobody on the
highway could've seen us from there. Nobody jumped
out of the woods in commando gear. We made plenty of
creaks and cracks getting to the front door. If anybody
was inside, they'd sure as hell know we were coming.

The door was padlocked—one of those loops slotted
through a metal hinge. Dumb.

I got Allison to hand me a Phillips head out of my
backpack and removed the base of the hinge in less than
a minute. We could've gone through the window pretty
easily too, but I wasn't ready to break glass just yet.

We went inside the hut.

Allison said, "Yuck."

It was dark. It smelled like rotten food and sour
laundry. In the light of my pencil flashlight it was difficult

to piece together exactly what we were seeing, what happened here. There was an unmade single bed against the left wall. A portable stereo against the right littered all around with CDs and cassettes. The CD carriage was sticking out—the "drink holder," as my brother Garrett called it. The floor was covered in grass mat that was starting to tear into separate squares. The curved roof was covered with black cloth that just made the space seem more claustrophobic. In the back was a kitchenette and a phone and one shuttered window and a tiny walled-in area that must've been the bathroom.

When our eyes adjusted to the dark Allison went into the kitchen and lifted a pan of half-scrambled eggs from the electric grill. They were rubberized in places, crystallized in others.

"Two eggs for breakfast," Allison said. "Every day, no exceptions."

"He left halfway through making those," I said. "What do you think—about two or three days ago?"

Allison shuddered, put the pan down. "Something like that. So the bastard's alive."

She sounded less than thrilled. She gave me a tentative smile. "I guess I figured that. It's just—"

She hooked her thumbs in her borrowed Banana Republics, looked around at her feet where men's clothes were strewn around as if somebody had walked through a laundry pile. Then she kicked one of Les' shirts with a vengeance.

I went into the bathroom. A man's toiletry bag was in the sink, next to a propane-powered Destroilet with directions on the lid about how to avoid a house fire when you flushed.

I got out my Polaroid and took a picture of the toilet. Nobody would believe me about it, otherwise. Then I took some pictures of the rest of the cabin—the eggs, the laundry, the scattered CDs.

I went to the kitchen counter and picked up the phone. The line was active. I set the switch from touch tone to pulse and pressed redial. I was pretty sure I got the number on the first listen but I hung up before it rang, then tried it again. I wrote the number on my hand and let the phone ring. No answer on ten, no answering machine.

Allison said, "Tres."

I turned. She was looking at me reproachfully, holding the frying pan with the eggs. As quietly as possible she said, "Well? This or the Mace?"

"Wha—"

Then I heard the creaking, from outside, like someone trying to climb the old porch steps with at least some semblance of stealth.

38

A shadow moved across the yellow curtain into the doorway and became Frank the Bubba, my courteous shakedown deputy from the night before. He scowled and smushed his nose against the screen door, trying to see into the interior gloom. He was wearing jeans and an orange Hawaiian shirt. More advanced surveillance techniques.

I looked at Allison. "You're a lot of fun. But right now I want you to put down the frying pan, okay?"

"Are you crazy?"

"Put it down."

Frank's eyes adjusted to the dark. He focused on me. I smiled and waved. He looked at Allison. Slowly, she lowered the pan and waved too.

"If we had a gun," she speculated quietly, "we could've shot him five or six times by now."

"Shut up," I told her. "Please."

Frank opened the door and came inside.

His face was lye-scrubbed red and his eyes were

bleary. His blond mustache whiskers spiked at weird angles. He looked groggy and irritated but not particularly surprised.

"That's right," he said. "You two really need to be here."

The walkie-talkie on his belt made a click, then a metallic crackling sound. He kept his eyes on me while he picked it up. "Never mind, Garwood. False alarm."

The garbled response sounded vaguely like Elgin's voice. I couldn't make out what he said but apparently Frank could.

"Yeah," he said. "It was nothing."

Frank turned the volume knob down to zero.

"False alarm?" I asked.

Frank scanned the room, tapping the walkie-talkie against his thigh. "Elgin has some ideas what he might do if he ever sees you again. I don't want him to get too excited."

Frank looked around for a place to sit, opted for the bed. He sank into the foam mattress, hesitated, then crossed his legs and began to pry off his left boot.

"Got to excuse me," he grumbled. "Feet are killing me."

Allison said, "You want us to rub them for you?"

She was leaning against the kitchen counter, head on her hand like she was bored. She glanced at me and said, "*This* guy managed to get you on the pavement?"

Frank's ears turned the same color orange as his Hawaiian shirt. He raised his eyebrows at me. "New woman?"

"Allison Saint-Pierre. She's charming, really."

The name registered, maybe the reputation, too. Frank gave me a weary look of condolence. He switched legs and tugged off the other boot. His socks were two slightly different shades of blue.

"I didn't like what happened last night, Mr. Navarre. I didn't like it worth a damn."

"Try being the one with your nose in the gravel."

A smile flickered underneath the mustache. "You

don't get what I'm saying. People bother Mr. Sheckly, I got no problem pushing them around a little. That's not my beef."

"Reassuring."

Allison sighed. She fiddled wistfully with the Mace on her key chain, picking at the little plastic tab.

"Sheck takes care of his people," Frank continued. "It's a close-knit county out here. P.I.s come around all year long, sticking their noses into the Paintbrush's business, looking for paternity suits, blackmail photos, you name it. I don't have any problem dissuading them."

"Planting guns in their cars," I said.

Frank sat quiet for a long time, then apparently decided something. He sat forward, reached into his wallet, and pulled out a photograph.

"Look at this."

I took the photo. It showed Frank in white shorts and a different Hawaiian shirt, his arm around a similarly dressed plump blond woman. The woman was holding a white bundle that was either the world's largest Q-Tip pad or a well-swaddled baby.

"Got a family now," he said.

I smiled politely.

I handed the photo to Allison, who gave it the same bored once-over she'd given Frank.

"That means something to me," Frank insisted. "Gets me thinking in a different way. Taking care of friends, looking after people that've been good to the department—that's one thing. But throw-downs, and with a lady in the car—"

"Yeah," I agreed. "You really know how to draw the moral line."

He spread his hands. "All right. Maybe you don't want to hear it. I just wanted you to know—"

"That your partner didn't share his plans with you," I supplied. "Doesn't make me feel any better."

Frank stared into his empty boots, then sat up and began pulling them back on. "You don't understand how it is these days, Mr. Navarre."

"I understand two people have been murdered. I understand Tilden Sheckly's got some illegal business going on which he's very anxious not to have uncovered. I understand he's playing you for a fool, giving you the pissant jobs of shaking me down, doing surveillance on the least important places, where Les has already been scared away from. What am I missing?"

"He's chicken," Allison said.

Frank stared at her coldly. "You don't know me to say that. You don't know Sheck or what he's dealing with."

Allison laughed. "Like he's a victim?"

Frank's fists closed up and his eyes became unfocused. Something about his response bothered me. His anger turned into something more like embarrassment.

The walkie-talkie on his belt clicked.

He and I exchanged looks.

"I see two options, Frank. First is you help me out, tell me what's going on, maybe I can help you get to some people who will listen to your problems. The second option is you let Elgin in on this party and we see where it takes us. Which can you live with easier?"

Allison straightened up, smiling slightly, indicating that either option was just fine by her.

Frank stood. He looked around the tossed-up cabin one more time, then decided on a third option.

He picked up the walkie-talkie and turned on the volume. "Yo, Elgin, I'm trying again. I thought I saw something."

He took his finger off the button.

"You folks got one minute."

Allison pouted. It took a look of absolute steel for me to persuade her away from the kitchen counter and out the door.

As we walked past Frank his eyes stayed fixed on the back window. When I turned around in the doorway he was still standing like that, like a soldier at attention.

39

Allison and I hardly spoke on the boat ride back. We docked at Turk's, thanked Bip for the rental, and sloshed into the store with our lake-water-filled shoes. We went our separate ways in the little dusty aisles, then met back at Eustice's cash register.

I had nacho-flavored Doritos and a Nehi orange. Don't ask me why—when I'm stressed and disoriented I pick orange food. Never planned. It just happens. Sort of a dietary mood ring.

Allison had a twenty-ounce bottle of fortified wine.

I stared at the bottle, then at her.

"What?" she demanded.

"Death wish?"

"Fuck you."

Eustice shifted uncomfortably, tried to smile. "Ya'll have a nice evening."

We drove south, skirting the lake and heading toward the dam. The late afternoon sun was slicing through the tops of the live oaks, making the road furry with shadows and the lake glaring silver. Allison drank her grade A stomach destroyer and pushed my mother's purple glasses farther up on her nose and watched the scenery.

She only spoke when we failed to take the turn that led back to San Antonio. "We going somewhere?"

"One more stop on the Les Saint-Pierre tour."

"His body, I hope?"

I paused before answering, trying to keep down the irritation. "He's alive, Allison."

"Those deputy guys must've found him."

"They found the cabin. Knowing Frank and Elgin, they blew the surveillance somehow, let Les spot them before they spotted him. Les got out. He left Frank and Elgin sitting on the place, wondering when he would show up. That means Sheckly didn't kill Les, doesn't know where he is, and is anxious to find him."

"That makes one of us."

We drove over the dam. On the left-hand side the lake stretched out, twisted and glittery and dotted with little red racing boats trailing lines of wake. On the right-hand side the dam's cement walls sloped down to a valley of limestone chunks and tiny scrub brush and a much reduced Medina River, strained of everything except the sludge.

"Les left in a hurry," I said.

"Mmm."

"He was using the cabin as a stopover, someplace to complete his paperwork, collect his funds, settle into his new identity. Since he was flushed out prematurely, he'd need a place to go."

"Uh-huh."

I glanced over. Allison's head was starting to loosen on her neck, her jaw drifting up and down with the bumps in the road. She was frowning and underneath the purple sunglasses her eyes were closed. The wine bottle was empty.

"You okay?"

"I'm angry." She said it calmly, her face so relaxed that she almost didn't look like herself.

"Les left you. You can be angry."

"I didn't ask for your permission, Tres."

I raised my fingers off the steering wheel. "No, you didn't."

She wiped her cheek. "And I am not crying any tears for that bastard."

"No, you aren't."

We crossed the dam and headed around the east side of the lake. On the side of the road barefoot fishermen were making their way back to their cars. College kids were loading their water skis onto trailers. Allison continued not crying over Les Saint-Pierre and wiping her cheeks furiously. I kept my eyes on the road.

We were almost to the village of Plum Creek before she said, "So where did he go?"

"What?"

"If he got chased away from his hidey-hole before he was ready, where did he go? Hotel?"

"Too dangerous. Hotels remember long-term guests. There's a high risk he'd randomly run into somebody he knew. And he couldn't pay the bill without attracting notice—either by leaving a paper trail with a credit card or being conspicuous by using cash. No. More likely he'd pick somebody he trusted to put him up for a while. A best friend."

"Les has forty thousand of those."

"But people he'd trust to hide him?"

"Julie Kearnes," Allison decided. "Or the Danielses."

"The Danielses?"

She nodded, stretching out her legs and crossing them at the ankles. She stared down at her feet, now bare and white and wrinkled from the lake.

"Les started out treating them like pets or something. You know—simple folk. They needed to be groomed and cared for. Eventually he started liking their company. Willis is a sweet old fart most of the time, and Miranda's an angel. And Brent's a good listener, a little self-destructive like Les. Les became attached to him pretty quick."

"But you and Brent—"

Allison shrugged. "For the last month or so. I'm not sure Les knew and I'm not sure he would've cared if he did. With me and Brent it's just—it's not love or anything, sweetie."

She sounded like she was trying to reassure me, trying to explain away a minor illness she'd been fighting off.

"That the way Brent sees it?"

Allison laughed for the first time since we'd entered Les' cabin. "I imagine Brent sees me as some kind of trial to get past. I guess you haven't spent much time around him, Tres. He's sweet. He's also sensitive as a raw blister with all the stuff that's happened to him, tries to punish himself every time he thinks he might be enjoying life again. Been in his rut so long he's scared to come out, I guess. Sometimes I can't stand him. Sometimes it feels good to be with him."

"That's disturbing," I said.

"That I've slept with him?"

"No. Your assessment of who Les trusts enough to hide with."

"Because?"

"Julie Kearnes was killed. And the Danielses—is this phone number what I think it is?"

I read her the number on my hand, the last number that had been dialed from Les' cabin.

Allison stared out the side window. It was a quarter mile or so before she said, "The Danielses' ranch."

"Of course it may have been dialed months ago," I said, "before Les disappeared. It may have been an ordinary call to a client."

"Mmm."

We drove along, both of us trying to get comfortable with that idea.

We turned past the Plum Creek Dairy Queen.

The boat storage facility was uphill, a good fifty yards from the water. It was a gravel clearing fenced off with chain link and barbed wire with a large drive-through gate. Inside were storage sheds of corrugated metal and plywood, each just big enough to house a boat on a trailer. When I drove up, the gate was open and a family was hitching up their outboard to a Subaru four-wheeler. Or Mom was doing it anyway. The two kids were making like a trampoline in the backseat and the dad was studying a *Sports Illustrated* swimsuit edition in the driver's seat. Allison and I got out and helped Mom get the hitch in place and connect the brake lights. Mom gave us a nice smile and asked if she should just leave the gate open. We said sure.

Les' boat shed was A12.

The chain and padlock on Les' shed door were new. Fortunately the back wall of the shed was not. The metal peeled up easily on the bottom, giving us just enough space to crawl underneath.

The walls of the shed didn't go all the way to the roof. There was about a foot of space at the top to let in light, enough to see by. Les' boat was just like Kelly Arguello had said, a twenty-five-footer with a collapsed mast and the deck covered with a blue tarp. The tarp was tied on haphazardly but with a lot of knots and enthusiasm. We finally had to cut our way through.

I climbed onto the aft deck, then gave Allison a hand up.

The bench seats on board were white rubbery material embedded with silver glitter. There was a small empty cabin below, a closet really. No way more than one person could fit down there.

"Okay," Allison said. "So it's a boat. So what?"

"Hold on."

I went below and searched. Nothing. On the tank of a tiny toilet was a copy of *Time*, August three years ago. Not encouraging.

When I came back topside Allison was prodding the deck floor with her foot. Whenever she pushed down, the blue plastic showed a square of seams about two feet by two feet.

"Life vest compartment," I said.

She and I exchanged looks.

"Why not?" I agreed.

Two minutes later we were sitting on the bench with an unearthed ice chest between us.

It was a green Igloo big enough to hold two six-packs. When we opened it there was no beer, though. There were stacks of money. Fifty-dollar bills, the same as Milo had paid me with. About fifty thousand dollars' worth. There was also a computer printout of addresses—some in San Antonio, some in Dallas and Houston. Next to each address was a date.

In case of drowning, look up addresses. Throw large quantities of money. Les Saint-Pierre, the safety conscious ship's captain.

Allison hefted a stack of fifties. "What the holy fuck—"

"Later. Right now we get this to the car."

Allison looked dazed, but she helped me repack the ice chest, get it over the side of the boat, then wedge it under the storage unit's tin wall. On our way back to the Audi, each of us carrying one handle of the Igloo, we left the gate open for another family that was coming in to collect their boat.

Maybe they too were stashing money and addresses in their shed.

They smiled and waved their thanks. I smiled back.

Everyone is so damn friendly in the country.

40

The drive back started out well enough.

Allison was coming down off her twenty ounces of bad wine and was starting to warm up to the realization that we had fifty thousand dollars stashed under the backseat. By the time we got onto the highway she was recapping the afternoon in glowing terms, throwing out casual insults about her idiot husband and the Avalon County Sheriff's Department. She suggested we drive out to Miranda's gig at the Paintbrush, see if we could find any more deputies to beat up.

"But first better clothes," she insisted. She tugged on my T-shirt sleeve. "I'm not going with this. And you've got to have cowboy boots."

"I've worn cowboy boots exactly once. It was not a success."

"Tell."

"No thanks."

But she kept nagging until, reluctantly, I told her about the photo my mother still shows off whenever I'm

foolish enough to bring friends over—me two years old,
thigh-deep in the Sheriff's black Lucheses, trying not to
fall over, my cloth diaper sagging obscenely.

Allison laughed. "You're due for another try."

We didn't tell Rhonda Jean at Sheppler's Western
Wear about the diaper photo. We didn't tell her we
looked so bad this evening because we'd been breaking
into places all around Medina Lake. We just told her we
needed a quick change of clothes before the store closed,
in fifteen minutes.

Rhonda Jean smiled. A challenge.

Fourteen minutes later she had me outfitted in boot-
cut Levi's and a cotton pieced red and white shirt and
size eleven natural tan Justins. I vetoed the hat and the
rattlesnake belt that she promised me she could have
engraved with TRES on the back at no extra charge.
Allison came out sporting a white fringed shirt and black
boots and tight-fitting jeans that only a woman with an
excellent figure could've gotten away with wearing.
Allison got away with it pretty well.

Rhonda Jean nodded her approval, then sent us on to
the cashier. I paid with the last of the fifties Milo had
given me at Tycoon Flats.

Allison watched as I emptied my wallet. "You're paying out of pocket? With all we've got stashed in the car?"

The cashier gave us a very funny look. I smiled at
Allison and said, "Let's go, darlin'."

Back in the Audi we drove with the windows down.
The wind was almost cool now, whipping around the
front seats and sending the medicine pouch beads on the
rearview mirror into a little jellyfish dance. Allison had
taken off the sunglasses and her eyes seemed softer and
darker than they had been before.

I was starting to turn some things around in my head,
ideas about the addresses we'd found and the money and
the trail Les Saint-Pierre had left.

"You know much about the record industry?" I
asked.

Allison held her hands far apart, like she was bragging

about a fish. "Two years with Les Saint-Pierre, cowboy. What you wanna know?"

"CDs."

"What about them?"

"If you were importing them from overseas in large quantities, how would they be packed? Boxes? Crates?"

"Uh-unh. Spools."

"Cylinders."

"Yeah. Big ones. The jewel cases and covers are only added in the destination country, with local suppliers. It's cheaper that way. Why?"

"So much for keeping the business modest."

"What?"

I waited a half mile before responding. "We should talk about the money."

"What's to talk about? Les was stupid enough to forget it when he ran, it reverts to me. You want a finder's fee, sweetie?"

"Les probably embezzled that money from the agency."

Allison stared at me. "So?"

"So it isn't yours. I'll store it for a while, until I know what's what. Then, most likely, it'll go to the debtor's court."

"You're kidding."

I didn't respond. We had come all the way back to Loop 410 to hit Sheppler's and were now heading north again, ostensibly to go to the Paintbrush. I missed the Leon Valley exit and kept driving, circling the city.

"You're going to do Milo Chavez a fifty-thousand-dollar favor," Allison decided.

"That's not what I said."

"That's what it amounts to—bailing his ass out of debt and leaving me nothing. That's what you're thinking, isn't it?"

"I'm thinking you're overreacting again."

Allison stomped her shiny new boot against the floorboard. She crossed her arms and looked out into the hills. "Shithead."

We passed I-10, kept going. I exited on West Avenue and turned left, toward downtown.

"Maybe I should just take you back," I suggested. "Let you collect your car."

"Maybe so."

We drove in silence. West Avenue. Hildebrand. Broadway. Saturday night was unfolding all along the avenues—neon bar signs and low-rider cars and slow-cruising pickup trucks. The air was laced with the smell of family barbecues, pork ribs, and roasted peppers.

When we finally got back to Queen Anne Street I cut the engine and the lights. We sat there, staring at Allison's crookedly parked Miata, until Allison began to laugh.

She turned toward me. Her breath smelled faintly of fortified wine. "All right. Don't get the wrong idea, sweetie."

"What wrong idea is that?"

She reached over and pushed a couple of buttons on my new Western shirt. "That I didn't appreciate the day with you. I got a little upset, that's all. I don't want you thinking—"

"The money is staying in storage, Allison."

She blinked slowly, processing what I said, then decided to laugh again. "You think that's all I'm interested in?"

"I don't know."

"Fuck you, then." She said it almost playfully. She leaned toward me slowly, tugging my shirt, inviting me to meet her halfway.

Something twisted in my throat. I managed to move her hand away and say, "Not a good idea."

She pulled back, raised her eyebrows. "All right."

When she got out of the car she slammed the door, then turned and smiled in the window at me. "You and Milo have fun dividing up Les' estate, Tres. Thanks for the good time."

I watched her get in her car, start the engine and pull

off the curb with a grind and a thump, and drive away. I reminded myself that was really what I wanted.

I sat in the dark Audi, leaned my head against the back of the seat, and exhaled. *Feel lucky,* I thought. *You just spent seven hours with that woman and neither of you shed any blood.* But when I closed my eyes they burned. I tried to replay our afternoon ten different ways, going through all the placating things or the really nasty things I could've said. It made me feel even more dissatisfied and infuriated than I had been before.

I should've gone out to the Indian Paintbrush. I had plenty of new questions for Mr. Sheckly, some reports to give Milo, a lady to see who would be singing "Billy's Señorita" right about now, looking out at the audience with some very fine brown eyes.

Instead I got out of the car, my legs shaky from the long car ride, and wobbled toward my in-law apartment with the feeling that somewhere under the waterline, somewhere toward the prow, I had just been torpedoed.

41

 I tried to treat Sunday morning like the start of any other day. I did my tai chi, had breakfast with Robert Johnson, made a fifty-thousand-dollar deposit under my landlord's antique rosebush.

Then I drove to Vandiver Street before anyone would be awake at my mother's house, left the Audi out front and the key in the mailbox, and reclaimed the VW.

I headed south toward the State Insurance Building.

If the tower had been downtown it would've been invisible, but where it was—stuck in the middle of the flatlands south of SAC, surrounded by parks and one-story office complexes, it looked huge. The parking lot only had a handful of cars, one of them being Samuel Barrera's mustard BMW.

I punched the elevator button for level six and was deposited in front of a frosted glass door that still bore faint discolored outlines from the stencil letters that used to read: SAMUEL BARRERA, INVESTIGATIONS. Now there was a classy brass plaque above a classy ivory and gold buzzer. The plaque read I-TECH.

I didn't opt for the buzzer. I walked into the waiting room and went up to the little sliding window like they have in dentists' offices. The window was open.

The receptionist was so short that she had to crane her neck to see me over the top of the counter. Her hair was mostly calcified hair spray that curled away from her face in capital letter *U*'s.

"Help you?" she inquired.

I smiled. I straightened my tie. "Tres Navarre. I'm here to see Sam."

She frowned. People weren't supposed to come in on Sunday morning asking for Barrera, especially by first name. "Won't you sit down?"

"I will."

The sliding-glass panel shut in my face.

I sat on the sofa and read the latest company bulletin from I-Tech headquarters in New York. There was some propaganda about how well the company was doing snapping up private firms in various states and selling them back to their owners like McDonald's franchises. One ad aimed at outside readers told me exactly what it took to be "I-Tech material."

I was just assessing my I-Tech potential when the inner office door opened and Sam Barrera came out. He walked up to me and said, "What the fuck do you want, Navarre?"

I put down the news bulletin.

Barrera was wearing the standard three-piece suit, brown this time. His tie was a shade of yellow that miraculously matched. His gold rings were newly polished and his cologne was strong.

"We need to talk," I said.

"No we don't."

"I went out to Medina Lake, Sam."

The sunglass-metal quality in Barrera's eyes got a little harder. "You will be talked to, Navarre. But it won't be by me. You'd better tell Erainya—"

"There was more than a cabin out there, Sam. You missed something."

Just for a second, Sam Barrera wasn't sure what to say. It had probably been years since anyone dared to suggest he had missed something. It had probably never come from an amateur half his age.

"Parks and Wildlife," I said.

Barrera processed quickly. His face went through a chameleon phase—red to brown to coffee color. "Saint-Pierre had a boat? He registered a *freshwater* boat?"

"Would you like to know what I found, or would you like to threaten me some more?"

He was quiet long enough for the cement in his expression to resettle. "You want to come in back?"

He turned on his heel without waiting for my answer. I followed.

Sam's office was a shrine to Texas A & M. The carpet was plush maroon and the drapes were the same. On the mahogany bookshelf, pothos plants were carefully interspersed with Aggie diplomas and photos of Sam and his sons in their Corps uniforms.

On Sam's desk were photos of Barrera with his friends—law enforcement types, the mayor, businessmen. In one photo Barrera stood next to my father. The Sheriff's '76 campaign, I think. Dad was smiling. Barrera, of course, was not.

Sam sat down behind his desk. I sat across from him in a large maroon chair that was strategically designed to be too cushy and low-set. I had the feeling of being much shorter than my host, trapped in an interrogation cup.

"Tell me." Sam leaned forward and stared and waited.

"Bootlegs," I said. "Sheckly's been recording his headliner acts, creating master tapes in his studio, then shipping the tapes to Europe for production and distribution. More recently he's gotten greedier, started to import the CDs back into the U.S. That's why you and your federal friends have been stepping up the heat."

Sam brushed my comments aside. "What was in the boat?"

"First I want confirmation."

Sam curled his fingers. The wrath of God built up behind his eyes—a collected, intense darkness meant to warn me that I was about to be smitten from the earth. He looked around his desk, maybe for something to kill me with, and focused instead on the picture of himself and the Sheriff. Some annoyance crept into his expression.

"I suppose you will continue to screw things up unless I level with you, Navarre. Or unless I get someone to throw you in jail."

"Most likely."

"Goddamn your father."

"Amen."

Sam readjusted his belly above his belt line. He turned his chair sideways and stared out the window.

"The scenario you described is commonplace. Frequently someone at a venue records the shows. Frequently the recordings turn up as bootlegs."

He waited to see if I was satisfied, if I would give in now. I just smiled.

Sam's jaw tightened. "What is uncommon with the Indian Paintbrush situation is the scale. Mr. Sheckly is presently recording something like fifty name artists a year. The master tapes are sent through Germany to CD plants, mostly in Romania and the Czech Republic, then distributed to something like fifteen countries. More recently, as you said, his partners in Europe have been encouraging Mr. Sheckly to target the U.S. market, moving him from boots to pirates."

"What's the difference?"

"Boots are auxiliary recordings, Navarre—studio practice sessions, live recordings, cuts you couldn't get in the store normally. Sheckly's radio shows, for instance. Pirates are different—they're exact copies of legitimate releases. Boots can make money, but pirate copies undercut the regular market, take the place of legitimate work. They have massive potential. You make them well, you can even pass them off to major suppliers—department stores, mall chains, you name it."

"And Sheckly's are good?"

Barrera opened his desk drawer and got out a CD. He took the disc from the case and pointed with his pinkie at the silver numbers etched around the hole. "This is one of Sheckly's pirate copies. The lot numbers on the SIDs are almost correct. Even if the Customs officials knew what they were looking for, which they rarely do, they might pass this. The covers, once they're added, are four-color printing, quality paper stock. Even on the boots Sheck's taken precautions. The liner notes are stamped 'manufactured in the E.U.' This is meant to make one think it's a legit import, explain the difference in packaging."

"How profitable?"

Barrera tapped a finger on the desk. "Let me put it this way. It's rare that you have one syndicate controlling the manufacture *and* distribution of so many recordings in so many countries. The only similar case I know of, the IFPI confiscated the receipts of an Italian operation. For one quarter, one artist's work, the pirates pulled in five million dollars. It'd be less for country music, but still— Multiply the number of artists, four quarters a year, you get the idea."

"Business worth killing for," I said. "What's the IFPI?"

"International Federation of Phonographic Industries. European version of the RIAA in the States."

"Your client."

Barrera hesitated. "I never said that. You understand?"

"Perfectly. Tell me about Sheckly's German friends."

"Luxembourg."

"Pardon?"

"The syndicate is based in Luxembourg. Just so happens Sheckly made his connections in Bonn, does most of his business in Germany."

I shook my head. "Help me out, Barrera. Luxembourg is the little country?"

"The little country known for laundering mob money, yes. The little country known for maintaining loopholes in the E.U.'s copyright laws. The pirates love Luxembourg."

I sat for a while and tried to process it. I was determined not to feel out of my league, not to show Barrera I was going to run from the room screaming if he gave me one more acronym.

"Sheckly got himself into a dangerous association," I said.

Barrera came the closest I'd ever seen to a laugh. It was a small noise in the back of his nose, easily mistaken for a sniff. Nothing else in his face moved.

"Don't start shedding tears, Navarre. Mr. Sheckly's pulling down a few million extra a year."

"But Blanceagle's murder, and Julie Kearnes'—"

"Sheckly may not have ordered them but I doubt he had much of a conscience attack. It's true, Navarre, bootlegging is usually white-collar stuff, not very violent. But we're talking a large syndicate, into gunrunning and credit cards numbers and several other things."

"And Jean?"

"Jean Kraus. He's beaten murder raps in three countries. One victim was a young French boy, about thirteen, son of Jean's girlfriend. He decided to lift some of Jean's petty cash. They found the kid in an alley in Rouen, thrown out a fifth-story hotel window."

"Jesus."

Barrera nodded. "Kraus is smart. Probably too smart to get caught. He's over here encouraging Sheck's CD distribution network in the U.S. It's only a matter of time before Jean and his bosses start using Sheckly's trucking lines for their other interests—guns, especially. That's finally what got the D.A. and the Bureau and ATF interested. It takes a lot of fire-stoking to get them excited about stolen music."

"Your big league friends."

"We've got a case for mail fraud in four states, interstate

commerce violations—orders placed and filled with some
of Sheckly's distributors. Even that has taken years to
assemble, to get a judge interested enough to grant access
to Sheckly's bank statements and phone records. Throw in
the fact that Avalon County law enforcement is in Sheckly's
pocket—it's been tough going. Ninety percent of a case like
this has to be informants inside."

"Les Saint-Pierre. He made himself your solution."

"What?"

"Something his wife said. He was your in."

"To Julie Kearnes, yes. And Alex Blanceagle. And all
three of them disappeared as soon as they started talking.
We may lose the interest of the State Attorney's Office if
we don't get more soon, something solid. Now it's your
turn. What was in the boat?"

I took out the addresses I'd found in the ice chest—
locations with dates next to them. I handed them to
Barrera.

Barrera frowned at the paper. When he was done
reading he looked out the window again and his shoulders drooped. "All right."

"They're distribution points, aren't they? Dates when
shipments of CDs will arrive."

Barrera nodded without much enthusiasm.

"You've got locations," I prompted. "You know what
Sheckly is doing. You can stage a raid."

Barrera said, "We have nothing, Navarre. We have no
grounds for requesting a search warrant—no evidence
linking anyone to anything, just some random addresses
and dates. Maybe eventually, that information will lead
us somewhere. Not immediately. I was hoping for more."

"You've been building the case for what—six years?"
I asked.

Barrera nodded.

"Chances are Sheckly knows," I said, "or he's going to
know soon that this information is compromised. You
don't move on it now, they'll move the goods, change
their routes. You'll lose them."

"I'll go another six years rather than get the case

thrown out of court because we acted stupid. Thanks for the information."

We sat quietly, listening to the A & M Fighting Aggie clock tick on Barrera's back wall.

"One more thing," I said. "I think Les fled to the Danielses. Or at least he considered it."

I told Barrera about the phone call from the lake cabin.

"He would be stupid to go there," Sam said.

"Maybe. But if *I* got the idea Les might've enlisted their help, Sheckly's friends could get the same idea. I don't like that possibility."

"I'll have someone go out and talk to the family."

"I'm not sure that will help the Danielses much."

"There's nothing else I can do, Navarre. Even under the best of circumstances, it will be several more months before we can coordinate any kind of action against Mr. Sheckly."

"And if more people die between now and then?"

Barrera tapped on the desk again. "The chances of the Daniels family getting targeted are very slim. Sheckly has bigger problems, bigger people to worry about."

"Bigger people," I repeated. "Like thirteen-year-old boys who steal Jean Kraus' petty cash."

Barrera exhaled. His chair creaked as he stood up. "I'm going to say what I said before, Navarre. You're into something over your head and you need to get out. You don't have to take my word for it. I've leveled with you. Is this something an unlicensed kid with a couple of years on the street can handle?"

I looked again at the photo of Barrera and my father. My father, as in all his photos, seemed to grin out at me as if there was a huge private joke he wasn't sharing, almost certainly something that was humorous at my expense.

"Okay," I said.

"Okay you're off the case?"

"Okay you've given me a lot to think about."

Barrera shook his head. "That's not good enough."

"You want me to lie to you, Sam? You want to go ahead and arrest me? Avalon County would approve of that approach."

Barrera sniffed, moved over to his window, and looked out over the city of San Antonio. It was deadly still on a Sunday morning—a rumpled gray and green blanket dotted with white boxes, laced with highways, the rolling ranchland beyond a dark blue-green out to the horizon.

"You're too much like your father," Barrera said.

I was about to respond, but something in the way Barrera was standing warned me not to. He was contemplating the correct thing to do. He would have to turn around soon and deal with me, decide which agency he needed to turn me over to for dissection. He would have to do that as long as I was a problem, sitting in his office, telling him what was unacceptable to hear.

I removed the problem. I stood up and left him standing by the window. I closed the office door very quietly on my way out.

42

The day heated up quickly.

By eleven, when I exited the highway for Ranch Road 22 in Bulverde, the clouds had burned away and the hills were starting to shimmer. I took the turn for Serra Road, then drove over the cattle guard and pulled my VW under the giant live oak in front of the Danielses' ranch house.

No one answered the front door so I walked around by the horseshoe pit.

The back field looked like a playground for the Army Corps of Engineers—pyramids of PVC and copper pipes, crisscrossed trenches, mounds of caliche soil. The other night it had been too dark to see the extent of the work.

Leaning against a utility shed out beyond the chicken coop were three metal canisters a little smaller than cars—septic tanks. Two were dull silver and pitted with rust holes. The third was new and white but caked here and there with clods of dirt, as if it had been improperly installed and then dug up again.

The riderless backhoe squatted at the end of a trench, its shovel nuzzling the caliche. The backhoe was speckled with dirt and machine oil but looked fairly new, painted the green and yellow of a rental company.

I heard a tape playing out beyond the tractor shed. It was spare acoustic guitar and male vocal—like early Willie Nelson.

I walked that direction. The horse in the neighboring field watched me with her neck leaning into the top of the barbed wire while she chewed on an apple half.

When I got closer I realized the tape I was hearing was one of the songs Miranda performed, only changed for a male singer. When I got around the other side of the shed I realized I wasn't hearing a tape at all. It was Brent Daniels singing.

He was sitting in one of two lawn chairs against the far wall of his tractor-shed apartment, next to the chicken coop. He was facing the hills and strumming his Martin for the hens.

His hair was tousled into a thin wet black mess, like he'd just showered. He wore a T-shirt and denim shorts.

There was a stack of Dixie cups and a bottle of Ryman whiskey on the tree stump next to him. He'd made a bold start on the bottle. He was singing his heart out and for the first time I realized just how good he really was.

He didn't hear me coming up, or he didn't care. I stayed about twenty yards away and listened to him finish the song. He gave the impression that he was singing to somebody on the hilltop over on the horizon.

When Brent finished he let the guitar slide off his lap, then he picked up the whiskey bottle and poured himself a cupful. He slugged it down and glanced at me.

"Navarre."

"I thought you were a recording."

Daniels frowned. "You want Miranda, she's in Austin, mixing the demo. Willis is out getting more finger pipes."

"In that case, mind if I join you?"

He deliberated, like he wanted to say no but was so out of practice turning down social requests that he didn't remember how. He held the stack of Dixie cups toward me. I took one off the top, then sat in the other lawn chair.

You could see a long way off. The hills in the distance were green. The sky was blue the way amusement park water is blue—an unnatural, dyed-for-the-tourists kind of look, with foamy little scraps of cloud. A couple of turkey buzzards circled about half a mile to the north, over a clump of trees. Dead cow or deer, probably. To the east there was a brown zigzag of haze from someone's brushfire.

The Ryman whiskey burned its way down my throat.

"Les' brand, isn't it?"

Brent shrugged. "He gives it out. Door prizes."

I wanted to ask some questions but the country air, the country mood, had started working on me. I realized how tired I was, how tired I'd been for the past few weeks.

The midday sun was warm but not unpleasant, just enough to burn the last of the dew off the chicken wire and get some warmth into my bones. The hills invited quiet spectating. The reasons I had come out to the ranch house started unknitting in my head.

"You play out here often?"

Some shadows deepened around Brent's eyes. "I suppose."

"Y'all got another gig tonight?"

He shook his head. "Just Miranda. She's got a show-up scheduled with Robert Earle Keen at Floore's Country Store. I suppose Milo's going to bring her back down for that."

I dabbed the flakes of Dixie cup wax off the surface of the liquor. "Miranda doesn't drive at all, does she?"

I hadn't even considered that fact until I said it. I hadn't questioned it Friday night, when I'd given her a lift into town, or the other times when she'd gotten rides with Milo or her father. The fact that I had just naturally accepted it, not even thought about it as odd, disturbed me for some reason I couldn't quite put into words.

"Not that she can't," Brent said. "She doesn't."

"Why?"

Brent glanced at me briefly, declined comment.

He picked up his guitar again and picked the strings so lightly I almost couldn't hear the notes. His hand changed chords fast, contorting into various claw shapes on the fret board.

"You ever get frustrated with her playing your songs?" I asked. "Getting all the attention for your music?"

Brent kept playing quietly, looking at the hills as he worked his fret board, occasionally twitching his eye as he reached for a harder note. His face and his hands reminded me of a deep-sea fisherman's as he worked his rod and reel.

"She was grateful at first," he said. "Told me she couldn't have done it without me—that she owed me everything. She gives you those bright eyes—" He smiled, a kind of sad amusement. Suddenly he looked like his father, a leaner version, less gray, weathered a little sooner and a little more harshly, but still Willis' son. "Guess *you're* the cavalry now, ain't you, Navarre?"

"You never thought much of Milo hiring a private eye."

"Nothin' personal," he said. "Seems to me Les has ditched us, Milo's trying to prove he's got things under control. It's not—I appreciate—" He stopped himself, not sure how to proceed. "Miranda was talking about you yesterday. She seemed to feel a lot easier about things—said you were a good man. I do appreciate that."

He meant it, but there was an uneasiness in his tone I couldn't quite nail down. "Something about her Century Records deal is bothering you."

He shook his head uncertainly.

"Has Les tried to call you?"

Brent frowned. "Why would he?"

"Just a thought. You don't figure he would've contacted Miranda?"

"Les is gone for good. That's pretty obvious, ain't it?"

"Is that what Allison's hoping?"

Brent played a few more chords. His focus moved farther away by a few hundred miles. "It never should have happened between me and her."

"None of my business."

Brent shook his head sadly.

For no reason I could see he decided to start singing again. It was a pretty tune—one of his slow ones, "The Widower's Two-Step."

Coming straight from Brent the song was a hundred times sadder. I could almost feel the weight of the tractor-shed apartment on his back, imagine a young woman in there, pregnant, dying from some condition I couldn't even remember the name of.

I got myself another Dixie cup full of whiskey. The liquor made a warm heavy coating around my lungs.

When Brent finished the last verse we were quiet for a long time. The sun was nice. The circling buzzards and the horse pawing up the field and even the frantic, coked-up movements of the chickens were all getting more and more fascinating the more I drank. I could've settled into that lawn chair for the rest of my life, I figured.

"You get any money from the songs?" I asked. "Allison was saying something—"

Brent nodded. "Quarter royalties."

"A quarter?"

"Half to the publisher."

"And the other quarter?"

"Goes to Miranda as co-writer."

"She co-wrote the songs?"

"No. But it's standard," Brent said. "The artist who records the song gets half credit for writing it even if they didn't. Looks better on the album that way. It's a trade-off for them choosing your material."

"Even if she's your sister?"

"Les said it's standard."

I watched the turkey buzzards. "Seems like Miranda could've made it unstandard."

He shrugged. I couldn't tell whether he cared or not. I wondered what conversations Allison had had with him about that.

"Les ever stay at the ranch house?" I asked.

He nodded reluctantly. "Once. I was following him back from a gig one night, he run himself off the road from all the drink and pills. Had to convince him to come back here and sleep it off. He wasn't a happy fella. He talked a lot about self-destructing that night."

"How'd you handle it?"

Brent played a chord. "Told him I'd been there."

He sang another song. I drank more. My feet were pleasantly numb and I was enjoying the sound of Brent Daniels' voice. I felt easy and comfortable for the first time in days. Not thinking about whether I wanted to become a licensed P.I. or a college teacher or a neon blue bearded lady for Cirque du Soleil.

Brent and I talked some more in between songs. It was like having a bilingual conversation—shifting in and out of singing and talking until there stopped being a difference. After a while Brent started doing other people's music—"Silver Wings" and "Faded Love" and "Angel Flying Too Close to the Ground." Stuff that reminded me of my dad's record collection. God forbid maybe I even mumbled along with Brent as he sang.

Things got blurry after that, but I remember during one of the silent places saying, "Les hasn't played straight with anybody this whole time. He wouldn't be worth protecting."

I wanted to look at him, see his reaction, but my eyes were closed and I was enjoying them that way.

"I gave up on protection a long time ago," Brent said.

His voice was a sad sound, the chords bright and airy behind it.

The last thing I remember, he was singing something about a train.

43

I woke up with the feeling that somebody had hooked me to a reverse IV. All the fluid had drained out of my mouth and my eyes and my brain. When I moved my head everything turned white. I realized, belatedly, that I was feeling pain.

I sat up on the metal cot and rubbed my face where it had pressed itself into the texture of the rayon. One of the yellow curtains was open and light was pouring directly onto my chest.

Other things came into focus—a folding card table with a bucket of silverware on it. A wooden bunk bed, the bottom bunk stripped to the springs. A *Playboy* wall calendar that was still stuck on Miss August. The walls were the same inside the little tractor-shed apartment as they were outside—rough wood, painted red. What few pictures there were hung from bare nails. Brent's carving knife was stuck directly into the wall above the tiny sink. There was no oven—no kitchen to speak of. Just a hot pad and a coffeemaker and a mini-refrigerator.

It was possible that a woman might've lived here once, but you couldn't've proved it.

I tried to get up.

I tried again.

When I finally succeeded I realized where all the fluid in my body had drained to. I looked around for the rest room.

It was a tiny closet behind a shower curtain. Everything was close together. The sink overlapped the toilet tank and the shower drained directly into the tile floor so you could, conceivably, use the toilet and take a shower and brush your teeth all at the same time.

I only tried option number one.

It wasn't until I rummaged in the medicine cabinet, hoping for aspirin, that I found some reminder of the woman who had once lived here—orange prescription bottles, at least ten of them, all typed faintly with the name Marla Daniels. Insulin A. Prenatal vitamin supplements. Glucophage. Several other names I hadn't ever heard of. Some were open, as if she'd just taken her prescription this morning. As if nothing had been touched in the cabinet in two years. In the corner, behind the container of white Glucophage tablets, was a baby teether still in its plastic wrapper.

I picked it up. Little glittery shapes—diamonds, squares, stars—floated through the liquid inside the plastic ring, sluggish and sterile.

Behind me Brent Daniels said, "You're up."

I closed the cabinet.

When I turned Brent was trying his best not to notice what I'd been doing. He fingered the edge of the shower curtain.

His hair had dried, and his face was clean-shaven. Except for the eyes, he didn't look like a man who'd been drinking as heavily as I had.

"Miranda called," he told me. "Said Milo was going to be mixing for the rest of the afternoon and did I want to pick her up early. I could, or—?"

"I'll drive up."

Brent nodded, like it was bad news he'd been expecting. He gestured behind him with his chin. I followed him out into the apartment, which was just big enough for the two of us.

Brent opened a cabinet above the little refrigerator and retrieved a bag of flour tortillas and a can of refried beans.

"Hungry?"

My stomach did a slow roll. I shook my head no.

Brent shrugged and cranked up the hot pad. I stared at the picture that was taped inside the pantry door—a black and white of a woman with short brunette hair, a slightly moonish face, an almost uncontainable smile, like she was being tickled.

"That Marla?"

Brent tensed, looked around to see what I was talking about. When he realized I meant the picture he relaxed.

"No. My mother."

"You were how old?"

He knew what I meant. "Almost twenty." Then, like it was something he was obliged to add, something he'd been corrected on many times, "Miranda was only six."

Brent threw a tortilla directly on the hot pad. He watched as it began to puff up and bubble. The tortilla was probably old and flat but after a minute on the grill it would taste almost as good as fresh. The only correct way to heat a tortilla.

"Willis might not be too happy with you driving to pick Miranda up," he speculated.

"But you don't mind."

He flipped the tortilla. One of the air bubbles had cracked open and the edges had blackened.

"Maybe I will take some," I decided.

Brent made no comment, but got another tortilla out of the bag.

"I don't mind," he finally agreed. "Dad . . ." He trailed off.

"He's got an unpredictable temper, doesn't he?"

Brent was staring at the picture of his mother.

" 'Billy Señorita,' " I said. "The only song Miranda wrote herself—it was about your parents."

Brent stirred up the refried beans. "The fights weren't as bad as that."

"But scary to a six-year-old."

Brent stared at me. He let a little anger burn through the dead ash. "You want to think about something—think how Willis feels, hearing that song every night. Put him in his place, all right. Worked like a charm."

I did what Brent said. I thought about it.

Brent added a little pepper and a little butter and salt to the beans. When they were smoking he spread them on the flour tortillas, folded them, and handed one to me. We sat and ate.

I stared out the side window into the tractor shed. An enormous orange cat was sleeping on the seat of the rusty John Deere. A couple of doves were in the rafters above. My gaze shifted over to the ceiling above me.

"What's up there?" I asked.

"Attic now. Used to be the sewing room."

"Sewing?"

Brent looked at me, a little resentful that he had to say anything else. "Marla."

I turned my attention back to my bean roll.

"I want to tell you something," I decided.

Brent waited, not concerned one way or the other.

Maybe it was his passivity that made me want to talk. Maybe the midday whiskey hangover. Maybe it was just easier than telling his sister. Whatever it was, I told Brent Daniels pretty much the whole story—about Sheckly's bootlegging, about Jean Kraus, about how people that were in a position to give information on Sheckly's business were disappearing, either by choice or not.

Brent listened quietly, eating his bean roll. Nothing seemed to shock him.

When I was done he said, "You don't want to go telling Miranda all this. It'll kill her right now. Wait for her to finish her tape."

"Miranda may be in danger. You too, for that matter.

What was Jean Kraus arguing with you about—that night at the party?"

Brent smirked. "Jean, he'll argue about anything. That don't mean he's going to kill me and my family."

"I hope you're right. I hope Les doesn't bring you folks the kind of luck he brought Julie Kearnes. Or Alex Blanceagle."

Brent's eyes started collecting shadows again. "Miranda doesn't need this."

"But you're not concerned. You don't worry about Les making problems for you."

Brent shook his head slowly.

He was a hard person to judge. There could've been a lie there. Or maybe not. The weathered face and the years of hardness covered up just about everything.

"Tough for me to let somebody in here," he said finally. He stared off at the rough red walls of the apartment.

I sat there for another few seconds before I realized he'd just told me to leave.

44

 By the time I picked up Miranda at Silo Studios, another promised cold front had edged its way south and stalled, pressing humid air and gray clouds over Austin like a sweaty electric blanket.

The folks seventy miles north in Waco were probably cool and comfortable. Then again, they were in Waco.

Milo Chavez was too busy to speak to me. He and one of the engineers were glued to the sound board, listening in awe to the new vocal tracks Miranda had laid down over the last two mornings.

"Fifteen takes," Milo mumbled to me. "Fifteen god-damn takes of 'Billy's Señorita' and she blew it away in one try this morning. My God, Navarre, losing that first demo tape was the best thing that ever happened to us."

He laid his hand on the little BOSE speaker like he was consecrating it.

Chavez agreed to let me take Miranda back to S.A. early as long as I got her to her appearance tonight on time. Miranda said she was starving. She suggested lunch on the way back to town. I had a conscience attack and called my brother Garrett to see if he could join us. Unfortunately he could.

When we got to the Texicali Grille we found Garrett at an outside table. He'd pulled his wheelchair under one of the metal umbrellas and Dickhead the parrot was waddling stiffly back and forth on his shoulder. Danny Young, the owner of the Texicali, was sitting backward in the chair across the table.

Danny was a family friend, connected to the Navarres through a network of South Texas kin and near-kin that I never could quite remember.

Many years back Danny had moved his restaurant business from Kingsville to Austin and decided to grant himself an honorary double degree in alternative politics and burger-flipping. He announced that the half of Austin below the Colorado River must secede from the growing yuppiness of the north, so he hoisted a green XXXL T-shirt up the flagpole at the Texicali and started calling himself the Mayor of South Austin. I think Danny's political platform said something about flip-flops and salsa and Mexican beer. I'd told him he could annex San Antonio anytime he wanted.

Danny's hands took up most of the top of the chair back. His graying brown hair was pulled into a ponytail and when Garrett said something about Samsung Electronics moving to Austin, Danny laughed, flashing the silver in his teeth.

"Hey, little bro." Garrett waved at me. Then he saw Miranda and said, "Damn."

She was dressed seven hours early for her fifteen-minute spot at Robert Earle Keen's Halloween Night Show. She'd chosen a cotton blouse made of big orange and white squares, a black skirt, tan boots, lots of silver jewelry. Her hair and makeup were airbrush perfect. Most of the time I would've called the look too much, too Big Hair Texas for my tastes. This afternoon, on Miranda, it worked for me.

I shook hands with Garrett and Danny.

I started to introduce Miranda but Danny said, "Oh, hell, we've *jammed* together."

Miranda laughed and gave Danny a hug and asked him how his washboard playing was coming along. Danny told Miranda she'd sounded just fine on Sixth Street last month.

Garrett kept looking at Miranda. He wasn't having much luck getting his mouth closed.

The parrot eyed me cautiously, like he was forming a vague memory of unhappier times, before Jimmy Buffett and ganja.

"Noisy bastard," he decided.

Danny gave Miranda one more hug, then asked us all what we were having. Garrett told him just about everything, especially Shiner Bock. My stomach went into a little gallop, reminding me about the large quantity of whiskey I'd subjected it to for lunch.

"Make mine iced tea," I corrected.

Danny looked at me funny, like maybe he didn't know me after all, but he went inside to place the order.

"The renowned Miss Daniels," I introduced. "My brother Garrett."

Miranda said, "Pleased to meet you."

Garrett shook her hand, looking at me while he did it. He asked me some silent questions. I just raised my eyebrows.

Garrett gave Miranda one of those toothy grins that makes me wonder if he goes to the orthodontist to get his teeth unstraightened and sharpened on purpose. "Love your tunes."

Miranda smiled. "Much obliged."

"I thought you only *liked* them," I reminded Garrett. "I thought she wasn't Jimmy Buffett."

Garrett told me to shut up. So did the parrot.

Miranda laughed.

"Here, asshole." Garrett fished something out of the wheelchair's side pocket and handed it to me. It was about the size of a computer disk, wrapped in brown paper and sealed with a black and white peace sign sticker.

When I started to protest, he held up his hands in defense. "Did I say anything? Take the damn disk—it's nothing. Some security programs I thought you could use. Don't even consider it a present."

Miranda looked back and forth between us, a little confused.

"Nothing," I promised her.

"Absolutely nothing," Garrett agreed. "Everybody turns thirty. Forget it."

It was Miranda's turn to open her mouth. She looked at me indignantly.

"I'm hoping somebody will gift me a noose," I said. "For my brother."

"You didn't—" Miranda started to say something else, then realized she didn't know quite what.

Garrett was still grinning. "He's embarrassed. Getting old. Not having a day job yet."

"Or maybe hanging is too quick," I speculated.

"Dickhead," squawked the parrot.

Miranda looked back and forth, at a loss for words. It's a look I've seen a lot from women who find themselves between two Navarre men.

"End of subject," I announced. "Tell Miranda how you're reconfiguring your computer to take over the world."

Without too much more encouragement Garrett started telling us about the bastards running RNI, then about his latest unofficial projects. After a while Miranda stopped staring at me. The conversation swung around to Jimmy Buffett, of course, which segued into Miranda's pending fame-and-fortune deal with Century Records. Garrett tried to convince Miranda that she could do a bang-up cover of Buffett's "Brahma Fear" on her first album. After the second round of Shiner Bocks, Miranda and Garrett had just about worked out the arrangement.

During the conversation I sipped my iced tea and

subtly moved Garrett's gift off the table, then into my backpack. Out of sight, etc.

When the food came Danny sat with us for a while. We ate Texicali burgers heavy with salsa and Monterey Jack and watched the afternoon traffic speed down South Oltorf. Dickhead the parrot sat on Garrett's shoulder, holding a tortilla chip in his claw and eating it piece by piece. He hadn't yet learned to dip it in salsa. That would probably take another month.

After a while Garrett said he had to get back to work and Danny said he had to get back to the kitchen. A few raindrops started splattering the patio.

"Nice meeting you," Miranda told Garrett.

Garrett wheeled his chair sideways and the parrot shot its wings out, correcting its balance. "Yeah. And hey, little bro—"

"Say it and die," I warned.

Garrett grinned. "Nice meeting you, too, Miranda."

When we were alone I started shredding the wax paper from the burger basket. Miranda put her boot lightly on top of mine.

Yes, I was wearing the new boots. Just happened to be in front of the closet.

"Hard to like them sometimes," Miranda said.

"What?"

"Older brothers. I wish I'd known—" She stopped herself, probably remembering my injunction to Garrett. "Here you drove all the way to Austin to pick me up, spent half your day."

"I wanted to."

She took my hand and squeezed it. "The taping went really well today. I owe that to you."

"I don't see how."

She kept a hold on my hand. Her eyes were bright. "I missed you last night, Mr. Navarre. You know how long it's been since I missed somebody that much? Can't help but change my singing."

I stared out at the traffic on Oltorf. "Has Les contacted you, Miranda?"

Her grip on my hand loosened just slightly. She had trouble maintaining her smile. "Why would you think that?"

"He hasn't then?"

"Of course not."

"If you had to get away for a few days," I said, "if you had to go somewhere safe that not too many people knew about, could you do it?"

She started to laugh, to put the idea away, but something in my expression made her stop. "I don't know. There's the show tonight, then tomorrow is free, but then the tape audition on Friday—you don't seriously think—"

"I don't know," I said. "Probably it's nothing. But let's say you had to choose between keeping your schedule and being sure you stayed safe."

"Then I'd keep my schedule and take you along."

I looked down at the table.

I turned over the bill and discovered that Danny Young had comped the meal. He'd written "Nothing" in black marker across the green paper. The Zen waiter.

Miranda turned my palm up so hers was on top.

Raindrops starting ping-pinging more steadily, a slow three-quarter time against the metal umbrella.

"Anyplace else you need to go in Austin?" she asked. "As long as I got you up here?"

I watched the rain.

I thought about Kelly Arguello, who would probably have some more paperwork for me. She might be sitting on her porch swing in Clarksville right now, clacking away on her portable computer and watching the raindrops pelt the neighbor's yard appliances.

"Nothing that can't wait," I decided.

45

Two hours later we were back in San Antonio, in Erainya's neighborhood. I had promised Jem I'd come by Halloween evening, but it only took Jem a couple of blocks worth of trick-or-treating to decide that Miranda was the one he *really* wanted to play with.

She raced him up each sidewalk. She laughed at his knock-knock jokes. She showed the most appreciation for his costume. Jem was tickled to death when Miranda offered to be his Miss Muffett.

"She's good with kids," Erainya told me.

Erainya and I were sitting on the hood of Erainya's Lincoln Continental, watching the action.

There was plenty of it in Terrell Hills that evening. The neighborhood Anglo kids were traveling in twos or threes, dressed in their store-bought princess and ninja outfits, their pumpkin flashlights switched on and their plastic jack-o'-lanterns stuffed with candy. The bubba-esque parents strolled a few feet behind, drinking their Lone Stars, talking on the porches, some of the dads with little portable TVs to keep track of the college football games.

Then there were the kids imported from the South Side traveling in groups of ten or twenty, unloaded from their parents' old station wagons into the rich *gente* neighborhoods to gather up what food they could. They dressed in old sheets and maybe some smeared face paint, sometimes a plastic dime-store mask. The bigger kids, fifteen or sixteen years old, did their best to cover their hairy arms and their faces. They let their younger siblings do the asking. The parents always stayed well back on the sidewalk, and always said thank you. No Lone Stars. No portable TVs.

Then there were the oddball loners like Jem. He was skipping awkwardly along in his bulbous homemade spider costume, the black fur coming off on the boxwood hedges and the wire arms flailing and catching on the paper skeletons people had hung from their mesquite trees. By the third block he didn't have much costume left, but nobody seemed to mind. Especially not Jem.

I watched Miranda chasing Jem back down another sidewalk. Both of them jumped over a mesquite that grew flat across the front yard in the shape of a wave.

Jem showed off the pralines and watermelon slice candy he'd scored, then kept running with Miranda close behind.

"Way to go, Bubba," I told him.

Miranda flashed me a smile. She went after Jem like she'd been doing it all her life. Or all of Jem's, anyway.

Erainya muttered something in Greek.

"What?" I asked.

"I said you look like a Turk, honey. Why so sour?"

She was wearing the standard black T-shirt dress. When I'd asked her why no costume she'd said, "What, I need to *look* like a witch, too?" Her arms were crossed and she was grabbing her sharp elbows. Her expression was a little softer than usual, but I suspected that was just because she was tired.

Over Erainya's objections, Jem had told me about

their flush job at six that morning. He loves the can-I-use-your-phone-so-I-can-locate-this-boy's-parents routine. According to Jem the skipped husband's girlfriend opened the door right away and even offered them a Coke. Erainya had collected an easy day's fee from the wife's lawyer.

"I'm not sour," I protested.

Erainya tightened up her body a little more, extended one finger toward me like she was going to jab me with it. "You got a nice lady with you, next week you get to come back to work with me—what's the trouble?"

"It's nothing."

Erainya nodded, but not like she believed me. "You had it out with Barrera?"

I nodded.

"He give you reasons why people might be dying over this business with Sheckly?"

"Yes. And reasons why it was over my head."

We watched Jem wiggle his spider arms for the guy at the next front porch. The guy laughed and gave Jem an extra handful of candy from the large wicker basket he was holding. The guy also watched Miranda appreciatively from behind as she walked down the sidewalk. I wondered how much force it would take to fit the wicker basket onto his head.

"Don't listen to him," Erainya said. "Don't let him cut you down."

I looked at her, not sure if I'd heard correctly.

She examined her talon fingernails critically. "I'm not saying you did good, honey, getting involved the way you did. I'm not saying I like your procedures. But I'll say this just once—you should do P.I. work."

It was hard to read her expression in the dark.

"Erainya? That you?"

She frowned defensively. "What? All I'm saying is don't let Barrera treat you second class, honey. Cops make the worst P.I.s, no matter what he tells you. Cops know how to react, how to be tough. That's it. Most of them don't know the first thing about opening people up.

They don't know about listening and untangling problems. They don't have the *ganis* or the sensitivity for that kind of work. You got *ganis*."

"Thanks. I think."

Erainya kept frowning. Her eyes drifted over to Miranda, who was racing Jem down the steps of the last porch on the block. "How bad is the girl mixed up with this case?"

"I wish I knew."

"Is somebody going to get hurt here?"

"Not if I can help it."

Erainya hugged her elbows and, just once, kicked the tire of the Lincoln with her heel, hard. "You could do worse, honey."

Jem and Miranda came back at full tilt, Jem running past me and Miranda running right into me, grabbing my forearms to stop herself.

She had a little praline crumble at the corner of her mouth. Sneaking some of the loot.

"Hey," she said.

Jem said he was ready to drive to another neighborhood now.

A Latino family of twelve walked by, the parents saying pretty much the same thing in Spanish. The father looked empty-eyed, like he'd been driving around since way before sunset. The kids looked tired, the mother a combination of hungry and uneasy, doing her best to skirt her kids around the Bubba fathers with the portable TVs and the little blond kids with costumes that cost more than all her family's shoes put together.

Erainya frowned down into Jem's candy bag, carefully chose a Sweetarts, the sourest thing she could find, and looked back up at me reprovingly.

Then she ruffled Jem's balding furry headpiece and told him to get in the car.

46

"We *ain't* going to make it."

Miranda didn't sound concerned, exactly. More like she was getting a taste for tardiness and wasn't quite sure if she liked it or not. She'd never been late to a gig before. Somebody else had always driven. Somebody responsible. No side trips to trick-or-treat with four-year-olds.

"I thought this was supposed to be impromptu," I said. "Drop in on Robert Earle. Sing a couple of songs. Casual."

"This took Milo about a month to arrange, Tres. Century's got A & R folks coming from Nashville and everything. Milo will *not* be thrilled."

She tried to fix her makeup again, not an easy task in a moving VW at night, even with the top up. She'd wait until we passed under a highway light, then check her lips in the two seconds her face was illuminated in the visor mirror. She looked fine.

During the next lighted moment I checked my watch.

Nine o'clock exactly. At Floore Country Store, two miles farther up the road, Robert Earle Keen would just be starting his first set, expecting to be pleasantly surprised halfway through by his old buddy, Miranda Daniels. Milo would be pacing by the entrance. Probably with brass knuckles.

We zipped along with the front trunk rattling and the left rear wheel wobbling on its bad disc. I patted the VW's dashboard.

"Not this trip. Break down on the way home, please."

Of course I told the VW that every trip. VWs are gullible that way.

Miranda put away her makeup. She stared out at the ragged black line of huisache trees blurring past. "I like your brother Garrett. I like Jem and Erainya."

"Yeah. They grow on you."

She circled her hands around her knees.

"Thirty," she speculated.

"Hey—" I warned.

She smiled. "Is Garrett right?"

"Hardly ever."

"I mean about the way you feel—that you think you should've settled into a steadier job by now?"

The flashing yellow light that indicated the turnoff for John T. Floore's popped over the hill on the horizon.

"Don't let Garrett fool you," I told her. "Behind the tie-dye and the marijuana, he's the most Catholic person left in my family. He believes in moral guilt."

Miranda nodded. "I imagine that's a yes."

We turned left across traffic.

The Floore Country Store sat with its back to the highway, its face to Old Bandera Road and miles and miles of ranchland. A million years ago when John T. Floore opened the place it really had been a country store—the only option for a meal or groceries or a beer this side of an Edsel ride into San Antonio.

The "store" side of the business had long ago become a sideline to the bar and the country music, but a sign above the exit still read: *Don't forget your bread.*

Tonight the lights of Floore's back acre were blazing.
Pickup trucks lined both sides of Old Bandera Road. The
lime-green cinder-block front of the bar was even more
thoroughly covered with plywood signs than it had been
on my last visit. Some advertised beer, some bands, some
politics. WILLIE NELSON EVERY SATURDAY NIGHT, one of
them said.

We drove past, looking for a parking space. From
the road, Robert Earle Keen's music sounded like random booming and throbbing, a tape played backward
very loud. There was a crowd of cowboy-hatted folks at
the door.

I doubled back, drove past the farm equipment repair
shop, and parked on the opposite side of the bridge that
went over Helotes Creek.

Milo had apparently been watching for my car,
because by the time we got Miranda's guitar out of the
trunk and started walking across the bridge he was
already in the middle coming toward us, scowling like
the troll from the Billy Goats Gruff.

"Come on," he told Miranda, taking her guitar from
me without meeting my eyes.

"Sorry," Miranda tried.

But Milo had already turned and started back toward
the bar.

Miranda cleared a path for us pretty neatly. The old
man at the door tipped his hat to her. Several people in
line backed up to let her through, then had to back up
even more for Milo. A greasy-looking Bexar County
deputy with a graying Elvis haircut told her howdy, then
escorted us across the bar room and out the back door.

The twenty or thirty picnic tables in the gravel lot
were all jammed. So was the cement dance area. At one
of the tables by the back of the building, Tilden Sheckly
sat with several of his cowboy buddies. I caught his eye
and his standard easy grin as we walked past.

The only illumination on the dance floor was from
outdoor bulbs on telephone poles, colored Christmas

lights, and neon beer signs along the fence. Up on the green plywood stage, Robert Earle was singing about bass fishing. He'd gotten a beard and a classier outfit and a bigger band since the last time I'd seen him play.

Miranda turned to Milo. "Where—"

Milo nodded over to another picnic bench by the chain-link fence, about fifty feet from Sheckly, where a few young guys in slacks and white dress shirts were sitting. Not locals. One of them was even drinking a wine cooler. Definitely not locals.

"Just be yourself," Milo advised. "Do the numbers we talked about. Robert Earle's going to start you with a duet on 'Love's a Word.' Okay?"

Miranda nodded, glanced at me, then at the A & R men across the yard. She tried for a smile.

Milo handed her over to the deputy with the Elvis haircut. He walked her up to the stage. Robert Earle had just finished his bass-fishing song and was announcing over the applause that he'd just found out one of his oldest friends in the whole world was in the audience. He said he surely wanted to invite her up to do a little music.

A spattering of applause started up again, getting a little more enthusiastic when people saw Miranda coming up the steps. Apparently the crowd recognized her.

Milo waited long enough to make sure she'd gotten onstage safely and that her mike was working. Robert Earle started kidding with her about the last time they'd played together—something about eating mescal worms and forgetting the words to "Ashes of Love." Miranda kidded him back. If she was nervous she hid it well.

Milo shot me a quick, disapproving look. He walked past me, toward the table where the important people sat.

I stared at his back for a few seconds, then decided I might as well go inside and buy myself a birthday beer.

The interior bar was a walnut box that amazingly managed to hold the elbows of the bartender and six or seven customers without falling apart. Nobody was in costume, unless you count kicker clothes. Nobody had pumpkins or candy. Beers were displayed in a glass refrigerator case along with thick black wrinkly curlicues that according to one sign were dried sausage. $3.50 per ring.

I bought a can of Budweiser and no dried sausage. I walked outside again. I crunched over the gravel toward Sheckly's picnic table.

Onstage Robert Earle was plucking out an acoustic intro. Miranda was starting to sway. Without a guitar, her hands were loose at her sides, her fingers tapping lightly on the folds of her skirt.

When Sheckly noticed me coming he mumbled something to his lackeys and a round of laughter started up. The skin of Sheckly's left cheek, where Allison had landed the horseshoe, was corpse yellow, stained with Mercurochrome. The cut itself was covered with a line of beige squares that looked like strapping tape.

The man sitting next to him was almost as ugly, even without flesh wounds. He had pale skin, orange hair, a thick unintelligent face. Elgin Garwood.

"Hey, son," Sheck said. "Good to see you."

I slid onto the opposite bench, next to one of the cowboys.

"Surprised to see you here," I told Sheck. "Not minding the shop tonight?"

He spread his hands. "Sunday's my day to get out. I like to see the other clubs, keep tabs on who's playing."

I gestured toward the table of stony-faced A & R men. Milo was sitting with them now, trying to look self-assured, smiling and gesturing proudly toward the stage.

"Especially when reps from the record company come looking at Miranda," I told Sheck. "Keeps Milo on his toes, wondering if you'll come over and ruin the night."

Sheck grinned. "Hadn't thought of that."

Elgin was glaring at me.

I gave him a smile. "They let you off surveillance tonight, Garwood, or did Frank just get tired of your clown act?"

Elgin rose real slowly, keeping his eyes on me. "Get up, you son of a bitch."

The other cowboys glanced at Sheck, looking for a cue. Over by the fence, one of the Bexar County deputies on security was frowning in our direction.

"Go on, Elgin," Sheck said lazily. "Go inside. Get yourself another beer."

"Let me call Jean," Elgin said.

Sheck's smile stayed in place but his eyes dimmed a little. The fire sank a little farther back in his skull.

"Probably a good idea," I agreed. "At least your Luxembourg friends are professionals."

Elgin made like he was going to come across the table at me, but Sheckly raised his fingers just enough to get back his attention.

"Go on," Sheckly told him. "Don't call anybody. Go inside and get yourself a beer."

Elgin looked at me again, weighing the pros and cons.

"Go on," repeated Sheckly.

Elgin wiped his nose on the back of his hand. He went.

Sheck looked at the other cowboys and the communication was as clear as in a pack of jackals. They got up and vacated the table too.

Behind me, Robert Earle's twangy cowboy voice had given way to Miranda's piercingly clear tones. The song was just vocals and acoustic, the way she sounded best. She sang back to Robert Earle about why he was leaving her.

Sheck listened, his eyes on Miranda, his face complete concentration. When Robert Earle took over again, Sheck closed his eyes.

"That girl. You know I remember the first time she came up to me. One of the Paintbrush's community dances, the ones we do free for local folks every Wednesday. She said I should come down to Gruene Hall and give her a listen. Batted those brown eyes at me and I'm thinking—this is old Willis' girl? Little Miranda?" He let his grin spread out a little. "I suppose I went down to Gruene that next weekend expecting to get me something besides a little music, but I heard that voice—you just can't get away from it, can you?"

"Unless it gets away from you."

Sheck's grin didn't diminish at all. "Let's wait for last call on that one, son."

"You don't think Century Records is serious about her?"

Sheckly followed my eyes over to the table of A & R reps. Sheck chuckled. "You think that means anything? You think they won't evaporate faster than gasoline once they learn Les Saint-Pierre is out of the picture? Once they learn about my contract?"

"So why wait to tell them?"

Sheckly spread his hands. "In good time, son. Let's give Miranda a chance to come to her senses on her own. Way she was talking the other night, 'fore that fool Saint-Pierre woman went crazy on me—it sounded to me like Miranda was figuring out what's what. She knows Les Saint-Pierre left her in a bad spot. She's looking to cover her bases."

Miranda and Robert Earle's duet came to an end. The hooting and hollering started up. Robert Earle gave a twisted little smile when he saw the audience's response, then suggested into the mike that Miranda and him better give "Ashes of Love" another try. Miranda laughed. The couples on the dance floor yelled approval.

"How do you mean, covering her bases?" I asked Sheck.

He spread his hands. "Nothing to be ashamed of, son. Can't blame her. She just reminded me of my offer from a few months back—asked if she was still welcome to move out to the mansion."

"*She* asked *you.*"

"Sure. I said it might be a good idea, seeing as—" His eyes got that distant look in them again, like somebody had just opened the oven door and let a draft blow past the pilot lights. "Just might be better for her out there, where I can look after her, seeing as Les Saint-Pierre got her into such a muddle, gave her and Brent and Willis all these fool ideas about where her career should go."

"Fool ideas about how to push you out of the picture."
Sheck nodded. "And that."

I drank my Budweiser. The top of the can smelled like sausage.

"Ashes of Love" went into full swing. Robert Earle's band backed up the vocals with a good beat, bass and drums and heavy rhythm guitar. When the first verse came around Miranda let loose—her voice went up half an octave and about a million decibels to the kind of energy level she'd had at the Cactus Cafe. Her eyes closed, one hand on the mike and the other clenched at her side. Robert Earle stepped back, grinning. He played his guitar and mouthed "Ooo-whee." On the now-packed dance floor, the audience responded in kind.

It was impossible to have a conversation—not because of the volume, but because it was impossible not to want to watch Miranda.

That was just as well. I wasn't sure what to say to Sheck right then, what to think. I was staring at the lady onstage, thinking about a night a million years ago in a Victorian on West Ashby—in a guest room that had smelled like daisies and freon with a small cool bed and a body I hardly remembered. What I could summon up was lighter than the aftertaste of cotton candy.

The song finally came to an end. The applause was loud and appreciative. Over at the picnic table with the wine-cooler-sipping Century reps, Milo Chavez was looking confident, pleased. He'd even managed to get one of the reps to crack a smile.

I looked back at Sheckly. "You wanted to level with me the other day. Let me return the favor. Samuel Barrera thinks you're as bad as your European friends. When he takes them down you're going to go down just as hard."

Sheck raised his eyebrows placidly. "How's that, son?"

"I don't think you're a killer, Mr. Sheckly. I don't think Julie's and Alex's murders were your idea. I think you're a mediocre black marketeer who let things get out of control. You let some greedy professionals take over your operation and crank it into high gear. Now you're scared. You're out of your league and your local people are getting nervous. I think a year from now Jean Kraus is going to be sitting in your office, calling the shots. Either that or he's going to be long gone and you're going to be left with a very large mess where Avalon County used to be. Your friends decide Miranda's caused them any of their present troubles, you think you can really keep her out of the cross fire?"

Onstage Robert Earle and Miranda had slowed down the pace again. Keen was taking the lead on Brent's song, "The Widower's Two-Step," which Robert Earle obviously knew well. It sounded strange coming from him, though, with an edge of quirky dark humor that made the tragedy in the song seem unreal. It was now just another my-momma-died-and-my-hound-dog-went-to-prison country song. I didn't like the way it played.

Over at the bar Sheckly's friends had recongregated with a few new recruits, all waiting and watching for some sign to come in for the kill.

Sheck's face was dark. He hadn't looked at me while I spoke. He was concentrating on Miranda again, but not with any pleasure. He reached up and dabbed at the edge of the bandages on his cheek. When he finally spoke his tone was forcibly light and completely unnegotiable.

"Don't press your luck no more, son. You hear?"

It wasn't a threat. It sounded as close as Sheck could get to earnest advice. It was also very definitely the end of the conversation.

As I left, Tilden Sheckly's buddies flowed back around the table. They tried their best to reconstruct the joking atmosphere they'd had before—popping new beers, lighting cigarettes, talking in loud voices at my expense. Their boss smiled stonily, looking nowhere in particular, like the majority of his mind had already checked out for the evening.

Robert Earle and Miranda were harmonizing onstage. Couples were slow-dancing. Milo was entertaining the

Nashville bigwigs with funny stories and a new round of wine coolers.

I nodded amiably to the Bexar County deputy on my way inside. My birthday Budweiser was empty. One down, twenty-nine more to go.

47

At the break I stood outside the entrance of the bar, watching the occasional headlights go down the road. Tilden Sheckly and his friends had left long ago. About fifty other people had arrived, many of them excited when the ticket-taker told them Miranda Daniels was in the house. Nobody got particularly excited to see me at the door. Nobody asked for an autograph.

A few minutes after the canned music began, Miranda appeared at the entrance, followed by a cadre of smiling cowboys. She thanked them and begged off drink offers until they finally drifted away. Then she came over to me, smiled, and circled her arm through mine.

Without speaking we started down the hill toward the Helotes Creek Bridge. After a hundred yards, the night closed around us. The sky was still overcast but in the south the reflection of city lights made a dull shine. We stopped at the bridge.

Miranda went to the metal railing and leaned against

it. I joined her. We were about eye level with the tops of the stunted mesquite trees that filled up the dry creek bed below. You couldn't see much, but you could smell the wild mint and anise, steamed into the air by the warm day.

"Milo said it sounded good," Miranda mused.

"It sounded great."

Miranda didn't have to lean too far to press against me. "He doesn't approve of you, does he?"

"Robert Earle Keen?"

She bumped against me, playfully. "Milo. I thought he was your friend."

"He's worried about your record deal. You've got a lot on the line and Milo's afraid Sheckly's going to ruin your chances. He's unhappy I haven't found a way to get Sheckly to lay off yet."

She ran her hand along the metal rail until it met mine. "That's not all, is it?"

"No. Last time Milo and I worked together—there was a woman. It took three or four years before we could speak to each other again after that. He's probably afraid I'm getting distracted again, with somebody he's got a stake in."

"Are you?" There was a warm, husky undercurrent in her voice.

I stared into the mesquites. "We should probably talk about that. We should probably talk about why you decided it would be useful."

It was impossible to see her face in the darkness. I had to read her momentary silence, the sudden absence of her hand and her side against mine.

"What?" she asked.

"You said it Friday night—it looks like you're along for the ride. Everybody worries about taking care of you because they're sure everyone else is going to mess up the job. You cultivate that kind of dependency pretty well— it's gotten you a long way."

"I don't . . ." Her voice faltered. It sounded compressed, still slightly playful, like she had crossed over the

line in a teasing game and was just starting to realize the
person yelling "stop" really meant it. "I'm not sure I like
the way you're talking, Mr. Navarre."

"The funny thing is I don't blame you," I said. "I
want to see you make it. You've had a pretty shitty
family life up to now—you did what you could to get
yourself somewhere. You figured out ways to keep your
dad in check. You got Sheckly to be your standard-
bearer. You got your brother to sell out his songs to you.
When Sheck's patronage became too confining you got
Cam Compton to give you information that could shake
you free, then you encouraged Les Saint-Pierre to try a
little blackmail scheme. When things started getting scary
you figured it might be useful to have me around your
finger, so you gave me Friday night. Now you're getting
unsure about your chances with Century Records so
you're hedging your bets with Sheck again. We're all
stuck on you, Miranda. Milo. Sheck. Me. Even Allison.
We're all running around tackling each other and
treating you like a football, and here you are quietly
calling all the moves. Congratulations."

"I don't believe you just said that."

I ran my hands along the metal rail. "Tell me I'm
wrong, then."

Far down the hill, a new song started up from Floore's
backyard. I could decipher the bass guitar, an occasional
fiddle line above it.

Miranda said, "You think that I was with you Friday
night just because—" She let her voice twist, fall silent.
Everything in me said I should respond, offer an immediate retraction.

I resisted.

A breeze lifted up from the creek bed. It brought a
fresh wave of hot anise smell with it.

"I won't let you think that," she insisted.

She folded herself against my chest and pushed her
arms under mine, wrapping fingers around my shoulder
blades.

"That's not a denial," I said.

She turned her face into my neck and sighed. I kept
holding her, lightly. There were little specks of sand in my
throat.

I'm not sure how long it was before the Danielses'
white and brown pickup truck drove by us on the bridge.
It slid down Old Bandera almost soundlessly, riding the
brakes all the way, and double-parked sideways in front
of Floore's.

I made my voice work. "Were you expecting your
brother?"

Miranda pulled away, letting her hands slide down
until they hooked into mine. She looked where I was
looking, saw her father fifty yards away, getting out of
the passenger's side of the old Ford. The man coming
around the front through the Ford's headlights wasn't
Brent—it was Ben French, the drummer. The two men
walked together into the bar.

A premonition started twisting into a solid weight
somewhere inside my rib cage.

Miranda said, "Why—"

She turned and started walking back toward the bar,
trailing me behind her.

Willis and Ben and Milo Chavez met us at the corner
of Old Bandera, under the streetlight.

Daniels looked haggard and old, not just with
drinking, although he'd obviously been doing that, but
with anger and a kind of washed-out emptiness, the
dazed way people look when they're coming off a crest
of grief and waiting for the next surge to hit. He leaned
on his cane like he was trying to drive it into the ground.
Ben French looked equally haggard. Milo's face was dark
and angry.

As we took a few final steps to meet them, Miranda's
hand tightened on mine.

"I thought you were in Gruene tonight," she asked
her father.

"Miranda—" His voice cracked.

"Why are you driving the truck?" she demanded.

Willis stared at Miranda's hand in mine, confused, like

he was mentally trying to separate whose fingers were whose.

"Navarre," Milo put in. He nodded his head back toward the bar, willing me to come with him, to leave father and daughter alone.

Miranda's hand stayed fastened on mine.

"What's happened?" Her voice was sterner than I'd ever heard it, impatient.

"There's been a fire at the ranch," Willis managed to say.

"A fire," Miranda repeated. It was a whisper.

Milo kept looking at me, willing me to step away.

"Where's Brent?" Miranda demanded. But her voice was thin now, glassy.

When no one answered at the count of five, Miranda tried to ask her question again, but this time her voice cracked into small shards of sound.

Willis Daniels looked down at his cane, saw that he hadn't yet driven it into the ground, and wiped his nose with tired resignation.

"You'd best drive with your friends," Willis suggested.

Then he turned to go back to the truck, Ben French holding his arm.

48

The old tractor shed had cracked open like a black eggshell.

You could still see huge scars the fire engine had made coming through the gravel and mud, the barbed-wire fence it had plowed through in order to get around the back of the house. All that was left now were three Avalon County units in the front yard, their roof lights rotating lazily, cutting red arcs across the branches of the granddaddy live oak. The medical examiner's car was pulled around the side of the house, parked diagonally over the horseshoe pit.

Around the back of the house a generator whined, cranking out juice for the floodlights that illuminated the sooty wreckage of Brent's apartment. The smell of wet ashes was cloying even from twenty feet away.

Miranda and her father stood on the back porch, talking to a plainclothes detective. Miranda's face was bleached and vacant. Every few seconds she would shake her head for no apparent reason. Her orange and white blouse had poofed out from her skirt on the left side and wrinkled like a balloon frozen on dry ice.

I looked over what was left of Brent Daniels' front wall. Inside, the hosed-down ashes made a thick, glistening surface, almost a bowl shape. Sticking out of the sludge were lumps, objects—pieces of wood that had miraculously remained unburned right next to large pools of melted metal.

The south wall, to my right, was still almost full height. Most of the wood had bubbled and blackened, but one upper cabinet had come open post-fire, revealing a perfectly intact set of dishes. The paint on the inside of the cabinet was pink. The photo of Brent Daniels' mother had been preserved.

Fires have a rotten sense of humor.

Jay Griffin, the medical examiner for Avalon County, had staked out an area where Brent's cot had been, the place where I'd slept that afternoon. Jay and two other men with white gloves were poking into the ashes with what looked like plastic rulers.

Milo walked back to me from the toolshed, where he'd been interrogating one of the deputies. "You overheard?"

I nodded. I'd overheard. Barred door, from the outside. Clear traces of incendiaries on the outer walls, pooled inside where the windows had been. One victim lying on the cot—perhaps drugged, perhaps already dead. No struggle to get out, anyway. The M.E. had mostly charred bones to work with. Maybe some dental work. It takes a lot to burn a human body. Somebody had gone the extra mile.

I looked out into the fields, unnaturally lit up by the spotlights. It made me feel like I was back in a high school stadium night game, all the shadows long and elastic. Third and ten.

The chickens in the coop were little red feathery lumps—dead from the heat. The woven straps on the lawn chairs sagged in the middle where they'd melted.

Farther out, two rusted, dirt-caked septic tanks leaned against the shed. The new tanks had apparently been sunk into the proper places, ready to store gray water for the garden, to make sure the ranch's toilets flushed properly. I'm sure that would've been a big comfort to Brent Daniels, the man who wrote most of Miranda's soon-to-be hit songs, knowing he'd spent his last afternoon filling in sewage lines.

"Ten gets you twenty," Milo said, "it'll go down as an accident. A suicide, maybe."

On the porch, Willis Daniels was nodding vaguely, grimly, to something the detective was telling him. Miranda had her fingers curled tight against her palms and was pressing them against her eyes.

"They couldn't," I said.

I had already filled Milo in on my latest findings. He had expressed no surprise at the information Sam Barrera had given me, no surprise that the authorities wouldn't be riding to the rescue in time to save his record deal, only a sour regret that Les hadn't gone through with his blackmail plan. I had not told him about my conversation with Miranda.

Milo turned over a charred board with his foot, so the unblackened side of the wood faced up. "One damn signature. All that leverage and all we need is a goddamn signature—not even an admission that Sheck's contract was forged. Just a waiver. We've got to do something ourselves, Navarre. Friday—"

"You're still thinking about your deadline. After this."

"Come on, Navarre. If Century hears—"

I kicked the board away. It skittered through the wet grass.

"Probably good publicity. Be happy, Milo. You won't have to pay Brent his twenty-five percent for the song rights."

"God damn it, Navarre—"

But I was already walking away. It was either that or take a swing at Milo, and I wasn't the right combination of angry and drunk and stupid for that. Not yet.

I didn't look where I was going.

I pushed through a couple of newspaper reporters

who were trying to interview a deputy lieutenant, then halfway to the porch I ran into a burly plainclothes officer who was helping the evidence technician raise a camera tripod.

Before I could apologize Deputy Frank turned around and told me to watch it.

Whatever other angry comments Frank might've been about to make, he swallowed them back like live coals when he recognized me.

"You going to get that, Frank?" the evidence tech said behind him.

Frank looked me in the eye. What I saw in his face was too much information, too many questions that all blurred into something incomprehensible. White noise. His expression was the visual equivalent of picking up a receiver and listening to the shriek and hiss of a modem.

He looked away. "Yeah. Sure."

Then he turned and helped the evidence tech lift the tripod.

I walked up the steps to the back porch.

Willis had just asked a quiet question and the county detective was responding in an equally quiet, gentle voice. The detective had a slick curve of black hair combed almost into his eyes, like a crow's wing glued to his forehead.

"We don't know," he said. "We probably won't—not for a while anyway. I'm sorry."

Willis began to say something, then thought better of it. He glared at the blue-painted floorboards. He looked twenty pounds thinner—most of it taken from his face. The skin around his eyes was unnaturally gray, the wrinkles that ran from the edges of his nose into his mustache and beard so deep his face looked carved.

When he saw me his grief turned into something heavier, something more active.

I walked over to where Miranda sat on the porch railing. She was hugging her arms. Her carefully curled hair had disintegrated into simple tangles again and her gig-perfect makeup job was completely scoured away.

I didn't ask how she was doing.

She only acknowledged my presence by a change in her breathing—a shaky inhale, then a long exhale. She tried to untense her shoulders. Her eyes shut.

The detective was asking Willis a few more questions— When had he left for Gruene Hall that evening? Was he sure Brent had planned on staying home all night? Had Brent had any unusual visitors lately? Had Brent been seeing anyone special? Or broken off any relationships?

At the last question Miranda opened her eyes and glanced over at me. The composure she'd been knitting together over the last hour started to unravel.

Willis wasn't listening to the detective's questions. He was watching me, and the way Miranda was crying. I tried hard not to feel the way the old man's eyes were attaching themselves to my face.

"Do you want to leave?" I asked Miranda quietly, then to the detective, "Can we leave?"

The detective frowned. He lifted the crow's wing off his forehead, then let it fall back into place. He said he supposed there wasn't any problem with us going.

Slowly, Miranda collected enough energy to stand. She steadied herself against the porch beam.

"All right," she whispered. "I can't—"

She looked at the blackened tractor shed, the spotlights. She seemed unable to complete the thought.

"I know," I told her. "Let's go."

"The hell you will."

Willis Daniels' words took even the homicide detective by surprise. It wasn't so much the volume as the acid tone, the suddenness with which the old man stepped toward me.

"*You* killed him, you son of a bitch." He pointed his cane at my feet and made ready to smash my toes. "It was something you did, wasn't it? Some trouble you stirred up."

Miranda moved a few inches behind me. There was no hesitation, no faltering in the way she did it. It was obviously a maneuver that had long ago become instinctive for her.

The detective looked back and forth between us, interested. "You want to explain?"

Willis glared at my feet.

The detective looked at me.

I gave him an explanation. I told him some of the things that had been happening to Miranda since Century Records became interested in her. I told him I'd been hired to find out what I could and that as far as I knew Brent Daniels would've had absolutely no reason to be in the line of fire. I gave the detective my name and number and address and said sure, I'd be happy to talk more.

"But right now," I said, "I'm getting Miranda out of here."

The detective looked at Miranda, then looked at me. His eyes softened just a little. He said all right.

"This is her home," Willis growled.

I found myself stepping toward the old man, grabbing the tip of the cane that he'd raised toward me. The tension along the shaft of wood was uneven, his grip on the other end weak. With not much force I could've taken it away, or thrust it back. Anything I wanted.

"Tres—" Miranda said.

Her fingers dug into my shoulders with a surprising amount of force.

I pushed the tip of the cane away, lightly.

"Call me whenever," I told the detective.

The detective was reappraising me moment by moment, like I was a tie game in progress. Sudden death overtime.

"I'll do that," he promised.

Miranda's fingers relaxed.

As I walked back down the steps, holding Miranda's hand, Milo Chavez was arguing with one of the newspaper reporters—something about family privacy. I couldn't tell if he was arguing for or against. Deputy Frank was still looking at me, giving me white noise with his eyes. Jay Griffin the M.E. had lifted something long and black and thin from the ashes of the tractor shed and was turning it. In the spotlights the forearm looked surreal, like a piece of black glazed ceramic, nothing that could ever have been part of a human body.

49

The next morning vendors were selling offerings for the dead all along General McMullen Road. The parking lot of the orange stucco strip mall was lined with battered pickup trucks and delivery vans, all covered with wreaths, crosses made of blue silk flowers, pictures of Jesus, flowery frames empty and ready for the insertion of the beloved's pictures. There were tables of foodstuffs—*pan muerte*, the bread of the dead, fresh tamales, tortillas, black cat-and pumpkin-and skull-shaped cookies.

Dia de los Muertos was tomorrow. Today—All Souls' Day—was just a warm-up. Otherwise we would never have been able to turn into San Fernando Cemetery without getting choked in traffic.

The circular maze of one-way drives wasn't empty by a long shot, though. In every section of the cemetery people were unloading the trunks of their cars—coffee cans of marigolds, picnic baskets, all the things their *antepasados* would need. Old men with trowels were cutting weeds away from the marble plaques, or digging holes for new plants. About half the graves had already been adorned, several buried so thick in flowers they looked like a florist's waste dump.

The less conventional graves had fake cobwebs covering them, flowers planted in jack-o'-lanterns, little cloth ghosts dangling from strings on the tombstones. Others were fluttering with ribbons and spinning sunflower and flamingo-shaped pinwheels.

"Good Lord," Miranda said.

She was dressed in jeans and her boots and an oversized U.C. Berkeley T-shirt she'd borrowed from my closet. Her hair was pulled back in a clasp. Her face, clean-scrubbed and devoid of makeup, looked pale and younger. She wasn't back to normal by a long shot— about every hour her hands would start trembling again, or she'd suddenly start crying, but there were pauses when she seemed surprisingly stable. She'd even given me a weak smile when I'd brought her *huevos rancheros* for breakfast-in-futon. Or maybe what made her smile was the way I looked in the morning after sleeping on the floor with the cat all night. She wouldn't tell me.

We drove around a huge mound of rocks topped with a life-sized stone crucifix. At the base of Jesus' feet a brown mutt dog was taking a nap. We kept driving toward the back of the cemetery, then circled around.

I was looking for a maroon Cadillac.

I finally found it in the center of the cemetery.

Ralph Arguello was about twenty yards from the curb, standing over his mother, a large woman in a brown sack dress who was kneeling at one of the graves, planting marigolds. Ralph was easy to spot. He was dressed in his outfit of choice—oversized guayabera shirt, jeans, black boots. His black ponytail looked freshly braided. The butt of his .357 had snagged on the edge of the olive shirt, making it anything but concealed. He was holding a bunch of silver Mylar balloons decorated with pictures of trains and cars.

I parked behind the Cadillac. Miranda followed my stare.

"*That's* your friend?"

"Come on."

We walked between grave markers—most of them flat plaques, mirrored gray granite that reflected the sky perfectly. The mottoes on the tombstones were trilingual—Latin and Spanish and English. The decorations were something totally different—somewhere between ancient Aztec and modern Wal-Mart.

Ralph turned toward us as we walked up. His thick round glasses looked cut from the same material as the Mylar balloons and the tombstones.

It was difficult to tell whether he looked at Miranda or not.

"*Vato*," he said.

I nodded.

We waited for a while, not saying anything else while Mama Arguello completed saying the rosary over the grave.

At first I didn't realize where we were, what part of the cemetery.

Then I noticed how close together the grave markers were, that each space was no more than two feet wide. They went on like that, row after row, for what looked like a good half acre. Nearby was another marble Jesus, this one surrounded by kids. The Spanish inscription: *Suffer the Children.*

The decorations around us were sprinkled with Halloween candy, toys, flower arrangements shaped like lambs. Mama Arguello finished her prayers and then took the cluster of balloons from Ralph and tied it on a stake in the grass. The engraving on the marker said: "Jose Domingo Arguello, b. Aug. 8, 1960, d. Aug. 8, 1960. *In recuerdo.*"

The hook on the stake had frayed knots from past years of balloons—all baby-blue ribbons, some perhaps decades old.

Mama Arguello smiled and gave me a hug. She smelled

of marigolds—a pungent scent like perfume from a jewelry box buried for a hundred years. Then Mama Arguello hugged Miranda, telling her in Spanish that she was glad we could come.

It didn't really matter that Mama Arguello didn't know Miranda. Mama A. had stopped caring about things like that about the time she stopped being able to see. Her glasses, Ralph assured me, were just for show. With or without them, the world for Mama had long ago become a series of blurry spots and lights. It was now mostly about smells and sounds.

"Come with me," she told Miranda. She dug her pudgy brown fingers into Miranda's forearm. "I have some tea."

Miranda looked uncertainly back at me, then at Ralph. Ralph's grin couldn't have made her feel any easier. The old woman led her back to the Cadillac, where she started unloading things into Miranda's arms—a thermos, a picnic basket, two pots of flowers, a large wreath.

Ralph made a small laugh. When he looked down at the tomb marker his smile didn't waver at all.

"My older brother," Ralph told me.

I nodded. Jose Domingo. An old man's name.

I wondered how many hours Jose had lived, what he thought up there in heaven of the thirty-plus years of infant's gifts and balloons he'd been receiving at his grave site.

"You got more family here?" I asked Ralph.

Ralph waved his hand toward the east, like it was his real estate.

"Take us two days, me and Mama. Start here and work our way around. Yvette's right over there. We have lunch with her, man."

Yvette. Kelly Arguello's mother. I exchanged looks with Ralph, but he didn't have to tell me about Kelly not being here, or about what he thought of her defection.

He watched Miranda struggling with the *ofrendas* Mama Arguello kept handing her. Mama was giving her directions in Spanish, telling Miranda stories she couldn't understand.

Miranda began smiling. At first it was strained, grieved. Then Mama told her about who a particular bottle of whiskey was for, a real *cabrón*, and Miranda laughed despite herself, almost spilling a plate of cookies balanced in the crook of her arm.

"The *chica*'s in trouble?" Ralph asked.

"I don't know. I think she might be."

I told him what had been happening. Ralph shook his head. "*Pinche* rednecks. *Pinche* Chavez. You don't see him out here today."

"Can you help, Ralphas?"

Ralph looked at his brother's tombstone, then reached down and yanked out a piece of crabgrass at the edge of the marble. He threw it behind him carelessly. The weed landed on one of the unadorned graves, behind him. "This lady mean something to you?"

I hesitated, tried to form an answer, but Ralph held up his hand.

"Forget I asked, *vato*. How long I known you, eh?"

From another person, it would've irritated me. From Ralph, the statement was so honest, the grin that went with it so blatantly amused, that I couldn't help but crack a smile. "A long time."

"Shit, yet."

Miranda came back, burdened down with gifts for the dead but more at ease now, smiling tentatively. She followed Mama Arguello as she led the way to the next ancestor. Miranda looked back at me and asked, "Coming?"

We went to visit Yvette, about half an acre away. Her tombstone was an upright piece of white marble, rough-finished around the edges. The stone was almost engulfed in a large pyracantha bush that hung its branches down in the shape of an octopus. Each branch was thick with red berries the size of bird shot.

Across the drive from her grave, a new hole was being dug. The riderless backhoe had scooped out a perfect coffin-sized trench in the lawn and was now standing there, abandoned.

I stared at the backhoe.

Miranda helped Mama Arguello spread a blanket next to the grave and set out some paper plates of cinnamon toast and cups of steaming tea that smelled like lemon.

The cold air swept the steam from the tea. Mama set out a plate and a cup for Yvette's grave, then began telling the tombstone how well Kelly was doing in college.

Ralph listened without comment.

Miranda was shaking her head, looking across the cemetery at similar scenes here and there, at different grave sites. There were tears on her cheeks again.

"Today is better," Ralph told her. "Tomorrow—*loco*. Worse than Fiesta."

Miranda brushed her hand under her eye, dazed. "I've lived in San Antonio my whole life—I never—" She shook her head.

Ralph nodded. "Which San Antonio, eh?"

A few feet away, a family unloaded from a long black town car. The grandmother had wraparound sunglasses and walked stiffly, like this was her first time out of the nursing home in a long time. She was escorted by a woman with orange-and-brown-streaked hair and a pink sweat suit and lots of jewelry. A couple of teenage girls followed, each with an expensive warm-up suit and a smaller version of mom's hairdo and jewelry ensemble.

They walked to a grave where the colors were white and green, the wreath a flowery Oakland A's logo. On the tombstone was a flower-framed picture—a teenage boy in an open coffin, his face the same color as the white satin, his A's jersey on, his hair combed and his pencil mustache trimmed and a look of pride sculpted on his dead face. Gangbanger. Maybe fifteen.

"Ralph has a rental house nearby," I said. "I've used it before."

Miranda looked beyond the cemetery, into the surrounding neighborhood of run-down stores and multi-colored one-room houses. The tears were still coming.

"Is it safe?"

Ralph started laughing quietly.

"Nobody you know would ever look here," I said. "That's the whole point. You stay with Ralph, you'll be safe."

Miranda thought about that, then looked at Mama Arguello, who was offering her some lemon tea.

"All right," Miranda said. And then, like her timer had run out, she curled her head against her knees and shivered.

Mama Arguello smiled, not at all like she knew what we were talking about, then she told Yvette's tombstone how nice it was to have visitors, how fresh the *pan muerte* tasted this year.

50

When I got back to 90 Queen Anne a gold foil package the size of two glass bricks was sitting on the porch. The card said: *This will look perfect on your desk at UTSA. Good luck today. Happy Birthday.*

Mother's writing. She made no mention of my failure to come to her Halloween/by-the-way-it's-Tres'-birthday party the night before. Inside the wrapping was the *Riverside Chaucer*, new edition. A seventy-five-dollar book.

I took it inside.

I stared at some tentative notes I'd made two mornings ago for the demo class I was about to do. After last night, the whole idea seemed absurd, trivial—and oddly comforting. Students were going to attend classes today. Assistant professors were going to yawn and drink coffee and stumble through boring routines and most of them wouldn't even smell like house fires. They wouldn't see blackened bones every time they closed their eyes. They wouldn't catch themselves humming songs by the recently murdered.

With a kind of dread, I realized I wanted the class to go well.

Robert Johnson was of course sleeping on the outfit I needed to wear, so I did the tablecloth trick. Robert Johnson flipped, got to his feet, and glared at me. It took me five minutes and a full roll of Scotch tape to remove the black hair from the white shirt. Five more minutes to tie the tie with Robert Johnson helping.

After that it's a blur.

The demo lesson did go well, I guess. I chose "Complaint to His Purse" and did the most radical things I could remember from graduate seminars—break the class into small groups, ask them to read the poem aloud while holding their wallets, ask them to write a modern-day interpretation. We had a few laughs comparing Chaucer to a phone solicitor, then trying to find a Middle English phrase that was the equivalent of "suck up." Most of the students didn't even fall asleep.

Despite my dress clothes I probably looked like I had slept on the floor the night before and spent my morning in a cemetery, but that was okay. Most of the students looked that way too.

Professor Mitchell shook my hand a lot in the hallway afterward and told me how he was sure I'd get the job. The other professors filed out without saying anything. They frowned just as much as they did during my earlier interview. Maybe tracing the etymology of "suck up" had been too much.

I drove out of the UTSA visitor parking lot feeling tingly and hollow. I was halfway down I-10, doing an impossible seventy miles per hour, before I even realized I had gotten on the highway.

I took the first exit, pulled the VW into a strip mall parking lot, and shut the ignition.

I tried to get my heartbeat under control. I didn't have much luck.

I couldn't place the feeling right away—sort of like an electric generator spinning in my intestines. Not going anywhere, not hooked to anything, just making useless electricity. It was a few more minutes before I recognized it as shock. I'd felt this way a year ago, after I'd killed a man. I'd woken up a few nights afterward with this same feeling—disconnected inside, like someone else had just vacated my body and left me the shell. I told myself this was only a college lesson, for God's sake.

I started the car again. I decided to take comfort in the mundane and drove next door to Taco Cabana for enchiladas to go.

When I got back to 90 Queen Anne my favorite car was parked conspicuously across the street. Deputy Frank had the window down on his black Ford Festiva and was rubbing a finger along the top of his mustache while he read a magazine.

He might've been a little more obvious if he put wavy-hands on his windshield wipers, but only slightly.

I parked the VW and walked across to his car. Frank pretended to ignore me.

In his passenger's seat was your normal stakeout gear—junk food, a camera, bottled water, a tape recorder and shotgun mike. He had his suit jacket off so the shoulder holster was in plain view. There was a black briefcase between Frank's knees.

He flipped a page of *Today's Parent*.

"Colic," he said, like he was talking to himself. "It's driving me crazy."

"That's rough," I agreed.

I waited. Frank turned a couple more pages. He read like he was looking at assembly instructions, his eyes flicking back and forth around the pages in no particular order, looking for the schematics on proper baby-building.

"You supposed to be keeping tabs on me?" I asked.

Frank nodded, tapping his thumb on a picture of a new super-absorbent diaper.

"Sheckly?"

Frank nodded again.

"You want to come in for some enchiladas?"

Three times was a charm.

Frank put down his magazine, picked up his briefcase, and got out of the car.

We walked around the side of the house. My landlord Gary Hales was standing in his living room, watching out the window as I brought the man with the shoulder-holstered gun and the black briefcase onto his property. Gary loves it when I do stuff like that.

I opened the door of the in-law and Robert Johnson padded up, bumped into Frank's leg, then stepped back indignantly, his super-keen animal senses suddenly warning him that I wasn't alone.

"Hey, blackie." Frank bent down and scratched Robert Johnson's ear.

Frank apparently passed inspection. Robert Johnson began rubbing the side of his face vigorously on Frank's shoe.

Frank glanced around the room, still in read-schematic mode, until his eyes came to rest on the exhibition sword in the wall mount. "Tai chi?"

I nodded, surprised. Nobody guesses correctly.

Frank waved at the futon. "Okay?"

"Sure," I said.

He sat, putting his briefcase on the coffee table. I went into the kitchen and took out the two foam boxes of enchilada dinners. Robert Johnson materialized on the counter instantly.

I got out three paper plates in wicker plate holders. Two enchiladas for me, one for Frank, one for Robert Johnson. Flour tortillas and beans and rice and grease all around.

I took the food into the main room, set Robert Johnson's on the rug, and handed Frank his.

Frank sat forward on the futon. He rolled a tortilla into a tube, dipped it in enchilada sauce, and bit the end off.

"Enough's enough," he said. "The briefcase has some prelims from the M.E. on Brent Daniels, some paperwork I borrowed from Hollywood Park on Alex Blanceagle. There's also some other cases from the Avalon Department where"—he stopped, considering—"where Sheckly's name has figured prominently."

"And you're showing all this to me?"

Frank read the wall. He chewed his tortilla. "Some guys I know at Bexar County—Larry Drapiewski, Shel Masters—they tell me you're solid."

I tried not to look surprised. Larry and Shel didn't always tell me I was solid. The adjectives they used about me much more frequently had to do with gas or liquid. Frank must've caught them at a weak moment.

"You should be giving this to Samuel Barrera," I suggested.

Frank gave me a brief smile, then he slid the briefcase toward me across the table.

"But Barrera would feel obliged to say where he got the information," I continued. "You need someone who can take a little heat off you."

He finished his tortilla, wiped his fingers, then stood up.

"Shame you didn't come home today," he speculated. "I'll wait until midnight, then decide to call it quits. Agreed?"

I nodded. "Good luck with the colic."

Frank actually smiled. "Yeah. And, Navarre—I hear things at the department. Elgin, some of the other guys who were at Floore's last night. They're hoping you come back into Avalon County sometime when they're on duty. If I were you, I wouldn't do it."

When Frank was gone, I kicked off my Justins and let my toes expand to their normal size. Robert Johnson came over and discovered that his head fit perfectly in a size eleven boot. He shimmied in up to his waist and stayed that way, his tail flicking back and forth.

"You're weird," I told him.

His back legs padded a few times. The tail flicked.

Then I remembered I wasn't supposed to be home.

That left several options, none of them pleasant. I reclaimed my boots and headed out toward Monte Vista.

51

When I got to the Saint-Pierres' house the realtor was just leaving.

"Mr. Saint-Pierre?" she asked.

Her tone was mildly amused. She held the front door open for me with just her fingertips, up at ear level, the way my mom used to hold up my dirty T-shirts, asking if I could get them in the hamper for once.

"Thanks," I said.

"I made some sketches." She wedged her clipboard snugly under the arm of her rotten-apple brown blazer. "The house has marvelous flow patterns."

"I've always thought so."

She nodded, pursed her lips, then appraised the front of the house one more time. "Well, I'll get back to you."

"Allison gave you a time frame?"

"She said immediately."

"Perfect."

She gave me another amused smile—probably never met a talent agent before—then offered me her business card. Sheila Fletcher & Associates. The ink was the same color brown as her jacket and her nails. She waved three fingers at me as she walked down the driveway and got into her Jeep.

Sure enough, the interior of the house had great flow patterns now. Easy when there was nothing to flow around. The white sofas and the artwork pedestals were gone. The Oaxacan wall hangings had been removed so the walls were all white paint and windows. Six million moving boxes were stacked by the door.

The bar was still set up, however, and there were two glasses on it, one sticky with lipstick and bourbon residue, the other half full of tepid water. The fireplace had been used the night before. The smell of smoke lingered from the poorly working flue. After the previous night, smoke was not a smell I was glad to encounter.

I went upstairs and started checking the bedrooms. The first was packed. In Les' room the four-poster bed was stripped, the rolltop desk taped shut, his closet empty. I opened one of the moving boxes packed in the corner. Les' Denton High School yearbook was on top.

"What the hell are you doing?"

I turned and found Allison was in the doorway.

She'd raked her blond hair into stiff wet rows, rinsed but not shampooed. Her complexion was pasty, the corners of her eyes unhealthy red. Her figure was totally hidden under a man's white dress shirt and baggy khakis. Maybe they were Les'. The shirt was speckled with some light brown liquid.

"Glad I caught you before you left town," I said.

She glared at me. "Get the hell out, Tres. Isn't it enough—"

She faltered. She waved her hand vaguely north, in the direction of the Daniels ranch.

I nudged the moving box with my foot. "The realtor says you're moving out immediately."

"Is that any of your business?"

"Possibly."

She grabbed her forearm with her opposite hand like

she was covering a wound. She looked past my shoulder. "I'm renting the house, all right? I can cover the mortgage that way until the sale can happen. It's about the only choice I had."

"What happened to taking over the agency?"

Allison laughed. Her voice was suddenly quivery. "Milo's been real busy with Miranda, but not too busy to bring in some lawyers. Why don't you ask him?"

She stepped inside and sank down on the edge of the stripped mattress. She stared at the boxes of Les' things.

"Who did you have over last night, Allison?"

"That is *definitely* none of your business."

"You're going to need an alibi."

She opened her mouth. She searched for something to say but couldn't quite find it.

"Arson with murder is almost always to cover traces," I said. "Homicide done hastily, by somebody who flew off the handle. Who does that sound like?"

She made a small croaking sound. "You think—"

"I don't think," I said. "But it doesn't look good—you packing up and moving out. If I was the detective in charge of Brent's murder, maybe with Tilden Sheckly paying me to find a convenient solution, I'd start with you. Your husband disappears, your lover gets torched, you've got a history of violent, unpredictable behavior. I doubt many people would come to your defense."

She hugged her arms. "I've got nothing. Brent is dead. Les is gone, Milo's got the agency, and I've got nothing. Just leave me alone, okay?"

She leaned forward until her face was almost over her knees.

I counted to ten.

It didn't help.

"Get up." My own voice sounded strange. "Come on."

I grabbed Allison's upper arms and lifted her to her feet. She was heavy—not dead weight, but her bones seemed to be lead. I had to use most of my strength to keep her from twisting out of my grip. Finally she succeeded and pulled away. She stood there, wet-eyed, rubbing the white stripes on her arms where my fingers had been. "You *fucker.*"

"I don't appreciate the self-pity. It's not going to get us anywhere."

"Just get out, Tres. You hear me? I used to think you were all right."

She glared at me, willing me away, but the anger was unsustainable. She took a long shaky breath and looked around at the boxes again, the rolltop desk, the blank walls. Finally he sank back down onto the bed.

"I'm so tired," she murmured. "Just go away."

"Let's get you out of here. Let's do something constructive."

She shook her head apathetically. When I sat next to her, Allison leaned against me—nothing personal, just like I was a new wall.

"I'm moving home to goddamn Falfurrias," she said. "Can you believe that? This house can buy me about six of the nicest houses down there. I can raise cows. Listen to crickets at night. Isn't that insane?"

She looked up at me. Her eyes were watery.

"I'm the wrong person to ask."

She laughed the word *shit*. "You never give me a goddamn straight answer, do you? Where is Miranda?"

"Staying safe."

"In your apartment? Sharing that little futon?"

"No. Not with me."

Allison looked at me uncertainly. She heard the finality and the edge of bitterness in my voice and she didn't know quite what to do with it. She started to get up but I held her shoulder, not forcefully.

I'd like to say that from there events took their own course and I was caught by surprise. But they didn't and I wasn't.

I kissed her.

For once Allison Saint-Pierre didn't put up a fight. She eased into the kiss with a kind of exhausted relief.

After a long time she leaned back into the bed and I went with her. She bit and kissed and breathed in my ear as I tried futilely to work the first button on the massive white dress shirt until she laughed and whispered, "Forget it."

She sat up just enough to get the shirt off overhead. Then she pressed against me again and felt twice as warm, almost feverish. Her back was all goose bumps.

We rolled around on Les Saint-Pierre's bed and with each new angle the most exposed piece of clothing was kicked or pulled or cursed away. I think Allison stopped crying by the time the clothes were all gone. Her skin was uncomfortably hot except for her fingers. Those were ice-cold.

There was some unstated agreement that this love-making would require nonstop movement, not necessarily frenzied but definitely continuous. Stopping would lead to thinking and thinking would be bad. We took turns crushing each other into the slick, uncomfortably bumpy surface of the mattress, little pinprickers of rayon stitching needling us in our backs. The room was air-conditioned but we quickly became sweaty and noisy until the sounds became an uncontrollable cause for the giggles and then almost as quickly stopped mattering. We rolled a little too far, off the side of the bed. I remember something about a pain in my elbow but that didn't matter much either. We readjusted and sat facing one another, Allison's chin at the level of my mouth and her feet curled against the small of my back. Allison hugged me very tight with her arms and legs and buried her face in my neck and trembled quietly, as if she were crying again. I inhaled sharply and joined her and my body didn't know to stop the movement until Allison's muffled voice spoke into my neck. "Please—okay. Okay."

We stayed still then, feeling each other breathe until the rhythm of our lungs slowed and the hardwood floor began to feel uncomfortable. Our skin separated in places like candle wax being peeled away.

Allison smushed her nose against my cheek and rubbed around until her lips connected with mine. When I kissed her the second time I kissed teeth.

"When you say 'let's do something constructive,' Mr. Navarre—"

"Shut up."

She laughed, pulled her face away, and cupped my ears lightly with her fingers. "Didn't happen."

"Of course not."

She kissed me again. "You're still holding out on me for fifty thousand dollars."

"You're just trying to get the money."

We showed each other how much we detested each other for a while longer.

At some point I remember looking up and seeing the Latina maid in the doorway, but when I opened my eyes for a better look she was gone, just a momentary vision of bored, aging eyes in an impassive face, showing more irritation than embarrassment at the gringos on the floor of the stripped bedroom, giggling foolishly and muttered little "I hate you"s. Maybe to the maid we were just one more item she would be glad to be rid of when the house passed to more respectable owners.

52

"I liked the Audi better," Allison told me.

We were sitting in the VW with the top up, the windows open, but not a bit of circulation coming through. The afternoon had turned thick and gray and lukewarm. Nothing interesting was happening at the warehouse across the street.

"What is this?" I asked. "Number seven?"

"Five," she corrected, pushing up the sunglasses. "It just feels like seven."

I borrowed the list of addresses from her, a photocopy of the document we'd found in Les Saint-Pierre's boat shed. I scanned the page. A total of twenty-three addresses just in San Antonio. At this rate it would be way past Friday before I even had time to find them all, much less figure out ways to get inside and see if they had value to the case against Sheckly. Sam Barrera could have probably put his agency into high gear and gotten the job done in one afternoon if he hadn't had legal restrictions to deal with. Sam Barrera could go to hell.

So far all the addresses were storage facilities or trucking yards. Not all of them said Paintbrush Enterprises on the gates but I had a suspicion Tilden Sheckly or his friends from Luxembourg had a stake in each, one way or another.

Each address had a date next to it. Allison and I had started the search with the location closest to today and worked our way forward in time. We were now on November 5, four days from now. The address was in a light industry park in the elbow of land where Nacogdoches met Perrin-Beitel and became, in true Texas creative thinking, Naco-Perrin.

The storage facility consisted of a pair of long parallel buildings, painted army green with mauve trim. The inward-facing walls were lined with steel roll-up doors and stubby loading docks and were just far enough apart that a semi-rig could back in and deposit its freight box on either side. The asphalt between the two buildings was scarred with large black semicircles from truck tires. It looked like somebody had been in the habit of drinking from God-sized Coke cans there and hadn't had the sense to use coasters.

The complex was ringed with ten-foot chain link, no barbed wire at the top but a security guard in a booth at the front gate and good night lighting all the way around. In the day, traffic on the back side of the industry park was heavy—a constant stream of cars cruising Naco-Perrin's ugly strip malls and fast-food restaurants. On the entrance side of Sheckly's facility, traffic was lighter. The only neighbor was a sulfur-processing plant across the street, acres of weed, and mountains of moon dust.

At the moment the guard at the gate wasn't very interesting to watch. He was reading a little magazine, *Security Guard's Digest* probably. The gates were closed and there were two detached freight boxes in the yard in front of closed loading doors. No business in or out.

Allison sighed. "This is better than staring at the walls at the old house. But only slightly."

Before we'd left Monte Vista, Allison had started

referring to her home of two years as *the old house*. When she'd plopped into the shotgun seat of the VW she'd insisted that she was completely all right, over Les, finished grieving for Brent, ready to help me, and convinced that our afternoon together had been nothing but a nice little break from reality. I wasn't buying any of it and I don't think she was either, but it did let us set aside weightier issues so we could concentrate on watching empty loading docks.

I was about to suggest trying address number six when a white BMW sedan cruised past us on Nacogdoches. It slowed, then turned at the gate. The security guard immediately discarded his magazine and came out to the driver's side window.

"Ignition," I said.

Allison sat up and looked.

Jean Kraus rolled down the BMW's window and spoke to the guard, who nodded. Jean spoke again, smiling, and the guard nodded even more vigorously.

The guard trotted up to the gate, unchained it, and swung open one side. The white BMW drove through. Jean Kraus parked next to the first trailer and he and two other men extracted themselves from the sedan. Jean was dressed for success—an Armani suit, beige, with a little black tie and plenty of silver accents. The other two men I didn't recognize. One was well built, Anglo, with curly brown hair and dress slacks that didn't match the sleeveless T-shirt. The third guy was taller, older, a black sweat suit and the remnants of black hair.

Jean seemed to be pointing out some things to the men, giving them the tour. After a five-minute conversation and some head nodding and a few looks at the loading bays, all three got back in the BMW and left.

"They're moving cargo out," I said. "Getting rid of it early."

Allison looked at me. "Are we being constructive yet?"

"We're on the outskirts."

I started the engine of the VW.

We followed Jean's BMW for a few miles down Perrin-Beitel before it became too difficult. The traffic was bad, Jean was a little too jumpy a driver, and my orange bug was anything but nondescript. To stay with him I had to risk discovery. I fell back and let him go.

"Does this mean we don't get to beat the shit out of anybody?" Allison wanted to know.

"I'm sorry, honey."

Allison pouted.

It was starting to get dark when I dropped her back at the *old house* in Monte Vista. Allison insisted on staying there and she insisted on staying there alone. I didn't argue very hard with the second part. Seeing her get out of the car, I started developing a funny empty feeling in my intestinal basement that either meant I very much wanted to stay with her or I very much didn't. You get to feeling those extremes and not being able to tell them apart, it's time to go home by yourself and feed the cat.

I watched her walk all the way up the sidewalk and go inside and I watched the door for a long time after that. The door didn't reopen.

When I got home I showered, picked the cleanest things I could find out of the growing pile of laundry, then made two calls.

Ray Lozano answered at the Bexar County M.E.'s office.

"Raymond. This is Tres."

A moment of silence. "As in the guy who owes me the Spurs tickets?"

"Yeah, about that—"

"Save it, Navarre. You keep making promises and I keep believing, it'll just make me feel bad."

"Faith is an admirable quality, Raymond. You like the Oilers?"

"What do you want?"

I read Lozano the notes Frank had given me from the Avalon County autopsy of Brent Daniels.

"So?" he said.

"What can you interpret?"

"They were lucky to get as much tissue as they did, given the state of the body. It sounds like this guy was dead before he burned. No soot particles in the bronchi. No carboxy-hemoglobin in the fluids. This guy didn't go down breathing smoke."

"And the lack of a positive ID?"

"Somewhat unusual, given that they know the victim, but it's early. They have to be one hundred percent sure. If you have to wait for X-ray records from a big hospital, or wait for the odontologist, maybe the anthropologist to come down from Austin, it can take up to ten days. Sometimes more. It doesn't sound like there's really any doubt, though. The size is right, compensating for shrinkage; age and sex are right."

"What about these trace chemicals?" I read off some hard-to-pronounce compounds the M.E. had found in the few remaining fluids of Brent's body.

Lozano ticked his tongue a few times. "I'd have to check with a toxicologist. Was this guy an alcoholic?"

"Probably. Yes."

"Okay—that gives you a setup for liver damage, poor sugar processing. If the guy came in contact with certain other drugs in a large enough dosage, they could trigger the kind of chemicals you're seeing there, only that would mean the subject was in a diabetic coma before he died."

"A coma. You mean like if he came into contact with diabetes drugs? Gluco something-or-other?"

"Glucophage. Absolutely."

I was quiet so long Lozano finally said, "You still there?"

"Yeah. You think—would somebody OD on these, for suicide?"

Lozano blew air. "Not unless they were mainline stupid. Chances are pretty good the drugs wouldn't kill you, they'd just turn you into a vegetable. I know one nurse at the Medical Center that happened to, man—alcohol and diabetes medicine. They're changing her diapers three times a day now. Plus it wouldn't make sense—a guy goes comatose, then dies, then becomes a crispy critter."

"Okay."

"That information helpful at all?"

I probably didn't sound too enthusiastic when I said, "Yeah. It's helpful."

"Now what was that about the Oilers?" Lozano started to say. But the phone was already halfway to the cradle.

Milo Chavez was even more thrilled to hear from me.

"Tell me Miranda is safe," he demanded.

"Miranda's safe."

"Tell me I shouldn't kill you for taking off with her like you did."

"Come on, Milo."

"I had a couple of Avalon County dicks in the office this morning, Navarre. They had some questions about how Les and I got along with Brent Daniels, why I might've hired a PI and what kind of work you did, whether you were licensed or not. I didn't like the direction they were going."

"Avalon County homicide couldn't detect its way out of a *cascarón*, Milo. They're just trying to rattle you."

"They're succeeding."

I told him about my afternoon—about the autopsy files from Frank, then about the warehouse address I'd visited on Perrin-Beitel.

"I know that place," Milo said. "This is good, isn't it? The RIAA guy, Barrera—he'll need to move on it now, right?"

"You ask Barrera, he'll tell you nothing's changed. There's still no evidence, no probable cause for a search. Just the fact I saw somebody there who I didn't like isn't enough. Barrera's willing to hold out another few years if it means strengthening his legal case."

"I've got until Friday," Milo muttered. "And you're talking about years."

"Barrera's technically correct," I said. "There's nothing

they can move on in what I've found. At least not right away."

"Technically correct," Milo grumbled. "That's just great."

"We'll figure out something," I promised.

"And Les?"

That one was harder to sound confident on. "Consider him gone. For good."

Milo was silent, probably trying to formulate some kind of B plan. When he spoke again his voice was strange, tightly controlled. "I'll need to talk to Miranda. If we're going to have to come clean with Century when we bring them the tape, I need to talk to my client about strategy. She needs to know the risks. Maybe—"

"I'll bring her by later tonight," I promised. "It'll take a couple of hours."

"My office at nine," he suggested.

"Okay. And Barrera is good, Milo. The people he is working with are good. They will eventually put Sheckly's ass in a sling."

The other end of the line was deadly calm.

"Milo?"

"I'm fine," he said.

"Let it go, Milo."

"All right."

"Your office at nine."

Milo said sure. As he hung up he was still speaking, muttering unhappy and angry thoughts. I had the feeling I was no longer part of the conversation.

53

Mendoza Street ran along the eastern edge of the San Fernando Cemetery. On the left-hand side of the road the graveyard's chain-link fence tilted and bowed at irregular intervals, like a football team had been using it for blocking practice. Evening ground fog had thickened on the cemetery lawn, diluting the tombstones and the air and the trees into one grayish smear.

On the right side of the street was a line of box houses with brightly painted wood slat siding and burglar-barred windows and worn tar shingle roofs. The yards were squares of crabgrass, some gravel, some display areas for broken furniture and tires. There were no kids in sight, nothing of value on the porches, no windows open, few cars parked on the street except those that had been stolen from other parts of town, then stripped and abandoned here. There were plenty of those.

Number 344 was a turquoise one-bedroom in slightly better repair than the houses around it. Ralph's maroon Cadillac and a baby-blue Camaro were in the driveway.

The front yard was white gravel, decorated with bottle caps. The burglar bars on the screen door and windows were painted white and shaped like ivy, though they were so ornate and thick they reminded me more of a fused curtain of bones.

I rang the bell and stood on the porch for about twenty seconds before Ralph answered the door, mid-laugh. Somewhere behind him I could hear Miranda laughing too. The smell of mota smoke wafted out the door.

"Eh, *vato*." Ralph's glasses shimmered yellow in the porch light.

He stood aside to let me in.

The living room was bare except for one brown couch opposite the window. The interior walls were stark white and the floors hardwood and several bullet holes in the ceiling had been imperfectly spackled over. Drive-by souvenirs from the house's previous owner. Ralph had gotten the place cheap because of that.

Through an archway I could see Miranda sitting at a dining table across from another woman. They were both laughing so hard they were wiping away tears. Miranda was still dressed as she had been this morning—in jeans, boots, and my T-shirt. Her face had more color, though; her posture was a little less weighed-down. The other woman was a young Latina with long coppery hair and a bright yellow dress that showed lots of leg. She wore black pumps and silver earrings and makeup.

When the women saw me they both smiled.

Miranda said my name like it was a pleasant memory from twenty years ago.

The other woman got up and came to give me a hug. "Hey, vaquero."

She kissed both my ears, then stepped back to appraise me.

"Cally," I said. "How you doing?"

"*Asi asi.*" Then, still in Spanish, "You've got a nice lady here."

I looked at Miranda, who was still smiling and wiping her eyes. There was only one lit joint in the room—in

Ralph's hand—but there were assorted munchies on the table—bags of tortilla chips, a steaming canister of Ralph's homemade venison tamales, a plate of Ralph's special *pan dulce*—the kind with the green flecks in the icing. Uh-oh.

Ralph saw my expression and spread his hands. "Everything's cool, *vato*. Just relaxing, doing the grief process, right?"

I stared at him.

Ralph shrugged, turned to Cally. "Eh, *mamasita,* let's go out back, get Chico to take you home."

Cally said good-bye to Miranda, gave her a hug, then kissed me one last time. Ralph gave us an amused grin, then led his lady friend out the screen door.

In the floodlit backyard, Chico of the yellow pirate bandanna and the easily kicked balls was working on a half-assembled Shelby. Ralph kept the car out there just for his grunts—sort of like the block table for kids at the doctor's office. Chico stopped messing with the fuel pump and quickly wiped his hands when Cally and Ralph came out.

I sat across the table from Miranda and turned the plate of laced *pan dulce* around. "How many?"

Miranda blinked very slowly. "Two? I don't remember."

"Great."

My face was apparently good enough to warrant another laugh. She held her hand over her mouth, quivered silently for five beats, and then did a little snort on beat six.

"I guess I shouldn't ask how you're feeling," I ventured.

"I'm sorry," she said. "I just—it feels good to laugh, Tres. Cally's so nice. Ralph is really lucky."

"Sure," I said.

"Have they been together long?"

I hesitated. "Actually they're more like business partners."

Miranda frowned. She reached for another *pan dulce* before I moved the plate.

"Better not," I said.

"Oh—right." She went for the bag of Doritos instead, examined the plastic edges. "Ralph and Cally told me not to be mad at you. They talk about you pretty highly— said you usually knew what you were talking about, even if it wasn't fun to hear."

Outside, Ralph had finished giving Chico his orders. Ralph tossed him a set of car keys, then swatted Cally's behind by way of farewell. She grinned, then followed her yellow bandannaed chauffeur around the side of the house, out of sight.

"I spoke to Allison today," I said.

Miranda smiled ruefully. "My best friend in the whole world."

I told her about Allison moving out, about the addresses we had tracked, about how I had some new information on Brent's murder.

Miranda tried to pull her expression together, to anchor herself on my words. Her attention disintegrated quickly.

There was a small hole in the upper corner of the Dorito bag, much too little to get a chip through. The problem was too much for Miranda's stoned sensibilities. Finally she started breaking up chips inside the bag with one finger, getting them small enough to fit through the hole.

My story faltered to a stop.

Miranda looked up, probably wondering why the sound of my voice had gone away. "What?"

"Milo wanted to see you tonight, to talk strategy. Maybe I should call him, tell him tomorrow would be better."

She processed those words.

"Milo wants—" Her voice trailed off, like she was just remembering that name. "My brother is dead and Allison's leaving town and Milo wants to talk about Century Records."

A car engine started in the driveway. Seconds later the headlights of the baby-blue Camaro slipped through the living-room window, over the couch and across the living-room table, then disappeared down Mendoza Street.

Miranda moved a small piece of tortilla chip across the table with her finger, like it was a checker. "We should talk, Tres. Before we see Milo."

"I know."

"The things you said last night, the way you made me out . . ."

The screen door screaked open and Ralph came in alone.

I turned back toward Miranda. "Like I said, tomorrow would be better. I'll call Milo."

"*Pinche* Chavez," Ralph put in. "This lady need help it ain't going to come from his sorry ass."

He looked at Miranda. She rewarded him with a faint smile.

I walked to the phone. Ralph sat where I had been sitting and helped himself to the tamales. As he pried off the canister lid a cloud of steam and cumin and spiced meat smells mushroomed up. He pulled out three of the tamales and began unshucking them. He told Miranda not to worry about a thing. We'd be taking care of her.

Gladys answered the phone at the agency office.

"Milo in?" I asked her.

Gladys sounded like she was shuffling furniture, or maybe moving quickly into another part of the office.

Her tone was low and urgent.

"He's out," she whispered. "You mean you don't know—"

"What do you mean, out?"

Our questions cross-fired and tangled. We both backtracked and waited.

"Okay," I said. "Tell me what happened."

Gladys told me how Milo had canceled his dinner meeting with an important client, then stormed out of the office. He'd thrown his pager on Gladys' desk on the way out, telling her "Don't bother." He'd said he had some business to take care of. Gladys had been worried enough to check Milo's desk, which she'd been forbidden

to do but which she apparently knew well enough to
notice what was missing—the handgun Milo kept in the
middle drawer. She had just assumed, me being the most
disreputable person Milo knew, no offense of course,
that he'd gone somewhere with me. Gladys was about to
tell me something else, something to justify her prying,
but I cut her off.

"How long ago?"

"Ten minutes?" she said, plaintive, apologetic.

I hung up and looked at Ralph, then at Miranda.

"What?" Miranda said.

"Milo just left the office with a gun," I said.

My words took a while to impact, and even when they
did the effect was dull. Miranda's brown eyes slid down
to my chin, then my chest, then to her own hands. She
pushed the Doritos away. "You know where he's going?"

"Yes."

"He's trying something dangerous. For me."

"Yes."

Ralph ate, looking back and forth between us. His
expression had all the depth of someone watching a bar-
room TV program. When he finished his tamale he wiped
his hands and then spread them, a here-I-am gesture.

"Maybe so," I agreed.

Ralph slowly broke into a grin, like I'd given him an
answer he'd been expecting for days.

I looked at Miranda. "You could stay here. Ralph is
right—he and I could take care of it for you."

Miranda flushed. Anger seemed to be burning the
marijuana slowness out of her eyes. "I'm coming. Just
tell me where we're going."

Ralph straightened up in his chair so he could take out
Mr. Subtle, his .357 Magnum. He clunked it on the table
and said, "Dessert."

54

The night sky was bright with thunderclouds and the air smelled like metal. The raindrops were infrequent, warm and large as birds' eggs.

Ralph pulled the maroon Cadillac in behind the VW on the north side of Nacogdoches, about half a block down from the entrance of the storage facility.

He met us by the chain-link fence of the sulfur-processing plant. The wind was whipping around, pushing Miranda's hair into her mouth. Her white Berkeley T-shirt was freckled with rain.

"Bad," I told Ralph.

Across the street the gates of the floodlit facility were open crookedly. Sheck's huge black pickup truck was just outside. The security booth was empty; Milo's green Jeep Cherokee was parked at a forty-five-degree angle across the entrance, its fender crunched against the booth's doorway and its driver's side door open. If the guard had been in the booth, he would've had to crawl over Milo's

~~hood to get~~ out. From this angle I couldn't see the yard between the two buildings.

Monday night. Traffic along Nacogdoches was light. What cars there were turned into the industrial parkway before getting to our block. Two blocks down, five or six teenagers were waiting at the VIA bus stop.

Ralph looked at the yard. "No cover worth shit. Chavez, man—stupid ass isn't worth saving."

"You can back out," I said. "No obligation."

Ralph grinned. "*¿Mande?*"

I nodded my thanks, then looked at Miranda. She was hugging her elbows. Her brows were knit together. On the ride north she had managed to shake off most of the effects of the laced *pan dulce*, but she still had a withdrawn, slightly puffed-up demeanor, like a very cold parakeet on a perch. She shifted her weight onto one leg and lifted the other boot behind her knee. "What can I do?"

I think it was meant to sound brave, gung ho. It came out plaintive.

I got out my wallet and gave Miranda one of Detective Gene Schaeffer's cards, which I'd had the unhappy fortune to collect on many occasions.

"You can stay here if you want," I told her. "Be our anchor. Ralph has a cell phone. You hear any trouble, any shots, call that number and ask for homicide, Gene Schaeffer. Insist on talking to him. Tell him where we are and what's happening and tell him to get on the phone with Samuel Barrera and get down here. We're giving them probable cause to enter. Do you have all that?"

Miranda nodded uncertainly.

Ralph looked at me, produced his fallback gun, a Dan Wesson .38, and held it toward me. "I know what you're gonna say, *vato*. But I got to offer."

"No thanks."

"I'll take it," Miranda said.

She did, gingerly. She held the gun correctly, pointed it down, unlatched the barrel and rolled it, checking the cylinders. She closed it and looked at me defiantly. "I'm not being an anchor." Then to Ralph, "Take your own damn cell phone."

Ralph laughed. "This lady's all right, man. *Vamos.*"

He got out Mr. Subtle. We crossed Nacogdoches and walked toward the gates, staying close to the fence.

By the time we got there rain was coming down heavy enough to make a high-pitched pinging against the corrugated metal roofs of the storage buildings. In the yard were the same two freight boxes that were there that afternoon, but this time they were attached to semi-rigs with the motors running. One loading-bay door was open. No one was on the dock, but looking underneath the first truck we could see long shadows from two pairs of legs on the other side—men talking between the trucks. One of them wore jeans and boots. The other had slacks, dress shoes.

I turned to Miranda. "Last chance."

But it was already happening too fast. Ralph knew when to take advantage, and he knew there wouldn't be a better chance to close some distance. He went right, walking quickly toward the cab of the truck. I moved left to the side of the building and began jogging toward the first loading dock. Miranda followed me.

The gunshots came when we were almost to the dock. I was running forward before I fully registered what I had heard. Two shots, both incredibly loud, from inside the warehouse, followed quickly by two shots from the right, behind the first truck. Those had been almost as loud—the report of a .357. Ralph had taken advantage of timing again.

We met Ralph under the loading dock, where metal slats had been laid across from the cement to the truck bed. The dock was only about five feet high. We had to crouch to avoid being seen from inside. Ralph had his gun out and was shaking his head, whispering Spanish curses and looking mildly displeased. Behind him were some low-pitched groans, almost muffled in the rain and the truck engines.

"*Cabrons* tried to get smart. One of them might live, I think."

I looked under the truck. On the opposite side, thirty yards away, the man in the slacks and the T-shirt who had been with Jean Kraus in the BMW earlier in the day was curled up on the asphalt, a pistol about ten feet away from him—kicked there by Ralph, probably. The man was making the groans as he tried to stop the bleeding in his thigh. He was kicking himself along the pavement with his good leg, like he was trying to get somewhere, but he was only succeeding in making small circles. His fingers clutched his leg where the blood was seeping through, soaking his pants and smearing the pavement. He had gone at least one complete circle in his own pool because the blood was on his face and in his hair too. In the outdoor lights the sticky places glistened purple.

Red-haired Elgin Garwood was ten feet closer to us. He was very dead. A .357 round had eaten a fist-sized chunk out of his chest, just to the left of his sternum. He was staring at the sky and rain was running off his forehead. His 9mm was still in his right hand.

My ears roared. I tried to think but the engines and the rain and the after-echo of gunfire made it impossible. Inside the warehouse, an argument was going on. More groaning. Was it possible they hadn't recognized the gunfire outside as a separate problem? Maybe the echo inside the building . . .

A carload of high school kids drove by on Nacogdoches, oblivious, grins on their faces, heavy metal music blaring.

I held my breath, then popped my head up for a brief look into the warehouse.

A two-second snapshot—Tilden Sheckly and Jean Kraus arguing. Sheckly with a gun stuck in the waist of his pants. Kraus' Beretta in his hand. The apparent subject of the argument, a mountain of wounded human being on the floor in front of them. Milo Chavez, the soles of his very expensive shoes pointed toward me, one hand clutching at his shoulder, maybe his heart. A single line of blood ran away from his body, stopping after two feet to seep into and around a legal-sized document that Milo had apparently dropped, then continuing.

I ducked back down and pressed my back against the cement wall of the loading dock. I closed my eyes and tried to memorize the placement of things.

When I opened my eyes again I was looking at Miranda. Her face was pale, her hand pressed lightly over her mouth. She was staring under the truck, watching the man kick a circular path through his own blood, watching the other one with the hole in his chest, the one who had brought his wife Karen to Willis' parties.

She started shaking.

"Get the hell out, Ralph." I grabbed the cell phone from him, then, with much greater hesitation, traded it with Miranda for the .38 Wesson. "You just killed a cop. An Avalon County deputy, but still a cop. Miranda goes too—Miranda makes the call to Schaeffer, neither of you were ever here."

Ralph's face hardened. The lenses of his glasses gleamed solid yellow. He rubbed his thumb along the safety catch of the .357. "That's too bad, *vato*."

"No," I said.

But I couldn't stop it. Ralph crouched just low enough for the shot. The muzzle blast flared, illuminating the underside of the truck. The man who had been kicking a circle in his own blood stopped kicking. A new red pattern, less circular, began seeping into the asphalt around his head.

I counted three very long seconds. Miranda crouched next to us, stone still. Her face had the dazed, unhappily sated look of someone who was just realizing that she'd overdone it at the banquet table.

Ralph turned to me, gave a very small, cold smile. "Ain't standing in no lineup for Milo Chavez, *vato*. *Lo siento*."

Then he was gone, Miranda whisked into his wake and pulled along willingly or no, and I didn't have the luxury of thinking.

~~There had~~ been a third shot. Jean Kraus would be coming out.

It had been almost twenty years since I fired a gun. I moved five feet to the left and turned, lifted above the lip of the loading dock just enough to see and fired a round toward the roof, roughly in the direction Sheck and Kraus had been standing. Sheck was still there, but now partially crouched behind a large wooden crate. Kraus was twenty feet closer to the entrance. When I fired he almost fell over himself backtracking. I didn't have time to notice if Milo was still breathing.

I ducked and moved toward the side steps of the loading dock.

I yelled, "Sheckly! Two men are down out here. The police have been called. We've got about three minutes to work this thing out."

Miranda and Ralph had disappeared through the gates. There were no sirens. Yet.

A huge drop of rain caught me on the nose, forcing me to blink. Inside it was silent until Sheckly let out a strained noise, a poor imitation of a laugh. "You just don't give up, son, do you? You think I'm gonna stop to sign ole Milo's papers right now I'm sorry—I'm a little busy."

I was at the top of the steps now, my body flat against the wall just outside the entrance.

"You wanted Chavez shot?" I called. "Was that your idea? If I was you, Sheck, I'd put some distance between myself and Kraus right now."

I crouched, looked in, and nearly got my head shot off anyway. Kraus had targeted effectively. I fired back stupidly, ineffectually into the air and ducked around the corner again. My hand was already numb from the recoil. The smell of primer was in my nose. God, I hate guns.

In my third snapshot look I had noticed a few new things. There were rows and rows of large cylinders stacked upright just behind Kraus. Each was about seven inches in diameter and five or six feet high, wrapped in brown paper and capped on either end with plastic, like huge canisters for architects' drawings.

The other thing I noticed was Sheckly. He had been standing again, making no attempt to find cover. And he wasn't staring at the entrance, looking for me. He was staring at Milo Chavez's chest. Chavez's hand had fallen away from the shoulder and was now limp at his side. That was not good.

Jean Kraus called out, "There is nothing we can't discuss, Mr. Navarre." His voice was collected, genial, a little too loud to be trusted. "Your friend needs a doctor's attention, I think. Perhaps we should call a truce."

"Go on, Navarre," Sheckly called. "Get out of here."

"Let's discuss it," I called. "Like Kraus says. Did he tell you about the thirteen-year-old French boy he killed? Kraus discussed his way out of that one real well. I imagine he'll do the same here—get safely to another country and leave you with the wreckage and the bodies, Tilden. How does that sound?"

Kraus' voice came back a little bit louder and a little less genial. He made sure I heard the action on the Beretta as he chambered the next round.

"I have my gun pointed at your friend's head, Mr. Navarre. At present he can still be saved. Throw your gun into the doorway and come into the warehouse and perhaps I will reconsider my options. Do you understand?"

Sheckly said something very insistent in German, an order. Kraus responded derisively in the same language.

Sheck barked the same command again and Kraus laughed. Somewhere very far away there were sirens. The rain kept falling in my face, soaking through my shirt.

"No good, Sheck," I yelled. "Give it up and I'll make sure they listen to you. Let Kraus and his associates be the ones they lynch. Otherwise we're talking multiple murders and Huntsville and a bunch of guys in Luxembourg laughing their ass off about you. What's it going to be?"

"*One*—" Kraus started to count.

Milo Chavez managed a noise, a low mumble that might've been a scream if not for weakness and shock.

Sheck barked something else in German and Kraus yelled *"Two—"* and I gave up hope and came barreling into the doorway to fire when guns went off.

Not mine.

I remember Jean Kraus raising his Beretta toward Sheck and Sheck drawing his .41 faster than anything I've ever seen and both men firing. Three rapid red bubbles expanded and burst in the back of Kraus' white turtleneck. Kraus lurched backward into a forest of upright CD spools and sent them crashing to the floor. Plastic caps shot off and three CDs spilled out like metallic poker chips, slishing colorfully across the cement. *Three.*

The aftermath was incredibly quiet. The rain drummed on the corrugated metal overhead. The truck engines hummed. I swear I could hear the rattle of Milo's breath.

Sheck stared at me. His eyes were dull. He wiped the sweat off his lip with the back of his gun hand, took a step back, and stumbled against the crate where he'd been hiding a moment before. There were giant sweat rings like half-moons under the arms of his denim shirt. One of his boots had come untucked from his jeans. His hat was knocked sideways at a funny angle and he was bleeding—from the scar Allison had given him a few days ago, now burst out of its little squares of tape, and from a streak of blood on his arm, where Jean's bullet had grazed through the shirt, ripping the fabric and a layer of skin neatly away.

The sirens were getting louder.

I looked at Jean Kraus' body in the CDs. He was bent over the tubes of music at a funny angle, his head too far back and his chest too far out. One of the canisters had fallen into the crook of his arm so he seemed to be holding it like an oversized spear. One leg was folded unnaturally behind him. His eyes were open as black and fierce as ever.

I crouched next to Milo and looked into his face. I couldn't tell anything. He continued to breathe, and to bleed. The wound was in his shoulder, probably no internal organs hit. His eyes were glazed and unfocused.

I looked at Sheck.

He was breathing shallowly, like he was trying to remember how. When he looked at me and laughed, the noise sounded more like a pained whimper, like he was getting something cauterized.

"I can talk, son," he told me. "I'll talk. Hell, I've weathered worse."

As the sirens approached and I tended to Milo's wounds Sheckly paced around the warehouse, kicking at the pirate CDs, laughing and mumbling to Jean Kraus' corpse that he'd weathered worse, like maybe if he said it a few hundred more times he might come to believe it.

55

Tuesday and Wednesday were a blur.

I remember cops, Milo Chavez in the hospital, more cops. I remember sleeping in an interrogation room for several hours, speaking to Sam Barrera and Gene Schaeffer on several occasions and meeting Barrera's nice friends from the FBI and ATF. When I dreamt I dreamt about giving pints of blood over and over and asking for donuts and water and getting nothing but little smiley face stickers that said: I'M A DONOR.

I woke Thursday morning on the futon at 90 Queen Anne, wondering how I got there. Vague memories started surfacing about a ride in the back of a mustard-yellow BMW, someone who smelled like Aramis cursing my father's name as he trundled me out of the car and dragged me up the stairs and tucked me roughly into bed.

I blinked the crust out of my eyes. Robert Johnson was curled around my feet. The TV was on.

I stared at the pretty colors and the plastic faces of

anchorpeople. Slowly the sounds they were making became English.

They were recapping the story of the week, telling me things I already knew. We'd had the second largest bust of pirate and bootleg audio CDs in U.S. history, right here in the Alamo City—$1.5 million netted in cash over the last two days and 350,000 titles by over ninety country artists—all precipitated by a police response to gunfire at a North Side warehouse Monday evening. Three men had been killed before police arrived. One of the victims was an Avalon County deputy who'd apparently been in collusion with the pirates. The other two victims were Luxembourg nationals. A falling out among thieves, one reporter had called it.

Tilden Sheckly, country music entrepreneur, had been taken into custody at the scene and was cooperating with authorities about his connections to the European smuggling ring. He had led Customs officials to three separate warehouses full of merchandise and cash and several boxes of automatic weapons that the ATF claimed were the first shipments of a fledgling gunrunning operation, piggybacking off the CD distribution network. Several recent murders in the San Antonio area had now been linked to the Luxembourg organization and at least one foreign national was still at large, wanted for the slaying of the Avalon County deputy Elgin Garwood. The anchorman showed the wanted man's face—the third man who'd been in Jean Kraus' BMW—and gave a name I didn't recognize. The murder weapon had been found several blocks away—a .357 caliber pistol, wiped of prints, unregistered.

A search was under way for locally based talent agent, Les Saint-Pierre. According to Samuel Barrera, RIAA's contracted private investigator and hero of the day, Mr. Saint-Pierre was not a suspect in any crime. Rather, Saint-Pierre had disappeared while acting as an informant for the authorities and was, sadly, presumed dead.

As for Tilden Sheckly, he was a small fish. When pressed the SAPD spokesman confirmed that Sheck stood a good chance of lenient charges if, as promised, he could help authorities in several states and at least three E.U. countries with information on his Luxembourg partners.

I turned off the TV.

I managed a shower, then some cold cereal.

Around ten o'clock I called a friend of mine in the *Express-News* entertainment section and got the rest of the story. The inside scoop in music industry circles was that Les Saint-Pierre had actually embezzled tens of thousands from his own agency and disappeared to the Caribbean. Some said Mazatlán. Others said Brazil. Many said he'd been working with the Luxembourgians. The agency he'd headed had collapsed over the last forty-eight hours, although one of Les' associates, Milo Chavez, had heroically confronted the pirates and blown the whole operation open. Chavez was said to be recovering nicely and putting together a lucrative deal for Miranda Daniels with Century Records. As a result of that, and the good publicity, Chavez had employment offers from several large Nashville agencies. Reportedly with Milo would came Miranda Daniels as a client and a large number of former Saint-Pierre talent. Milo had apparently underestimated himself.

According to my friend at the *Express-News*, the Miranda Daniels developmental tape featured strong material and was as good as a surefire gold record. It had a strong buzz going, whatever that meant. My friend expected the deal to go through with Century Records and Miranda to be on the *Billboard* charts by New Year's. He said the human interest angle really helped—first and foremost the recent tragic death of Miranda's brother, who had written some of her best songs. The murder of her former fiddle player helped too.

"The tabloids are eating this up," Carlon McAffrey told me. "You don't happen to have an in with this Chavez guy, do you? Or Daniels?"

I hung up the phone.

I did tai chi on the back porch until almost noon. Halfway through the long form my muscles started to

burn the right way again. The vacuous sick feeling in my
stomach faded. Once I got into the sword form I could
almost concentrate again. The phone rang just as I was
completing the last section.

I went inside and caught it on the third ring.

Kelly Arguello said, "Allen Meissner."

"What?"

"Get a pen, stupid."

I pulled one out of the crack in the ironing board.
Kelly rattled off a social security number, a Texas driver's
license number, a flight number.

"Meissner applied for the social security number two
months ago," she said, "at age forty-five. Got his license
at DMV two weeks ago, then plane tickets to New York
on American, booked for tomorrow. Good trick considering the guy died in '95. Meissner used to be an in-house
auditor for Texas Instruments."

"Holy shit," I said.

"You did say before Friday, didn't you?"

"You found him."

Kelly laughed. "That's what I've been trying to tell
you, *chico loco*. Your client's going to be happy?"

I stared at the flight number. "When was this reservation made?"

"Yesterday. Hey—this is good news, right?"

I hesitated. "Absolutely. You're incredible, Kelly."

"I've been trying to tell you that, too. Now about that
dinner—"

"Talk to Ralph."

"Oh, please, not that again."

I leaned down against the ironing board and ran my
fingers into my hair. I closed my eyes and listened to the
slight crackle of the phone line.

"No," I said. "I mean you should call him."

She spent a few silent moments trying to interpret my
tone. "What happened? What'd you two get into this
time?"

"You just need to call him, okay? Even better, get
down here. Spend a day with him, okay? He needs—I

don't know, I think he needs to be reminded you're around. Some niece-ly influence."

"Niece-ly is a word?"

"Hey. English Ph.D. here. Back off."

"This is the thanks I get for helping you?"

"You'll do it?"

Kelly sighed. "I'll do it. I'll also come to see you."

She said it like it was the deadliest threat she could make. I smiled in spite of myself.

"¿*Bueno?*" she asked.

"*Bueno,*" I agreed.

56

It was Friday morning before I spoke to Milo and Miranda again. I never found out how Miranda's things got picked up from the safe house on the South Side—Ralph just handled it somehow. Ralph didn't call me. That told me something.

Milo and Miranda arranged to meet me at the Sunset Cafe for breakfast. Gladys the ex-receptionist for the ex-Les Saint-Pierre Agency set up the appointment.

The Sunset Cafe was the kind of place you'd drive right by—an adobe one-room shack on the ridge rising from Broadway, wedged between an art gallery and an insurance office. Despite its name, the *cocina* opened early and closed early, serving egg and bacon and *carne guisada* tacos and strong coffee to blue collars. When I pulled the VW up the steep driveway and into the tiny parking lot, Milo's Jeep was already there.

The Daniels' brown and white Ford pickup was also in the lot, minus the horse trailer. Willis Daniels was sitting in the driver's seat. If he noticed me walking up, he didn't let on. At least not until I stood at the window for a few seconds.

The old man looked up from his book and smiled a tight smile. "Mr. Navarre."

He offered to shake, gentlemanly. His hand lacked any of the energy it had had when I'd first shaken it, outside Silo Studios a hundred years ago.

"You not hungry?" I asked.

The smile took on a kind of sad amusement. "I'd just be in the way. You go on."

He went back to his book, sighed. It would've been easier if he'd yelled at me, or frowned at least. I went inside.

Milo and Miranda were drinking coffee at the table by the window.

Saying Milo looked nice is superfluous, but somehow there was shock value in seeing him immaculate again after the way he'd looked on that warehouse floor, then in the hospital bed. His trousers were dark and freshly pressed, his white shirt crisp with starch. The bandages underneath the shirt made his left shoulder look bulkier than the right. He was wearing a diamond stud earring and his short-cropped black hair looked freshly trimmed along the edges.

He hooked a pink chair with his fingers and dragged it out from the table.

"Have a seat, Tres."

I sat between them.

Miranda was wearing lightly tinted round sunglasses. She'd chosen all white today—long skirt, blouse with just enough mother-of-pearl studs to put it into the Western category, white ankle-length boots. Even her hair, dark and curly, was pulled back in a white headband, making her forehead look high and her sunglasses that much more obvious.

She was looking into her coffee, holding it with both hands. She glanced up briefly at me, then down again.

"Here." I set my shoe box next to Milo's untouched plate of tinfoil-wrapped tacos.

Milo scowled, lifted the lid, then closed it again.

At a table across the way one of the construction workers had apparently seen what was inside the box. He said, "Holy shit" very quietly and nudged his friend.

"You brought me cash?" Milo asked, incredulous.

"That's the way I found it."

Milo looked at me, a little puzzled by my tone. "All right. Fifty thousand?"

"Half."

He looked at me longer.

"Problem?" I asked.

"Very possibly."

"The rest I'm giving to Allison. The way things are shaping up, it may be the only thing she gets out of this deal."

Milo let his eyes slide over to Miranda, who looked suddenly very sad.

"Allison," Milo repeated. "You know that this is agency money, Les' and mine. You know she doesn't have claim to it—why the fuck—"

"You want to talk to the IRS, go. I'm sure you were planning on reporting this recovered."

Milo closed his mouth. His eyes had the bull fierceness in them, but he was trying hard to keep it from the surface.

"I hoped we could be a little more constructive here. I didn't want—" He shook his head, disappointed. "Christ, Tres, it's not like we don't owe you something, but—"

He let me see a little bit inside, a little bit of hurt and discomfort, the sense that we were still friends.

I turned to Miranda. "You happy with your deal?"

The question took her by surprise, or maybe it was just the fact that I spoke to her at all.

She sat up, away from me just slightly. "I will be, yes. I'm grateful to you. But—"

She was steeling herself to say something, probably something she'd rehearsed with Milo before coming here.

She couldn't quite manage it. She swallowed and looked on the verge of tears. It was a look she did well.

"Miranda's relocating to Nashville," Milo supplied. "We both are."

I turned my attention back to him. "You both are."

Somehow the words seemed absurd. I felt like I was speaking Spanish, when I hit an unfamiliar colloquialism and the sense of almost being fluent came to a grinding stop.

Milo unwrapped one of his tacos, peeling back the tinfoil with the detached interest of a coroner. A plume of steam zigzagged up from the eggs.

"We've been lucky things have worked out as well as they have," he explained. "Very lucky. We owe you for that, but we thought it would be best—Miranda needs to be closer to the action."

I stared at Miranda. She wouldn't meet my eyes.

"We just wanted you to know," Milo continued. "There's a lot of outstanding problems from all of this. Until Miranda's career really gets going, things are going to be fragile. Miranda needs a clean break from everything that's happened."

I kept staring.

"She's lost family here," Milo continued. "She can't keep being reminded of that. We want to make sure you feel compensated, but you need to be out of the picture, Tres. I'm going to insist on that."

"Compensated," I said. Another foreign term. I looked at Miranda. "You plan on *compensating* the others, too—Cam, Sheck, Les? How about Brent and Julie Kearnes?"

Miranda wiped a tear away. She was wavering between sorrow and anger, trying to decide what approach would be the most effective.

"That ain't fair, Tres," she muttered, hoarsely. "It just ain't."

I nodded. "How long until Milo gets the clean-break message, from somebody in Nashville, some slightly bigger big shot who's decided he can look out for your interests better? A week ago you told me Allison was the only person who scared you to death, Miranda. I've met somebody scarier."

"Stop," Milo insisted.

He was strictly lawyer now. Our relationship was about thirty seconds old and would fade as soon as the conversation was over, like finger pokes on bread dough.

I stood to leave. The waitress came over and offered me coffee apologetically, apparently thinking she'd been too slow. When I didn't respond she raised her eyebrows, offended, and walked away.

"You kept your promise, Chavez," I said. "You made sure things didn't work out like last time."

I walked outside.

When I got to the car Willis Daniels didn't even bother looking up from his book. He was smiling his peaceful, Santa Claus day-after-Christmas smile.

Through the window of the Sunset Cafe I could see Miranda crying, Milo's huge hand on her shoulder. He was speaking to her reassuringly, probably telling her she'd done what she had to. That it got easier from here.

There was nobody in the VW to do that for me.

It was just as well. I would've slugged them.

I turned right on Broadway and headed for the airport. I had a plane to say good-bye to.

57

San Antonio's main terminal was lollipop-shaped—
a long corridor with a carousel of gates at the end.
At the center of the circle was a magazine kiosk
and a pricey snack shop and a souvenir stand where you
had your last chance to buy authentic Texas pickled
jalapeños and stuffed armadillos and rattlesnake-in-
plastic toilet seats.

The American flight for New York would be departing
from gate twelve. I was an hour early. A flight from
Denver had just deplaned—a few businessmen, a couple
of college kids, lots of pale retirees, winter Texans.

I got myself a four-dollar draft beer at the bar and sat
at a table behind a row of bromeliads, facing the gate. At
the table next to me a couple of out-of-uniform airmen
were trading stories. They'd just been let out of basic
training at Lackland and were heading home on leave for
a week. One of them was talking about his wife.

Nobody I wanted to see came to the gate. The desk
wasn't checking anybody's tickets yet. A couple of stew-

ardesses ambled out of the gate, all blond hair and long legs and wheeled luggage. The overweight captain walked behind them, appreciating the view.

Over by the window a little Latino kid who reminded me a lot of Jem was putting his face against the glass wall of the observation area. He blew his mouth against the glass until his cheeks puffed out, then ran a few feet and did it again. The glass was a smudgy drooling foggy mess for a good twenty feet. Dad was a couple of rows away, watching sports coverage on an overhead TV. He probably wasn't much older than I was. The kid was probably five.

Finally a ticket checker changed the signs on the gate display. NEW YORK. ON TIME. He clacked a few keys on his computer terminal, then joked a little with one of the airport custodians.

Passengers started to arrive.

The airmen got up and left, shaking hands. One was heading to Montana. I didn't know about the other.

I bought another four-dollar beer.

The little Latino boy got tired of sliming the windows and came over to climb on his dad. Dad didn't much care. Pretty soon it looked like Dad was growing a small pair of flailing blue Keds out of his shoulder blades.

Finally the newly christened Allen Meissner arrived, twenty minutes before flight time, just before the airline would start preboarding. He was wearing a cowboy hat that shaded his face pretty well and clear glasses and faded denim clothes that weren't his normal look. He'd dyed his hair a shade or two lighter and I suspected that his cowboy boots were a little taller than they needed to be. He'd taken lessons on how to disguise himself, just like he'd taken lessons on how to construct his new paper identity. He wouldn't have attracted any casual onlookers. He would've stood a fair chance of slipping by any random encounters with acquaintances, unless they knew who they were looking for. I did. He was definitely my man.

The new Mr. Meissner was traveling light—a single

backpack, dark green. It was pretty much exactly like mine.

I walked up behind him as he was getting his boarding pass.

I let him check in, answer the questions, mumbled thank you to the attendant. When he turned around he ran into me at such short range that my face didn't register. He started to plow around me, the way strangers do, just another bumper in the pinball game.

Then I took his upper arm and backed him up.

He focused on my face.

"Hey, Allen," I said.

I've seen a lot of shades of red in my time but never one quite that bright, quite that quick to take over a complexion. I'm not sure what Brent Daniels would've done if we'd met under different circumstances, but here in a crowd, without a backup plan, he was stuck. It was my call.

"Buy me a beer," I said.

For one second I really thought he was going to bolt. His knuckles on the strap of the backpack went white. Then he shoved past me, angry but slow—heading for the bar like a kid who'd been told to go to the principal's office and knew the way by heart.

We sat at the same table I'd been occupying. My seat was still warm. Brent slid across from me with a beer. One for me—none for him. He passed the beer over and then waited for my reaction, like I might tell him he could go now.

I didn't.

"New York," I said. "Where then?"

Brent let out a little hiss of air. He looked strange with the fake prescription glasses, older somehow. He also looked strange because for the first time, he'd taken pains with his appearance. Real pains. He was closely shaven and immaculately clean. Not bad for a guy who had been a charred pile of ashes a few days ago.

Apparently a few papery lies floated through his mind

before he decided not to try them. Finally he just said, "I don't know."

"Les hadn't thought it that far ahead?" I asked. "Or you just don't know what he had planned?"

Brent shook his head. "What do you want, Navarre?" He didn't sound very anxious to hear the answer.

"I don't need a confession," I said. "I know the basics. Les had to go somewhere when he got scared away from his hiding place on Medina Lake. He'd already decided you were a kindred soul—you'd spent time together, you didn't give a damn, you knew what it was like being a shell. You also knew what it was like getting suckered into something by Miranda."

I waited for him to contradict me. He didn't.

"Les came to you and you agreed to put him up in the upper room of the apartment. Maybe a week and a half ago?"

Very slightly, Brent nodded.

"At some point, Les got drunk. Then he got stupid. He was a pill popper. He thought he recognized something in your medicine cabinet—something cosmetically similar to one of his favorite drugs. He took it and collapsed— diabetic coma. Maybe he didn't die right away. Maybe he stayed in a coma for a while, but eventually you realized you had a dying human vegetable on your hands. Les already had plans, had an identity, had money and an escape and everything he needed to get a new start. A man in his forties, with money and no connections. Les didn't need it anymore, so you decided you'd take it. Brent Daniels didn't have much of a future, did he? And he sure as hell didn't have much of a past. You burned his body in that tractor-shed apartment along with Brent Daniels' identity."

Again I could only judge the truth of what I said by Brent's eyes. Nothing snagged in his expression. He let it roll over him, not pulling back, not giving any indication anything was wrong. Or maybe he was just too dazed to let any reaction show.

"That's why Les never collected his fifty grand from

the boat shed. He wasn't alive to do it, and you didn't know anything about it. How much *did* you know about, Brent? With the keys to Les' new identity, maybe a change of photo or two—you could have whatever you wanted. To make it work, you must have access to at least a few of the late Mr. Meissner's accounts."

"You want to go now?" he asked. It was clear the "you" was actually "we," that he expected somebody to put on the cuffs.

"No," I said.

Brent stared at my beer. He let his shoulders sag down under the weight of the backpack.

"No?"

Total disbelief. Incredulity. I felt some of that myself, but I still shook my head. I heard myself saying, "You've got ten minutes. Maybe I think you deserve it. A lot more than Les Saint-Pierre did."

Brent stayed frozen at first. Then slowly, testing the theory, he got to his feet.

"One thing," I said. "One thing I need an answer about."

He waited.

I drank some more beer before I tried to speak again. Then I met Brent's eyes.

"There's another possible scenario. One I don't want to accept. The scenario where you gave Les those pills intentionally, knowing what they'd do to his alcoholic liver. Les was dead a lot longer than just a day or a few hours—he was dead long enough for you to really put the plan back together. Those septic tanks in the backyard— one of the newer ones had been buried, then dug up again just before the fire. That wasn't just coincidence. It wasn't just holding gray water, either."

Brent waited.

"Tell me that's not the way it was. It wasn't intentional."

Brent shook his head. Then said, almost inaudibly, "It wasn't."

He shouldered his backpack a little more firmly.

He met my eyes.

"I couldn't stand to hear those songs sung," he said. "It was a mistake, letting them out. If I heard them on the radio, Miranda singing them . . ."

He closed his eyes so tight he gave the impression of a man about to pull the trigger next to his temple.

"Catch your plane," I said.

It was hard sounding convinced, sounding like it was really the best thing. It was even harder watching him walk away, but I did. The last I saw was his cowboy hat, just before the Latino kid riding on his dad's shoulders stepped into line and started bouncing up and down along the gateway tunnel, waving his arms out to the side like he was an airplane, obscuring my last view of Brent.

The stewardess smiled and rolled her eyes at the skycap with the empty wheelchair next to her. Kids.

I got up and looked down at the beer Brent had bought me, what was left of it. I dumped it in the bromeliads and walked away.

58

My phone conversation with Professor Mitchell at UTSA lasted exactly thirty seconds. He offered me the job. I said I was honored and I'd have to think about it.

"I understand, son." He tried to make his tone not too obvious—that he didn't understand, that he thought I was an idiot for even hesitating. "When can you let us know?"

I told him next week. I told him I had another kind of class to finish up between now and then. He said fine.

After hanging up, I spent a long time staring at the crepe myrtle out the kitchen window. It was a relief twenty minutes later when Erainya did her customary unsyncopated rat-tat-tat on the screen-door frame.

When I opened the door Jem laughed and just about launched a two-layer cake into my chest as he came in. Fortunately I caught the cake while it was still in one piece and raised it up, allowing Jem free rein to tackle me.

Robert Johnson mewed a complaint and disappeared into the closet. He probably remembered the last time the Manoses had come over.

Erainya stepped in and looked around my apartment. "So you're still alive. You don't call why—you forget the number?"

Jem was explaining to me about the cake. He told me that we'd have to wait until I really finished my hours to eat it but he'd made it himself with his food coloring kit and I wouldn't believe the colors inside when I opened it up. The outside was forbidding enough—lumpy gray frosting that looked like the product a cement finger-painting session, the layers uneven and off-center so the cake seemed to be leaning away from me on its plate.

"It's just about the nicest cake I've ever seen, Bubba."

Jem giggled, then went to find the cat.

In the top of the closet a shoe box moved.

Erainya was still waiting for an answer to her question. She was giving me the look-of-death treatment, her black eyes bugging toward me and her talon fingers tapping her forearm.

"I got ten hours left," I told her. "That's about one job. You figure we can avoid arguing that long?"

"It's twenty," she reminded me. "And I don't know, honey. You going to get yourself sidetracked again?"

"Professor Mitchell is probably wondering the same thing."

Erainya frowned. "Mitchell who?"

"I said, yes. I'm willing to finish up. You?"

Erainya thought about it, weighing the pros and cons. "I suppose the Longoria case could've gone better if I'd had a dumb-looking guy for a decoy, honey. I supposed there's advantages. Maybe you got a little raw potential. Nothing amazing, you understand. And what about after the twenty hours?"

Jem came back over with Robert Johnson hanging by his armpits from Jem's hands, Robert Johnson's toes fully extended and the tiny white V on his crotch showing and his face looking like he would die from mortification any second.

Jem looked troubled. "Where's Miranda?"

He'd just made the connection, remembered his trick-or-treat partner and remembered that she had some vague association with Tres when she wasn't being Jem's Little Miss Muffett.

Erainya waited to hear an answer to both questions, hers and Jem's. She was chewing on the inside of her mouth, her lips turning sideways.

"Miranda had to go, Bubba. She's going to be a singer in Nashville. Isn't that cool?"

Jem didn't look impressed. Neither did Robert Johnson. Both turned and left. Probably going to play wet-kitty/dry-kitty in bathroom.

"You need anything, honey?" Erainya's voice was softer now, so much so that I had to look to make sure she had really been the one speaking.

She frowned immediately. "What?"

"Nothing. And no. Thanks."

Erainya looked out the window at the afternoon in progress. Gary Hales was in the front yard, watering his sidewalk. Across the street a red Mazda Miata was just pulling up in front of the Suitez house. The Mazda was loaded so heavily with cardboard moving boxes that the trunk was half-open, precariously fastened with a criss-cross of cords. Allison Saint-Pierre looked across the street, trying to make sure she remembered which house was mine. Last time she was here she'd been drunk.

Erainya and I exchanged looks.

"Nashville, honey?"

"It's not that."

She did a backhand slap in the air. "Ah. I'll wrap the cake in Saran Wrap. Maybe it'll keep."

Knowing how Erainya applied Saran Wrap, I had the feeling the cake would keep several centuries.

I went outside.

Allison saw me coming and sat on the hood of the red Mazda and waited. She was holding a backpack—my

backpack, the one I'd left with the maid at her Monte
Vista house.

Allison was already warming up her head shake as I
walked across Queen Anne Street. By the time I got to
her she was going pretty well with it.

"What is this?" she demanded. She held the backpack
up by one shoulder strap.

"A very old backpack," I said. "A souvenir. I figured I
didn't need it anymore."

She sighed through her nose. "I mean what's *in* it,
sweetie. You lost your mind?"

"It's Les' money," I said. "Or part of it. He forgot the
stash, we found it. I figured you're right—some of it
should go to you."

Allison's eyes couldn't quite get a fix on me. They were
wandering around the space where I was, not really
seeing. She looked sloppy today, moving-time sloppy—
her hair pinned up and her T-shirt streaked with old cobwebs and her legs below her cutoffs scraped and
smudged with dirt. Her face was etched with tiny white
wrinkles like cracked glass.

"You're just *giving* me twenty-five thousand dollars,"
she said, incredulous.

"Twenty-four thousand three hundred," I corrected.

"I know." She'd counted. The fact that I had too made
her even more incredulous. "Is this because—"

I shook my head. "It's not because of anything. I
know what Les' estate looks like. I know that his name
isn't going to be worth as much as you hoped. The court
is going to be paying off his debts first, and I doubt
there's going to be much for you. You're broke."

That didn't seem to answer her question. She knew all
that already. She kept staring at me, mad now.

"So give this to the judge, like you said," she said.

"I don't know the judge. I know you."

She finally lowered the backpack. She still looked
angry. "Exactly."

A car went past. Behind me Gary Hales' watering hose
sprayed across the cement and droplets thudded into

the grass. He must've been busy watching us. His aim was off.

"Still going back to Falfurrias?" I asked.

"You sure you want to know?"

We locked eyes. I looked away first.

"Damn you." She was shaking her head again now, trying to stay angry but with a tiny smile starting to form.

"Pardon?"

"You've got to go and keep the damn door open, don't you? You've got to give me just enough to think that maybe all men aren't complete shits. Why the fuck did you do this?"

"Think about Les," I suggested. "There's still a strong case."

She sighed.

"You were right," I told her. "About him running off, about getting away free and leaving everybody else with the mess. You were right all along."

"Big comfort."

She turned and threw the backpack in the shotgun window.

"Besides," I said, "it was twenty-five thousand."

She frowned. "What?"

"The amount—I was going to give you twenty-five thousand dollars. I scammed seven hundred. You can blame me for that."

She stared at me.

I pointed my toe in the air. "Reimbursed myself for these here boots. Paid my rent. They cost about the same amount."

Allison cracked a smile. "I've seen your apartment. The boots were a better deal."

Then she came up and put her arms around me. Her fingers traced my skin, remembering exactly where the sword tip scar was, circling around it. She kissed me long enough for Gary Hales to water the tree, the street, the front bumper on my VW. Long enough for me to forget how to breathe.

Then she pushed lightly away, bumped my forehead with hers.

"Come down to Falfurrias sometime," she said.

"And you'll introduce me to your four brothers?" I managed to say.

She grinned. She tweaked my ear with her fingers and it stung.

"*Them* you could handle, sweetie."

After the red Miata drove away I stood in the middle of Queen Anne Street until a family Land Rover drove up and tapped its horn. Excuse us.

I moved to the front yard, looked at Gary Hales.

"That one's gone," I told him.

"Ye-uh," Gary agreed. Disappointed.

Fortunately I'd paid my rent. That gave me thirty days to find either more money or more blondes. I figured the odds were about even.

I went inside to see about some cake.

About the Author

RICK RIORDAN is the author of three Tres Navarre novels—*Big Red Tequila*, winner of the Shamus and Anthony Awards, *The Widower's Two-Step*, winner of the Edgar Award, and *The Last King of Texas*. A middle-school English teacher by day, Riordan lives with his wife and family in San Antonio, Texas.

If you enjoyed Rick Riordan's second Tres Navarre mystery, the Edgar Award-winning THE WIDOWER'S TWO-STEP, you won't want to miss any books in this critically acclaimed series. Get the first, BIG RED TEQUILA, winner of the Shamus and the Anthony Awards, at your favorite bookseller's.

And turn the page for an exciting preview of the latest Tres Navarre suspense novel, THE LAST KING OF TEXAS, available now.

THE LAST KING OF TEXAS

Rick Riordan

Dr. David Mitchell waved me toward the dead professor's chair. "Try it out, son."

Mitchell and Detective DeLeon sat down on the students' side of the desk, the safe side. I took the professor's chair. It was padded in cushy black leather and smelled faintly of sports cologne. Walnut armrests. Great back support.

Mitchell smiled. "Comfortable?"

"I'd be more so," I told him, "if the last two people who sat here hadn't died."

Mitchell's smiled thinned. He glanced at Detective DeLeon, got no help there, then looked wearily around the office—the cluttered bookshelves, file cabinets topped with dreadlocks of dying pothos plants, the tattered Bayeux Tapestry posters on the walls. "Son, Dr. Haimer's death was a heart attack."

"After receiving death threats and being driven out of the job," I recalled. "And Haimer's successor?"

Detective DeLeon sat forward. "That was a .45, Mr. Navarre."

When DeLeon moved, her blazer and skirt and silk blouse shimmered in frosty shades of gray, all sharp creases and angles. Her hair was cut in the same severe pattern, only black. Her eyes glittered. The whole effect reminded me of one of those sleek, fashionable sub-zero freezer units, petite size.

She tugged an incident report out of the folder in her lap, passed me a color Polaroid of Dr. Aaron Brandon—the University of Texas at San Antonio's new medievalist for one-half of one glorious spring semester.

The photo showed a middle-aged Anglo man crumpled like a marionette in front of a fireplace. Behind him, the limestone mantel was smeared with red clawlike marks where the body had slid into sitting position against the grate. The man's hands were palm-up in his lap, supplicating. His blue eyes were open. He wore khaki pants and his bare, chunky upper body was matted with blood and curly black hair. Bored into his chest just above his nipples were two tattered holes the size of flashlight handles.

I pushed the photo back toward DeLeon. "You homicide investigators. Always so reassuring."

She smiled without warmth.

I looked at Mitchell. "You really expect me to take the job?"

Mitchell shifted in his seat, looking everywhere except at the photo of his former faculty member. He scratched one triangular white sideburn.

The poor guy had obviously gotten no sleep in the last week. His suit jacket was rumpled. His rodent-like features had lost their quickness. He looked infinitely older and more grizzled than he had just six months ago, when he'd offered me this same position for the first time.

It had been mid-October then. Dr. Theodore Haimer had just been forced into retirement after his comments about "the damn coddled Mexicans at UTSA" made the *Express-News* and triggered an avalanche of student protests and hate mail the likes of which the normally placid campus had never seen. Shortly afterward, while the English division was still boxing up Haimer's books and interviewing candidates for his job, the old man had been found at home, his heart frozen like a chunk of quartz, his face buried in a bowl of dry Apple Jacks.

I'd decided against teaching at the time because I'd been finishing my apprenticeship with Erainya Manos for a private investigator's license.

My mother, who'd arranged the first interview with Mitchell, had not been thrilled. *A nice safe job for once,* she'd pleaded. *A chance to get back into Academia.*

Looking now at the photo of Aaron Brandon, who'd taken the nice safe job instead of me, I thought maybe the whole "Mother Knows Best" thing was overrated.

"We offered you this position last fall, Tres." Mitchell tried to keep the petulance out of his voice, the implication that I could've saved him a lot of trouble back in October, maybe gotten myself killed right off the bat. "I think you should reconsider."

I said, "A second chance."

"Absolutely."

"And you couldn't *pay* any reputable professor enough money now."

Mitchell's left eye twitched. "It's true we need a person with very special qualifications. The fact that you, ah, have another set of skills—"

"You can watch your ass," Detective DeLeon translated. "Maybe avoid making yourself corpse number three until we make an arrest."

I was loving this woman.

I swiveled in Aaron Brandon's chair and gazed out the windows. A couple of pigeons roosted on the ledge outside the glass. Beyond, the view of the UTSA quadrangle was obscured by the upper branches of a mesquite, shining with new margarita-green foliage. Through the leaves I could see the walls of the Behavioral Sciences Building next door, the small red and blue shapes of students making their way up and down steps in the central courtyard, across wide grassy spaces and concrete walkways.

Icicle-blue sky, temperature in the low eighties. Your basic perfect Texas spring day outside your basic perfect campus office. It was a view Dr. Haimer had earned through twenty years of tenure. A view Aaron Brandon had enjoyed for less than ninety days.

I turned back to the dead man's office.

Yellow loops of leftover crime-scene tape were stuffed into the waist-high metal trash can between Brandon's desk and the window. On the corner of the desk sat a pile of ungraded essays from the undergraduate Chaucer seminar. Next to that was a silver-framed photo of the professor with a very pretty Latina woman and a child, maybe three years old. They were all standing in front of an old-fashioned merry-go-round. The little boy had Brandon's blue eyes and the woman's smile and reddish-brown hair.

Next to the photo were the death threats—a neat stack of seven white business envelopes computer-printed in Chicago 12-point, each containing one page of well-written, grammatically correct venom. Each threat was unsigned. The first was addressed to Theodore Haimer, the following six to Aaron Brandon. One dated two weeks ago promised a pipe bomb. One dated a week before that promised a knife in Brandon's back as a symbol of how the Latino community felt about the Establishment replacing one white racist with another. The campus had been swept and no bombs had been found; no knives had been forthcoming. None of the letters said anything about shooting Brandon at home in the chest with a .45.

"You have leads?" I asked DeLeon.

She gave me the subzero smile. "You know Sergeant Schaeffer, Mr. Navarre?"

I said, "Whoops."

Gene Schaeffer had been a detective in homicide until recently, when he'd accepted a transfer promotion to vice. Sometimes Schaeffer and I were friends. More often, like whenever I needed something from him, Schaeffer wanted to kill me.

"The sergeant warned me about you," DeLeon confirmed. "Something about your father being a retired captain—you feeling you had special privileges."

"Bexar County Sheriff," I corrected. "Dead, not retired."

"You've got no special privileges with me, Mr. Navarre. Whatever else you do, you're going to stay out of my investigation."

"And if the person or persons who killed Brandon decides I'm Anglo racist oppressor number three?"

DeLeon smiled a little more genuinely. I think the idea appealed to her. "You cover your ass until we get it straightened out. You can do that, right?"

How to say no to a job offer. Let me count the ways.

"I'd have to talk with my employer—"

"Erainya Manos," Dr. Mitchell interrupted. "We've already done that."

I stared at him.

"The provost is more than agreeable to retaining Ms. Manos' services," Mitchell said wearily, like he'd already spent too much time haggling that point. "While you're teaching for us, Ms. Manos will be finding out what she can about the hate mail, assessing potential continued threats to the faculty."

"You're wasting your money," DeLeon told him.

Mitchell continued as if she hadn't spoken. "The campus attorney's office has employed private investigation firms before. Confidence-building measure. Ms. Manos considered the contract a more-than-fair trade for sharing your time with us, son."

"I bet."

I looked at DeLeon.

She shrugged. "Say no if you want, Mr. Navarre. I've got no interest in your P.I. business. I'm simply not opposed to the campus hiring somebody who can stay alive for longer than three months."

I gave her a *Gee thanks* smile.

I sat back in the late Aaron Brandon's chair, understanding now why Erainya Manos had cheerily let me take the morning off. You have to cherish those open employer-employee relationships.

Mitchell was about to say something more when there was a knock on the office door.

A large young man leaned into the room, checked us all out, focused in on me, then wedged a plastic bin of mail through the doorway.

"You're the replacement," he said to me. "Thought so."

I'm of the opinion that you can categorize just about anybody by the type of vegetable their clone would've grown from in *Invasion of the Body Snatchers*. The guy in the doorway was definitely a radish. His skin was composed of alternate white and ruddy splotches and gnarled with old acne scars.

On top of his head was a small sprig of bleached hair that matched the white rooty whiskers on his chin. His upper body sagged over his belt in generous slabs of red polo-shirted flesh. His face had upwardly smeared features—lips, nose, eyebrows. They did not beckon with intelligence.

"Gregory," Professor Mitchell sighed. "Not *now*."

Gregory pushed his way farther into the office. He balanced his mail bin on his belly and stared at me expectantly. "You have my essay?"

"Gregory, this isn't the time," Mitchell insisted.

Gregory grunted. "I told Brandon, I said, 'Man, some people are really late with the grading but you take the cake. You ever want your mail again you get me my essay back.' That's what I told him. You got it graded yet?"

I smiled.

Gregory didn't smile back. His eyes seemed out of focus. Maybe he wasn't talking to me at all. Maybe he was talking to the pothos plants.

"I don't have your essay," I said.

"It's the one on the werewolf," he insisted. The mail bin sagged against his side. I'd disappointed him. "The Marie de France *dit*."

"*Bisclavret*," I guessed.

"Yeah." Unfocused light twinkled in his eyes. Had I read the essay after all? Had the pothos read it?

"*Bisclavret's* a *lai*," I said. "A long narrative poem. *Dits* are shorter, like fables. The essay's not graded and I may not be the one grading it, Gregory."

He frowned. "It's a *dit*."

Professor Mitchell sighed through his nose. "Gregory, we're having a conference . . ."

DeLeon took off her gray blazer and folded it over the top of her chair. Her bone-colored silk blouse was sleeveless, her arms the color of French roast and smoothly muscled. Her side arm was visible now—a tiny black Glock 23 in a leather Sam Brown holster. When Gregory saw the gun, his mouth closed fully for the first time in the conversation, maybe the first time in his life.

DeLeon said, "Dr. Navarre told you it was a *lai*, Gregory. Were there any other questions?"

Gregory kept his mouth closed. He shifted his mail bin around, looked at Professor Mitchell like he was expecting protection, then at me. "Maybe I could check back tomorrow?"

"Good idea," I said. "And the mail?"

Gregory thought about it, checked out DeLeon's Glock one more time, then dipped a beefy hand into the bin. He brought out a rubber-banded stack of letters that probably represented two weeks of withheld mail. He threw it on the desk and knocked over the silver-framed photo of Brandon's family.

"Fine," Gregory said. "Package, too."

The package hit the table with a muffled clunk. It was a manila bubble-wrap mailer, 11 by 17, dinged up and glistening at both ends with scotch tape. It had a large red stamp along the side that read INTRA-CAMPUS DELIVERIES ONLY.

While Professor Mitchell shooed Gregory out the door, DeLeon and I were staring at the same thing—the plain white address label on the mailing envelope. AARON BRANDON, HSS 3.11. No street address or zip. No return. A computer-printed label, Chicago 12-point.

I remember locking eyes with DeLeon for maybe half a second. After that it happened fast.

DeLeon put a hand on Professor Mitchell's shoulder and calmly started to say, "Why don't we go—" when something inside the package made a plasticky, *crick-crick-crick* sound like a soda bottle cap being twisted off.

DeLeon was smaller than Mitchell by maybe a hundred pounds but she had him wrestled to the floor on the count of two. I should have followed her example.

Instead I swept the package off the desk and into the metal trash can.

Nice plan if I'd been able to get to the floor myself. But the trash can started toppling. First toward my face. Then toward the window. Then it went off like a cannon.

In the first millisecond, even before the sound registered, the force of the blast frosted a huge ragged oval in the glass, then melted it in a cone of metal shards and yellow ribbon and flames, ripping through the wall and the mesquite outside and shredding the new leaves and branches into ticker tape.

I was on my butt in the opposite corner of the office. My ankle was twisted in the walnut armrest of Aaron Brandon's overturned chair and my ribs had slammed against a filing cabinet. There was an upside-down pothos plant in my lap. Someone was pressing a very large A-flat tuning fork to the base of my skull and my left cheek felt wet and cold. I dabbed at the cheek with my fingers, felt nothing, brought my fingers away, and saw that they glistened red.

Except for the tuning fork, the room was silent. Leaves and pigeon feathers and pages from essays were twirling aimlessly in the air, curlicuing in and out of the blasted wall. There was a fine white smoke layering the room and a smell like burning swimming-pool chemicals.

Slowly, DeLeon got to her feet. A single yellow pothos leaf was stuck in her hair. She pulled Mitchell up by the elbow.

Neither of them looked hurt. DeLeon examined the room coolly, then looked at me, focusing on the side of my face.

"You're bleeding," she announced.

It sounded like she was talking through a can and string, but I was relieved to register any sound at all. Then I heard other things—voices in the plaza below, people yelling. A low, hot sizzle from the remnants of the blasted garbage can.

I staggered to my feet, brushed the plant and the dirt off my lap, took a step toward the window. No more pigeons on the ledge. The bottom of the garbage can, the only part that wasn't shredded, had propelled itself backward with such force that an inch of the base was embedded in the side of the oak desk.

Distressed voices were coming down the hall now. Insistent knocks on neighboring doors.

Mitchell's eyelids stuck together when he blinked. He shook his head and focused on me with great effort. "I don't—I don't . . ."

DeLeon patted the old professor's shoulder, telling him she thought he was going to be okay. Then she looked at me. "A doctor for that cheek. What do you think?"

I looked out the hole somebody had just blasted in a perfect spring day. I said, "I think I'll take the job."